BURIED, BUT NOT FORGOTTEN

By

Tammy D. Thompson

Copyright © 2001 by Tammy D. Thompson
All rights reserved.
No part of this book may be reproduced, restored in a retrieval system, or transmitted by means, electronic, mechanical, photocopying, recording, or otherwise, without written consent from the author.

ISBN: 0-75962-223-X

This book is printed on acid free paper.

Dedications

I would like to dedicate this book, my first book, to my grandmother Gertie Jewell, and my grandfather, Theron Jewell, who are now gone to be with our Lord. They always held a special place in my heart, and always will. And I'd give anything for them to still be here to share my excitement. Even though I know they're looking down on me smiling, I want them to know that they are still in my heart and on my mind. I'd also like to thank Pennie Lewis and my sister Jill Hanna in the preparations of this book. I couldn't have done it without them. You know, a talent is a gift given from God, and what we do with it, is our gift back to him. I want to reach my full potential and return such a special gift. Thank you to everyone who believed in me and never gave up, because I never did.

CHAPTER 1

It was cool and windy on the day my brother, Lewis Laney, was laid to rest. The leaves were blowing like feathers in the wind; and as the casket was lowered, everyone wept at the loss of someone so young, who had died so soon. All that remained was my mother, father, my sister and me, Beth Laney. There were also a few friends who would hold his memory in their hearts forever. Though Lewis had always left a lasting impression, he left one which would be his last—a spot in the ground that held his hardened body, trapped in a wooden box for eternity.

The sadness lingering around me was almost too much for me to take. With puffed eyes and scorned hearts, everyone attending was speechless and devastated. The cool wind twisting around and around was blowing through my hair like a tornado. And my mind was not with me, but somewhere far, far away. Instead of remembering, I was only trying to forget. Though it seemed unnatural, I was beside myself as I turned away from the crowd of people mourning so desperately.

As everyone walked away, I stared in the direction of my brother's grave. I was standing there emotionless and cold. No tears were showing. I kept wondering why I didn't feel for my brother's death. It was like I wanted to wait until I was alone to release my true feelings instead of letting them out in the midst of everyone. My eyes were glassy and troubled, and no feeling could be seen by others. Everyone looked at me as if I were the most unfeeling person on the face of the earth—there was no love, no hate, only emptiness.

My sister, Melissa, was different. She wept continuously until her eyes were swollen shut, and her hands were clutched tightly together as if to hold in her fear and anger about the wrongs which had been done Lewis. Because of a small mistake from the hospital, Lewis ended up paying a huge price-his own life. You could tell by looking into her dispirited eyes that her pain fell much deeper than my own.

Melissa, and our mother, Alice, were in pure agony; unlike my father. My father, David, was calm. But everyone knew he'd soon realize what had happened, and then have to deal with it. Then he would know his son was gone forever. And when he came to that realization in his own heart, then I knew his rage would reach out to find someone to blame for Lewis's death.

I sensed every eye focusing on me. I stared up at the sky and my hands hung loose by my side. I didn't know how I felt inside. I made no contact with others. I didn't want to be held or talked to. I had crawled into a deep tunnel, too deep for me to get out of on my own. I desired no kind words or unnecessary mention of my brother.

I was the youngest of three, and I wanted to think I was grown, but mother and father knew all to well I wasn't. I had been pretty unstable in my thinking for a long time. No one knew why. Explanations for it were unknown. Everyone just thought I had a mental problem which couldn't be helped, but I tried not to listen to what people said about me. The more I listened, the more unconcerned I became about what people thought. It didn't matter anymore. All that mattered was how I viewed myself.

After Lewis' death, we all went on with our lives. Melissa married and moved away. I was left alone with my mother and father. I never could talk to them as friends, and I usually kept my fears and problems deep inside. My shyness and incompatibility with others, left me feeling alone quite often. And after my senior year of high school, I decided to change the direction in which my life was headed. All I saw behind me were dead ends and failures. That was all I'd ever seen. The only positive things happened to someone else. And my self-esteem dropped lower and lower each time I'd try something, and fail. I needed a change. I wanted to do something to make everyone, including myself, proud. My inner problems were triggered by something, but I didn't know what. The more I tried to figure it out, the more confused I became. My family had never been close, and I had very few friends to speak of. A change was exactly what I needed.

After long hours of thinking, I found a way to change my feelings about a lot of things. I found the answer looking out my window one evening at sunset. The beautiful colors the sky projected, shed new light on my grim and gloomy thoughts.

My thoughts were about going to college, away from everyone that made my life a living hell for so many years. I had a feeling new friends and a new scenery might do me a bit of good.

Those thoughts were settling to my soul as I laid back on my bed, in the dimness of my room, just staring at the ceiling as if it were some kind of crystal ball. For a change, I was making some kind of decision without a push from others.

It was almost fall and I wanted to get away as soon as possible. I told my parents what I wanted to do, and I was surprised at their reaction. Instead of being against my plan, they thought it would be a good idea. I was overwhelmed. I never would've guessed they wanted me to go. That made me doubt their love and concern. At first I thought I was too much trouble, and going away would solve their problems sooner than they expected. But I didn't care. Leaving would mean drifting away into a dream land of happy, young college students, that might be able to show me how to live a little and get the most out of life. Because up until that moment, I felt as though I hadn't lived at all. My feeling was that I was only floating around in the atmosphere being pushed whichever direction someone else wanted me to go. I didn't feel it was a life, but more of an existence.

Time flew by, and the day for me to leave came quickly. My bags were packed and sat at the foot of the stairway. As I slowly walked down the stairs, my mother and father met me at the bottom. It seemed as though they had smiles of relief on their faces, and that bothered me more than I wanted to admit. I was anxious about the change, but I was also afraid I'd have trouble making new friends. I had no idea of what the next few years had to offer, but I knew it had to be more than what the past eighteen years had given me.

Walking to my car, I looked back momentarily. My parents stood there waving. They didn't even bother to carry my luggage down for me, but I tried to put that thought out of my head as quickly as it arose. I wanted to focus on what was ahead of me, instead of dwelling on things which I could do nothing about. So I got into my car and drove away. I waved to them until they were out of sight. Then I knew I was on my own.

I drove in peaceful solitude. I looked forward, and never took one look back.

I wanted to forget about my adolescent instability, and make new, impressionable memories with people who would be my future hope. I wanted to succeed in something other than being a failure, and I wanted to be good at whatever I decided to be. There was no doubt in my mind that I could if I just put forth the effort. And, at that point, I was willing to put forth as much effort as possible to come out on top.

The drive seemed longer than the tallest mountain is high, but soon enough I pulled up in front of a beautifully landscaped, gigantic building with a Gothic look to it. The daffodils in the entrance way to the college seemed to smile at me as I stared peacefully at them. I parked in front of the steps, and stepped out of the car. Leaning on the hood of my car for a moment, I wondered if I'd like my new life. Though no one can tell the future, there was a warm feeling inside my heart. It was a feeling telling me to change my life forever. The coldness of home disappeared almost instantly when I arrived, and as I took a deep breath, I entered that beautiful building with high hopes.

First I checked in at the office so they would know I'd arrived. Then I went to find the dorm I'd heard such terrible things about. I knew nothing could be as bad as living at home, besides, what some may consider terrible, others might consider the same thing a God send.

I got my key and walked to the end of the hallway. I found the room number and slipped the key into the door. As the door slowly squeaked open, I saw another girl sitting on one of the twin beds unpacking her things. It was so tiny. There was barely enough room to walk, but I was determined to keep a positive attitude, so I started talking to my new roommate. She had a friendly disposition about her, and I was trying to display the same in return. Conversation started slow, but soon enough we introduced ourselves.

"Hi. I'm Beth Laney. I guess we're roommates," I said nervously.

"Yeah, I guess. I'm Amy...Amy Trotter. Nice to meet you Beth," she said with an equally nervous voice.

Unpacking didn't take long, but straightening took the longest. It was hard to find a place for everything. If things weren't just right, there wouldn't have been enough room to walk around; so we put our heads together and figured out the best way to organize everything. When we were finished, we rested for a moment on our beds. I sighed as I sat there quietly, and Amy began to laugh. She had a perfect smile. It was so cheerful, it made me want to smile right along with her, and that was exactly what I did.

"You know, as small as this room is, we sure have a lot of junk in here; and it all fits," she chuckled.

I went along with her and grinned a bit, "Yeah, it is small, but I guess it won't be that bad."

Tammy D. Thompson

    We talked for a while and got to know each other. She was very interesting to talk to. She talked like she had such a perfect life. Her parents had a lot of money, and the way she talked, she got everything she ever wanted, but there was something making her unhappy. It seemed to me that anyone with that kind of a life would have nothing to be unhappy about. She told me she decided to go away to college to make a life for herself instead of always taking what someone else had worked hard for. She didn't believe in getting anything the easy way. She wanted to climb the ladder of success until she reached the top on her own talents and hard work. I admired her for that. Most people wouldn't think that way. Most people would take what they could get and keep going back for more, but not Amy. I didn't know exactly how I compared to that. I didn't remember much from my childhood, and I wasn't sure it was happy enough to remember, but talking with Amy helped me to look ahead.

    I started feeling more enthusiastic about school the longer we talked. And I couldn't wait to see all the people who would be my new friends. I wanted to work as hard as I could to make as many friends as possible. I'd never really worked hard to keep any friendship, but I saw what a benefit it could be to try. It could help me make my way back up to reality and push me to the top, where I always wanted to be. I guess one definition of friendship, is one who gives love and support. And that was exactly what I needed. Love would give me strength, and support would give me the courage I needed to reach the top.

    Dinner time was closing in on us and our stomachs started making crazy noises. But instead of eating at the school cafeteria, we decided to go to town and see what we could afford on our weekly allowance.

    We fought the crowd of people coming in and out of the dorms and hurried to Amy's car. We made our way through the traffic coming into the college. There were people everywhere, and I watched everyone as we entered the middle of town.

I felt closed in as we drove around in that small town; but, at the same time, it gave me peace. I began to think I had moved to a close knitted community.

Amy's car was great. It was a burgundy Corvette convertible with gray leather interior. With the top down, the wind blew our hair. When we stopped, we looked at each other and started laughing. It looked like we had been struck by lightning. But we primped a little, and went inside a small fast food restaurant in the center of town.

We had an interesting conversation while eating. There were two guys who looked like they might go to college with us. One was medium height with black hair and eyes any girl would die for. The other was just the opposite. He was very tall, slim, and his blonde hair was as shiny as a new spring day. They were both attractive, but in different ways. And I let my interest stop there. Though they kept staring in our direction, I continued to talk about school. Amy looked at me a bit funny, but didn't say a word about it until later that night when we got back to our room.

When we arrived back, we turned on the television and sat on our beds. Then Amy asked, "Beth, what was it with those guys? At first you acted like you liked one of 'em, then you...well, you acted like you were scared to say you were attracted to him. Are you scared of guys? I know that sounds crazy, but the expression on your face was like you didn't want to be interested, whether you were or not."

"It's not that. I just want to concentrate on my schoolwork and my future. I don't have time to fool around. That's all I'd be doing if I got involved with anyone right now."

With a slight pause, she replied, "I guess you're right. That *is* why we're here, but still...oh never mind."

You could tell she was bewildered by my attitude, but she shrugged it off for the time being. I wasn't even sure what I was talking about. My mind was so twisted and confused about where I was and where I was headed, that I just made myself believe everything I'd said to her. Once I got settled in, I knew I'd come to my senses eventually. I just hoped getting comfortable with a new environment, wouldn't take long.

I was very tired from the drive, and knew I had to be up early for registration, so I told Amy I was going to turn in for the night. I got ready for bed, crawled under my warm covers and closed my eyes. Still, I couldn't sleep. As tired as I was, I kept thinking about what Amy had said to me. I wasn't sure why I didn't try to talk to those guys. I was interested, that was a fact, but something held me back. I had always been that way. There was something I never wanted to admit to anyone. I had just turned eighteen years old and had never had a boyfriend or even been out on a date. It wasn't because I'd never been asked, I had; but I didn't have any desire to go. There was nothing in my heart that led me into getting involved with anyone. Strange as it may seem, I couldn't explain it. I just dealt with it every minute of every day.

Soon, Amy turned out the lights and went to bed. She left the radio playing softly, and the song on the radio made my mind wander. It was an old song that always made me cry. I didn't know why I always cried when I heard it. Nestled warmly in bed I listened to the radio, huddled in a ball like I was afraid, and eventually I fell asleep.

Before the alarm sounded in the morning, the light glared from the window and woke me. I was never one to get up early, but for once, I did. I stirred for a few minutes, got my clothes together, and headed for the showers down the hall. It was different, but not too uncomfortable since it was a girls' dorm. I wrapped up in my terry robe and went to shower. I was startled as a man came around the corner with a tool belt wrapped around his waist.

"Sorry ma'am," he said, exiting out the side door.

I gathered myself, then went in, showered, and got ready for my first day at college. When I started walking towards campus alone, I peered at all of the strange faces around me. Amy wasn't too far behind me. And I could hear her high pitched voice over everyone else's. She was a character. I knew there would never be a dull moment with her around. After knowing her for only one day, I could tell she was very personable and friendly to everyone she meets. I felt blessed to be given someone like her as a new found friend.

Almost late for registration, I hurried across the campus with Amy running behind me. We reached the building just in time. The line was a mile long, and I knew it would probably take forever to get registered, not to mention the fact that I was still juggling what I wanted to take my first semester. Then, to my surprise, the two guys we'd seen the day before, were directly in front of us. They looked at us and smiled. They were even better looking up close. Amy and I whispered a few things to one another about them, and moments later they started talking to us. I couldn't believe it. Though I had always thought myself unattractive, boring and unnoticeable; I didn't feel that way at that moment. I felt like someone was actually interested in me. And oddly enough, I was interested too.

"Hi. Didn't we see you yesterday?" one of them asked.

"Yes, I think so. I'm Beth...Beth Laney." I responded.

"I'm Eric Norris. I just moved here from North Carolina," he said with a smile.

About that time, I looked up and Amy was talking to the other guy. She was so chipper. I chuckled a little. I knew there was no telling what she was saying to him.

She was so straight forward, so unlike myself.

"Where are you from?" he asked.

"I just moved here from Dallas." I answered, blushing a bit.

His gleaming eyes were hard to ignore as he continued talking. "That was quite a drive. I flew down. I just wanted to get away from home for a while—far away from home. You know, it makes you feel more on your own when you're away."

"I know. That's me. I wanted to do the same thing. Maybe not for the same reasons. Getting away does make you feel like you're growing up instead of being a kid at home," I replied with a smile.

When registration was over and we got our books, we went back to the room to see where we wanted to go from there. It was still early, and I didn't want to spend the rest of the day in that little bitty dungeon of a room. While we were changing clothes, the phone rang. Amy quickly answered it, and handed it to me. I wondered who would be calling me. I didn't think anyone even knew our number.

"Hello," I said curiously.

"Are you that good-looking blonde I was talking to in line today?" exclaimed a sexy voice.

"I don't know. Am I?" I answered playfully.

He laughed and replied, "Yep, it's you. I'd never forget that seductive voice of yours."

"Oh, come on. Don't be crazy. I've heard better lines than that before," I said.

"Doesn't hurt to try, does it? Listen, I was thinking," he said softly.

"And what were you thinking?"

"I was wondering if you wanted to go for a bite to eat and maybe drive around and see what there is to see in this little town," he asked sweetly.

"Oh, I don't know. I was going to...I mean, I was getting ready to..." I said, as I tried to stall until I knew exactly what I wanted to do.

There was silence on the phone line for a moment then, "If you don't want to..." he said, as I interrupted.

"No, it's not that. It's just that...I don't know Eric. You caught me off guard. I'm here for school and that's all, nothing else," I said regretfully.

He cordially took no for an answer, and we both hung up the phone. Amy stood there staring at me as if I had just committed a murder.

"What Amy? What?" I said with Amy standing there like a stone statue just staring at me.

"What's wrong with you? He's so cute, and you just turned him down for a date. You've lost your mind. I know that you've lost your mind. You should've told him you knew someone who'd go. I can't believe you did that," she said in disbelief of my actions.

"I just didn't want to go. I have other things I need to do. I need to..."

She interrupted, " You need to do what?"

"I don't know, Amy. I don't know what's wrong with me. You're right. He is cute, and I just turned him down," I replied, sitting on my bed and staring down at the floor.

Amy came over and sat down beside me. She put her hand on my shoulder and said, "Listen. I know there's something really bothering you; and, if you decide you need someone to talk to, just let me know. I'll be here."

I looked at her and smiled. I could tell she was going to be my rock to hang onto when storms came to throw my emotions into a whirl-wind. Her outlook on life was a bit of an inspiration when it came to rebuilding the way I wanted to live mine. Her smile made it hard to keep a frown on my face. I had to smile along with her or I knew she'd joke around until I did. That's just the way she was.

Classes started the following day. I was more nervous than I'd ever been. All those unfamiliar faces and a maze of classrooms made me half crazy. So, to relax myself, I picked up a book which I'd started, but never finished. I read until my eyes could barely stay open. And although it was early, I decided to take a little nap. But every time I would almost doze off, voices up and down the hallway would wake me. And through all the noise, Amy sat there as solemn as she could be, undisturbed.

The sun fell as the moon and stars came out little by little, and I started to think about how content I'd felt since I'd arrived. I felt at ease physically and mentally, and I was more than ready to create a new lifestyle for myself and meet new people.

With happy thoughts running rampant through my mind, I changed into my nightgown. I looked forward to the following day more than I thought I would in the beginning, and I wanted to be well rested. I was always told you can't learn well if your mind, body, and soul aren't properly rested. I believed that completely. I didn't want to be nodding off my first day of college. I wanted to look intelligent, although I wasn't sure if that was exactly true.

The following morning, I quickly got dressed and fumbled out of the dorms I had my books in one hand, my purse in the other, and my schedule somewhere in between. When I went to one building, I needed to be in the one next to it. I ran in so many circles I almost got dizzy. I stopped for a moment and leaned against a bench. Feeling confused and bewildered, I glanced up.

There was Eric. He smiled and reached over and took my books from me. "You got a load there Beth. Need some help?" he asked caringly.

"Well, I could use some directions."

"I'm new here too, remember, but I'll do the best I can. Come on," he said taking my hand and walking me toward my first class.

"Thanks." I said, taking back my books, and walking into class. I felt as if all eyes were focused on me. I didn't know how to sit or how to act. Then I felt a hand on my shoulder, "Come over here Beth," Eric said guiding me to two empty seats.

"What are you doing in here?" I asked.

He just smiled and wrote on a piece of paper.

> 'I glanced at your schedule yesterday, and wanted to get close to you, so I took your same classes. PLEASE, go out with me Beth. You're beautiful.'

I looked up at him and tried to look angry because he copied my schedule, but inside I was truly impressed because he wanted to be near me so much he would take a creative writing class. Since I was good at writing, I knew I could always help him if he needed it.

After class I went ahead of him, although I had no earthly idea where I was going.

He ran up behind me and grabbed my hand.

"What is it you want? Do you just want me to go out with you? If that's all, then I will," I said.

"No. I want to get to know you. I want to know your wants and your fears. I want to know what makes you who you are. I felt something the first time I saw you that I can't explain, and when you turned me down I felt lower than I'd felt in a long time.

I've always gone after what I wanted, and now I want you," he said convincingly.

"Ok. When do you want to pick me up?" I said, giving in to his flattery.

He just smiled and leaned over and kissed me on the cheek.

Though still a bit confused, I hurried beside him to the next few classes until the last one was over for the day. I started walking in the opposite direction, then

Eric turned to find me quite a ways away from him. He ran until he reached me, took my hand, placed a slip of paper in it, and went on his way.

I hurriedly opened it and read the poetic words he had written during class.

> As a flower blushes in full bloom
> There's none a flower like you,
> For your lips are like soft petals
> And your eyes are skyline blue.
> Your cheeks shine with each tender smile
> And your hair flows like a willow tree,
> Strong and beautiful is what you are,
> But stronger you and I would be.

I stood there in a daze as Amy came up behind me. She saw the paper in my hand and knew I was intrigued by something too good to be true. I handed it to her and she read it carefully.

"Oh my God, he's a poet. How romantic," she said, looking happier than me.

"It is quite impressive, isn't it? To be honest, it sort of blew me away. I've never had a man do anything like this for me before. To be honest, I've never had any man do anything for me before," I said, wondering if I was doing the right thing.

We gossiped about it all the way back to the dorm, and my heart was very touched by all of the trouble Eric had gone through to get my attention. No one had ever done so much just to get my attention. I knew if I let him go, I'd be throwing away someone everyone else would call "a keeper."

All afternoon I waited for him to call, but the phone didn't ring. "He's just like the rest of 'em, liars," I said to myself, heading for the door to go out for a walk. But before I could get out the door, the phone rang loud and clear. I ran to the phone, but stopped myself. I wasn't going to act as if I were waiting for him. I wanted him to think I could care less if he called. About three or four rings later, I slowly picked up the phone and answered.

"Hey cutie. Did you read my note?" he asked.

"Yes," I said "very impressive."

"I like to write. Does that surprise you? You see, I had creative writing on my schedule, but I just switched it around to be near you," he said.

"I guess we have one thing in common, I love to write. That's about the only thing I'm good at," I said.

He was quiet for a moment, as if he were thinking of the right words to say.

"How soon can you be ready to go?" he asked.

"Where are we going?" I said curiously.

"You'll have to find out when we get there. It's a surprise, but I assure you, you'll love it," he said.

"Give me an hour, but how do I dress? Casual, or dressy, what?" I asked him.

"Whatever you want to wear, I'm sure you'll look beautiful. I'll be there in one hour." he said, hanging up the phone.

Since I was already dressed, I went to the mirror and checked to make sure I looked just perfect for him. I wanted him to want me, but I wasn't sure I could do anything that would prove I liked him as well. I couldn't believe I had never been with a man. There probably weren't very many girls my age who hadn't. Embarrassing as it might have been, I was proud of it at the same time. I was holding myself for someone who I knew would never hurt me. I wanted to make sure before I gave myself totally. 'Cause once I gave myself totally to someone, I'd never be able to get it back again. And I never wanted to give something away that could never be gotten back unless I was sure it was worth taking the chance.

Before I knew it, an hour had passed and I went out in front of the dorm to wait for him. I sat down on the front steps and stared at all of the beautiful trees and playful squirrels who were around the swing in front of the student building. It was amazing. They weren't afraid of anyone. They would walk right up to you, look at you, then run away again. My wondering turned into nervousness as I saw Eric pull up in a brand new, red pick-up truck. It was beautiful as it sat there shining from one end to the other.

He walked up and took my hand. I stood and he led me to his truck, then let me in on his side. I slid over by the door and he just looked at me and smiled as though he knew he'd gain my trust eventually. Little by little he was, but I wasn't going to show that part of myself to him just yet. I wanted to make him work for any trust I may show him. And as charming as he was from the very first impression I had of him, if he were to stay that way, I knew it wouldn't be long before my heart was his.

Every little bit Eric would look over at me as if he were admiring the view. I was embarrassed by all of his attention. No one had ever been that nice and caring to me before. It was a new experience for me. I figured I'd better enjoy it while it lasted because I knew it couldn't last very long. There was a chance he would turn into a bastard just like every other man I'd known, but for the moment, I just couldn't picture him as being a bastard to anyone. That just didn't seem like the kind of person he was.

We drove for a while when he finally stopped. He parked beside a clear-water pond on the edge of town. The only sounds were the sounds of nature, soothing nature. He got out of the truck and came around to open the door for me. He took my hand and helped me out. We walked over to a clearing where he had a picnic basket, a blanket, and some wine glasses. My eyes filled with the anticipation. I hadn't known him long, but he seemed like the type that usually got what he wanted and knew how to get it. At least he had a good technique if nothing else.

We sat and talked for a while. He took all the food out of the basket, poured the wine, then made a toast.

"To you, and to what the future has to hold," he said.

We toasted and he leaned over slowly. Spooked by him, I jumped up and started walking towards the clear water. When I reached the edge of the pond, my reflection in the water was like looking into a mirror. There was fear in my eyes, but why? It drove me crazy. I really liked him, but why was I afraid? There was no reason. His presence was so placid and his smile exhilarating. I had to take a deep breathe and come back to earth to re-evaluate my feelings and my abrupt actions.

He caught up with me and asked, "Beth, what's wrong. Did I do something wrong?"

"No. It's not you. I know you've probably heard that before, but it's true.

I don't know what's wrong with me. I feel like I'm losing my mind," I said, leaning against his chest.

He held me tightly, and it felt good to have someone hold me in that way. He really was concerned about me. I could tell, but I still couldn't get past what was buried deep within my heart, that thing that keeps eating at me every time I want to get close to someone.

We went back over to the blanket. With my head on his stomach, he stroked my hair like my sister used to do when I was younger. It felt good. I felt at peace. The moon shone down on us like the eye of God was watching each movement we made. And as long as God was watching, I had no doubt things would be just fine. And as long as I was lying next to Eric, I felt safe. For me, that was a feeling I wasn't used to, but one I could learn to live with.

"You probably think I'm crazy, but..."

"Beth, no. You're not crazy, just confused. I am too," he interrupted.

Smiling at him, I leaned over and gently kissed his soft red lips for just a moment, a moment I wanted to relive over and over. The gleam in his eyes almost met the light of the moon, and the pounding of his heart made me worry that he already had too many feelings for me. My heart was also pounding, but I was able to control the feelings in my heart. I had to. I had no choice.

There was an unmistakable feeling in the air that something was overtaking both of us. I could feel it in the flinches of his chest, and in the soothing sound of his voice when he spoke to me. We talked for so long, that we fell asleep before we knew it. The first light of the sun in the morning woke us. When I opened my eyes, I saw the many colors of the sun as it rose to greet us for the morning. It was beautiful. It was an experience I seldom had the pleasure of seeing.

"Eric. Wake up. Look. Isn't it breathtaking?" I said as his sleepy eyes slightly opened.

He raised up and put his arms around me and held me close. His embrace took my breath away. I didn't want to let go. I wanted to hang onto him until the sun came and went a million times over. I wanted to see those brilliant eyes looking into my heart and my soul each time I met a new day.

Unaware of what time had passed, I looked at my watch and jumped up quickly.

"We have to go. We'll be late for class. Come on," I said, hurrying to the truck.

We scurried in and Eric put the truck into high gear. We were flying. Then I began to laugh for no reason. Maybe it was the excitement of the moment which took me in, but whatever it was, I knew one thing. He was so much fun. His expressions were so unique and his personality overtaking. By the time we reached the dorms, I was ready to jump out and get ready for class; but, about the time I reached for the handle, he pulled me to him. He gave me a kiss like none

I'd ever known. It touched me all over like a million bolts of electricity running through each and every part of me. Shivers ran through me like a roller coaster, that was virtually unstoppable. I pulled back and glanced at him. He knew he had stolen my heart with that one moment, that one kiss, but where would it lead? As hard as I tried to deny it to myself, I knew it just the same. He reached deep enough inside of me to make me realize there are some men that care about how you feel. Some men are sensitive and admirable in the way they treat someone who means everything to them. And I was impressed by his gentleman like actions and also by the gentleness of his touch.

CHAPTER 2

The first few weeks of school was more exciting than anything I had ever experienced before. Eric was becoming a normal part of each day. Every morning he called just to make sure his voice was the first voice I heard when greeting the day. And when I walked out the doorway to go to class, he would be standing there to carry my books and to hold my hand as we walked together. Though the cafeteria was noisy, when we'd go eat lunch, all we could hear was what the other had to say, and gazed into each other's eyes as if no one else was around. I had promised myself I'd never get entangled in something so complicated, but I was being sucked in by some kind of power stronger than the strength of my own mind. The light behind his gleaming eyes made me want to dig further and further until I could find out where that light was coming from. But there was this feeling inside of me that told me it was coming from deep in his heart—the place where all of his spirit, caring, concern, and love dwelled. I wanted to reach that place to see exactly what made him the person he was. What his childhood was like. And what gave him the values he held so precious and true. I wanted to know everything about him. Though I felt like I'd known him a lifetime, there was so much I didn't know about him.

And that was the part of him I wanted to explore until I knew every significant moment that made him the loving person he was.

The days were getting pretty routine. And I was a bit frustrated about my school work. My creative writing class was the only class I was passing with flying colors. My concentration was wandering a little too much on other things. And I needed to redirect my attentions on what I was there to do. I was there to get a degree and make something good of my life. I carried each moment as my last, because I knew the moment I took time for granted, it would be taken away from me by the powerful hands of the almighty above. My brother was proof of that. Though I hadn't thought about him much, I was still pretty upset in my own way. The way it happened was a bit unexpected and put the family in an outrage.

Time got away from him far sooner than he ever thought it would. He'd been in the hospital for minor surgery. Everything was supposed to have gone smoothly, with no complications, so the doctors said. But one mistake was made which cost him his life. One of the nurses came in and gave him a pain shot with a needle that wasn't clean. It didn't take long for the infection in his body to spread. No one quite knew what type of infection he received by the needle, but we all knew the end result was his death. My mom and dad were still trying to sue the hospital, but all the money in the world wouldn't change what happened. No apology would turn back the hands of time. I've learned all too well that time keeps ticking no matter if you're living your life happily or wasting it away on sorrow and depression. The way I looked at it, each minute is a gift given from God. And each experience we go through, traumatic or exhilarating, is a lesson given from the almighty, lessons we should learn from and live with. That made me think. I wanted to spend all the time I had left in the world working for a goal, a dream. And once I reached that goal, I'd have time to sit back, smile, and see what I'd accomplished. My dream was to be a writer. I wanted to be known. I wanted to be looked up to by others. But most importantly, I needed the self recognition of doing something worthwhile and important. I'd always felt it was worthwhile to take a pen and piece of paper and just begin to write. Sometimes it would be poetry, and other times it didn't make sense to anyone but me; but that was okay. I saw it as a way of therapy...a way to heal hidden wounds deep in my heart. Usually that was exactly what it did. The refreshing feeling I've always had after writing down my feelings is something that could never be described by words, only by the contentedness it brings.

For a change, I decided to lie down around 2:30, and rest after my last class, instead of running around and spending money I didn't have. I closed my eyes and fell asleep. A dream pulled me far away. I could barely see my hands in front of my face. It seemed never ending. The more I walked, the longer it became. A crossing appeared. A pale moon showed through a fog for a short time and then it disappeared. Walking over the bridge, I closed my hands into a fist. Appearing in front of me was a figure too hazy for me to recognize. I walked closer and then...I awakened; startled and in dismay. I looked at my surroundings and knew I must've had another terrible encounter within my dreams. Though I couldn't remember any faces or details, I knew it had frightened me deep inside. Trying to shake it off, I turned to the window. Without thinking, I started to shriek.

Eric's face was staring at me. He had climbed up the tree directly outside my window. I guess he thought he was going to surprise me, but I think he was the one who got surprised. I frightened him just as much when I bellowed out such a horrifying scream.

"Damn it Eric. What in the hell are you doing?" I yelled..

With the window open, he climbed in and looked shocked that I was angry, rather than happy to see him. But his timing wasn't the best it could've been. I was shaking, my heart pounding and anger was my first feeling when I saw him.

"Hey. What's wrong. I thought I'd surprise you, not startle you. Are you alright?" he said, trying to pacify me.

I just looked up at him with eyes full of fire. I didn't know exactly what I was angry about, but my blood was boiling. I guess his timing was just too off the wall at the moment. I had a feeling my dream was trying to tell me something, but nothing made any sense. It all seemed so scrambled up inside my mind. Such a short nightmare left me shaken. And Eric added to my nervousness with his unpredictable actions.

We sat down on the bed and I told Eric what I had dreamed. The sincere and caring look he gave me, made me feel silly that I was frightened at all. Just to look at him was all I needed to return back to reality and escape that dark road of fear. And as soon as Amy got out of class I figured she'd laugh about the whole thing.

"It was just a dream. It doesn't mean a thing Beth. Just try not to worry about it. Anyway, I'm here now, and you can hold onto me all you want," he said, putting his hands on my face and gently kissing my forehead like a father to his little girl.

With my head resting on his shoulder I felt secure, at least for the moment, and that was all I needed. The warmth I felt each time I was close to him was immeasurable. A million bon fires could never add up to the warmth inside his heart.

For a while, he just held me. I could feel his heart beating against my chest, and that made my heart beat with much the same rhythm. I closed my eyes and kept wishing that moment would never leave us. Feeling him next to me was like an eternity of happiness and contentment. I never wanted it to end, but I knew it would sooner or later.

For nights on end, I'd dream that very same dream over and over again. And the last time I dreamed it, the person in the shadow reached out for me in a terrifying way, tried to grab me, but my feet were fast and I just ran away. It was like whoever or whatever it was wanted to haunt me. Although I didn't know what was haunting me, I wanted it to leave me alone.

I couldn't make any sense out of it. It was very strange. I knew there was something that was in my subconscious making me have these odd dreams, but the more I tried to force it out, the less I seemed to know. When I'd let my guard down, my memory would get triggered by someone or something around me. I didn't want to have to worry about something that was probably just my imagination, but until I could find out exactly what was stalking my mind, I knew I'd continue to worry.

I walked around in front of my dorm just thinking. Eric tried to join me, but I wanted to be alone. I wasn't the type of person to be the least bit rude about anything.

I never wanted to hurt anyone's feelings. And I never wanted my feelings hurt, so I thought it was cruel to do something to someone you wouldn't want done to you. I tried to be subtle while telling Eric to leave me alone. I didn't want him angry with me, but I felt like I needed the time to pull all my thoughts and my feelings together and sort them out.

"Eric, do you mind if I walk alone today. I just need some time to think. It's not about us, it's about me. I'll call you when I get back to the room. It won't be long, I promise," I said softly.

He peered at me with those beautiful eyes and replied, "I guess, but you'd have a more enjoyable walk with me with you."

I smiled back at him, and my heart was full of warmth from his soul to mine. He always gave me that feeling. His touch was always tender and his voice mesmerizing. My heart was almost filled completely with the vision of he and I as one body combined. Though I tried to keep holding back, I wanted more than anything to have him forever. Each time I looked into his eyes, it seemed as though I could see the future. It was like watching a home movie of our future together. I wanted him, but at the same time, I wanted to get to know myself. For so long I'd been walking around in a body that had no idea where it had been, or where it was going. There was a part of my life which had been missing and I knew until I found that unknown link, I would never be able to give myself to anyone wholly. I knew until I understood my weaknesses and explored my strengths, I'd never be able to understand what was going on in the deep dark corners of my mind. What I needed was a shining light to lead me to my destiny, my past, and my future. I needed that yellow brick road to follow to happiness and to fulfillment, and someone by my side to hold my hand each step of the way. I needed someone to be able to stand with me and tell me everything would be alright. Sometimes words from a loved one can partially mend a broken fence of life. And in time, can fully mend it, until it's like brand new. The only problem I had, was that I'd never had that special loved one to do that for me. I never felt as though anyone cared enough to reach out for me with a loving hand of help. After a while, I stopped looking for someone to help me, and started trying to help myself. For everyone knows that the only person you can really count on, is yourself.

Eric was who I needed beside me, but the rest was unknown. The way I felt for him was the only thing keeping me sane at the time, and I didn't want to lose my rock and foundation. Just the thought of him made me smile. Just a glance would fill my heart until it was overflowing with bliss. Sometimes I'd be in class or in the shower, and when a memory of he and I would cross my mind, a faint grin would turn into a smile. Until I met him, no one could ever do that for me.

My walk was peaceful and full of serenity. The beauty which surrounded me had to have been touched by God's hands. The leaves were so delicate and shining, and the birds sang beautiful melodies from heaven. A cool breeze swept through me until it wiped away every bit of sadness and fear. I just stood there and stared up at the sky, through the clouds and past the birds that were in such perfect flight. I kept hoping God would give me a sign that everything would be as I'd always dreamed, a life full of hope, rather than despair, and of love, rather than loneliness. I knew he could hear my thoughts and feel my agony of the unknown. And I knew one remarkable day a tremendous light would shine down and guide me until I reached that golden rainbow only few people see in a lifetime. But, I, Beth Laney, would be one of those few, because I knew I would try, be patient, and it would be mine. I'd realized at that point in my life, attitude was everything.

Still walking, I stopped at a nearby swing. Smiling, I was proud of myself, for that was my first day of positive thinking. It was the first day optimism trampled my pessimistic side, and left my heart with a new birth of hope; a hope I hadn't seen in a long time. I didn't want to go on looking at life from the darkest side. I wanted to face the light and see everything that could be grasped within my own abilities. And with that thought floating around in my head, I sat back to enjoy the beautiful scenery God had placed so perfectly in front of me.

The crackling of leaves came from directly behind me, and a set of large hands covered my eyes entirely. At first I felt a short flare of panic, but then I realized those big warm hands couldn't have been anyone's but Eric's. I reached up and placed my small frail hands over his and gently removed them. I turned half way around and Eric was standing there with that picturesque smile across his handsome face. He began to rub my neck intensely to release all of the tension that had built up inside of me. And it worked remarkably. Soon enough he came around and sat beside me. He sat as close as he could get and the warmth transmitted between us was electrical. It started at my heart and worked its way out, and I knew if heaven was anywhere near, I had to be there at that very moment. Because I felt like I must have had a dozen angels hovering over me telling me to dwell only on the moment at hand and not think of anything else.

"I have a great idea," Eric said.

With a smile I replied, "What, more surprises?"

"Maybe, come on," he said, pulling me up from the swing and going towards his truck.

With Eric you never knew what was going to come up next. Maybe that was one reason he became such a big part of my life in such a short time. His gallant way of doing things always made one minute to the next very enticing. I always felt like a princess in a fairy tale when he would sweep me up and take me somewhere. Sometimes I could almost picture a pedestal in front of me, as if he were lifting me up higher and higher. Of course, even though I knew I was no princess, he was still my prince.

We drove for just a moment, and finally we pulled up to this cabin just a few minutes from town. It set back a little in the woods, and the nature scene was astounding. It was exquisite the way everything had it's place in such a solitary environment. The animals seemed fearless and I had never seen so many different kinds of flowers blooming in such an isolated domain. I could've sat there and stared at it forever. It would've been easy to just shut out the rest of the world. The trees were smiling at me, it seemed, and the sky cradled both Eric and I like tiny babies.

"Come on, I want to show you somethin'," he said.

We walked up to the cabin carefully. The ragged steps up to the porch were worn and hazardous looking, but Eric made sure I didn't fall. He held onto me until we were on safe and untarnished wood. When he opened the door, to my surprise, the interior of that old cabin was clean and beautiful in a rough kind of way. The was furniture was wooden and coarse. The bed in the corner was small and old fashioned with a square wooden headboard and footboard. There were several candles set around here and there, but no lights anywhere. It was beginning to get dark so I began to worry a little more than I should've. I'd always been a little uneasy in strange places. It wasn't spooky in the least, but just different from what I'd been used to.

Eric went over to the first candle and lit it, then the next and the next. By the time he was finished, the light in the room gave a very romantic atmosphere. Overwhelmed with awe, I went and sat down in a rough wooden chair over by the table that matched it perfectly. I glanced down and there was a picture that looked very old. I picked it up and stared at it for a moment. I didn't recognize the people, but it looked as though it was taken in that very cabin long ago. The background in the picture looked so fresh and clean. Eric came over and hovered over my shoulder.

"They look so much in love," I said, staring at that piece of the past.

"Like us?" he said.

"Eric, I..."

To feel something was one thing, but for me to reveal it was another. My fear still dwelled deep inside of me. I wasn't sure telling all would be the best thing to do. And I wasn't sure he'd understand what problems were buried that I still didn't quite know what they were. I wanted to deal with them alone first, and then reach for help if necessary.

"What, Beth? We've been seeing each other for a while now. I know you feel it too. Don't act like you don't because I can feel it each time I hold you and I see it when our eyes meet. I've felt it for sometime now. I know you love me. I just wish you could tell me. I've wanted to tell you since the first day I saw you. I know it sounds silly, but I knew somehow I would see you again; and I was right," he said with a sincere look on his virile and perfectly shaped face.

I stood up and kissed him gently on the cheek and then laid on his shoulder for a little more security before I let loose everything I'd vowed not to. Just holding him told me he would never betray me. And the warmth from his body melted into mine like the sun warming and nourishing the flowers. In a way, he was nourishing me with his love and affection. He always seemed to try to cover me and protect me like the darkness over the night. Though it may sound strange, even sitting alone, at times I could still feel him near me. His spirit and caring always dwelled around me even when he wasn't there. And when we would see each other, the feeling grew and grew until I'd realized I'd jumped into deep water without thinking. But for once, I wasn't frightened to swim. In fact, I wanted to learn how to swim.

Though someone else might feel as if they were being interrogated, I felt like someone had just lit a light inside my heart. He lit a candle to show me the way on the pathway of love, and I intended to follow it step by step, and side by side.

CHAPTER 3

Taking my hand, with the cabin dimly lit, Eric led me to the window which held a spectacular view of the lake below. The reflection of the trees onto the water made them look twice as beautiful. And the florescent beams from the moon were shining down on the tiny waves, making small streaks of light all over the lake's surface. Like in a painting, it was something that was hard to take your eyes off of.

With Eric's hands around my waist, he squeezed me tightly. It was an embrace that made me feel very protected and free of dismay. I wanted him to hold me like that until he could hold on no longer. I covered his hands with mine and we just stood there in a steady, but slow rocking motion; like the rocking of an infant-back and forth.

His fingers crawled around my stomach like a spider on its' prey, and the higher he went, the more nervous I became. It wasn't that I didn't want his touch, but being with a man was an experience I'd never had before. It was so scary, and yet comforting at the same time. My mind was boggled by the intensity of the moment, but flattered by his soothing gestures.

His warm kisses on my neck made sporadic sparks fly within my body, and the tension was easing little by little. I was beginning to let go entirely and started giving in to all of his aspirations. At that moment, I threw away the blinders which kept me from wanting love in my life, and replaced them with the trust I held in him. I reached down into my heart and destroyed them fully. At least that way, I knew I would be able to see things clearly without looking at everything through muddy water. I had to see things clearly. If I didn't, my mind would get bogged up to the point where I would be unable to see right in front of me. I wanted to see what was coming next. I needed to know the consequences of my actions.

Still looking out the window, I knew what would happen next and it frightened me. I had never been with a man because my fear always kept me from it. But my fear was giving into passion and my heart was being taken by a swift, but loving hand...a hand I knew would never hurt me..

Turning around anxiously, Eric held my face up with his fingertips and smiled his irresistible smile. Our eyes stayed on one another, only building up to the moment when I would give all of myself to him. But the apprehension was still there. Trying to push it further and further away didn't seem to facilitate. All I was able to do, was block all of the fear from inside away from the moment at hand, and hope it would stay away.

He looked down to the floor and back up again. And as he kissed my cheek gently, he started to unbutton my shirt one by one, very carefully. My hands were shaking and my knees felt like they were going to collapse. My palms were wet with anticipation, but my heart was still very cautious. It had to be. I was cautious for my feelings, but, at the same time, I wanted to jump into a deep sea just to see if I could swim well enough to keep my head above the dangerous waves of love which sometimes turn into traitorous storms of deception. But deceit was not what I saw ahead of me. He never once made me wonder if he was being honest with me. He never once lead me to believe something that wasn't true. His heart was full of honor.

His hands slipped my shirt off my shoulders swiftly, but gently, and then I took the initiative. Instead of being slow and steady as he'd been with me, I rapidly took off his shirt and dropped it on the floor. Eric went over to the bed and pulled back the handmade quilt and brought a candle over to light the way. Before we reached the bed, we were already undressed and full of anticipation. I could tell he was nervous because of the way he shook when held me in his arms before we laid down. It was like a shiver of cold, but it wasn't cold in the least. In fact, it was getting very warm in that small cabin, and I knew before it was over, the heat would get much worse. I could already feel the sweat forming on my forehead the closer we became. It felt like we were sticking together like glue from the perspiration between us.

We crawled into that tiny bed and Eric covered me like a blanket. Our bodies were close and our hearts were beating a thousand times faster than ever before. I had never felt such anticipation. Nothing had ever left my heart beating so that it felt like it would burst. I felt like I needed to tell him I'd never been with a man before, but I was afraid he would think I was strange. But the honesty within me, made me utter that he would be my first sexual experience.

"Eric, I've never..."

He interrupted, "I know. It's ok. We'll go slow. Remember I love you."

"I love you too," I said as he started to make love to me.

He was very slow and easy, and his touch made me feel even more secure than I did before. I knew he would never be with me if he didn't want or if he didn't love me. I knew he loved me. His actions always made that so very clear. And his words completed his actions.

To hold that moment secure in my mind, I closed my eyes and tried to feel all of the love Eric was giving me. Our bodies worked together like a well oiled piece of machinery, and for a moment, all of the fear and frustration that had been my bedfellow for so many years, was gone, dissipated. All of the fear was replaced, for a moment, by love and encouragement from someone who could very well be my future, someone who could be my soulmate until my time is up on this earth. And since no one knows when their last moment will be, I wanted each moment to be treasured.

Everything was going so smoothly when a flash of fear came as a vision in my mind. The darkness was overwhelming me. A dark figure shadowed me as I lay in bed. The closer he became, the more fear welled inside of my soul. As his hand reached down, and I felt a touch in the genitals, I burst out in tears and in rage of the solicitude that bound me. My eyes were clinched shut and anxiety took over. The tremble throughout my body was undiminished by love or by anything or anyone around me. I felt like a child trapped in a time that had nothing left for me but desperation and loneliness. Sweat poured off my body as I laid there curled up in a ball rocking too and fro. As my eyes were being pried open, in front of me, was the man who was trying so hard to be loving, caring and tender. But at that moment I felt separated from him. His touch seemed obscene, and his kiss terrifying. As shivers of the unknowingness of what was happening came over me, I blocked out everything but the sound of the crickets outside the window. It seemed to calm me, to separate me from my confusion.

Eric reached over to hold me, but I pushed myself further away from him. In my mind, I had traveled many miles away with no idea where I'd gone. All I knew was that there was something unfinished inside of me. There had to be something that needed to be looked at with passion and solitude. I knew Eric must've thought I had lost my mind, because that was exactly what I was thinking. I wanted to know what was happening to me just as much as he did.. I wanted to know why I couldn't live my life without fear. It was like there was an important piece of a puzzle missing; but nowhere to be found. And that was the one piece I needed to know exactly who I was and what I had become. All of the flashes and images in my mind were driving me insane. I just couldn't seem to put them together. I couldn't make one clear picture out of them. They seemed so jumbled up; so unclear.

"Beth, what's wrong. Tell me damn it. I have a right to know what's going on. You've been pushing me away since the first day we met and all I've done is make excuses for you. I need to hear the truth, not an excuse," Eric said, his eyes filled with anger, but at the same time, concern.

I burst into tears and buried myself in his arms of security. I didn't know what to say. I wasn't sure what was going on, so I knew I couldn't tell him. I had to find out where that hell hole, I'd been living inside, was, for the first time in my life. An explanation seemed impossible, and words were hard to come by. As he waited for an answer I thought of what I could say to make him realize I was just as lost as he was. I knew he might not believe me, but I had to try to make him understand.

"Eric. I can't tell you. I can't tell you because I don't know myself. I just keep seeing these images, these visions, and they're scaring the living hell out of me. I've got a fear inside I can't control. It's not you. I'd never be afraid of you, you know that. You're the only one who keeps me from losing my mind, but...but still, still I'm afraid. This dark figure I keep seeing is the key, but who or what it is? I just don't know. Please don't give up on me. I've already told you I love you, and that's the first time I've ever really felt this kind of love. I don't want to lose it so soon after I've found it. I love you Eric."

He took my hands and pulled me to him, firmly. He stared into my eyes, and I saw an emptiness that would only be filled with my happiness. My unhappiness was very apparent, and it seemed like he felt just as lonely and confused as I did. I didn't want to transfer my fears and anxiety to him, but I could tell that he really did love me. I always heard when someone loves you, really loves you, your pains are their pains, and your happiness is theirs as well. Feeling a tear gently flow down my cheek, that teardrop had two meanings. At first it was fear of the unknown, but then it changed to the tear of happiness in knowing I was truly loved. It was astounding. Just him being there gave me the shelter I needed to stand tall until I reached what was trying to be my downfall. And I had to keep reaching and reaching until I found out what mysteries had been hovering all around my soul from the first time I envisioned fear itself. It was a strange feeling.

We got dressed, and the silence in the room was blaring at me. I just wanted to get back in my own bed and think about what was going to happen next. I was even more confused then than ever. Besides feeling loved, I also felt betrayed. And for no reason at all, in my subconscious, I blamed Eric for all of it. It wasn't fair, but I had no one else to blame for what was happening to me. He was the only one around, so I guess it made perfect sense to blame him. But instead of blaming him, I should have been thanking him for giving me his shoulder to cry on and his arms which he'd wrapped around me over and over again..

Eric took my hand and we started to walk to the car. Before we reached it, Eric stopped and looked up at the sky for a moment. A hush surrounded us as the sensuous chill of a brisk breeze soothed our skin after such a discouraging evening together.

"Look. The stars are shining so beautifully. Beth, I've always thought the stars had a hidden lesson in them. You know, they're up there in a pitch dark skyline, and they still shine just as bright, and twinkle just as much every single night. That's always amazed me.

Every time I get really depressed, I look up to the sky at night. You know, as dark and gloomy as the night may seem, the stars above just keep shimmering, keep shining as bright as if it were the light of the sun. And I bet if all the stars were side by side, they'd overpower the darkness and bring light to everyone. Just like us. If we stay side by side, we can overpower the dark and bring back light and that would keep it just as bright every hour of every day. We can keep darkness away by putting the light from our hearts together as one flame," he said, letting passion roar from his heart.

"Oh Eric, I know you're right. I just hope we're two stars that'll stay close together and never shy away each time the sky gets darker. I hope that light doesn't turn to dim and leave me all alone. I need you," I said, embracing him sincerely.

Eric's words touched me and made me think. I knew he was right, but the uncertainty of him being around forever, left me confused and frightened at the same time. Eric always seemed to keep reminding me that he cared, and the words 'I Love You' filled my mind with wonder of the days and years to come. Although I'd never been quite sure of anything, I wanted to force my heart into trusting someone if just one time.

From then on, day after day, hour after hour, everything was pretty much the same. Amy and I became best friends and Eric completed the triangle. School started putting a strain on me. I guess I never realized how hard it would be. I even started failing creative writing, one thing I would've never believed. My strongest interest was beginning to deteriorate before my eyes, but my personal life was unexpectedly wonderful. I was doing something I swore I would never do, I was putting everything else ahead of my hopes and dreams of being a well educated and looked up to professional. As someone once told me, "Dreams are like the wings of an eagle, wounded, it can't fly, but if they're protected, there is no limit to how high you can go, or where you can travel."

In a way, I felt like I was wounding my own eagle of dreams, but still able to protect them, I wanted to repair the damage and start to fly once more. Some things are worth the trouble they cause you, and I knew my education was one thing that would be hard, but at the same time, I knew it would give me great rewards in the future; rewards that could never be matched by anything else..

There was one thing which had bothered me. I hadn't talked to my parents in such a long time. I didn't even know if I would know their voices if I heard them. So one night I sat down with my magical pen and blank paper, and started to write them a letter.

Dear mom and dad,

How are you doing? I haven't talked to you in so long that I'm not sure what to say. How's Melissa? I wish I could talk to her. Please give her my address and maybe she'll write to me. Christmas is soon, so I guess I'll see you then.

Love Your Daughter,
Beth

When I put the pen and paper down, I felt a loss of words. I'd never felt a loss of words, so I thought. I picked up the phone about the time a knock came at my door.

"Coming," I yelled, putting on my old terry clothe robe.

When I opened the door, there was a dozen long stemmed yellow roses. They were exquisite. The baby's breathe that was nestled in the midst of the flowers, gave it a lavishing look. I picked them up and steadfastly put my nose up to the soft pedals. The scent lingered throughout the room, like a garden had been placed in it. Imagining the sun was warming my back as I leaned down on a radiant group of blossoms, my eyes were closed and my heart taken. I could also imagine a pathway through the garden which led to a stream of clear white water. The soothing sound of the water put me into a trance. It was as though I could feel a zephyr of coolness like I had moved myself to another place.

"Beth, what are you doing?" Amy said, looking down at me.

I was leaned down as if my imagination had come true. To be honest, I was a bit embarrassed. Amy probably thought I'd gone off the deep end. But my imagination just got away with me. It seemed to do that quite often.

"I was just...well. Look what I got," I said, trying to gear away from my embarrassment.

"I bet I know who those are from," she said with a shifty smile.

Looking at the expression on her face, I wondered what she was thinking. She acted as though she knew something, but wouldn't dare tell me.

"Hey, what's goin' on? You know somethin' don't you? I mean, there was no card. I'm not a mind reader, you know," I said.

"Come on Beth, you know who they're from. Who else would they be from? " She said, still with a look on her face that didn't seem completely honest.

"Well, I don't care. They're lovely, and I'm keepin' them no matter who they're from," I said, lying down on my bed to study.

It wasn't long before the phone rang. I glanced up at the receiver and then at Amy.

"Answer it. It might be your secret admirer," she said secretively.

After about five rings I finally picked up the phone and answered. "Hello." I said, knowing who it'd be.

"How'd you like the roses? " an unfamiliar voice asked.

"Eric, is that you?"

"Who's Eric? I guess I should be jealous," the voice said.

A bit frightened, I hung up the phone, but it wasn't just a moment before it rang once more. I had no idea who it was. I wanted it to be Eric, so I answered it again.

"Why did you hang up? I wanted to talk to you. I've been admiring you from afar ever since the beginning of the semester. I never could get close to you because of that guy you're always with," he said in a threatening voice.

"Who are you?" I asked sharply.

"Not now. You'll find out soon enough" he said hanging up the phone hurriedly.

Amy looked confused. "I would've sworn Eric sent them. I just talked to him the other day and he said."

"What did he say? Come on Amy. Tell me," I demanded.

She stammered around somewhat and then answered me, "He wants you to spend Christmas with him. He wants to fly you down to Carolina with him so you can meet his family. But you didn't hear it from me. I just thought he might've sent you flowers to butter you up before asking you to go. I have no idea who just called. I'm just as surprised and stunned as you are," she said.

Disturbed a little, I just stared at Amy with a blank expression on my face. I didn't know what to think. It was enough that I was having to go through something unknown already, now I was having to deal with some kind of psychopath on the rampage. I knew it had to have been just someone playing a prank on me, but you never can tell. Crazy people are born everyday. I just hoped none of them set their sights on me. That was all I needed to finish pushing me over the edge.

I stormed out the door and ran down the hall in confusion. Everyone I passed looked at me as though I was from a time warp or something. When I reached the doorway that took me outside, I stopped abruptly. I placed my hand on the door and slowly pushed it open. The bench across the street always gave me a peaceful feeling, so I went over and sat down. I only saw one or two people out walking, but I didn't think twice about it. I'd never been one to let paranoia keep me from anything, though it slowed me down sometimes..

I lowered my head to think and I felt a hand surprisingly touch my arm. But when I started to turn around, whoever it was touching me, turned my head straight so I couldn't see them. They didn't say a word. All I could hear was breathing and I could feel it the same on the back of my neck. It'd only been a few seconds, but it seemed like an eternity. The longer I sat there in the darkness, the more apprehensive I became.

Then he laughed. It was Eric. "Scare ya?" he said, continuing to chuckle kiddingly.

"You Bastard! You inconsiderate bastard!" I cried out.

Not knowing about the strange phone call and roses, he looked at me as though he couldn't believe my reaction to him. I was shaken up completely, and my heart was beating unusually fast. I felt faint. The trees around me seemed to swim around my head, and when I attempted to stand, I fell to the ground. Eric went into hysterics. There were a few people walking by, and one of them called an ambulance. Eric or no one else knew what had happened to me.

A full day passed before I woke up. The doctors were bewildered. They said there was no sign of anything possibly wrong with me, but for evaluation, they kept me for another day just to be safe. I wasn't even sure what happened. I wanted to know. I knew if it was my fear that did it, I wanted to do something about it. It always seemed as though when I would start to get my life together, something would happen to paralyze me. At that point, my security was Eric. He was my warm blanket in the coldest of nights. And most importantly, he was the only one who ever proved to me his love was completely unselfish. He always seemed to light the way in the darkest of nights, but I knew one day, one hour, one minute, his light of love wouldn't be there and I would have to face the darkness with only my security of being who I am. And I wasn't sure I knew who I was. I wasn't even sure if I wanted to know. There were so many things that were like fill in the blank in my life. It made it more of a guessing game than anything. And I didn't want to have to guess when it came to the rest of my life. My time was too valuable for me to guess at anything at all.

Someone once said that the fear of not knowing is the biggest fear of all, and I at that point in my life, I believed that with all my heart. I always seemed to fear something which was invisible to me, something which played a game of hide and seek. It was always something in my mind that scared me. Sometimes, I think I made it all up just for an excuse to draw back inside that shell hidden deep in my soul. No matter, something was happening to my mind, to my soul.

It was like a puzzle. There were so many pieces to put in place that confusion set in before it was finished. I wanted to find the final pieces of the horrible puzzle scattered all around me. I knew that with my luck, when it was all over, there would be one piece missing, and that piece would be the link to who I am inside. But I also knew if I was lucky, all of the pieces would fit and I would have a whole life without any mystery, without any doubt about what I wanted to do in the future and where I had been in the past. No one needs that kind of strain on their subconscious. But I wondered, at the same time, if everyone knows where every piece of the puzzle fits in their puzzle of life. No one knows everything. Maybe I wasn't as crazy as I thought I was.

I knew when I returned to my confusing life, I would have to make a decision about what I needed to do to make myself whole again. And at that point I was ready to do so. All I needed was a little bit of help through it all...just a little help.

CHAPTER 4

Eric came to pick me up once the doctors decided I was well enough to go home. Seeing him was light of the sun after being in a dark tunnel. His eyes were fused with mine as he came closer to me. I was sitting on the edge of the bed; He took my hand, and gently led me down the hallway. Frightened as I was of him at times, he made sure I felt no fear at all. In fact, I felt more peace than ever before. The feel of his warm hand holding mine was one no words could express completely. But I knew once reality set in, my apprehension would cover me and my spirit. Hard as I tried, I always seemed to regress back into my old state of mind, instead of moving forward. I tended to dwell on past worries and hardships, rather than look forward to what bright roads might be in the pathway of life ahead of me. Light always seemed so very far away. Sometimes my courage would dissipated before I would consume the full renewing of such a light. And often times the tunnel was just far too much of a stretch for me to make.

Although the doctors said I was doing fine, Eric thought it necessary to take me to his room until I felt well enough to be alone. Even though he didn't know what was wrong with me, he still tried his best to be with me no matter what, and that was what I needed the most. He wanted me to be comfortable and to feel safe. It was as though he could read every thought scurrying across every inch of my brain at the exact moment I would think it. It amazed me sometimes the things Eric knew before I could say a word. Sometimes I thought he was a mind reader. I could be looking out the window of his truck quietly, and he'd look over at me as if he knew what I was thinking. It was a heart to heart connection I'd never experienced with any other person. Oddly enough, sometimes I did the same thing. Our souls were joined from the first day we met. I always knew

God had a plan for everyone, and everyone has someone special picked just for them. God's plan for me was to be with Eric and he with me. And if that wasn't God's plan, it should've been.

As we drove down the road, Eric looked over at me constantly. He always did that. He acted like he was a peasant and I was his queen. I guess every woman wants to be put up high on a pedestal at one time or another, but I'd never been used to that kind of treatment until he came along. Nothing he ever did surprised me. It usually bothered me when someone stares, but when he did it, it made me feel good about myself.

We pulled up to his dormitory and stopped abruptly. As he grabbed my things, he looked up at me and smiled.

"Come on," he said. "I'll show you where I live."

Hesitantly I followed behind him. He reached back and grasped my hand firmly, as if to calm my nerves. I could tell he knew I was a bit uneasy about staying with him. I felt well enough to stay in my own bed, but I didn't argue with him. When we reached his room, we looked at one another. I knew I wasn't ready for anything to happen between us just yet, and I wanted to make sure he knew it as well.

"Eric, I don't want you to think just because I'm staying with you means I'm ready for-I'm just not ready for that. I hope you're not mad, I said apologetically.

He grinned a bit and touched my face in soft strokes. "You didn't think that was the reason I brought you here did you? Come on Beth. I'm not that kind of person. I want you here so I can make sure you're alright. I worry about you. I don't care about anything else right now. All I care about now, is you."

I felt silly at his reply, and wished I hadn't said anything about it. I should've known he wouldn't do anything to hurt me, but at the same time, something told me to make sure he understood before we did something both of us were not ready for. The memory of what happened the last time we tried to be intimate lingered through my head. I guess I wanted to dust the settle before stirring up any more.

We went in and although it took me a while to relax, I finally felt comfortable being there with him. We talked for hours. Conversation was never ending each time we would talk. In fact, sometimes we'd never ran out of anything to say. But as tired as I was, I had to go to sleep. My body was exhausted and my mind was moving in slow motion. When I suggested we turn in for the night, he agreed and gave no argument.

He laid me down on his narrow bed and he sat beside me until every worry I had, drifted far, far away. I was unable to see anything but tranquility. It didn't take long until the tranquility which protected me, led me to badly needed sleep. I could hear Eric breathing at a steady pace, and every once in a while I would feel his warm breathe near my face as if he wanted to gently kiss me, but not wanting to wake me at the same time. Ever so often I would slowly open my eyes and close them back again just so I could see him staring lovingly at me. After a while I dozed off feeling God had placed me in good hands. Eric's devotion to me was immeasurable. And his sensitivity was like none I'd ever seen in any other man, not even in my father. My father was man of few words, and those few words were never "I love you." He never had the desire to express himself in that way. That was why it was very hard for me to see someone whom I'd know for such a short time, express more caring for me than my own family ever did.

Peace blanketed me all night long. As long as Eric was near me, I felt fine. And he always seemed to be nearby no matter where I was. I think that was one thing he tried to make me realize. He always told me, "Just look over your shoulder, and I'll be right there whenever you need me. That's a promise." It took me a while, but those words finally sunk in enough to where I believed them.

The bright sunlight through the window finally woke me very early the next morning. I glanced over and Eric was lying sideways on a chair fast asleep. He looked like a child as he was slowly breathing in and out, in and out. He didn't move, and silence welled up around us. Maybe it was just me, but I didn't consider silence to be my companion, it was more like an adversary hiding behind a mask of accord. But I could see that mask and the true peace of things seldom showed its' face in the way I viewed this masquerade party of sanity. For sanity was one asset I knew I did not possess. But with the same thought, time would give me what I needed to regain what sanity I used to grasp onto tightly. Praying to seize your sanity is probably the most spoken prayer, but less admitted than any other, because I knew in my heart I wasn't the only person in the world losing their mind for an unknown reason. I was a one of a kind, but not in that way. There had to be others just like me. I hoped so.

I sat up and tried to sneak away cautiously without disturbing his placid sleep, but as I reached the doorway.

"Where ya goin?" he ask softly.

Looking at him as he rubbed the sleep from his eyes, I replied "I need to go back to my room, and besides you could use some productive sleep. I know that chair isn't the most comfortable bed. But I did feel good being in the same room with you all night. I felt like I had a guardian angel watching over me while I slept. Maybe that was why I slept so wonderfully. Just knowing you were in arm's length made me feel too safe to be scared of anything."

He stood up listlessly and came over to me. Without a word he took me in his arms and laid his head on my shoulder as if he were planning on never letting me go. And for a split second I didn't want him to let me go, but I had to if I was going to jump back into reality. Holding onto his perfectly shaped body was marvelous, but I realized I couldn't stay in that spot and in that position for the rest of my life. I had to move on and let the smoke fly behind me.

Finally we released, and all we could do was smile at one another.

That moment seemed more like a fantasy than anything at all, because everyone knows that moments where contentedness fills yours soul, will not last forever. It fades slowly until it utterly disappears. But it never hurts to fantasize every once in a while, especially when the fantasy is so remarkable.

I left Eric's room and returned to my own. Amy was just leaving to go to class. She ran up and embraced me tightly.

"Are you okay. I've been worried sic since the other day. I called the hospital twice. They said you were going home today," she said concerned.

"I'm fine. Eric picked me up and he insisted I stay with him last night. I've been with him all night, but it's probably not what you think. He's been a real friend. I guess that's what I need most right now."

She smiled and told me she'd always be there for me. Of course, I knew that since the first day I met her. I always knew we'd be able feel each other's happiness and pain. I'd never had a friend like her. God must really think I'm special to send me such a caring person, I thought.

When she left, a picture came into my mind as if it were yesterday. I was just a child sitting on the front steps of the old frame house I used to live in. And next door lived a little girl about my age. She didn't live there for very long, but we became good friends in a very short time. As hard as it was for me to make friends, it was easy with her. And the ironic thing was that her name was Amy. I never knew her last name, but when she left I felt as though she left with a part of me. We would always say the same thing at exactly the same time. It was like we were thinking from the same brain, the same wave length. But until now, I'd never found another person who treated me with that much respect. But Amy did. I was very grateful for her loyalty, and her honesty with me. She was one reason I began to question the thought of never trusting anyone. And I thought she might be the one to change my mind about Eric. I thought maybe she'd reassure me he was the man to turn my life around. God knows how hard she tried to tell me since the first day I met him. She seemed to see it before I did.

Considering I was exhausted, I skipped the remainder of the day's classes but intended on returning the following day. And later that afternoon, Eric came by after all of his day's curriculum. I was sitting upright on my bed watching television when he came knocking on my door. When I let him in, he walked quietly over to my desk and sat there with a blank look on his face. Not sadness, or even a smile, but somewhere in between the two.

"What's this?" he said picking up a little black address book of mine.

"It's all of my family's phone numbers," I said, bewildered by his curiosity. "Why?"

Quiet for a moment, he looked up at me as if he wanted to ask me something.

"What Eric? What's on your mind?"

"Ever thought about tellin' your parents about everything? I mean about the hospital and uh...everything?" he said hesitantly.

"No. Hell no. What's this interrogation for? What does it matter to you if I tell my parents or not?" I said with a harsh voice.

"I just thought..."

"You shouldn't think so much. This is my life and I can do whatever I want to with it. If I decide to tell my parents about my problems, I'll do it. But they already think I'm crazy, so why support what they already think is true."

Eric lowered his head as if he was sorry he ever brought it up in the first place. "I'm sorry Beth. I didn't know it would upset you so much. I didn't know that you and your family were."

"What? Not the perfect little family like yours—little white picket fence, mom, dad, brother, sister and a little dog named spot. No, I've never had a perfect family, not anywhere near perfect," I said as a tear began to swell up in the corner of my eye. "My mom and dad could've cared less what I did or who I did it with. All they cared about was their perfect little son. He was always so perfect, and now that he's dead, he means even more to them than ever before. I was only there for decoration, I was the child that completed the so-called traditional family. You don't understand. No one understands. I don't know myself sometimes."

    I couldn't believe he had upset me so much just by asking about my family, but it had always been one subject I never liked to discuss. I just didn't have anything to say about anyone who didn't have anything good to say about me. And kind words were always the last things I would hear out of the mouths of my family members. My sister Melissa was always there for me, but she left home far too soon for me to grow up a normal child. She was probably the only person whoever thought I counted for something. She was always so naive, but I guess that was what kept her so sweet and caring. Just her presence made me feel better. But once she was gone, I was lost. My only contact to the real world of family had left me. And all I was left with, was my mom and dad who still cared more about my dead brother than they did me, even though I was alive and with them. Maybe that was the part that bothered me so much. The way I always looked at things was through rose colored glasses, only seeing the good in all. Many people do that, but the vision is so different when you look at it clearly and not so distorted. It is so much different. Only then do you see people for exactly who they are.

    Eric looked like he had lost his best friend, so I got up and went over and held his head against my chest. I felt bad for lashing out at him like that. He didn't deserve that kind of treatment from me. He was only trying to be helpful and I treated him like he was being nosy, instead of compassionate. I didn't know what I was doing. I was probably only an inch away from pushing him out of my life, but I didn't know how to control my anger and frustration without lashing out at someone. I didn't want him to be my target. He was too good to me for me to react to him in that way.

We went over and laid down on the bed, but this time it didn't seem to bother me. Not a sound was being made, but with his arms wrapped around my waist like a safety net, I was fine. His touch was lethal at times, but other times it was indispensable. It was like untamed animal. At first you fear it, but after a while, you are familiar with it, then you learn to love it as your own.

Eric began to caress the curves of my body, slowly, but intensely. He pulled my hair back and began to run his tongue up the center of my neck until it sent shivering chills down and down. He turned me to where I was facing him, and as soon as his lips touched mine, he pressed hard, hard kisses—not sweet or subtle at all.

The more stimulated he became the harder his kisses were. His hands roamed like an octopus. And his fingers worked hard to unfasten the buttons on the jeans I was wearing. A black darkness came over by body and I was frozen in time, another time. I began to shake like I was freezing from cold, but Eric didn't cease his actions. Again I saw a shadow, a dark shadow, one I couldn't make out. But the room I was standing, in the dimness, had a cold breeze blowing through it. The Dismay of this gloomy figure stiffened me up until I could hardly breathe. I gasped for a breathe, then a hand, a large hand reached out for me, with sounds of terrifying laughter from a distance. When I tried to run from the laughter I found myself fighting off the man who was lying next to me. I was swinging my arms as if trying to beat Eric off me. When I realized what I was doing, my face was red from tears of the horrible vision I thought had left me for good, an illusion I thought I'd never have to face again. But there it was, once more, staring me in the face when I'd begin to feel a little peacefulness.

Eric started to speak, but I didn't give him the chance. I stood, went to the sink, washed my face, then turned to him with a look of quandary. Not sure of what was going to come out of my mouth next, I paused to gather my thoughts. And when I was sure of what I wanted to tell him, I began to speak very straight forwardly to him.

"Eric, I don't want you to say anything. I've got a problem. I don't know what it is, but I want to find out, and as long as I'm with you, I can't find out. Every time I'm with you, I get scared. I'm not scared of you exactly. I don't think. But I'm scared of something. I feel like I've been put in a tunnel with many different ways to go, but unsure of which direction to take. If I go one way I see you and your loving smile, but if I turn another way, I see all of these images of something that's trying to haunt my thoughts and my dreams. I feel like it's striping away every bit of sanity I have left. At times, it seems like I should be put in a padded room and left alone.

I know you must think I'm crazy, but please understand. If I stay away from you for a while, maybe I'll be able to figure out what's happening to me. I want to know if I'm going crazy, or if there is a explanation for it," I said, willing to sacrifice everything just to know.

As he started to speak, I told him to leave. I didn't want to hear his voice. And staring in those brilliant eyes only made me want to change my mind about everything I'd just said. I knew that solitude was my best friend at that moment, and Eric was only an interruption, one in which I couldn't take the chance on ruining the discovery of what I was looking for.

He stood up and reached out to touch my hand, but I turned away. I didn't want anything to shift my decision. And I knew if he touched me, I would melt into him like hot butter all over again. So he left without saying a word. The look on his face was inconceivable. I would've never thought I'd have so much influence on anyone, especially someone of the opposite sex. No other man has ever cared enough to be hurt by words from me. I never knew I had that kind of power within this fragile body and soul of mine. And I never realized someone could love me enough to do exactly as I asked without any questions or harsh words of ending.

Weeks passed and each time I saw Eric, I'd turn and go the other direction. My visions of darkness during the daytime and night seemed to dissipate. And I began to feel better about things. It all started to seem like just a bad dream, like it was never real at all. It had to have been all in my imagination, I thought. My schoolwork began to improve and I started spending more time with Amy. She was my inspiration to wake up each day. Her crazy jokes and crack up's only make me feel more at ease as each day went by. And sitting alone one afternoon I picked up my notepad and pen and began to write:

Loneliness, just a word to immortalize your soul
And separate you from happiness
Loneliness, feeds you hard times
Where there used to be love and laughter,
And gives nothing to the life being lived.
It holds sadness and regret
Where bliss used to roam
And the sad thing with loneliness
Is that it creeps into the cracks of your heart
Until your heart wants to be alone
For being lonely is just a feeling
That some create a way to live
And those that keep it locked inside
Have nothing there to give.

I sat my pen down and stared at the words I'd just written. And for the first time, realized I'd found some therapy for my feelings, for my fears. I recognized the difference between facing my anxiety and running away from it. I'd run away for so long, I never learned how to face anything; And never wanted to until then.

That night I found slumber much earlier than usual. Since I had been sleeping much better, I wasn't scared to close my eyes and face the darkness, but this time it was different. Though secure with repose, when I closed my eyes something strange happened. I began to hear whispers from somewhere, no particular direction, and found myself trapped in the midst of smoke and fire. Flames were coming up all around me and it seemed real enough that I could almost feel the heat from the inferno. Once again, like before, I heard laughter, but this time it was loud, overbearingly loud. It didn't seem to be closer, but louder and louder, minute by minute. It was almost like I could recognize the voice, but not quite. I listened carefully because that was one nightmare I was going to face head on and not run from, as I had done in the past.

I yelled, "Who are you damn it!" But the laughter just got louder until I couldn't stand it anymore. I could feel the sweat pouring off me as though I'd actually placed myself in the nightmare itself. I didn't want to wake because I knew the moment I opened my eyes I would be in another state of confusion, as many times before. But it didn't take long until I took myself out of that horrible atmosphere and came back to reality. I woke screaming as loud as I possibly could. To my surprise, and embarrassment, there stood Amy trying to calm me. She looked terrified. I wasn't quite sure what she thought was happening, but I knew she was wanting to help me no matter what it was. The look on her face was solace, forcing me to release what had only been a dream and grasp for the new day at hand. I didn't have a very tight grasp on life, but I did the best I could under the circumstances.

I reached out to her and she hugged me securely until my nerves had settled down. I was shaking furiously. And that was the moment when I decided I needed to get some help before I ended up losing my mind. It was the only thing left for me to do. I gave up the man I had fallen desperately in love with, all for nothing at all. I had taken my own life through a tailspin, and still felt as though I was standing in the dark. There had to be something which was beyond me, to explain my aberrations. Because I knew everyone was not like me. Not everyone around me was looking over their shoulder to make sure they weren't going to get snatched up by some maniac, or afraid to sleep because of what might be lurking in the midst of their dreams. That all sounds crazy to other people, but not to me. It seemed to be my way of life.

I stumbled my way through the day in a state of confusion. But once I reached my room, without thinking, I reached over and started going through the phone book for help. I came across a lady whose name was Dr. Penny Downs. She was a psychiatrist, a shrink. I stopped at her name because I had heard one of my teachers recommending her to someone. And if they thought highly of her, then I figured she had to be pretty good. That looked like my only alternative at the time, so I called and set up an appointment to meet with her and see if I felt comfortable talking with her. I knew I'd feel more comfortable finding out why I was going nuts with a woman rather than a man. It was still a hard first step to take, but the call seemed easier than I imagined. I thought the person on the other end of the line would say "Here's another nut comin' in," but they seemed really nice and that put me at ease a little. I knew I had no choice. It seemed all too clear what I had to do.

I was to go the following day after my classes were over, and I was full of anticipation and nervousness. Amy kept asking me to tell her what was going on, but I dodged every question. It wasn't that I didn't think she wouldn't understand, but I just didn't want her to think bad of me. She'd been the only one, besides Eric, who'd been there for me each step of the way since I arrived on campus, and what she thought meant a lot.

That night as I laid down, I said a pray to the God above:

Dear God,

    Please give me peaceful sleep tonight. I know if anyone has the power to do that, it's you. And please put an amount of strength in my soul that will lead me through this dark hole I'm in. I need you to help me, and with you beside me, everything will come out full of light and joy. This is all I ask, in your name………Amen.

When I closed my eyes that night, surprisingly enough, my prayers did more good than I thought. I didn't dream, I only fell into a deep hole of rest. Stillness covered my body until I was full of certainty of the relief I'd feel when I woke. And just the knowing of finding out what terror had stricken me, led me down the right pathway for the first time in a long time. And for a moment, I could see a little light at the end of the tunnel.

CHAPTER 5

The day was at hand. And it was time for me to journey down that long dark road which I had been stumbling down for months. I knew I had to talk to a stranger, and I didn't know what I was going to say to her, or if she would think I was completely crazy as everyone else did. I was hoping I wouldn't be paralyzed with fear and not say a word. That was my first thought. There was a chance my fear would take a greater hold on me than I wanted it to. There was no way she could help me if I didn't have nerve to tell her what I'd been going through. What I had to do was take a deep breathe over and over until all of the tension of my anxiety was overcome. Then I knew I could confront my problems, and try to learn to trust the stranger I was going to confide in. I had to learn to trust her before I let her see into my heart and into my soul. Although trust was one word I always had a problem with, I was willing to try. If all I did was try, at least I would know inside I gave it my best shot, but if I didn't try at all, then I was only leading myself onto another dark road with no light at the end.

While dressing, the phone roared in my ear. Though Eric had done what I requested of him, not contacting me, I had a feeling he was on the other end of the line. I didn't want to answer it for that reason. I stared out the window for a moment and reached for my purse. And when I walked out the door, the phone was still ringing off the wall, but I just kept on walking 'till I could no longer hear it. I missed him desperately, but I learned to do things to get my mind off him each time his memory would ambush my thoughts. In other words, I was on the go all the time. Because I began to think of him more often than I wanted too. It was like the vision of his face was etched in my mind like scriptures in stone, almost impossible to remove. All I could see was the beautiful color of his eyes everywhere I looked. On a clear day, the few clouds hovering above would sometimes make a shape that would remind me of times we spent together lying on the grass by the pond nearby. I just couldn't seem to forget as easily as I thought. I still felt his touch, and his warm breathe lingered over me each time I would close my eyes. But most of all, what I remembered, was how desperately he wanted to make love to me just so he could show exactly how much he loved me. He gained my trust from the very beginning, but the only problem I had left was that I didn't trust myself. I didn't want to hurt him just because my insecurities were shooting at me from every direction.

After reaching my car and starting to town, I tried my best to clear my head. Getting closer and closer to the doctor's office, my nerves shook each inch of me. I didn't know what to expect or how I'd react to anything she might say to me. When I pulled in and parked, I sat there a moment in silence, just readying myself for the confrontation of what would hopefully be a new friend. After gathering my thoughts, I got out of the car and walked slowly towards the door.

When I went in and told them I was there and what time my appointment was, it wasn't long before my name was called.

"You can see the doctor now," the receptionist stated.

With a slight pause, I stood up. Each step into Mrs. Down's office was like a million. And when I reached the chair sitting in the corner, I sat down solemnly just staring down at my feet like a child hiding away inside herself. Every bit of flesh on my body trembled, not with fear exactly, but trembling. When I heard the door shut behind me, the softest voice came soon after, as soft as the petal of a beautiful rose.

"How are you today Beth?" Dr. Downs asked delicately.

Forcing myself to look up at her, I answered, "I'm fine."

"Well," she said "Are you ready to get started? I'm sure you're ready to find out whatever it is that's bothering you, and hopefully I can help."

My eyes wondered all over the room as she spoke. It was dim, but not frightening in the least. The fixtures seemed so home like, and the feeling all around was nothing but the serenity of wanting to help someone in need. The lights against the walls were covered with some kind of material to tone down the brightness in the room. The window directly ahead of me was slightly open and letting in a cool slow breeze which gave me a comfortable feeling. I knew she was talking to me, but her voice seemed a million miles away. I had to focus more on what she was asking me. I felt like I'd been removing myself from that room and concentrating on other things to keep from having to face what I was really there to uncover. Putting it off only made things worse, so I pivoted on her lips as she talked.

"Now, Beth, close your eyes and relax," Mrs. Downs said tenderly.

I leaned back in the chair and slowly shut my eyes. The dimness turned to dark, but the breeze was still running through my hair like a swiftly moving spring. And the feeling of nervousness still surrounded me as I listened to her. She told me to start telling her about my life as far back as I can remember, so I sat there and thought for a moment and tried my best to think back. It was very hard. So many memories I'd had as a child seemed to have vanished as I grew older. And other memories seemed as vivid as if it were yesterday. There were only certain memories contained in my mind and the rest was a mystery.

"Well," I muttered hesitantly," I remember my sister and I, when we were young, about seven or eight, brushing each other's hair. I always loved it when Melissa fixed my hair. It always made me want to fall asleep. It was so relaxing. We'd do it for hours. And she loved to do it as well. I always looked at her as being my best friend since I had no friends to speak of at that time. Melissa, well, she was more like an angel to me. I felt like she was my protector sometimes. Sometimes when I'd be sad or upset about something, Melissa was the only one who'd ever pick up on my feelings. Everyone else just wheeled around me as if I were some kind of obstacle in the way of where they were going or what they were doing.

I used to have long, almost white hair as a child. I always loved it. I thought it was pretty. It turned eventually, but it was so white for the longest time. Some of the kids used to kid around with me and call me snow white, until I learned to stand up for myself a little, then they left me alone. But kids always found somethin' to bother me with. Sometimes they'd call me slow or stupid. I had to learn to deal with it in my own way. I guess that way, was just staying away from everyone. Then they couldn't because I wasn't there for them to gawk at."

"What else Beth? Is there any other memories that stand out in your mind?" the doctor asked.

"I remember my father. He was always so serious about everything, but even though he never said it, he loved all of us. He worked hard to give us everything, but.."

"But what Beth?" Mrs. Downs asked curiously.

" I don't know. Sometimes I think that he had the philosophy 'Give a child what it wants, but forget about all the love and attention.' I mean, my mother feared him at times, but other times it was just the opposite. Dad never hugged us or kissed us to let us know he cared. In fact, he never really did anything to show us any type of affection. He would go into his little rages sometimes, but that was when we all learned to stay away from him until he cooled off a little.

"I never feared either my mom or dad, probably because they never acted like I existed. As long as I kept my room clean and the dishes washed, I was invisible. Sometimes I wonder if I didn't like being invisible."

Mrs. Downs wrote a few words down and looked back up at me with caring eyes. "You talked about your sister, your mom and your dad, but did you have any more brothers or sisters besides the ones you've already talked about?"

"Yeah," I said shortly.

"Well, do you want to talk about them?" she asked soon after.

With a blank look on my face, I answered, "I had a brother. His name was Lewis, Lewis Laney, but, uh...he was killed. I mean he died not long ago. He was older than me and we were never close. I really don't even like to talk about him. He's dead. He's gone!"

Mrs. downs looked at me like she'd stumbled across some kind of stepping stone. I didn't know what else to say about Lewis. I mean, the way I looked at it, he lived and he died. He never did anything for me. We never talked. He never even led me to believe he cared about me. Why should I have talked about him. He was my brother, but, at the same time, he was a stranger to me.

"Beth, tell me more about your childhood. I'm very interested in the way you made friends. You seem like you'd make friends very easily, and maybe even have several boyfriends. Is that how it was?" she asked as if she was trying to pry something out of me.

"Actually Mrs. Downs, my childhood was awful. I was always the girl that no one picked when choosing teams. When it came to friends I had almost none. The only people who claimed to be my friends were those who wanted something from me in return. I felt left out so often. Like I said before, I just separated myself from everyone. I was tired of being laughed at and talked about.

There was one girl that was a good friend, but it was only for a short time. She moved away soon after we got to know each other. I missed her for a long time. Maybe that was why I was afraid to make new friends. I guess I was scared that I'd lose them too. The only person I considered a real friend entered my life in a flash and left the same way.

That was harder on me than anyone ever knew. I think Melissa knew, but she didn't harp on it, I guess, because she thought it might just make things worse than they already were.

Of course, I never thought anything could ever get any worse than they had already gotten. My only friend, the only one who didn't judge me, left me, deserted me."

Sitting quietly, the tapping of a pen on her desk made me look up. "I want to see you again in one week Beth. Just relax. Remember I want to be your friend, and I won't leave you. Don't forget that. We have just started, and before it's over, we're gonna free you of your problem, and maybe build a friendship along the way. Okay," she said reassuringly.

When I stood to leave, I felt Mrs. Downs' hand on my shoulder. She stopped me to tell me something. "Beth Laney, I can tell you're a very special young lady and I know you're going to feel better before we're through. My daughter would've been about your age now, I believe you and her would've favored her so much. I'm so glad you came here. As far as me helping you today, I'm not sure of that, but I know you helped me. My daughter died when she was born, at least that was what I was told. I would've sworn I heard a cry, but that's beside the point. Sometimes I forget because I never attempted to have any more children, but today you helped me remember what kind of person I would've wanted my daughter to be. Thank you for your help. I never thought I'd say that to a patient, but thank you," she exclaimed with peace showing on her face.

She placed her delicate arms around me and carefully embraced me as a mother would her child, with such care. And when she did, I felt a sigh of relief. I was so scared to talk to a stranger, but she wasn't a stranger at all. She was like someone I'd known for many years. And the thing that impressed me the most about her, was that you could tell her sincerity was genuine. You could tell she meant each word that flowed from her lips. All of the uneasiness slowly faded and I stood there completely calm.

As I left her office, it was strange, but I couldn't wait to come back and talk to her again. I could tell she was interested in everything I had to say. And until that point, everyone that knew me thought I was crazy, but not Mrs. Downs. She was actually trying to help me in any way she possibly could. I had this gut feeling she and I would end up being more than physician and client, we would be friends, something I could always use more of.

My mind wandered as I drove back to my room. I began to think of Eric. I missed him so much, and for once I wasn't too ashamed to admit it. The way I was handling the situation with Eric, was wrong. I should've known by then you can't push someone away and expect them to be waiting for you. It doesn't work that way. And I wanted to mend what I'd ripped into as soon as I could get the chance to do so. If it had been up to me, I would've done it very, very soon, before he strayed to someone who wasn't hanging on the edge of their rope. If I didn't take hold of my sanity soon, Eric would just be a memory I would never want to forget. His eyes would stare at me in my sleep, and his fingers would caress my body when I'd feel scared and alone. If there was ever a light to lead the way in my life, the light was coming from his heart straight into mine. I couldn't explain it. He acted as though he would always be there for me, but so many times people take things for granted, especially other people, and that's when you have to stop and smell every rose and kiss every tiny baby, just so you can enjoy each miracle our God created for us. He didn't create these things for us to pass up and never notice. He put them on the face of the earth so we'd have something wonderful to view and to admire. Because when you pass up such wonderful things, your life passes swiftly without anything to show for it. That was one thing I didn't want to be guilty of. I wanted my life to mean something. I wanted my compassion to be much stronger than my animosity. But most of all, I wanted to look back at every second of my life and smile at how I redirected my anger and also how I helped others along the way. Because I've always believed helping other people made your heart grow stronger, and in the long run, I knew I would be justly rewarded for all that was done for the good of others. I was never one to think of only myself, but also, for a long time, I had no one else to think of as well.

I was in such bewilderment when I started paying attention to my driving, I had to swerve to miss a vehicle which was headed straight for me. It took me a moment to capture my breath. Then I stared out at the brilliant picture of nature that surrounded me like a warm blanket in the midst of a hard snow. It was amazing to me that everything was in perfect order. Nothing seemed out of place. The leaves blew as if they were doing dances in the wind and the birds sang like harmonious orchestras. I was taken in totally. I could always look up at the sky above, and I'd feel peace inside. That was just me.

When I returned, the campus was crowded from one end to the other. I looked at my watch and it was almost time for supper. Everyone was rushing to see who could get in line at the cafeteria first. I knew I would never rushed to eat there. So I always fixed something in my room or didn't eat at all. It never made that much difference to me. Besides, my appetite, hadn't been the best. I had more important things to focus on than what I was going to have for breakfast or supper. I just didn't care.

To my surprise. I saw Eric sitting on the swing quietly as everyone hurried by. He was sitting there staring at the ground below him. I knew he had to be just as depressed as I was. If he missed me half as much as I'd missed him, he had to be full of complete and total loneliness. Because that was all my heart had been filled with ever since I told him to leave me alone. I never meant to hurt anyone, but in the end, I hurt both of us unintentionally.

Without hesitation, I strolled over to him, not making much noise at all. There were so many people walking by that he didn't even notice me. I stood there for a moment just looking at him. His face was sullen and full of pain, and the confidence he'd always had since I'd known him, seemed to have disappeared in the dust of confusion. I was apprehensive to say a word because I wasn't sure if he'd ignore me or if he'd embrace me like I wanted him to. I wanted his tender arms to clasp around my waist and just hold me there like that until he just couldn't hold on any longer. I felt like I'd hurt him to the point where he might not want to return to that same valley of pain. I never did it intentionally. I was only trying to protect myself. I was trying to find myself before I explored someone else.

In a moment, Eric looked up and our eyes met like a sunrise to the edge of the sea. His eyes were red and teary, and his hands were shaking as he held them tightly. I took a step and sat down next to him. I wanted to reach over and put my hand on his, but, he seemed so uneasy with me. He acted as though he didn't want to step back into the same snake pit after already being bitten once. That was just the way he looked at me. And for once, I didn't blame him. I wouldn't have blamed anyone for not setting themselves up for another fall. And with me, Eric seemed unsure if there was another cliff up ahead for him to plummet down from. There was no way I could make him believe there wasn't. The only way, was to show him. And that was exactly what I intended to do.

I gathered my nerve and scooted closer to him. Then I placed my hand over his and squeezed it gently, but reassuringly. I wanted him to feel the electricity from my heart to his through my touch. He always felt it before, and I still felt it. The silence of the moment made me tremble with the fear I might have gone too far in protecting my own heart and not worried enough about someone else's. Though putting a shield around myself was something I'd always done, I had this feeling it was time to pull the shield away and learn to take chances. A poem I had written ran through my thoughts:

ONE CHANCE

One chance may be all that's given

To us as time goes by,

And some take advantage of that chance
While others don't even try.
For they think something better's coming
When that may be all there is.
Just one chance to make a life.
Just one chance to live.
So when something wonderful comes along
Don't turn your head away.
Reach out and try to touch it,
Each minute, every day.
For some chances only come around
Once in a million years.
So if you grasp them tightly
You'll have a smile and cast all tears.
One chance, One fear,
Soon all chances just disappear.

At last, he unclenched his hands and held my hands tightly. They were so warm I could've held onto them forever. I felt his pain as he kept hold of me and I was sure he could feel mine as well. I didn't know what to say to him. For once, I was speechless and at a loss of words. He too, didn't speak. I guess we both thought that neither one of us needed to say how we felt. It was in the air all around us. And even those who walked passed us, knew just by looking, that God made he for I, and I for him.

"Beth."

"Don't Eric. I know. I was stupid. Lets just sit here and enjoy the moment. Lets not confuse it with apologies or conversation. I just want to sit here with you and think about how lucky I am that you'll still have me next to you. I want to remember this day as the one where I stopped thinking of myself and begin to think of the one person I love dearly...you," I said, putting my head on his shoulder and closing my eyes.

The sun was gradually falling out of sight as we sat there. Then we waited until the stars showed themselves to us and picked one star out of a million to wish upon. Some wishes come true. And I believed if we wished a wish at the same time, it would surely have to come true. If we were to pick the same star, it would have to mean he and I would never separate, for that one star would be guiding the both of us; Him watching over me, and me watching over him.

Glancing up at him for a second, he leaned down and barely touched his lips with mine. The tenderness was overpowering. Again and again he did the same thing. With my eyes closed, I added those kisses to the dreams I already have of him. I had so many moments in my mind of he and I, that if you could've looked inside my heart, there would've been a mini-scrapbook of all of the time Eric and I had known one another. To most people it would seem like a short time, but I'd known him long enough to know he was one I never wanted to miss my chance with. For if I was to let him go, my light in the darkness would be gone and my happiness in sad times would disappear. I needed him and he needed me. We knew what we were doing—falling deeper and deeper in love every day.

CHAPTER 6

Darkness finally fell as we sat there quietly. And the only thing sweeping through my mind was what would happen the next moment? For when you try to look so deeply into the future, it tends to get blurry and you lose sight of what's really important—the moment at hand. Tomorrow may never come and next year is a million miles away, but the moment being lived, is what you should always count on. Never count on next week, next month or next year. Sometimes a moment is all you have to express your feelings. That was why I made up my mind I was going to do something completely out of character. I was going to jump in deep water which I had only waded in before—making love. I wanted him know me inside and out. I wanted him to want me. His touch did so much for my self-esteem. The more I felt it the better I felt about myself. He was good therapy for my heart and for the way I viewed everything and everyone around me.

He took my hand, leaned his forehead against mine, and kissed the tip of my nose lightly. Romance couldn't have been any better than it was at that moment. He drug me out of dismay and sheltered me from fear. But most of all, he never gave up on us.

As his head lowered, he muttered softly, "Well, I guess I better get back to my room. I'll see you in the morning for breakfast, won't I?"

With a bit of hesitation, I replied, "Eric, I want to be with you tonight. I want us to make love with no interruptions like before. I just want to be near you. You're the only one who ever makes me feel like a person, like I really matter. Until I met you, I didn't think I mattered at all, but, somehow you convinced me that I do mean something. You convinced me I'm not just wandering around on this earth with no friends to care about me. I love you, but even before I knew that for sure, I knew you were my friend. I knew you would stand with me no matter what obstacles I came up against. And if showing you physically, is how I can prove my love for you, I want to lie with you in the darkness and feel you next to me. I want to show you. You might know, but I want to show you. Give me the chance to prove something to you. Something I've never wanted to prove to any other man."

His eyes lit up like a shooting star. He looked as though he couldn't believe what I'd just said. I guess he thought I'd never want to be with him in that way again because of what happened before. But as I've always been told you can't overcome your fears until you face them head-on. That was one thing I'd always had a problem with. I was too scared to face any fear, no matter how minor it might've been. But to start new and fresh, facing my fears was one tiny step which would lead me to a staircase of renewal, a walkway to recovery. I never saw that walkway until Eric came into my life. He showed me a direction, but, until then, I was too afraid to follow his map of love.

"If you still want to be with me Eric, I'd be so honored to be able to lie next to you 'till mornin'. And I'd be even more honored to have you hold me until I feel totally secure about everything. I love you. more than anything. When I was without you, I realized that. You were the one who made me want to get up in the morning, and each thought of you helped me through the day. I can't explain it. You must have some mystical power, because each time you touch me, It feels like I'm being freed from many anxieties and fears. Even though they're still hidden deep inside of me, they seem to hesitate to rise to the surface when you're holding me, " I said looking at Eric gazing.

With no words, we began walking in the direction of his dorm. The sun had already gone down and the darkness was, for a change, peaceful and serene. The cool breeze passing by us couldn't change the warmth I felt inside. I wouldn't have minded walking with him all night long. As long as he held my hand, I knew I'd be just fine. Every little bit he'd look at me and smiled. And I'd smile at him in just the same sensitive way. It was strange. We didn't have to speak. The words were spelled out in each touch. The fire was transferred through our fingertips, and the anticipation of making love to one another was in the air which surrounded us.

The moon hovered above us with such exquisite light. It amazed me sometimes about the moon. Though the blackness of night showed reverence, the moon seemed to overshadow it to the point where darkness was calm and quiet instead of dreadful and full of anxiety. My mind wondered too many different thoughts before we reached our destination. It always did that. I was told by my sister Melissa once that I think too much. And she was probably right. My thoughts sometimes confused me, but moments like the one in the palm of my hand, I wanted to think, and I wanted to thank God for what I had.

When we reached his door, he turned to me. "Are you sure this is what you want to do. I mean, I understand if you're not ready for this again. I want you to be ready whenever we make love wholly. You're everything to me and I'm in no hurry. I don't want to rush anything because I know we have a lifetime to make our minds up Beth, look at me. Look me in the eye and tell me one more time that you are ready to give up one thing you'll never be able to get back-your virginity."

Those words from him were like words from heaven telling me that God approved of he and I. I hoped he approved, because I had a feeling no other man could ever love me with so much compassion and understanding as he. There was probably someone out there who would attempt it, but Eric was like a saint in my eyes. If there ever was a saint, he was standing right in front of me.

Looking up at him, I spoke in the most faithful voice. "I want you. And to give you myself, is something I want to do for you and for myself. You deserve to feel all my love for you in the best way I know how to give it. I'm not sure what to do or how to act, you can guide me so I'll know. Eric, I trust you completely. I won't tell you I'm not scared, because I am. It scares the living hell out of me, but it's you Eric. Why would I be scared of you? Why would the one person who has given himself to me, heart and all, frighten me? Please, just believe me. I wouldn't lie to you. If I wasn't ready for this, I wouldn't have said anything about coming with you tonight. Just hold me and make this a night I'll never forget."

The key slowly turned opening his door revealing his bed in the corner of the room, so neatly made and cozy. He went directly to his stereo and turned it on very low. A beautiful melody was playing which set the mood perfectly. He had pictures of cars and things hanging all around, and no clutter surrounded us at all. A few photos of his family were sitting on his dresser, and homework, left to do later, was scattered all over his desk.

He had a large rug in the center of the room. It was thick and cushioned like a huge pillow draped around our feet. His bed was small, almost too small for one, but under the circumstances, I knew we'd make do with what we had. The window was slightly cracked for a little extra comfort, and the blinds were wide open, letting in a little glare from the street light on the corner.

Eric went over and closed the blinds and turned back towards me. Each step he took made my heart pound harder and harder until I thought it might burst, but when he reached me, I suddenly calmed. Standing there face to face, saying nothing, made me wonder what he was thinking. I always wondered that about people. I always wanted to know what was going through someone's mind when silence filled the air. Sometimes I'd think they were looking at me in disgust, but other times, I was unsure. Facial expressions can tell a lot about what's on a person's mind. I learned that a long time ago. I guess my curiosity seemed to get the best of me. For I've always believed, if there's not an ounce of curiosity inside you, then something's wrong. Everyone gets curious about something some time in their life, I knew I did.

Eric asked, gently putting his arms around my waist, "Can I have this dance?"

I smiled and nodded happily, then we began to slowly move across the floor. I could hear guys going down the hallway making all kinds of men noises, but the beauty of the moment drowned them out almost completely. I laid my head on his shoulder and relaxed. My feet didn't even seem to touch the floor. It was like he was carrying me. With each movement, the deeper I felt for the man I was clinging onto tightly. With each sway as the music changed ballads, I felt our bodies melting into one another. I only hoped when I opened my eyes, I wouldn't find myself lying in my bed alone. This would be one dream I wouldn't mind having over and over again, but I wanted it to be real.

His lips began to touch my neck with soft kisses as he swept his loving hands across my back. I shivered a little as all the tension quickly left my body. With my fingernails, I scratched his back in a slow circular motion. I felt so at ease in his arms. He held me tightly, but at the same time, he was very gentle. He treated me like I was fragile, but wanted to hang on tight enough to be sure not to let me go. I knew I never wanted to let him go. Even times when we might not be together, he would be in my thoughts just as much as if he were lying right next to me. His sensual touch made me want to close my eyes and savor each ounce of goodness and love I was feeling. I wanted to enjoy it as long as it lasted, which I hoped would be no less than forever.

He led me to the side of his bed, and to my surprise, he reached over, took the pillow which was lying there, and threw it on the rug in the middle of his floor. Then he unfolded a blanket which was lying neatly at the foot of his bed, and placed it beside the pillow. It seemed as though he didn't want us to be cramped up in his bed, so he created our own little, warm bed in the floor.

"What?"

"Shhhhhhh," he said quietly. "Trust me."

We got down on our knees, then he gently laid me down like a mother to her tiny baby-gently. He hovered over me like an angel protecting someone from harm. The dim lights in the room still left enough for me to see his face and his eyes as he stared down at me. He cautiously put his body on top of mine with our two hearts intertwined in between. I felt each inch of him, from his toes all the way up to his sexy chest and manly hands that seemed to wander all over my body. I didn't care. I wanted his touch. I wanted his attention. And most of all, I wanted the love he had so much of to give. His heart was overflowing, none like I'd ever seen before, but lucky to have it as mine, I embraced it, promising myself never to release it until eternity had found its' end.

"Beth, you're so beautiful. I wish you only knew how beautiful you really are. I know you never thought of yourself in that way, but if you could look in the mirror and see yourself the way I feel you, beauty is all you'd see. If you could reach deep down into your soul and see what I so often feel, you'd know. You'd know you're even more beautiful on the inside. Oh God, what did I do to deserve this? What did I do to deserve you and all you've given me? There's a lot of things I never told you about myself, but I've had problems. But, Beth, when I saw your face that very first day, I knew you'd help me escape from all I ran from to begin with. You're beautiful in my eyes, and the beauty I see in you will never change in my sight. When you're a hundred years old, the outer beauty may have faded, but the part of you that really matters, will still be there, your heart, your caring heart," Eric said stroking my hair.

I didn't know what to say, for I'd never thought I was beautiful at all. But somehow, when he said it, I felt beautiful. I felt wanted. And the expression on his face said it all. The way he looked at me, told me he was being sincere. Though I never doubted it, I could see his honesty deep in his eyes. His eyes could always tell me what was true. Like a crystal ball, I could see visions of the future when I looked deep enough. And the future I saw, was one I couldn't wait for.

Pausing for a moment, I said, "Eric...when I look at myself, I don't see beauty. I see someone who's trying to sort her life out, someone who has just learned what real love is, and last but not least, someone who wants to become somebody. That's what I see. The way you look at me sometimes makes me wonder if you're blind, but then, if being blind makes you want to be with me, then I want to be your guide from now on."

Eric smiled, and started to speak, but I interrupted.

"Let's not talk. Lets make love. I want to make love to you with all of the passion I have inside of me," I said seductively.

He looked surprised, but pleased. From that moment on, everything was extraordinary. He must have had electricity running through his fingertips, because each time he'd touch me, I felt a bolt of electricity run through my heart. And with each tight embrace, I could feel us dissolve into one existence.

I sat up and grabbed the bottom of his shirt and slipped it off as easily as I possibly could. I wanted the night to last forever. Before I knew it he was sliding my shirt off and kissing my shoulders with such ease. It felt so good. Each time his lips would touch my skin, I would quiver from the warmth of his breath. He started easily, but as each moment surrendered itself to time, his anxiousness took over.

His fingertips stroked each inch of my flesh so tenderly until it was almost too much to take. And as I laid there quiet and still, I enjoyed his touch, his tenderness and grasped onto it with all I had in me.

In no time at all our clothes were scattered around, but we didn't want to rush making love. I didn't want to do it hurriedly. I wanted to take as much time as we both needed, to make sure we were full of the passion of love.

The music played softly and the lights were dim, but we had to make sure we took our time with what came next. For a while he just laid there beside me and held me close to him. That relaxed me more than I thought it would. I wasn't sure if I would have one of my strange dreams, but if I did, I knew the passion of our love would surely scare it away. I hoped it would anyway. It didn't want anything to discontinue a moment as tender as the one we'd become a part of.

The covers over us were soft and warm, but it wasn't the covers that kept me warm at all. Eric's body let out so much heat that we didn't need a blanket. The warmth given between he and I was enough. The anticipation made me start to sweat a little and it did with Eric as well.

He took my breasts in his hands very sensitively and his breathing started to get heavier, moment by moment. I closed my eyes and as he began to kiss my breasts, I felt a sensation I'd never felt before. It went through my whole body. My nipple began to get harder and harder as his tongue ran across it over and over again. I'd never felt that kind of pleasure before in my life. Then he began to move down lower and lower, and for a moment, I wasn't sure what was happening. I was frightened in a way, but I knew Eric wouldn't do anything to hurt me, so I just relaxed and let it happen. I began to arch my back as he went all the way down. It was, at that point, I wanted it. I wanted it more than anything. He made me feel so good. I felt like I was in a dreamland just waiting to wake up, but it wasn't a dream. It was all happening. I was being made love to with more passion than I'd ever known in all my life. He was incredible.

Finally he raised up and started to make love to me entirely. He and I were moving together in perfect motion. The pain I felt was overpowered by the inconceivable feeling of love that was all around us. He gave no hard thrusts, only slow sensual movements as if he wanted to make sure I was ok. It was wonderful. I never imagined how it would feel to be with someone in that way. The sensations of he and I together as one body was a miracle given from God.

Then I started feeling strange. The sensations started getting stronger and stronger until I just wanted to scream out loud. That was when he started taking it a little faster and then faster. Oh God, it felt great, but at the same time, I felt drained. Sweat was dripping from each and every pore of my body.

He laid over beside me once more and we just laid there and stared up at the ceiling. Trying to catch our breath, we enjoyed the silence. He stroked my shoulder in the darkness as I rested my head on the center of his chest. I couldn't believe I had actually gone through with the one thing I had been so frightened of for so long. It was nothing to be frightened of at all. In fact, I'd never done anything which made me feel so loved and cared for. And the pleasure was something which couldn't be transformed into words. I felt it, but I couldn't explain it even if I tried. It was that powerful.

The silence dwelled until Eric spoke.

"Are you ok?" he asked.

"Oh, Eric, I never realized it would be like this. I'm sorry I didn't give you the chance before. I know I can trust what you say now. I know you'd never hurt me," I said gleaming with pure happiness. He could tell I was happier inside than I'd been in a long time. My heart had to keep telling my mind it was real, it was really happening, but it still seemed like one big fantasy come true. It was as though all my dreams of Eric and I being together sensually, came to life in an instant, and it was astounding.

We both agreed we needed some sleep, so we closed our eyes and fell off into a peaceful slumber. It couldn't have been anything but peaceful for me. Lying in his arms for the remainder of the night was all I could've asked for. I could hardly go to sleep for reliving what we had just done. He and I were fused together for a little while, long enough for me to know what I wanted to do from that day on.

Buried, But Not Forgotten

When morning came, the sun was trying to creep through the blinds in his window. I sat up and stretched a little, and moments later Eric did the same. The day seemed brighter than any other day before. The sun seemed brighter, and the air blowing through the window was so much fresher. I took a deep breath in and out and felt like a new person. I was a new person, at least in one aspect of change—the changing of the heart.

"Mornin' beautiful," he said, sweetly kissing me on my cheek.

I don't know why, but I acted a bit embarrassed. "Goodmorning."

I leaned over and rested on him for a moment and he held me close once more. It was more of a reassuring hug than anything. I could tell he just wanted to let me know the night before meant just as much to him as it did to me. We were both glowing inside and out. We had created a bond between us which no one would ever be able to take from us, a bond connecting our hearts. It was enough just knowing he loved me, and I knew he didn't have to guess at what I felt. I didn't want to play any more games. I only wanted to be honest, and I also wanted to be there for him whenever he might need me. My goal in life had changed a little since my experience with Eric. It transferred from being focused only on a career, to happiness and a career. I knew that was how it should be. Because I guess if home life isn't happy, your career can't make up for it.

I had to break the mood by getting up and dressing. I was almost late for my class as it was, so I had to hurry and get back so I wouldn't be late another day. When I reached the doorway, he came up behind me and put his arms around my waist. He pulled me to him as if he never wanted to let go, and I never wanted him to. We had connected in a way I had never done with anyone else. I believed in my heart he was my true soul mate and love. We had connected in many ways, but mostly by love, trust, and true companionship.

Walking back to my room, the birds sang all around me and the atmosphere was almost poetic. I had always loved the scenery and sometimes I'd even go outside just to stare at the squirrels and birds. Sometimes I'd just watch the trees sway to and fro until I was in a peaceful trance. It was so tranquil. I never remembered anything like that back home. It was always so noisy and busy at home. There was never time to stop and find something beautiful to admire. I was never given any time to do anything, except clean house and remain out of sight after all was done and finished with.

When I walked in my room, Amy was getting dressed for her first class, but I hadn't even started getting ready.

"Gonna be late again, huh Beth?" Amy said chuckling a little afterwards I smiled and replied, "Maybe one day I'll make it on time, and when I do, you know that there has to be something wrong with me."

Amy looked at me in a bewildered kind of way. "Something happen last night? You look different. You look happier than normal."

"Ah, me and Eric just stayed up all night talking. We always have such good conversation," I said, a grin was smearing across my face which had already turned ten shades of red.

"Yeah. I don't have time for you to tell me now, but when I get back, I want to hear every single, dirty, filthy, sexy detail," Amy said.

"Well, you better be ready for a long talk then, because I have a lot to tell you. Amy, I think he's the one. No, he is the one," I replied in a small daze.

Amy just rolled her eyes at me as if to say "You're crazy," and left. I was moving in slow motion when I should've been in fast forward. I only had fifteen minutes to get ready and get to class, but I just couldn't motivate myself to go. The only thing that made me want to go was the fact that all my classes had my favorite person in them. With that thought, it didn't take me very long to throw on some make up, change clothes, and be out the door in a flash. He was a great incentive in and out of the classroom.

Dashing across campus, I was startled by a group of jocks that happened to be crossing my path. They were always such jerks to every female that walked by.

"Hey baby," one of the guys said.

"Leave me alone. I'm late for class," I cried out trying to pass them.

They laughed a little and another one of them taunted, "Scared to be late for class. Come on, I'll walk you to class."

That same guy grabbed my arm as if he was going to drag me in the opposite direction of where I was headed. About that time I heard a very familiar voice come from behind us.

"Let her go!" Eric insisted, as he boldly walked up.

The guys laughed a little more, still not releasing me.

Eric became angrier as he spoke, "I said let her go, she's not bothering anyone, so I suggest you don't either!"

He let go of my arm and left a mark where he had held it so tightly. I ran over to Eric and held firmly onto his arm. As they walked off, they continued to laugh, and that made me so angry. I hated guys like that. They thought they were such studs that any girl would want them, but I was one who never wanted anything to do with them.

Eric peered at me compassionately, "You alright? I'm glad I was late for class to, no tellin' what they would've done if I hadn't been here."

"Yeah," I said picking up my books from the ground and looking at him with a sigh of relief. He had perfect timing.

As we continued on to class, he never released my hand until we reached the classroom. We sat right next to one another in every single class, so we were never very far apart from each other. I felt good about that. He was close to me, that was all that mattered.

The day flew by, and our last class led to thoughts of where we would spend the remainder of the day. I knew I needed to study, so I told Eric I wanted to go to the library for a while to catch up on some of my homework I'd been neglecting for days. He agreed, and I went back to my dorm to get some things I needed, while he did the same. We were going to meet each other at the library.

It didn't take long for me to get what I needed, so I went over a little earlier than we had planned to meet. My first subject to study was English. I was supposed to compose a poem about something dear to me. The teacher didn't name a subject. She said it was open to anything and everything as long as it was clean enough to read in the classroom. So I thought and thought about what I wanted to write about. Then it hit me. I could write about my encounter with Eric, but just talk about my feelings and not literal actions. So that was exactly what I did. My mind went to work and I sat there with my pen and pad in front of me for a few moments before anything came out of my jumbled up mind.

WITHOUT A DOUBT

The moments that I spend with you
I'll remember "till I die
And your smile caresses my heart and soul
For that smile will never lie
Your kiss reassures me
That your love will always be around
And I feel that very love
When there's not a sound.

Memories of what we've shared
can never be erased
And from this day forward I promise

You will never be replaced

For without a doubt-I love you
Without a doubt I want you near
Without a doubt your in my thoughts
Even when you're not here.

WITHOUT A DOUBT-I love you!

CHAPTER 7

Sitting quietly after I'd written the poem, I looked down at it to see if there was anything that needed to be changed-a word or phrase which could be made better. I'd always been a perfectionist when it came to writing. And I wanted to make sure every word was just perfect for the sentence it was in. That was just me. Then I folded it up and put it in my folder as Eric strolled up to the table where I was sitting.

"Hey! Been here very long?" he asked.

"Not too long. I was just doing our English assignment. Remember, we have to read our poems aloud in class tomorrow."

He had this look on his face as though he had completely forgotten about it, but Eric was just as good a writer as I was, so I knew it wouldn't take him long to come out with something just like I did. He took out a pen and piece of paper and began to write hurriedly. I was fast when it came to writing anything, but Eric was much faster than I was. It wasn't five minutes before he had it ready. He looked up at me and handed it to me to read.

"Read it. It's about you, come on. Read it," he said anxiously.

"I wrote about you too," I replied handing him the poem I had written before he arrived.

We both looked down and started to read. I was surprised at what words he put down on paper.

A ROSE

Her face was like petals

And her eyes shined like the sun

Her smell was like a rosebush

From the day we both begun.

So delicate and peaceful,
She drifts along with the wind.
She needs her love and nourishment
The warmth of the sun will send.

I smile each time I see her
Glowing petal cheeks and smile.
For that is one Rose
That I would walk the extra Mile.

I'd cross the highest mountain
To pick that one from a crowd.
For I've never seen a rose so lovely
For that rose I'm proud.

She's the rose I found abandoned
By those who cared not about her love,
But I have a rose in you my dear
For your beauty was sent from above.

You're a rose, You're my rose!

A tear started to form in the corner of my eye as I finished the beautiful poem Eric had written for me, and about the same time, Eric looked up. He too had read the one I had written about him. He reached his hand over and placed it on top of mine. Our eyes met melting together as one. It seemed like I could see deep down into his soul. And I was sure he could do the same. For once, someone was thinking of me in the same way I thought of them. His thoughts were harmonious with mine, and that was a wonderful feeling to have.

"Beth, that was great. You feel that way?" he asked, like he didn't already know.

I smiled and replied, "You know I do. I didn't have to say it did I? I know you can see it every time you look at me or touch my hand. Because I can tell the way you feel before you ever say a word."

We remained like that for a moment, and then we realized we were there for a reason. We opened our books and began to catch up on all we had put aside for days. I was glad I had neglected my studies because what I neglected them for, was far more important to me. When I first arrived, I believed my school work was more important than anything, but suddenly I changed my mind. There was something more important to me after my new found experience with a man who could possibly be the one I would spend the rest of my life.

It took us hours to get done. I swore to him I would never let things get that behind again. It was much harder to catch up than to do them right away. We laughed a little, and gathered our books to leave. There was hardly a soul in the library, and when we got up, he told me to come over to where he was. He was standing in the middle of one of the book aisles back in the corner. Curiosity got the best of me. I wanted to see what he was up to, so I got up and went over where he was. When I reached him, he pulled me close to him and kissed me passionately. I wasn't even scared we'd get caught. When our lips dismissed one another, we started to laugh.

"You're nuts," I said. "We could get caught. There's no tellin' what they'd do to us if they caught us in here doin' this."

"Come on, be adventurous," he persisted patting me on my butt as we walked back to the table to get our things.

We snickered all the way out the door. I bet everyone thought we had lost our minds. The few people which were studying kept looking at us as to say "Please be quiet."

Eric was such a maniac sometimes. He always liked to do something just for the main fact that maybe no one else had ever done it before. His wild and crazy side didn't come out very often, but when it did, I would always be totally embarrassed. He made damn sure of that. That was one thing I loved about him, though. When you always know what to expect from someone, it takes some of the thrill out of the relationship. And there were times when Eric would do things I never expected him to do. It would be just like him to stand up in a restaurant and yell " I love this woman!" I would never put it passed him. That was just the way he was. He was exciting and stimulating to me. He was surely a one of a kind. I liked the stimulation of having someone do something for me out of the ordinary and totally unexpected. It made things interesting, and it also made me feel like someone special.

Walking along, we decided to grab something to eat. I hadn't eaten all day long. At lunch we just sat on the swing and talked and never once thought about going to the cafeteria, so we hopped into his truck and went to the nearest fast food restaurant. As we ate, conversation never slowed down. We always had something to talk about. Our discussions went from school, to writing, and back to us again. It was never boring. And his wise cracks kept me smiling the entire time.

Every little bit, he'd lean over the table and gently kiss me with everyone watching us. I think he did that on purpose. He always wanted everyone to know we were together. And by the way he acted, everyone had to know. I never minded because I wanted everyone to know he was mine and mine alone. I didn't know what I'd do if I ever thought he was thinking of being with someone else. It wasn't that I thought he'd do that, but, in my experiences in life, anything is possible.

We took our time eating because we both knew we had to go back to our own rooms for a change. If we ever got caught in one another's rooms we probably would have gotten kicked out of the dorms, so we were in no hurry to finish.

It was getting late and we had to leave. Sleep from the night before was little, so we had to make up for the sleep we had lost.

He drove me back to the front of my dorm and dropped me off. We sat there for a few minutes in pure silence. I didn't want to leave him, and I could tell he felt the same.

He leaned over and kissed me on my cheek so sweetly and I got out slowly. As he drove off, I blew him a kiss and he turned and gave me one of his brilliant smiles I always love to see. His smile could always light up the darkest day and fill my heart with happiness all at the same time.

Flying on cloud nine, I walked in the dorm and down to my room. Amy was still up studying when I came in and sat down. She peered at me for a moment before she said anything. I knew what she wanted to ask, and I was more than ready to tell her. I wanted her to know how much I loved Eric and how wonderful things had been going. I wanted everyone to know.

"Now, lets hear it. I've wanted to know all day long. God, you look like you're glowing inside and out. This has got to be good," Amy declared, full of curiosity.

I smirked a little and replied, "Not much to tell."

"Come on Beth, don't leave me hangin' like this. You will tell me or I won't let you sleep a wink tonight."

"Alright, I'll tell you. I stayed with Eric last night."

"And..." she inquired, trying to hurry me along.

"It was extraordinary. For the first time, I gave myself to someone Amy. For the first time I really gave all of myself to someone without being scared of my feelings. His gentle touch still covers me and his warmth, I know will keep me warm tonight when he's not even here.

I don't know, it was like that dark cloud of doubt surrounding me for so long, was lifted for a short while, just long enough for me to show my affection the way I really wanted to. You know how much Eric cares, don't you Amy. Can you see it just like I do? I see yesterday, today, and tomorrow every time I look into his eyes. I can't put him out of my mind. It's like he's become a permanent fixture in my heart and my soul."

"I've always seen it," Amy agreed, as if to say 'I told you so.'

"You don't have to be a smart ass about it. I knew you were right from the beginning, but it just took me a while to really believe he was someone I could trust totally and completely without any doubt at all," I said, gleaming a smile.

Amy came over to me and gave a sincere hug. Her friendship was very important to me. Although we hadn't spent a lot of time together lately, she was still one person I knew I could depend on no matter what time of day or night. I knew she would be there.

"Listen, I'm very tired. As you know, I didn't get much sleep last night," I chuckled.

"Me too. I hope you have sweet dreams. I know you will if you dream about Mr. wonderful," she said.

I smirked a little on her smart remark, but she was always kidding around. She was just as glad as I was to know I had I finally decided to open up and try to love someone. I knew she could tell from the first day we met that it was hard for me to believe anyone or trust anyone. But I learned. It took me a little while to let go, but at least I let go enough to find a little happiness.

I kept closing my eyes, but sleep was hard to find. I tried and tried, but my mind kept going back to the night before. I wanted him holding me again so badly that I could taste it, and I had the strange feeling Eric was lying in bed having the same problem. I hoped he was anyway, because if he wasn't, what happened between us wasn't as real as I thought. I threw out that doubt as soon as it crossed my mind. That was the same kind of doubt that almost made me give him up for good. And I didn't dare let that happen twice.

Finally, the last time I closed my eyes, I fell asleep faster than I thought I could. The quiet of the room kept me at peace. There was no loud noises or terrible thoughts going through my head. So for a while, I thought of nothing. My slumber was nothing but slumber. I began to think all of those dreams were just my imagination playing tricks on me, but just before I woke, I started going through another dark tunnel. I didn't want it to happen again. I wanted it to leave me alone.

I shook and rolled around in my bed hoping it would make me come back to reality, but nothing helped. All I could see was a large hand reaching for me. There was no body, no face, and no noise. The closer it became the more sporadic and nervous I got. When it finally got close enough to touch me, I jumped, but it was only Amy trying to wake me. I laughed a little at myself for being scared of what turned out to be my roommate. I wasn't going crazy. I was letting my dreams sift into my reality.

All day long I thought about the appointment I had made to go see Mrs. Downs again the following day. I wasn't sure if I needed to go see her or not. I felt like I was getting better. I considered her a friend already and I didn't want to let her down. So I decided I'd go one more time just to tell her my fears were deteriorating. I wasn't sure if she'd believe me or not, but I had to explain to her how I felt.

The day passed quickly. I was busier that day than any other day before. Eric was just as busy. I saw him through the day, but after classes, we both went our own way to take care of business that needed to be done. His kiss at the end of the day gave me energy to complete my tasks, so that was exactly what I did. Amy and I had some things to get at the store, and a few other errands to run, but by the time we were through, it was late. I always hated coming back to the dorm at night. I didn't quite know what I was afraid of. I guess I was afraid of what lurked in the darkness invisible to me. I always imagined I'd be walking alone with no one anywhere in sight and a strange man would pop up from behind some bushes or from around a corner and seize me. But as long as Amy or someone was with me, it didn't bother me near as much. Amy just thought I was a little crazy when it came to things like that. But I knew there were crazy people in the world and I surely didn't want to meet up with any one of them.

Like always, Amy and I talked until we could hardly hold our eyes open. Eric had called somewhere in between our conversation about him, and what we bought at the store. Another night passed by as I balanced on the edge of peaceful sleep and nightmares. It was like I was barely keeping all the monsters away from my dreams. I could still see them, but they were faded out enough to where I didn't completely lose my mind. Just knowing Amy was right there with me, made me feel better. I would've rather had Eric there, but some things just couldn't be helped. I would've spent every night with him if it'd been up to me.

Waking the following morning, sleep filled my eyes until everything was blurry and unfocused. With a warm rag, I gently removed the tired sleep from my eyes and looked in the mirror. The whites of my eyes were red, irritated, and puffed underneath. I looked like an old women who'd been through hell, but without all the wrinkles. Although I had gotten plenty of sleep, it looked as though I hadn't slept at all.

Amy rolled out of bed about that time. She looked almost as rough as I did. We looked at each other and began to laugh. I was just glad that nobody could see me looking that way. It was scary enough me looking at myself, much less someone seeing me.

"I'm gonna shower. I'll be right back," I said, grabbing my towel and heading to the bathroom down the hallway.

It was early and not many people were up. I was the only person in there showering. I undressed and stepped into that hot steamy water. It felt wonderful on my skin, and so relaxing. The pressure of the water seemed to massage the back of my neck as I stood there enjoying it thoroughly. I smoothed the soap all over my body and began to rinse it off. With my eyes closed, I started to wet my hair and I could feel someone touching me. I turned around, but no one was there. So I continued bathing. With closed eyes once more, a scene flashed in my head of someone trying to reach in after me, only the scene I saw in my head, was me as a little girl. I actually saw myself in my own mind as a small child. Each time I looked around, no one would be there, but the presence of someone hovering around me like a ghost floating around in the air. I began to tremble, but I didn't know why. I got to the point where I was afraid to close my eyes. I just wanted to keep them open at any cost. I couldn't imagine what the image I'd seen was all about. But I did know one thing, the person I saw was me. I couldn't have been any older than seven or eight. It seemed so real. I knew there was no way I could have been making all of those things up in my confused mind. I couldn't hardly think straight. How could I make up something that unexplainable. I guess after all the craziness in my life, nothing was impossible to do. That was my explanation for it.

I quickly dried off and ran back to my room. I went over and curled up on my bed in the corner, trying to hold myself together for a moment. I passed Amy in the hallway, so it was very quiet in there. The phone rang loudly and I jumped up and answered it without hesitation.

The person at the other end of the line was my favorite person. "Hey good lookin'. Want to meet me somewhere and we can do somethin' crazy," he said in a silly voice.

"You're crazy. Have I ever told you that before?"

"Yeah, but keep on tellin' me. That lets me know you still love me," he replied with a little sarcasm in his voice.

I smiled as if he could see me through the phone, and told him I'd see him in class. Hanging up the phone, I leaned up against the wall and slid slowly down to the floor. I thought of how my mood always changed when I would see Eric, or even just hear his voice. It always put me back on track to my happiness that took me time to build within myself. It was nice to have someone to do that for me.

There was one more person that seemed to help me, and that afternoon I had another appointment with her, Mrs. Downs. For a little while, I didn't think I needed her help anymore, but I realized I needed her more then, than ever. I really didn't know her, but at the same time, I felt like I had known her all my life. It was strange. So I opened up my mind once more I wanted to be able to give her all the information she needed to help me the best she could. I wanted her to help me. I needed her help, and her friendship was important to me as well. Everyone knows you can never have too many friends, only too many enemies. And as far as I was concerned, I had made more friends in the time I'd been at college, than any other time in my life. Mrs. Downs seemed so caring to me, and I knew if I could have a friend like her to help me with my problems at the same time, then I wanted to build on that and not destroy it. So I readied myself for another encounter with the dark side of my life. Whether it would help, I didn't know, but I wanted to try. Mrs. Downs was only there to help, and the idea of having a stranger care about me more than my family ever did, tore me up inside, but also made me realize something. I realized that no matter what you think of yourself, there will always be someone who believes you are wonderful, whether you believe it or not. And to me, Mrs. Downs was one who believed that. I wanted to trust her. I needed to trust her. She was my link to happiness, and I didn't want to break the only link I had to the unknown and to my fears.

CHAPTER 8

The hour grew near for me to go and talk once more about things I was trying so hard to forget. Although the dreams I had didn't make any sense, they frightened me still. I was flustered because I had no idea why it was happening to me. At times, my mind seemed so far away, but other times, I was in complete control of everything I said and did. So often in a quandary about what was going right and then distorted once again, by all that troubled me, I'd just sit alone and think. Such sequence of inconsistencies in my life made me wonder if I'd gone completely insane. The only thing in my life that was halfway normal, was the way Eric and I communicated. Someone once told me "The skill of communication can take you further than the inferiority of silence." And after being able to talk to Eric about anything on my mind, I knew it was true. Communication must be the key to unlock any closed door. I had unlocked one door with Eric, and I believed it was time to turn the knob and open another with Mrs. Downs.

As I began to dress, someone slid a note under my door. I walked over and picked it up. I could smell Eric's cologne immediately. Just the smell of him put a smile on my face. As I opened it carefully, what was written didn't surprise me a bit.

Written on the small piece of paper was a short letter:

Beth,

I'm not sure what's going on with you, or where you have to go that's so important, but I wish you'd trust me and love me enough to tell me eventually. There's nothing you can't say to me. I told you before, I want to know you completely, and that means the good and the bad.

Please don't shut me out. I know you believe what I say, but, at the same time, you seem scared to let go all the way. Don't fear anything as long as I'm around. I would never let anything harm you—I PROMISE!!

Call me later—I'll be waiting to hear from you.

LOVE ALWAYS,
Eric

Putting the letter to my heart, and then smelling it once again, I danced around the room as though prince charming had come and swept me off my feet. Like Cinderella, I never felt worthy of a love like the one I had found, until then. He made me feel worthy of anything. And as I looked above, I spoke to God as I often did when I needed a little extra security in my soul. It was quiet, but I knew God could hear me. I asked him to help me through any pain trying to swallow me, and to hold me tight in the night when I was all alone. There were times when I wasn't sure if he was listening, but then, I knew he heard every word I'd whispered because as soon as I said "Amen," the tree beside my window began to rub back and forth by the gestures of the breeze outside. To me, it was a sign from God he was watching me and was there whenever I needed him. Just knowing he heard my prayer, put much serenity inside of me where anxiety dwelled before. And that made all the difference in the world.

Walking down the hall to the lobby, I didn't have a clue what I was going to say to Mrs. Downs this time around, but somehow, like the last visit, she seemed to make me talk by the way she asked questions, by the tone of her voice, that soothing sound of hers. It seemed amazing to me how someone can talk you into something just by the way they speak, but she could. I didn't feel half as nervous about seeing her as I did the first time.

When I started to walk out in front of the dormitories, Eric walked up. He had a cheerful look on his face, as always; And when I saw him, I did too. Like the old saying goes, 'Smile and the whole world will smile with you.' Eric made that old saying come true.

"Where ya headed?" Eric said, peering at me with those splendid eyes of his.

With a little hesitation, I answered, "Oh, just to town to pick up a few things. Why?"

Looking a bit puzzled, he said, "I don't know, you've seemed a little preoccupied here lately. I was just wondering why. For some strange reason, I feel like you're holding something from me. I can tell. I mean, you don't look me in the eye when you're hiding something. Are you hiding something?" he inquired curiously.

"Eric, it's just something I need to deal with on my own first, and then I'll tell you what's goin' on. Please don't pester me about it. It's hard enough as it is. There are times when a person just needs to work some things out for themselves. I don't want to involve you," I said.

A hush fell over us for a moment. The tension was much more than I could stand. He looked like a sad puppy just begging, but I couldn't help it. As much as he meant to me, my sanity meant even more. If I wasn't able to grasp that once again, I knew I could never carry on with Eric. So, I tried to walk away from him.

"I'll see you after while, okay?" I said walking towards my car which wasn't very far away.

It began to rain heavily with no notice, so I ran as fast as I could to get in my car before I was completely soaked. By the time I reached it, I was drenched from my head to my toes. And as I got in and dried off a little, I looked back, and Eric was nowhere in sight. I figured he had ran for cover as well. My only hope, was that I didn't offend him, or make him angry. That was the last thing I wanted to do. I just wanted him to back off a little until I felt I could confide in him.

My shirt was so wet, it stuck to me like a magnet. And because it was cool outside, it didn't make it any better. There were people running everywhere trying to get in their cars or the dorms before they, too, looked like a wet dog. I snickered a little to myself as I took a towel lying in the back seat, to dry off. I knew I must've looked horrible, but I didn't really care. The only thing on my mind at the moment, was reaching Mrs. Downs office and trying to find some answers. I wanted to find answers to all of the questions which had been dancing through my mind for far too long. And I knew, if anyone could find answers for me, it would be Mrs. Downs, my new found friend.

Pulling out of the parking lot, the rain was coming down so rapidly I could hardly see. The rain poured down sideways in sheets, and the wind made for difficult driving. I could barely see in front of me, but I pulled out in a hurry, hoping I wouldn't have an accident with another car or even with someone crossing the road. My vision wasn't great, so it was just a guessing game at that point.

Making it off campus, I came to the first red light heading towards town. The rain beat down on my car harder and harder, like a flood was near, but I knew it wouldn't be long before it would shut off like a water faucet. It always did that. The sound of the rain did something to me. The sound of beating down rain seemed to trigger something in my mind. I was driving, but, at the same time, I began to think back. I saw nothing clearly, but I could hear the rain like it was yesterday.

A flashback showed me as a child sitting on my bed. The lights were out in the house, but there was a glimpse of light coming from the street corner lamp shining through my window. I had affixed myself in a different time, a different place. I could feel myself rocking to and fro against the headboard of my bed.

Then, I heard my door squeak open slowly..."Maybe it was daddy," I thought to myself, and then...a loud noise came from ahead of me. A car had stopped suddenly and swerved halfway across the road. It brought me back to the actuality of the moment. My mind had wondered away once again, but it was just like a memory, nothing to be frightened of. At least I didn't feel threatened like I usually did when my mind drifted to far away placed.

Still driving, I recalled a poem which I had written about fear. Though it was years earlier when I'd written it, I remembered like it was yesterday.

CASTING SHADOWS

Casting shadows in the night.
A dream forever lost.
Casting shadows in the night.
For sanity pays the cost.
Fear of dark; a gateway
Of hell's eternal fire.
Fear that sooner than you think
Your life will expire.
Casting shadows in the night
As you lay your head to sleep.
Casting shadows in the night
In your mind, such danger creeps.
Fear of noise; the unknown,
Of what may be lurking around.
Fear of danger looking
For a soul to place a frown.
Casting shadows; fear itself,
Never letting go of night.

Tammy D. Thompson

> *Until God shows there is hope*
> *As he gives us morning light.*
> *Casting shadows; casting fears*
> *Where there should be no fear at all.*
> *When we stumble in the darkness*
> *We then take a fall.*
> *For casting shadows; imaginary pain*
> *When all is said and done.*
> *We need to hold on tight*
> *For shadows try and make us run.*
> *Casting shadows; casting still*
> *Many dangers in the night,*
> *But still we find our sanity*
> *When God gives us morning light.*

Remembering those words written from within my heart, made me wonder if I wasn't still afraid of the same thing that feared me when I wrote those words down on paper. I was never really sure why I wrote it in the first place, but I figured it had to do something with what was in my subconscious.

Taking a deep breath, I sat relaxed in the car as I drove along slowly in the rain which continued to pound down on the windshield of my car. Relaxing and clearing my mind helped me to ready myself for another encounter with the source of my anxieties. I knew when I learned to face my anxieties head on, I would be able to live my life fully and completely without any interruptions from stray thoughts that might want to ravage through my mind at any unspoken moment. I guess that was what scared me the most, not knowing when it would attack my spirit and disillusion my mind. I was disillusioned enough. All I needed was someone to block out all of those notions, and replace them with something pleasurable and more conceivable.

Turning the corner, there was a small store. I pulled in for a moment to get something to drink. I opened the car door quickly and ran in before I got any wetter than I already was. And when I got inside, the only other people in there besides me, was the clerk and a man standing in the corner. I tried to hurry because I was almost late for my appointment, so I grabbed a drink and went towards the checkout. The man in the corner acted very strange as he looked at me, but I just glanced away and tried to mind my own business. I'd never seen him before. And the way he glared, puzzled me. He acted like he knew me from somewhere.

I paid for my purchase and looked outside as the rainfall almost came to a screeching halt. As I reached the door, the man who acted so strangely, jetted in front of me and ran out the door, as he said, "Excuse me, ma'am."

I was frozen in the spot in which I stood. "That voice...that voice." I thought to myself. It sounded so familiar, though I'd never seen him before. I didn't even think I'd seen him around campus. Then it hit me like a ton of bricks. "The man on the phone." I said to myself. "That was him. I know that was him. The one who sent the flowers. Oh my God. Who was he?" I pondered with a slight bit of frustration mixed with curiosity.

I got in my car and locked the doors hurriedly. I didn't know what to think. I knew it was him. I would never mistake that voice—such an offensive tongue. I'd almost forgotten about the incident with the flowers until that moment, and it all came back to me how it frightened me for so long. For weeks after getting flowers from an unknown, I walked around scared to turn a corner, frightened to answer the phone, and even too afraid to take a stroll on campus unless Eric was with me. But then it all started to come back to me.

Distracted by the stranger, I lost track of what time it was. I had sat there thinking about the past for longer than ten minutes, and was late for my appointment with Mrs. Downs. Pulling myself together, I drove several blocks, and I was there. The parking lot looked abandoned except for one vehicle parked on the far end. I knew it must've been Mrs. Downs car.

Not thinking of anything, I got out and shut the car door without looking around at all. Suddenly, someone came from behind me, put their hands on my shoulders and began to message them intensely. I tried to turn around to see their face, but I was forced to face ahead. I was paralyzed with fear. It was as though I couldn't make a sound because each time I opened my mouth to yell, no sound came. And then, he spoke in a low unmistakable voice, "Hey Beth! Goin' to see your shrink?" he laughed.

"Who...oo are you? What do you want with me?" I asked timidly.

"Oh, don't be afraid. I'm not the boogie monster, just your worst nightmare," he said, taunting me.

His grip got tighter and tighter until it began to hurt. His clutch was like the tight clinches of a bear trap, and his breathe was beating down on my neck. It disgusted me. Finally, I started to scream. I saw Mrs. Downs look out her office window, and then run out of the building as quickly as she could.

Before I knew it, I was being thrown down on the ground abruptly. And before I could turn to see where he went, he disappeared. My breathing was rapid, and my heart was beating ten times its' normal speed. As Mrs. Downs reached me, she crouched down beside me and held me tightly. I was shaking like a leaf and didn't know why such a horrible thing was happening to me. In a way, I wished I'd told Eric about everything. Maybe then he would've come with me and everything would've been just fine, but I didn't, and things were even more twisted than ever.

Mrs. Downs held my hand and led me inside. Her warmth and caring was so clear to see. I felt like she really cared about me. Just like before, it was like I'd known her for a lot longer than a week or two.

After comforting me, and making sure I was alright, she picked up the telephone and called the police. It wasn't very long before an officer came to take a statement from me. Since I didn't pay very much attention in the store, I couldn't quite say what the man looked like, but I did know his voice. If I didn't know anything else, I did know that much.

When the police were finished taking my statement and all of the information they needed, the officer left. I sat there still and quiet for a moment. Once again, the silence embellished my inferiority complex which had been with me all of my life. That was always something I could never get rid of. Though I was able to cover it up at times, I was never able to complete destroy it. And that man who tried to dig up all of the fears I'd buried, uncovered enough to set me back in my progress and recovery to the world of the sane.

"Mrs. Downs, I'm scared. I don't know what do to. For once I'd reached the point in my life where I was beginning to feel happy about my life, and about all of those around me, but now."

With a smile, she softly interrupted, "Beth, what you have to realize is that none of this is your fault. You just happen to be at the wrong place at the wrong time, that's all."

And then, I began to tell her about the roses, the phone call, and how it all tied together somehow. She looked puzzled, and as smart as she was, she couldn't explain it either. All she could do, was to comfort me until my nerves calmed a little.

Hesitantly she asked, "Are you feeling up to our session today, or would you rather come later on in the week?"

"No, I'm here already. I don't want to put anything off just because I'm scared. Besides, I know as long as you're here with me, I'll be just fine," I replied with a pale grin on my face.

"You're very brave. I can tell that by the determination I see in your eyes. I had that same determination when I was your age. You remind me a lot of myself when I was younger. It's good to see one person who wants to help themselves, while a million others just give up on any help at all," she said, leading me into her office.

Contrary to the visit before, she started things out much different. I guess I didn't know what to expect, but she asked me to do something which was always hard for me to do.

"Ok, Beth. Just relax. This time, I want to try something that may pull you out of your shell a little. Why don't you start today, by telling me anything, anything that's on your mind. From my experience, I know, the mind is where it all begins and to treat it, we have to know what you're thinking," she stated.

Staring around the room, I had no words. Nothing came to me. The only thing on my mind at that point, was Eric. Of course, he stayed on my mind, so it wasn't anything unusual.

"Well, it's Eric, my boyfriend. He's so worried about me. I haven't even told him that I'm coming to you, I guess, because I think he might think I'm crazy or somethin'. I don't know. He's an understanding man, but I'm not the type of person to unload my problems when he probably has problems of his own to work out," I said softly.

Never being an outspoken type of person, I felt strange just talking. But by talking about Eric and our relationship, it didn't seem as hard as I imagined it would be. In fact, it felt good to tell someone other than Amy about Eric and myself. The way I saw it, I could get an objective opinion on what was going right in my life and what was going wrong.

"Beth...Beth. Are you alright?" she asked.

"I'm fine. I was just thinking about Eric. You know sometimes I wonder if he's for real. Sometimes it seems like he's a fantasy, a dream that I just made up inside my head to make me feel like someone who matters. He's too wonderful to be true, Mrs.. Downs.

"When he tells me he loves me, I believe every word. And up until I met him, I didn't believe anything anyone told me, good or bad. The only thing I really believed for the longest time, was how insecure I was and how ashamed I was of who I'd become. And for that, I don't know why. But with Eric, it's different. He makes me want to climb mountains that I never believed I could climb before. He tells me I'm beautiful, but when I look in the mirror, I don't see it. He's an angel to me. You know, like a guardian angel. It seems like he's been my protector ever since I've been here in this small town. "Does it sound crazy? Do you think I'm crazy?" I finished solemnly.

She laughed a little and answered, "No it doesn't sound crazy at all, and you're not crazy, you're in love. And sometimes love is the best therapy of all for a broken heart, a broken soul, or even a broken spirit doesn't know where to go."

For some reason, I felt uplifted. It was more like a friend talking to a friend, rather than a shrink to her patient. She was becoming close to me each moment I spent with her. That was what made it all worth while. I'd discovered someone who related to me like no other had. When she looked into my eyes, I knew she could see deep down into my pains, and she could also see my love for Eric.

"Listen Beth, you need a little breathing room for a while. I know you need me, but Christmas is just few weeks away, and maybe time with your family during the holidays will help you discover something new...something you will disclose to me whenever you return," Mrs. Downs said sincerely.

Nodded and replied, "Maybe you're right. The trip might do me good, but with my family is not where I want to be. They've never been a real family to me. And if weren't for Melissa, I wouldn't go back at all. I miss her so much. I have to go see her, if no one else."

Mrs. Downs hugged me and gave me a wink. "Here's my phone number. If you have anything you need to talk about, please call me. I hope you have a wonderful Christmas. If I had a daughter like you to spend it with, I know mine would be the best Christmas ever."

A tear began to form in the corner of her eye as she turned away. And for a moment, I felt sorry for her. She'd never mentioned a husband, but she acted so alone.

"Mrs. Downs, if it's any consolation, I wish my mother was more like you."

She hugged me once more before I left, and for a moment, I felt like a tiny baby being cradled in the arms of a loving mother. Though she wasn't my mother, she was the perfect image of what I wished my mother had been like...kind, generous, caring, and unselfish.

She told me she wanted me to come back when I returned, and as I walked towards the doorway of her office, she pointed out, "Beth, a family is only a family when there is love dwelling in the hearts of all who are a part. When love is lacking, it's only an existence of strangers. If you show love, more than likely, you'll get the same amount of love right back. Don't forget that."

Her words were carved in my mind as soon as she spoke them. It made sense, but at the same time, I didn't want to show any kind of love to those who never put forth effort to show it the same to me. It was hard for me to love family, because from the time I was a baby, they treated me like I was someone else's child, an outcast, and a stranger.

By the time I walked outside, the sun had made its way through the dark clouds above. The light shined on me and warmed my skin as I walked to my car. Stopping for a moment, I remembered what had happened in that very same spot and it made me tremble, but then I just shoved it out of my mind, as I often did with dilemmas which bothered me.

Stopping for a moment at the park on the way back to my room, I saw a young couple with a small child which looked like he might've just started walking. They were laughing and hugging one another as if they were walking on clouds. It made me smile, but it also made me wish I had that kind of memory as a child. I wished I'd been given a hug for little things, but most of all, I wanted a family. As Mrs. Downs put it, there has to be love dwelling in all who are a part, otherwise it is only an existence of strangers. I believed that. She seemed so wise, and yet, she seemed so alone too. She talked about how she wished she had a daughter like me, well, when I'm with her, talking to her, I wish I'd had a mother just like her.

Staring once again at the couple across the pond, tranquillity consumed me. Though I'd not had the kind of family I desired, I was overjoyed for that tiny youngster ahead of me. The look on his face, I hoped, would never fade, and the caring in his mom and dad's eyes, I prayed would last forever. For the way I looked at things, all children deserve the chance to have a home, not just a house to dwell in. A house is a place where many uncaring people live together, but a home is anywhere you are where you're surrounded by people who love you.

Home is not where I was going to spend Christmas, I was going to spend Christmas in a house full of strangers, with the hope that one day it would transform into the home I'd always wanted.

> Hope is a blessing,
> > A present from heaven's king.
> And as you keep on hoping,
> > A many happiness will bring

For as soon as hope is lost
    So is lost your heart.
Success and disappointments,
    Your outlook always plays a part.
For when you see the sky as blue
    When clouds are heavily strewn,
Then the hope of a beautiful day
    Will never leave you alone.

CHAPTER 9

I began to get a little apprehensive about packing. I wasn't sure whether or not I wanted to go back to the house in which I was so desperate to leave in the first place. I wasn't sure if it would make me feel better about my family or if it would push me further away from them. Because in my mind, I felt like I'd found a new family—a family of friends who cared more than my real family ever did. Like a yo-yo, my feelings were going up and down and side to side about what I wanted to do. In fact, I almost had my mind up not to go, when a little voice inside my head started calling out to me, "Give them a chance, it's Christmas!" So I followed that small part of me which believed in happy endings. Though I wasn't sure of what would happen, I wanted to try.

I could still remember the day I left for school. Mom and dad seemed so relieved I was leaving. It was like they were holding their breath until I was gone. I Know it was probably only my imagination twisting my mind around like a roller coaster, but, I still believed that. I mean, they had my things waiting at the doorway as if to tell me to hurry and get out. But most of all, the look in their eyes, is what I remember most. Dad was quiet and solemn, and mom didn't pay much attention to anything, as if to follow along with dad's lead. I never understood their relationship. Sometimes it was as though they were playing follow the leader, and dad was always the leader. Mom never stepped out of line when it came to doing as dad said. I knew one thing for sure, I never wanted to be like that with Eric. In fact, Eric wouldn't let me even if I wanted to. He always said I was my own person, and not to ever let anyone tell me what to do or how t0o do things. And I'm sure he included himself when he said it.

Still, the day I left my old life and went to college, was the greatest move I ever made. But then, I was considering turning back the clock and stepping into a time machine, only to place myself right back into the desperation and pity I used to feel when I was a part of an unloving and uncaring family.

I began to feel bad about everything which crossed my mind. I guess because of Melissa. She was a wonderful sister, but she too left when I needed her most. I always knew it was so she could start a life of her own as well, but I still felt like she abandoned me for someone she'd only known a year. The way I looked at it, we were sisters, and blood should be thicker than passion any day.

Looking up at the clock, I realized time had slipped hurriedly away from me before I knew it. So putting my clothes in my suitcase, the whole time I was hoping I wouldn't forget anything.

The stillness of the room and the music playing low, let some wonderful memories creep up on me like a cool breeze on a splendid winter night. I could recall the first time I saw Eric sitting in that restaurant. And I also remembered the tug-of-war in which my heart played when I pretended I didn't want to know him, or meet him.

I remembered the night we went and sat by the lake with a picnic spread on the ground. He was smooth right from the start. But most of all, each little thing he did for me was like picture shows in the midst of my mind every time I'd try to concentrate. His attentiveness and personality took me in from the first time he kissed me with all of the passion which dwells in his heart. And the many times he gave me silly looks to make me laugh, are the times which helped me to pull myself out of a rut and back into living.

A tear began to fall as all of these recollections swiftly scrambled through my brain like a tornado—unstoppable. It devastated my heart just knowing I wouldn't be with Eric on a sacred holiday like Christmas. I wanted to be able to see his smile as Christmas morning showed itself to us. I wanted to be able to run to him with an embrace he'd never forget and wish him "Merry Christmas," in a loving way. But most of all, I knew it would truly be a joyous holiday if we were together. Just the thought of being apart from him made me feel sick inside.

Sitting down on my bed for a moment, I drifted into deep thought. The last conversation I had with Eric was one in which I was snapping at him. I didn't want things to be left like that. I wanted to see him smiling once more before leaving for home. Though I'd never been one to claim to be wrong, I knew this was one time I had to admit to treating him badly. It didn't take long for me to realize what I needed to do.

Reaching for the phone, a million things ran through my head about what to say to him, but before I could think, he answered the phone.

"Eric," I said hesitantly.

"Beth, I thought you were furious with me for prying into your business. I'm sorry."

It was so ironic to me. I was calling him to apologize, and he ended up apologizing instead. That made me feel even worse because I made him feel as though he was the one who was wrong, when in actuality, I was the one being hasty in my own actions. But I wanted him to know how badly I felt about the way I acted towards him.

"Why are you apologizing? I mean, I was the one who"

"Wait Beth, lets not argue about who should be apologizing to who, ok. I'm just glad you called. I know you're probably packing to go home, and I don't want you to leave until we put things back on track first," Eric said.

"I guess you're right."

We talked for a while and I realized something. Just talking to him on the phone wouldn't fulfill what I needed to carry me through the holidays. I needed to see him in person. I wanted to be able to tell him face to face how much I was going to miss him while we were apart.

"Want to meet me at the pond before I leave? There's a few things I'd like to say before we go different directions for the holidays," I inquired, hoping he'd have time to do so.

"You don't have to ask me twice. See ya in a bit," Eric said, hanging up the phone.

I was already dressed, so I started down to the pond. I walked slowly admiring each and every piece of beauty which crossed my path on the way. Of course, the friendly squirrels were always there with their playful attitudes, and the atmosphere in which surrounded me, showed nothing but peace and serenity. The way I figured it, the slower I walked, the more beauty I would view before I took off on my journey back to hell.

It didn't take long to reach the clear and hypnotizing water at the edge of the campus. A long train of recollections of times treasured, covered my heart, my mind and my soul. There had been many moments sitting by that very pond with Eric's arms placed gently around me. But also there were many times which I sat there alone just thinking of what I needed to do next in my life. That pond meant a lot to me. It was a like a statue I'd come to whenever my problems overwhelmed me. And it was also a special creation by God, whenever Eric and I wanted to be alone. It was many things to me. And I believed in my heart if I didn't have that pond to turn to when I needed peace and reverence, I probably would've gone crazy. It was my hope in silence and my inspiration in loneliness.

I looked out at the water, at two swans gliding along side by side. They looked like two lovers never wanting to be separated, for they never swam away from one another, but instead, closer and closer. It was an inspiration to see. It made me think of my love for Eric. Although we wouldn't be together physically at Christmas time, I knew our hearts would still stand side by side. And our souls would be combined as one soul forever. Just that thought took away the sadness and painted a smile where a frown had been. Knowing I'd come right back to him once Christmas was over, made me smile even more. Then I started thinking, two weeks wouldn't be bad, as long as I could talk to him every day. As long as I could hear his voice telling me how much he loved me, the spirit of the holiday season wouldn't be hard to keep within my heart. In fact, his voice is probably the thing I needed to put me into that frame of mind.

Although the campus began to look abandoned, and the pond still, I wasn't the only one left there. I heard footsteps coming from several feet away. I turned to see Eric bundled up in a thick jacket, and blowing smoke from the cold when he would open his mouth. With no hesitation I ran to him. He caught me, and lifted me up in the air, and then around and around, as if I were light as a feather. When he slowly let me down, I wrapped my arms around his neck tightly. I didn't want to turn loose of the man I'd grown to love so deeply. And I didn't want to have to say good-bye to him when it was the first Christmas we'd be able to spend together, not apart.

His eyes shimmered as he started to speak, but before he could say a word, I placed one finger over his lips, and then reached up to kiss him. His lips were warm even though the cold surrounded us completely. Barely touching, that kiss was one to remember. It was so sensual, but passionate in the way it affected my heart. I didn't feel like we needed to say a word, but, at the same time, there were things he and I both wanted to say before we said good-bye.

Eric held my hands tightly as he stared down at the ground. The sadness in his face was easily read, almost as easy to read as the sadness in my heart. Then he looked up at me, "Beth, there's so much I want to say to you, but if I did, it would seem like I'm saying good-bye forever. I know that's not what I'm doin', but right now, it feels like that's exactly what's happening. I've thought a lot about us and I've come to the conclusion that..."

"Don't Eric, it's hard enough for me to leave you without you makin' me all teary-eyed before I go. I know how you feel. You don't have to say it. I can see it every time I look at you. I can feel it when you hold me as tight as you can. And I know it each night I lie down to sleep, because I sometimes feel like we're dreaming the same dream. There's nothing you need to say that I don't already know. I promise you. You have made it all too clear what lies in your heart, and knowing that will help me through each time I don't have you there right next to me. I guess, because I know you are in my heart everywhere I go. That's all I need to be happy," I whispered. He stared at me as if I were a priceless painting and he admiring the view.

We walked along the edge of the water and peered into the reflection of he and I standing there side by side, almost one body. That was one vision I could never forget. His tall sleek body wrapping around mine like a protector, and his large hands clutched onto me as though he were holding a priceless diamond. A few moments of stillness made us melt into one another, even more than before, and the sounds of a few birds who had lost their way, sang to create the perfect music for the perfect moment. It would've been a sin to break such a beautiful scene, a scene to add to the collection of memories I already had of Eric.

But then, Eric gazed at me as if he wanted to say something, but then he turned his eyes away.

Curiously, I asked, "What's wrong? You act like you want to say something. Is there something on your mind? Come on Eric, it's me you're talking to, not a stranger. What is it?"

Eric gradually released my hands which he held so tightly, and turned away from me. For some reason, I felt the pain he carried inside. And though, not a mind reader, I knew what was creating such despondency with him. I put my arms around his waist and he held onto my hands firmly. His hands were trembling, and made mine tremble as well.

I turned him around, and tears filled his eyes like a river flood. They were unceasingly trickling down his pale frozen cheeks, and gloom encircle his being.

I felt helpless and unsure of what to do. I could reach for him, but I knew the reason he was sad. He seemed to be dwelling on the same thing I was. Neither one of us wanted to walk away from the other. And neither one of us wanted to say good-bye. I could see it in his eyes, and he could feel it each time he touched me.

Uncertain of what to say, I teased him a bit, "I love a man who can cry."

He looked up at me and grinned slightly, and placed his head on my shoulder gently. We sat down on the swing, and I cradled him like a tiny baby. I was hoping it would give him the comforts he needed as well as the comforts I'd been searching for to make me feel better about leaving.

We sat there for several minutes, when Eric stood up, wiped the tears from his eyes and turned to me. I felt a speech coming on, and how I loved his speeches about us.

I just sat there waiting for him to say something. He reached down and caressed my face tenderly, and those puppy dog eyes of his showed through. I just closed my eyes enjoying his touch. He kneeled down and kissed me lightly on my forehead, and then he stood once more.

It was quiet for a moment, but soon enough, Eric began to open up his heart as wide as he knew how. "Beth, I don't have to tell you how much I love you. If I were to never say those three words again, you'd still know. I've been thinking a lot these past few days, and you've been the center of each thought. You know, I never thought I'd meet someone I like you. I never thought I could find anybody who makes me as happy as you've made me. We started out rough, though. I gave all I had to you, and when I thought you'd never come around, you opened up to me in a way I'll never forget."

A bit blushed, but flattered, I responded, "You're right about one thing, Eric. If you hadn't been so damned persistent, I probably would've never opened up, but you kept on and on until I agreed to go out with you. I should thank you. I could've passed up a 'once in a lifetime' because of a little too much pride on my part."

We peered at one another, and Eric continued, "Anyway Beth, there's something I need to say to you that I never thought I'd care enough to say to anyone. Before I start, please keep an open mind. But most of all, keep in mind my love for you, a love which will only grow, and never die."

"Eric, you sound so serious, " I questioned, with a mind full of intrigue of what he had to say so desperately.

He walked me over to the very spot he and I had come to the first time we met at the pond. He kneeled down once more, but this time his face was peaceful and full of a happiness I hadn't seen in him in a long while. He took my hand and kissed it delicately, and looked up at me once more. But this time, his eyes were shining like the brightest star. I could almost see the universe deep inside of them.

With a small hindrance, he paused before he continued, but then he hesitated no more. A smile was drawn across his face as he spoke, "I have a present for you, but before I show it to you, there are some things I want you to know. I know I'm seldom serious about anything, but I've found one thing I want to be serious about, and that's you.

Beth, I just want to make sure you know how you changed my life. You always tell me how I changed your attitude, but you changed mine as well. Believe it or not, I used to look at women as obstacles in the way. I always thought it pointless to date, because of the way I tended not to trust any female, at the time, it did me no good anyway. I wouldn't let myself get close to anyone because of the fear of getting hurt. You see, my mom raised me, but she was drunk most of the time. As a parental figure, she wasn't much, but she tried her best. When I got the chance to move away and go to college, I wanted to go as far away as I could. Mom and dad begin to try harder when I decided to leave, and I hope to God they straighten things out. I love them both."

"But Beth, when I first laid eyes on you, I felt something inside I can't explain. It was like fireworks were doing a display inside of me. Not sure I'd see you again, I just hoped, and sure enough there you were that day at registration. You were such a sight. I told myself then that I wouldn't let this opportunity pass me by. I felt a connection with you even when you were turning me down. I don't know why, but I felt like you'd open up sooner or later. The rest is history I guess. It took me a while to get you to trust me, but now that I've convinced you, I never want to be away from you.."

Then he reached into his pocket and pulled out a beautifully wrapped box so tiny it fit in the palm of my hand.

"Open it" he said anxiously.

Like a child on Christmas morning, I ripped into it hurriedly. And underneath that beautiful paper and ribbon, there was a small box. Biting my bottom lip in nervousness, I opened it slowly. I couldn't believe my eyes. It was beautiful, the most beautiful ring I'd ever seen.

Eric reached for the box and took the ring out. Very slowly, he held my hand and slipped the ring on my finger. It fit perfectly. I'd never been speechless in my life, but at that particular moment, no words came. My heart was pounding so fast that I think it skipped a few beats along the way, and my hands shook from the surprise of the moment.

I wrote something for you and only you. I hope this will explain the rest.

> For years I lived unknowing
> Of what gifts God had for me.
> I walked the streets of life alone
> So blind, I could not see.

> But then you came and soon I knew
> Why I'd left what once was home
> And the first time I kissed your lips
> I knew I'd never be alone.
> For you light my darkest hours,
> You turn a cloudy day to clear.
> You complete the heart that makes me,
> As you wipe away each tear.
> I've been through sadness many times,
> And I've been tortured by pain and strife,
> But you'll lift me from hell into heaven's gates
> If you'd only become my wife.

Even before he was finished, my tears were visible. His way with words just melted my soul, and his sincerity took me further and further in love than I'd been one moment before.

Standing, he peered deeply into my eyes and asked, "Will you be my wife Beth Laney? Will you marry me?"

With tears still coming down, Eric wiped them away with his large, but gentle hands. It took me a moment to regain my composer before I said anything. For a change, my heart and my mind were saying the same thing, and then I answered an enthusiastic "YES! yes...yes...yes I'll marry you Eric Norris."

The gleam on his face couldn't be explained by words, only a feeling-happiness and love beyond all. And I, Beth Laney, would, one day, be Mrs. Eric Norris. What a thought. I'd gone to college to start a new life, and I found a life better than I'd ever expected.

Eric picked me up, lifted me in the air and swung me around until we were both dizzy. We fell to the cold ground, but the cold was insignificant because our focus was on one another and not what surrounded us. It was as though there was a huge bubble that he and I were the only occupants, and the rest of the world had diminished.

"When are you leaving?" he asked in a somber voice.

I gave him that 'up to something,' grin and began to run towards my room. "Well, we have enough time to."

It didn't take a second for him to catch on to my little hint, and then he ran after me. Right before we reached the dorm, he caught up with me and grabbed me with his large, strong hands, but I didn't resist. I loved his touch and the sincerity which went right along with it.

We wrestled a little all the way down the hallway until we reached my room. The place looked deserted because everyone else had already left to go home. I guess everyone was anxious to go, but not me. I knew where I wanted to be.

Eric took the key from my hand and unlocked the door. He glanced at me, and had a mischievous look in his as he turned the knob. Before I knew it, he was carrying me, acting out what a honeymoon would be like. Though premature, it was fun. One thing I always liked about Eric was the fact he could always make me smile. And, at that moment, I wouldn't have been able to rip that smile off my face for anything in the world.

Though still confused a little about what was happening, I didn't have a doubt in my mind about my answer to him. I couldn't imagine going through the rest of my life without him next to me. And knowing I wouldn't have to, just lit up my entire soul to where I was glowing inside and out.

I went over to the stereo and put in my favorite Reba McEntire cd. Her songs always inspired me, and lifted me up when I'd reach a low point in my life. Music is therapy for the heart, the mind and the soul, I'd always thought, but love is therapy for everything.

Turning around, I couldn't help laughing. Eric had undressed down to his boxer shorts and was lying on my bed like a male model would in a magazine. I got on my hands and knees and crawled slowly over to him while snickering the entire time.

"Want me to give you something to laugh about?" he teased, as he began to tickle me furiously.

"Stop...stop it Eric," I cried out, laughing all the while.

He quit for a moment and said, "On one condition."

"What condition is that?" I teased.

"On the condition that you agree to make love to me right now," Eric whispered.

I let silence take over for a split second, and then I replied, "Well, if I have to."

There was no more hesitation from either one of us. He leaned down and our lips let out electrical sparks like never before. I felt it all over my body. It was amazing what his kiss did to me. It seemed to take away from every fear, every problem and every emotional breakdown I'd ever had, and it placed me in a land of peace and tranquility. In short, it was the miracle of love from his heart to mine and then back again. Nothing was more powerful, and nothing was more clear in my mind than he and I being together forever.

His lips touched each inch of me as I just lay there and enjoyed the pleasure of him embracing all of me. The beating of my heart was rapid, and the fulfillment was total.

His hands massaged my skin until there was not one tense muscle left, and I was limp from his advances, one after another. I just wanted to lie there and be the follower while Eric led the way to making sweet and beautiful love with one another. It had been far too long since I'd felt him in that way, and I wanted it more anything that could have been given to me at that moment. He was all I wanted and needed. Like a lighthouse and the ships which are guided by it, I was a small ship in the darkness, and Eric was the lighthouse to show me the way.

Soon, we were moving in slow motion, enjoying each second we had left together before I had to leave him. And the slower we went, the more loved I felt. I didn't want to rush our love, I wanted to admire it and not take it for granted. For each time he stroked my hair, I felt his devotion, and each time he kissed my cheek, the truth was clear to see. It seemed as though I had rid myself of the fear which captured me for a short while, because the only visions I saw were visions of Eric and I becoming one soul, one body and one heart. We'd already become one soul and one heart, and were becoming one body as we made love wholly.

As the passion went from a flaming fire to a burning ember, we embraced each other firmly. His hands still stroked each strand of my hair and I continued to rubbed his chest in a circular motion. No words were needed. The only thing we both needed was the affection of the other.

When I glanced up at him, he touched his lips to mine in such a sensual way, that my heart began to race once more. Wanting to feel his body against mine overpowered my better judgment and I gave into him once more.

It seemed as though we were playing follow the leader, because for once, I wanted to lead. I wanted him to lie back and relax as I did, and just enjoy the last bit of passion we could give to one another before we went our separate ways on such a special holiday. The moment was still flaming, and I wanted to make sure the fire didn't go out just yet.

I hovered over him like a goddess, and made sure he and I were penetrating into one body once more. The look on his face told me he liked to be explored and taken over. And with my eyes closed, I felt his love with each motion, slow or fast, it didn't matter. I felt his love in every direction I turned.

As the ecstasy overcame both of us, I collapsed onto his chest and my breathing slowed little by little as I rested on the man who'd made my life so worth the living. Our bodies clung together like magnets from the sweat from such passion and desire.

"How do ya feel?" Eric asked boasting.

Smiling, I replied, "I've never been happier Eric. You're what I've been searching for, though I didn't know I was searching at all."

"I know what'cha mean Beth. I guess what people say is true. You find nothing but heartache when you search for love, but it's when you stop searching that true love will find you," Eric said elegantly.

"Well, I'm just glad I wasn't searching, or I'd never found you," I replied, covering one another with warmth and love.

I sat up on the side of the bed and looked out the window for a moment.

My mind started going ninety miles an hour, and I pointed something out to Eric, "Hey, see those two birds on that limb right there?"

"Yeah. Why?" he asked.

"Have you ever thought about what happens when one bird flies one direction and one flies another?"

"No, not really. What happens?" he replied just to humor me.

"Well, those two birds are like us in a way. I'm gonna go one direction, and you're gonna go another direction, but when it's all said and done, where will we end up? I'll come back to the same place I started off, with you. And you'll come back to me. Just like those birds. They may fly in different directions at times, but I'll bet you they always end up flying together," I said turning and smiling at him.

"You're a one of a kind, ya know it?" he declared, pulling me to him with a gentle hug.

Then he looked over at the clock in the corner. "You probably need to finish packing your things don't you?"

"I'm just about finished. All I have to do is throw in a few more things and I'll be ready to go." I replied as the smile on my face turned to a little sadness because I knew I'd have to leave him soon.

He saw the gloom in my face, and reminded me of what I'd just told him, "Remember, we're those two birds. We might be flying in opposite directions now, but we'll end up back together."

Just those words from him took the gloom away in an instant and helped put back the smile which he'd placed there. I knew there was no reason to be sad about anything. Nothing but good had happened to me since I'd met him, and I had the feeling he would make sure that was how the rest of my life would be as well. Knowing I would someday be Mrs. Eric Norris filled me up inside like a hot air balloon, and I didn't feel like I'd ever come down from the high I'd reached.

Eric reached for my hand on which he'd placed the dazzling ring he'd given me. He lifted it gently, and kissed the ring which shimmered on my finger, and then he kissed each finger one at a time. I felt like a princess who had found her prince charming. And when he was finished enriching my skin with the warmth from his sweet lips. I laid my head on his chest for a moment, and I could hear his heart beating so rapidly that it might just explode.

Time was slipping by, and I knew I needed to get on the road before dark. Although I hated to drive when it was dark, I had to. I'd promised my family I'd be home by morning, and I didn't want to let them down the way they'd let me down so many times. I wanted to show them that some people do what they say, instead of being all talk. But most of all, I wanted them to see how much I'd grown up. It had only been four months, but I felt like I'd been gone forever. They probably thought I was the same naive little girl who left that day, but I wasn't. In a short time, I'd learned a lot about myself, and about what I wanted to do with my life. I refused to be a failure. I wanted to succeed and show them the person I was proud I'd become. Finally, I was a woman who knew desires, hopes, dreams, and a new outlook for the future. That was the new me. The person I was drifted far away and had been replaced by a new soul who knew where she was going, and how to get there. That was what I wanted them to see.

I stood and headed towards my dresser to pack a few more things when Eric went to the window. He just stared out there as if there were something interesting to look at. I walked over beside him and he put his arm around me. We stood there for a moment without saying a word. Just his touch made me feel secure and loved.

Then he looked at me and said, "Let me help you. I don't want you to go, but I know you need to, and I want you to get there safely. The sooner you leave the sooner you'll be home."

"I could use a little help," I said, beginning to straightened my suitcase so everything would fit perfectly.

It didn't take us long to finish packing what little I had left. Eric closed my suitcase and gathered the rest of my things and placed them by the door. For a moment, it was like time stood still. He was across the room, but our eyes connected. In a way, I felt like we could see straight through one another. Then in slow motion, we walked towards each other with both hands reaching out. When we met, our fingertips touched and our eyes still hadn't left one another.

"Let me help you with your bags," he said sincerely, walking out the door and slowly down the hallway.

Wanting to leave him one last thought, I stopped him for a moment. "Eric, I love you, and I'll miss you far more than you'll ever know. Please don't forget that."

I could tell by the look in his eyes he wanted to cry, so I kept walking. The last thing I needed was an emotional good-bye. I didn't want to have to spend hours driving and crying at the same time. But from the way both of us felt, I knew that was exactly how it would end up.

Though it was a short walk to the car, we walked slowly so we could have a little extra time together. My car was just about the only one in the parking lot, and there was no one else in sight. Eric kept glancing over at me and grinning. But I could tell he was only trying to cover up the disappointment of me leaving him at such a special time of the year.

It didn't take long to reach my car. I took out my keys, unlocked the trunk, and Eric placed my bags in neatly. Closing the trunk of my car, he walked over and leaned against a light pole. He was staring towards the ground, and I could feel inside my heart exactly what he was feeling.

"Hey," I said reassuringly, "It's only two weeks. We can live without each other for two weeks can't we? Besides, you have nothing to worry about. There's no one else I'm even the least bit interested in back home, so don't get any crazy ideas running wild in your head."

We smiled and Eric placed both his hands on my face. He stared at me as if he were admiring me. He always did that. I guess he knew it made me feel special. But then again, everything he did made me feel special. Just his touch took away the cold and filled me with the warmth of peacefulness and love.

Eric told me he had something else for me. I couldn't imagine what else he could give me. He'd already given me the best Christmas present ever-himself. So I agreed to drive him to his dorm so he could go in and get it for me. He held my hand firmly until we reached his dorm, then he quickly got out.

Turning to me, he said, "Wait right here. Don't move. I'll be right back."

I sat there for a moment and the car started to warm up a little. My hands were just about frozen, so I clutched them between my knees to defrost them a bit.

It didn't take long for him to go to his room and come back down. He must've ran all the way up and all the way back down. He jumped back into the car in a hurry so the cold wouldn't creep its' way in. Catching his breath, he handed me a sealed card.

"Beth, I don't want you to open this until Christmas day. I want you to have something from me on Christmas morning. It means a lot to me that you'll at least feel my love through this even though I can't actually be there." he said with such sincerity in the tone of his voice.

I agreed to do as he asked, but at the same time, I felt bad for not having anything to give him in return. I know he knew how tight money was with me, but I felt like I could've gotten him something. He'd showed me his love so gallantly, and I wished I could do something special for him, to show mine as well.

Feeling guilty, I explained, "Eric, I didn't get you anything."

He just smiled and lifted up my chin with his tender hands. "Beth, you say you didn't have anything to give me, but you have given me something. You've given me the most precious gift I've ever gotten from anyone. You said yes to being my wife, my lover, my friend, and my lifelong companion. And that'll be the gift to last me a lifetime."

I couldn't help but to smile. With only a few words from his lips, he took away my worries and replaced them with wonderful thoughts of the future. I was lucky. I knew in my heart if the world were to come to an end right then and there, I would've lived a lifetime of love and happiness in only a few months. Eric was like a lost treasure in which I found without even looking. To me, he was like a jewel shining brighter than any diamond I'd ever seen. He was the sun which woke me each morning. And from that day forward, he would be the one who would complete my heart. Before, it was only half a heart, but when he came along, he made it whole.

We both seemed to be staling, putting off the inevitable, so I leaned over, slipped my mom and dad's phone number in his hand, and kissed him gently on tender warm lips.

There was nothing more that needed to be said. I was sure he knew how much I'd miss him, and I knew how much he wanted me with him. But I also knew I needed to go. Eric looked at me with his exquisite eyes, squeezed my hand and said, "I love you Beth. Merry Christmas."

"I love you too, Eric. And I will have a Merry Christmas because my favorite present is on my finger," I said as he pressed up against me tightly. Breaking away he opened the car door and went and stood on the side walk facing me. I wanted to run to him once more, but for the sake of spared tears, I watched him through the rear view mirror as I backed up and drove away. He looked like a stone statue with nothing but disappointment and loneliness expressed on his handsome face.

I waved good-bye as he waved back at me. The further away I got from him, the more pain I felt inside, and the more sick I felt. Though I wanted to be with him, home was where I needed to go. So I stared straight ahead of me, and headed for the place I used to call home.

CHAPTER 10

Driving cautiously, I finally reached the edge of town and headed for the main highway which would carry me home. I could still see Eric's face in my mind. In a way, he acted as though I was walking out on him, but I knew it was just because he wanted us to be together so desperately. The wave good-bye he gave to me, was almost like he was reaching out for me one last time. I guess he thought I might change my mind and go with him instead, but he also knew what I needed to do to make peace with my family. I'm sure they felt deserted when I seldom called or wrote, but I felt deserted as well. I may not have tried to contact them often, but they sure as hell didn't try to get in touch with me either.

Before I knew it, I had my heart raging from thoughts of them. I had prayed to God many nights about going back home. If anyone could help me, I knew God would. I just hoped he had placed an angel above me to make sure I handled every situation with them just right. I didn't want my temper to run away, but also, I didn't want them to run over me as they'd done so many times before. I wanted them to know who I'd become. But most of all, I didn't want them to begin judging me the moment I walked in the door. I had judged myself enough for everyone, and to have to go through judgment by someone else, would've been far too much for me to handle.

Only a few miles out of town, thoughts in my head begin to go around and around like a Ferris wheel. Would mom and dad look at me as if I were still a child, or would they accept me for the person I'd become? Would Christmas be one to remember blissfully, or would dad go into a rage and ruin what could be a wonderful holiday for the whole family? So many questions were jumping out at me like shadows in the night, and I didn't have one answer to any of them.

The fear I'd feel out of place, struck me more then anything. As I said once before, I never quite felt like I belonged, but there were times I felt like part of the family, just like everyone else. Though it didn't happen often, I enjoyed those few times in my childhood. For once, I didn't want to have to turn to solitude to be happy around them. There was a time when solitude was my friend and helped me through each hardship, but then solitude started to turn against me. The more time I spent alone when I was younger, the more lonely I became. I guess that was why I went off to college. I thought it would change my life, and I was right. It changed my life tremendously. From the moment I arrived on campus, I began to search my soul for my true self. The more I searched, the more I discovered, and that was worth the move in itself.

The darkness encircled me totally, and the atmosphere in the car as I drove, was peaceful. I finally realized the long hours of driving would do me some good. It not only would give me time to think, but it would also give me relaxation from all of the stresses I'd covered myself with. I knew that none of what had happened was my fault, and I had to get passed the feeling I was to blame for everything happening in my life. Though some things I brought on myself, there were other things which were forced on me without warning. But still, I believed in myself more than I ever had before. I guess the one thing which made me believe more than anything was Eric. I never thought there was a human being so wonderful on this earth, but I was proven so very wrong. I knew as long as I thought of Eric when I'd get frustrated, I'd be fine. Just to speak his name was like singing a beautiful melody.

Beginning to get a little tired, I decided it was time to stop for a bite to eat. I had seen a sign which said there was a restaurant a couple of miles down the road, so I drove straight to it hoping I'd wake up a little. I never was one to drink coffee, but I thought it might do me good to get a little caffeine in my system. At least it would keep me awake while I was on the road. There was a large neon sign which said Captains Cove, over on the left side of the road, so I pulled in and parked. I leaned my head on the back of my seat for a moment to rest my eyes. I felt exhausted. I wasn't sure I'd be able to drive the entire way without stopping for rest, but I had to.

I stepped out of the car and stumbled up the walk. The front door read, 'All Night Service'. I was glad because I needed a place to rest and I also needed some coffee to open my eyes for the rest of my drive.

There were only a few people seated and one waitress who looked as though she came off the show 'Alice.' She had red curly hair and she was gnawing on a mouthful of gum. It was obvious to see she wasn't busy, but still she acted as though I wasn't there. I waited for a few more moments, and right when I was about to say something to her, she walked over to my table with a sway in her hips. She looked like she was ready to round up a few men and carry them off to her trailer house probably just down the road. I'd never been the judgmental type, and I was intrigued by her attitude. She was a bit cocky, straight to the point, and had that 'Could care less,' attitude in the way she talked. I kinda wished I was more like that.

I was looking right at the menu, but my eyes were blurry and unable to focus..

"What'cha have Hun?" the waitress asked.

"Well..." I said hesitantly.

"Come on, Ain't got all night. My shift's over in twenty minutes, and I'm ready to smoke this joint." she said in a rude tone of voice.

"Gimme a minute. I'm tired and..."

She interrupted, "Tired? You don't know tired Hun. Tired is when you work twelve hours a day, seven days a week, with nothin' to show for it. That's tired."

Just to get her off my back, I quickly ordered, "I'll have coffee. That's all. Just coffee."

"One coffee," she sputtered hurriedly walking off swinging her hips.

I laid my head down on the table for a moment when all the sudden I was startled, "This ain't no motel missy. You wanna sleep, you find a bed, you're in a eatin' place right now. And don't get no hairs all over my nice clean table, ya hear."

"Hey." I said, while she started to walk off once again.

"Yeah. Did I forget somethin' Hun?" she asked.

"No, you didn't forget anything. I just wanted to ask you what your name was. My name's Beth." I said trying to calm her a bit.

She stopped chewing her gum for a second, I guess in astonishment that someone actually tried to start a conversation with her. It didn't seem to me she had many friends, not with that rude disposition of hers.

Finally she answered my question, "It's Belle. Real name's Isabelle, but most folks just call me Belle. Why you so interested?"

I just smiled at her and sipped my coffee, To my surprise, she gave a slight grin right back at me. I could tell she was just bottling up frustration and tension. And I guess I caught her on the night she decided to release it on someone. It didn't matter anyway, she seemed kinda nice. She probably was, but by her actions, you'd have never known it.

I sipped on coffee until I'd drank three cups in twenty minutes. By then, my eyes were wide open, and I felt like I was able to continue driving. But as I reached in my purse to get enough money to pay Belle, she walked over to me, "It's on me hun. Have a nice trip wherever you're headin' to."

"Thanks. That's awfully nice of you," I replied as I stood up and gathered my things to go.

"Well, it's not very often a stranger's nice to ya even when you're an ass to 'em. I bet ya got real character, don't ya sweetheart. Anybody who can be nice no matter what's goin' on, has got to have some kinda character. Wish I had it," she said as she walked off, punched her time card, and left.

She made me feel good about myself. I guess she was right. I'd always been the kind of person who tried to be courteous to everyone, even if they weren't nice in return. I guess the old saying, 'Smile and whole world will smile along with you,' was true. Sometimes being nice to someone whose rude, backfires, but most the time, it pretty much forces others to be nice too.

I looked out the window and saw Belle getting into an old, rusty, faded red, pick-up truck. When she started the engine, it was so loud that it could've been heard a mile away. And as she backed out, it sounded as if it were ready to fall to pieces. I heard it sputtering until she was out of sight.

I picked up my purse and stepped towards the front door. There was still one person left in the diner eating. It was on old man enjoying his own company. He looked lonely. But I felt alone as well, so I waved good-bye to him, just to be friendly, and entered the cold once more as I went back to my car. I fumbled with the car keys for a moment. It was dark, and my eyes never were that great. Finally I found the right key, opened the door, and got in quickly.

It was like an icebox. Even after I started my car, it took forever for the cold air to be transformed to warm.. Gripping both hands together, I waited until I was comfortable. When all of the cold was replaced by enough heat to defrost my fingers and my toes, I backed out slowly and left that little diner in the middle of nowhere. I was glad I stopped though, not just for the coffee, but I was glad I met someone interesting as well. The way I looked at it, you could never meet too many people.

Once again, I was on my way. It was pitch dark, and night time was not my favorite time to be driving. I would've much rather been snuggled up in my own, warm bed, lying next to Eric. But one thing was admirable. The moon was so large, it seemed to cover the entire sky. I could see a few clouds slowly floating in front of the light which it generated, so clearly. Not just the moon was noticeable. The stars were as clear as a new summers day as well. I could've picked out the brightest star with ease. It was amazing. They looked like a million fireflies hovering in the sky for beauty's sake. I could've stared at them all night.

To occupy myself, I turned on the radio. I always loved to listen to song after song, and try to remember certain times in my life. I sat there peacefully and drove along as I sang with the radio. It was a habit of mine. I was never able to listen to the radio, without singing right along. I know people must've thought I was nuts. But singing always tucked me away into a different place. Sometimes I'd even pretend to be a particular singer, and hold something in my hand as if it were a microphone. Afterwards, I'd laugh at myself for acting so silly, but it always broke any monotony which filled my life at that point and time.

One song came on the radio I remembered well. It was popular when I was about six years old, and it was never clearer in my mind as it was at that moment. I could still imagine mom and dad placing an eight-track tape in the stereo, and us kids dancing around like crazy. My brother and I didn't really like one another, but we'd dance together and try to do every step mom and dad did. We always ended up falling on the floor and laughing before the song was over. Then dad would get angry because we got on his nerves, and tell us to go to bed. The fun never lasted very long. Dad wouldn't let it.

Then I turned the radio to a station which had all night dedications. I listened to people describing their love for another, and then there were those who were dedicating songs to someone they wished loved them as well. One lovely song after another made me feel nothing but peace. I guess I was like that girl who dedicated a song to the man she loved and who loved her just as much. That was Eric and I. But I felt sorry for the ones who had no love in their lives. Love is so fulfilling, and for someone to have to live day by day without someone to share things with, it hurt me just knowing there were those out there who knew nothing but loneliness. If I'd never met Eric, I would've never known what I was missing out on, but Eric showed me what living was all about.

I started to yawn, and I looked up at the sign on the side of the road. I only had another twenty miles to travel, but I knew it would seem more like a thousand. I was beginning to tire once more, so I put my foot on the floor to get there a little faster. Though I was never one to speed, I was afraid I'd fall asleep before I made it to mom and dad's safely.

I'd made it about five more miles, when flashing blue lights came from behind. Since I'd seldom been stopped by the police for speeding, I got a little nervous. I didn't know what to say to them. My friends at college, had told me many ways to get out of a ticket, but I had too much honesty inside of me to lie to an officer of the law.

I looked in my rear-view mirror, and to my surprise, it was Travis, a guy I'd graduated with. It looked as if he was riding with another officer for training. When he stepped beside the car and asked for my license and registration, he looked at me and seemed surprised to see me.

"Beth...Beth Laney. I thought you moved away. That's what your folks been sayin'," he said politely.

Still nervous from being stopped, I started trying to explain, "Travis, I was headin' home from college for Christmas. I guess I wasn't payin' attention to my speed. I have no excuse," Then with a little hesitation I asked, "Are you gonna write me a ticket?"

The other officer patted Travis on the back and walked off, leaving him to make the final decision on what to do.

He tried to fool me, and said, "Well, I guess I'm gonna have to..let'cha go this time." And then he laughed a little.

With a sigh of relief, I rested my head on the back of my seat and replied, "Thank you so much. I don't know if I could handle another set back when it comes to money."

"Just be more careful. Okay?" he said as he walked off.

I took a deep breath, buckled my seat belt, and cautiously drove on. The police car followed me for a few miles, then passed, and I saw Travis wave as they went by. I was always told most of the people you go to school with, disappear after graduation, but I was glad not all of them had. I knew of a few people who had moved away, but as far as I knew, most of the ones I shared classroom after classroom with, were still around. Most of them attended the community college, and I guess the rest were still mooching off their mom's and dad's as they'd done for years. I wondered sometimes if they would ever have a life outside of the old neighborhood. I knew I did. And my own life was all I needed to worry about.

I passed an old barn which sat way off the highway. The few friends I did have, and myself, used to go there and hang out. We'd just sit on hay bales and gossip about the people we didn't particularly like. I never stayed out too late, even when I wanted to, because of the fear my father instilled in me. I always feared he would beat me if I arrived home one minute late. But I never found out what he'd do, because I never gave him the opportunity to do so. I always played the sweet innocent Beth they wanted me to be. But those nights in the old barn, were some of my favorite memories.

A few more miles took me, to what used to be, the main park where I lived. After a few years it turned into nothing but trash and the homeless. The city decided to find a new local for a better environment for kids to play. But when I was a small child, I remembered me and my sister Melissa going there often.

Since she was older than me, she'd push me on the swing set, and help me make designs in the huge sandbox right in the center of the park. Lewis was supposed have watched us, but he always ran off and left us until it was time to go home. Melissa and I never gave any thought to anyone trying to steal us away, we just enjoyed spending time, laughing and playing together. That was one thought which made me light up inside. I realized then, how much I'd missed my sister. I only hoped she'd be there for me to talk to when I got home. With my luck, Melissa probably wouldn't come in at all, and I'd be stuck there with mom and dad for Christmas. That was a thought which completely shook me. I couldn't imagine having to put up with them for two weeks straight, without any say-so as to where and when I could go or do anything. I knew they wouldn't see it the way I did, but I considered myself grown. I'd lived without them for months, and made it fine. I proved to myself I could manage my own life. I sure as hell didn't want someone else trying to manage it for me, especially them.

Making the turn off the highway towards town, I watched the fields on the side of the road as the wind blew the grass to and fro. The moon shone down on them and made it easy for me to see whatever might've been out wandering around in the wide open. For a split second, I saw a deer. It ran across the road in front of me. It was a beautiful, graceful, and naive doe probably looking for its' mother. I was always glad we lived on the out skirts of town because of the scenery, such as deer, playful squirrels, and hundreds of birds not frightened of anything or anyone. They all seemed so free. Just to look at them, you'd know they had no worries. What a thought, no worries.

The stretch was long, but peaceful. Each place I passed brought back glimpses of a memory. Most made me smile, but some were recollections I wanted forget. I passed one place particular which made a scene flash through my head over and over again like pictures from the past. It was the football field at the Junior High I used to attend. I was thirteen years old, and had just gotten my period. My brother always drove me to school, although every morning I begged my mother to take me instead. I felt strange because I had to wear a tampax inside of me, but mom told me it was all a part of being a woman. Anyway, one day Lewis and I were getting into his car, when I dropped my purse. It fell open and my female necessities rolled out. I quickly gathered them, put them back into my purse and jumped into the car rapidly. Lewis always agitated me about something, and I just didn't want him to know.

We were driving down the road, and Lewis started his aggravation as usual, but I wasn't in the mood for it in the least. I remember trying to ignore him, but the more I ignored him, the more he kept on and on.

"So Sis, guess your turnin' into a woman, huh." he laughed.

With a face full of hate, I replied, "Just leave me alone Lewis."

"Awe, the little girl is shy. Let me see what'cha got in there Sis," he said trying to reach for my purse.

About that time we reached the school. When he pulled over, I hurdled out of the car and headed towards the field where I used to go each morning before class. I always went there because I wanted to be alone. There were usually guys playing football on the field, so I'd just sit over on the bleachers until the bell rang and most folks went in. But on that day, I was humiliated. Lewis got out almost as soon as I did, and chased me to where I usually sat in peace. There were a few guys in my class pitching a ball around when I ran by. Lewis caught me, grabbed my purse, and slung everything out of it. Somewhere between my brush and make-up, were a few necessities. Everyone near us saw them. I felt like crawling under a rock and dying. I'd never been so mortified in my life. And I kept thinking he'd stop, but he continued to taunt me.

Lewis just kept yelling, "Beth got her period! Hey Beth, you're floodin' today."

I started to cry, fell down to my knees, and begged him to stop. Finally, he walked over to me and said uncaringly, "You pick'em up. You're a woman now."

Then he turned around and walked off. Before he reached his car, he turned back to me and began to laugh a horrible laugh. The echo of his voice across the bleachers, sent cold chills down my spine, as I collected my things. With a lowered chin, I slowly walked towards the school. I was sure everybody saw what happened and I couldn't bare to be gawked at because of it. Without much thought, I passed the school, and entered the woods nearby. There was a pond a little ways behind the school, so that was where I went and stayed for the remainder of the day. It was quiet, and no one could find me there I felt tucked away in a safe place, and didn't want to be found. I just wanted to be left alone. It wasn't supposed to be that way. At least I didn't think it was.

When I returned home, the Principal had called my dad. He told dad I'd skipped school that day. When I tried to explain, all he could do was to give me lash after lash until he thought I'd learned my lesson. He couldn't have cared less about what kind of explanation I had. He didn't care about what I had to say in the least. The only person he really cared about was his dear son, Lewis. What a memory.

I always tried to put times such as that one, in the back of my mind. I didn't want to be able to reach it. It was so inconceivable to me how horrible Lewis was at times, and seldom did I ever have a recollection of any kindness he had towards me. Though there may have been one or two times he showed a bit of concern, all of the hatred he embellished on me the majority of the time, overshadowed it entirely. I waited on torture from his harsh hands, never the kindness of a helping one.

Just a few miles from the house, I pulled up to a red light. It was in front of a restaurant we often ate, called 'Bogotti's.' My recollection of that spot, came to me as clear as if it had been yesterday. Lewis, Melissa, and myself were driving home after a game one night. Lewis was supposed to be watching after us, as usual, but he could care less about us being in the car. He carried on his normal activities as if we were invisible.

This car pulled up beside us and acted like as though wanted to race. Lewis took them up on their insinuation. When the light turned green, Lewis went from zero to sixty in nothing flat. What scared me the most, was that he'd been drinking. Melissa and I both pleaded for him to slow down, but he had his mind set on winning. He completely blocked us out. Melissa dove into the back seat with me when she saw a sharp curve up ahead. We held onto one another, and before we knew it, we were in the ditch and not a foot away from crashing straight into a huge Oak tree. Lewis hit his head and was taken to the hospital, but we were fine. The ironic part of the whole thing, was that dad didn't blame Lewis, he blamed me.

Dad scolded me and said, "Beth, if you hadn't been aggravating your brother, maybe he would've been watching the road. Now go to bed."

"But dad..." I said, frightened by the evil look he gave me out of the corner of his eye. "I wasn't doing..."

"Just shut up. I don't want to see your face. Go to bed. NOW!" he shouted while I ran up the stairs, went to my room, and huddled in the corner.

Melissa poked her head in for a moment and all she could say to me was, "I'm sorry Beth."

I guess I couldn't blame her. She was just as scared as I was. Neither one of us would speak our mind for fear we'd be severely punished. And Melissa didn't like Lewis either. Sometimes I wondered if he even liked himself. With his arrogant attitude, it was hard to tell what he thought about anything.

Returning back to reality, I was pulling into the driveway of those who would probably deteriorate everything I'd worked so hard to build up—my self-esteem. But I promised myself I wouldn't let that happen. I wouldn't let them destroy me like that. Once was enough. I didn't want to give them a second chance to do the same thing to me. That wall of love which Eric built around my heart, was strong enough to withstand any amount of pressure from any direction. I knew that, if nothing else. I'd become a much stronger person in only a short time, and refused to let anyone push me back in time. I didn't want to be that same frightened little girl again. I wanted to remain strong willed and able to handle any situation. Mrs. Downs taught me one thing through all my therapy with her. She taught me to be myself because that was the only person I could be, and still hold my head up with honesty and integrity.

Sitting in the dark silence for a moment, helped me gather my thoughts. After only a minute or two, I reached across the seat, grabbed my purse, and started to get out of the car. But as I picked up my purse, the envelope Eric had given me was lying there. I rubbed my hand across it as if it were Eric's face. I placed it in my purse and wondered what Eric might want to say to me he hadn't already said. But as I told him, I wouldn't open it until Christmas morning. As hard as it was be, I wanted to keep my word. He trusted me. And I trusted him more than anyone I'd ever come across in my life. He always made it so easy. But most of all, I wanted him to believe in his heart he could trust me with his life. I guess in a way, I placed my life in his hands by saying I'd marry him.

I looked down at my engagement ring, and I could hear him asking me all over again, the question every woman wants to be asked. And I could picture him on his knees as if he were a peasant begging for the queen's hand. But he wasn't a peasant at all. To me he was a king, and I was the one who wanted to serve him for the remainder of my days to come.

Finally, I pried myself out of the car and opened the trunk. As always, I packed far more than I needed. So one by one I pulled and tugged until I had all three bags lined up in a row beside one another. I looked up the walk, but it didn't seem real. It didn't seem like I was really there. It was more like one of my odd dreams I often had, but it wasn't. It was real. I was back home.

With my purse and one bag over my shoulder, and a suitcase in each hand, I waddled up the walkway. Though it wasn't a very long walk, it seemed like a million miles. The more steps I took, the more it seemed I had to take to reach the entrance way of that old house. When I reached the steps to the porch, I stumbled and dropped a couple of bags in the midst of my fall. Gathering them once more, I chuckled a little. I never was very coordinated. Sometimes I'd trip over something which wasn't even there. That's what my dad used to tell me anyway.

As I reached the door, I realized I couldn't ring the doorbell. It was far too early in the morning to wake mom and dad, so I searched for the extra key which was always hidden above the light, by the mailbox. The glass door squeaked from its' rusty hinges, as I slowly opened it, and I felt a little weary of standing out there that time of night. With that thought in mind, I took the key, opened the door, and let myself in. I tried to be as quiet as possible when I shut the door and locked it. Starting up the stairs, the light in the stairway came on and startled me. Dad peeked down as if he didn't know it was me. I'd told them I was coming, but they probably didn't think it would be at three o'clock in the morning.

"Dad, it's me...Beth. I just got in. I drove all night," I said softly so not to wake mom if she was still sleeping.

"Beth?" he said carefully making his way down.

I sat my things down, and when he reached me, I leaned over and tried to hug him. I put my arms around him, but he just stood there rubbing his eyes as if he were trying to ignore my affection. Stepping back a little, I was without words. And it was obvious dad was too. All he could say was, "H...How ya been? Ain't heard much from ya lately. We weren't sure what was goin' on. We would've called you more, but you know how your mother is about..."

Shaking my head, I interrupted him, "It's alright dad. I'm fine—just fine. To be honest with you, things couldn't be better. Can we talk in the morning? I'm really tired from the drive and I'd just like to crawl in a warm bed and sleep."

With nothing more than, "Yeah, in the mornin' Night Beth." he went back upstairs.

He mumbled a few other things I couldn't understand as he made his way up the stairs, but he always did that. He talked to himself all the time. Sometimes I wondered if he didn't think he was better company than mom or anyone else. I remember when I was younger hearing dad talking in his room. I'd walk in there and he'd be facing the mirror as if he were having a conversation with himself. It always struck me as strange, but that was just dad. He was always strange in his own way and seldom acted normal. I guess that was why we usually looked over many of the things he did and said. Sometimes he knew what he was talking about, but more times than not, he was totally lost. It could've been the alcohol, but none the less, we dealt with it for a long, long time. It was sad mom was still there living with it alone.

Still standing at the foot of the stairs, I couldn't believe dad didn't offer to help me with my things. He saw what a struggle I was having, but he just turned and walked away. It made me angry, but I put my anger aside as I drug my suitcases behind me-step by step. The regret from bringing all I had in my closet, hit me. I was exhausted by the time I got to my old room and unpacked everything little by little. Eric must've thought I was crazy. I bet he couldn't believe one person needed that much to wear in just a two week period. And the more I thought about it, I began to think the same thing too.

When I was finished settling in, I looked at my watch and it was already four o'clock in the morning. I couldn't believe it. I'd always been the type to make it to bed before ten. If I ever stayed up later than that, it was a special occasion. I guess that coffee Belle gave me was what kept me awake long enough to make it the entire way without falling dead asleep and killing myself. Besides, the diner I stopped at, had a unique atmosphere. I don't know what, but it had atmosphere. Maybe it was the country attitude Belle had which made that short stop in the middle of nowhere, a pleasant memory.

Taking time to sit down, I looked around the room which I had occupied for many years. In fact, that very room was where I spent the majority of my time. If I wasn't hiding away from the world, I was bound there by my parents for not being the perfect child they always expected me to be. The corner was my favorite spot for a long time. I often sat there and just rocked back and forth until I rocked all my problems far away. I was such a dreamer.

I leaned over to set my alarm, but then I changed my mind. I didn't want to get up any sooner than I had to. I knew Mom and dad would both leave for work early, and I thought if I only waited until they were gone, the house would have a peaceful aura about it for the first time. I wanted to be able to walk down the halls without hearing yelling from every direction. The yelling was not always directed towards me, but it was still there, and I hated having to live with that.

Pulling the covers back, there was a note lying on my pillow. I picked it up carefully and noticed the handwriting was my mother's. Curious why she wrote to me, I unfolded it, and began to read the words she'd written in her beautiful handwriting.

Beth,

I assumed you'd come in way after your father and I turned in for the night, so I decided to welcome you home in this letter. We missed you dear. I know you don't believe your father did, but you know your father. He always was a hard one to read. Anyway, Beth, I'll be glad to see you when I wake in the morning. I hope you're not disappointed we didn't call you everyday when you were at school, but you know your father. He always was more worried about the phone bill going thru the roof.

Sleep tight in your room. Because this will always be your room. Maybe the house won't seem so empty now that you're here for the holidays. I can tell it's going to be the best Christmas ever.

Get some rest, and I'll wake you for breakfast.

Love,
Your Mother

The letter was a complete surprise to me. It wasn't like her to do something so out of character. From all the years I'd lived under their roof, she'd been more like a robot, doing only what dad said to do, and never having her own opinions. And she had never done anything like that before. For once, I started to look up to her, instead of belittling her for being such a coward. Even though dad probably didn't know she wrote the letter, it didn't matter. She still tried to do something to let me know I was welcome. And she was right, it did make me feel a little more comfortable about being there, though not completely, enough for me to relax.

'what a day!' I thought.

I felt lost without my book I was used to writing in every night. I made it a habit to sit down every night and write about the day I'd had. Good or bad, I always wrote down what I felt inside. Though I didn't have it with me, I was still determined to continue my diary during my stay for the holidays.

I searched for a pen, and I finally found one in the very bottom drawer of my desk. Finding paper was just about as difficult, but soon enough I located a tablet with a few empty pages in the middle, I turned on the lamp in the corner of my desk, and began another entry of "One Day in the Life of Beth Laney". That's what I called it. I figured one day I just might be a millionaire because of it. You never know, someone might look at it as an interesting story, and publish it. Well, there goes my dreaming again.

I laid my pen and paper down on the desk after making my daily entry and read over it as I always did. And as I stood, I stretched and yawned just proving how tired I really was. I could barely keep my eyes open. And I didn't intend on getting up for breakfast. I remembered what time mom always cooked, 8 a.m., and that wasn't near enough time for me to get the sleep I needed to be completely rested for the day rapidly approaching.

I found my gown and laid it on the bed. When I undressed, I slipped on my jade silk night shirt. It felt so good on my skin. But what felt even better, was when I crawled into my bed, the one I broke in many years ago. It was still as comfortable, if not more, than it ever was.

I turned facing the window and I watched the trees sway to and fro until sleep took me in as its' guest for the remainder of the morning. Though I seldom dreamed dreams of peace and tranquility, that was one night in which nothing covered me but the hope of new beginnings.

CHAPTER 11

My first night at home, sleeping in the bed I'd slept in for years, brought an apparition of festive thoughts dancing through my head. Slow breathing led me down a road with flowers putting out a wonderfully fresh scent all over, and the cool breeze which whisked through my hair, also cleansed my soul. I felt nothing but adornment inside. The world was beautiful. At the end of the road, there was my house. Taking my time, as if walking in slow motion, I went towards it carrying nothing but a smile. I had such hopes of starting over with my family that my vision seemed clear to what I wanted to see.

There was my sister. Oh, Melissa, my sweet sister. She stood on the porch to greet me. Looking like an angel, she seemed to glow. I'd missed her so much. And as she took my hand, we turned and stepped into the house. It was filled with such light, and the smell of freshness everywhere, was pleasing. There were dozens and dozens of roses, my favorite flower, sitting around the living room like a florist shop. I just took in the incredible aroma which surrounded me, and I held my hands together.

Melissa told me over and over again how delighted she was about me wanting to spend the holidays with her and our parents. Mom and dad walked in from the kitchen and were holding a batch of freshly baked cookies.

"Want some honey?" dad asked thoughtfully.

With a slight hesitation, I replied, "Please. Thank you dad."

The atmosphere in the room was unbelievable. I'd never seen them act that way together before. And Melissa, she was different. I wasn't sure how, but she was different.

I asked to be excused as I went upstairs to freshen up. But as I took the first step, the light began to darken, and a faint moaning entrapped me. I looked back to see where Melissa, mom and dad were, but they were no where in sight. The sun had even faded out of the sky. Then I begin to feel a little tremble throughout my body. It was as though I were being watched—hovered over.

I looked behind me once more and the flowers were gone. All my beautiful roses along with their scent, had vanished into thin air, with no trace they'd ever been there. But there was a smell unrecognizable. It was stale and harsh. To me, it was the smell of death. All my prior thoughts that all was fine, had deteriorated into the reality of regret.

I shouted over and over again, "What's happening to me? What did I do to deserve this?" But no answer came from the pitch black ahead of me. All I heard was faint moaning from no particular direction, just all around. My head begin to spin around and around as I tried to climb the stairway, but I stumbled and hit my head.

Feeling the bump which had risen on my skull from the fall, I sprang back up, and ran into the darkness. But as I reached the top, I was no longer by the stairway. In astonishment, I stood in the middle of my room. The lamp was on just as I'd left it, and my covers were pulled back neatly as always. The light post outside, was shining through the window, as it did every night, and my suitcases, were unpacked and sat in the corner.

Shaking my head, I tried to sift out all of the fear and instill contentment once more, but no sooner did I take a deep sigh of relief, my door squeaked open slowly. I stepped backwards until I reached my window sill. I couldn't move any further. Even if I could've, I felt frozen inside and out. I couldn't move a finger, a toe, or even turn my head to look away from the doorway. I was lost in a tunnel of fear which, I had broken away. Though I wanted to break away once more, I didn't know how.

When the door opened entirely, someone stood there in the blackness of the hallway. A trace of their build was barely visible, and they neither moved forward or backwards. They stood like a stone statue, not moving a muscle, or saying a word.

As hard as I tried to shut my eyes, they wouldn't close, but began to focus closer and closer on the figure which stood watching me. Inch by inch my view became clearer and clearer. But right before I reached total vision of my perpetrator of fear, the door slammed shut and the dark figure was gone.

I laid down in my bed and a voice sounding far away said, "Sleep tight Sis." And laughter followed. It grew fainter and fainter until the laughter was no longer heard.

I tried to close my eyes, but as soon as I did, I was being shaken furiously. Frightened to see who was in front of me, I fought back.

"Beth! Get up. It's nine o'clock. Breakfast has been ready for an hour. Haven't you heard me calling for you?" mom grumbled.

I opened my eyes one at a time to make sure the nightmare was over, then sat up in my bed. Covered with sweat, I wiped my forehead. My heart beat rapidly and it scared me. I felt as if it were going to explode. But after a few long breathes, it began to slow to where my nerves weren't doing summersaults any longer. Mom stared at me as if I'd lost what I had left of my mind, then she sat on the edge of my bed. She'd never been the mother type. I mean, she'd never been one to sit down with me and talk to me about what was bothering me. Usually she'd just say, "It'll be fine honey," and then walk off. It was strange for her to come and sit down as if she wanted to know why I acted so shaky. She took my hand and realized I'd been frightened by something. Almost unable to speak of what I remembered of my dream, or nightmare as it was, I squeezed her hand and a tear formed and trickled down my face.

"Mom, I'm scared. I don't know what's happening to me. When I think the dreams have gone away, they only appear again when I least expect them," I said with all the emotion I had within my heart.

You could tell she was contemplating on whether or not to ask any questions. In fact, I was beginning to wonder the same thing myself. For once, I wanted to be able to talk to her without any walls separating us. For once, I needed her to listen to what I had to say. I thought she might've had some explanation for all of my strange dreams and visions. And if she didn't, I hadn't lost anything, but instead, gained a friend to talk to.

Finally, I guess her curiosity got the best of her, and she asked, "Beth, what are you talking about? You act like you've seen a ghost. And what about these dreams. You know honey, a dream is just a dream. When you wake, it disappears and can't hurt you."

I lowered my head, wiped my tears, and looked back up at her. She sat there waiting for an answer, but it took me a moment to find a good way to explain to her what had been happening to me. I didn't want her to think I'd gone over the deep end, so I took my time and carefully tried to explain where she would understand, not judge.

"Mom, it all started after I left home and went to college. It took several weeks, but I begin to have these strange images blink in and out of my mind. Most were only bits and pieces of a puzzle I haven't put together yet, but others were perplexing. I don't know mom, nothing I've seen has made any sense, but last night was different," I said, trying my best to explain.

She raised her eyebrows in bewilderment of the things I'd just told her and for a moment she said nothing. But then she implored, "Now Beth, like I said, a dream is a dream, nothing more."

"No mom. You don't understand. I have a problem, but I can't find out what it is without your help, without someone's help," I begged her.

"What did you mean when you said that last night was different? What happened last night. You slept well didn't you honey?" mom inquired, talking to me as if I were a two year old child.

Very tentative, I answered, "Well, it was a dream that started more peaceful than any I'd ever had before. Melissa was there to greet me as I arrived home, and you and dad were different in a good way. But then it got extremely bizarre."

Shaking her head, she stood and turned away as if she were going to leave.

"Mom. Please don't leave. I need to tell you. I need to tell someone." I begged, until she turned back and sat down once more.

"Go ahead dear. I'm listening." she whispered, trying to humor me.

"Like I said mom, then it got really bizarre. Everything turned to darkness and I kept hearing a moaning voice from somewhere I couldn't quite pinpoint. The strangest part was when I ended up in here, in my room. But when I thought everything was okay, my door opened. Little by little it inched its' way until it stood wide open. And, in the hallway, stood an unknown figure. I couldn't see a face, but when I tried to focus to where I could see who it was, the door shut. Then I laid down with hopes that it was just a crazy nightmare, but when I closed my eyes in my dream, I heard another voice."

"Whose voice was it Beth?" she asked.

"It was Lewis's mom. Lewis's. He said 'sleep tight Sis,' and then he just laughed and laughed until I couldn't hear him any longer. It petrified me as the sound of his voice sent chills completely through me. It was like he was trying to haunt me, mom. Tell me what's happening. I need to know. I know I'm not crazy. I'm not."

"Beth...Beth...calm down. You have some imagination," She chuckled, standing and walking towards the door. Then she turned to me again and said, "You're not crazy, but if you keep on making yourself dream things like that, you might end up that way before it's over."

Angry that she looked over my pain and found humor in it, I laid there quietly and I could tell my blood pressure was sky rocketing. It always happened when I'd get indignant over something I believed in thoroughly. And I couldn't believe she was so cold hearted. But the more I thought, I realized she had to be that way because of dad. People always say you act like those you're around the most. And if that were true, mom would end up hating the world just as dad did.

In no hurry to eat breakfast, I walked over and sat down at my desk. I watched out the window for a moment and saw children next door playing. There were two girls and a boy. It amazed me how they, as brothers and sisters, got along so well. I'd never known it myself. If I'd ever gotten along with Lewis, it would've been a miracle from God. He and I weren't meant to get along. From the time I was born, until the day he died, we treated one another like enemies. But with Melissa, it was different. We shared secrets and pretty much told each other everything, but we had our problems too. I guess I'd always been a bit jealous of her in a way. Between the two of us, she was the one mom and dad had faith in to make something of herself. I was told I'd be a failure as far back as I could remember.

You know, sometimes I looked at other families, and compared to mine they were strange. But if I'd been smart enough, I would've realized we were the ones who had the strange family. Mom was completely submissive to everything dad told her. Melissa played miss goodie two-shoes to impress mom and dad. Lewis was arrogant and unruly, but as mom always said, "He's just trying to let out his frustrations. He's really a good boy." Dad trampled through the house as if he walked on water, and expected everyone to kneel at his feet. But I was like a one person audience watching a lifetime of charades from the people who surrounded me every day. None of us ever seemed to fit together to complete a puzzle. There were always so many pieces missing. And as I still sat there and watched the family next door, I smiled. It was good to see children growing up with a normal childhood.

I picked up a pen and did my daily therapy...writing poetry. I stared straight ahead momentarily, and then back down. All my feelings at that moment flowed swiftly to the tablet in front of me from my fingertips which were full of emotion.

HEARTS & SPADES
STRANGERS

Though feeling I'm surrounded
By strangers in my home,
I look for light within the darkness
And hope the sun will soon be shone.
I tremble from insanity
Of what visions haunt me every night,
While still I am searching
For a little glimpse of light.
But still these many strangers
That I should know so well,
They stare at me with laughter
As my heart begins to swell.
I reach for their assistance,
But they turn and walk away,
Without a glance of caring.
Without a word to say.
I then clutch my hands so tight
And cringe from my own fear.
I comfort my own sadness,
And alone I dry my tears.
For the darkness could be brightened
By just a small amount of care.

> But tired, I turn revolted
> That no one's standing there.
> Around and around I look once more,
> As my vision slowly fades.
> My family, but still such strangers.
> I am hearts, but they are spades.

Oh how wonderful it felt to write. Looking back over those elegant words, expressed in the most sensitive way I knew how, I felt renewed inside. Just sitting in peace and writing down what confusion had welled up inside of me, it inspired me to make the best of a bad situation. I refused to lie back and be treated like a peasant when I knew I was better that.

With no dithering, I hurried to get dressed. I didn't know if they'd already left for work, or if they were still downstairs waiting for me, but it didn't really matter to me. After the way mom acted to me when I tried to talk to her, I wanted a little time to overlook the fact that she didn't care enough to listen.

With my shades pulled open letting all of the light from the sun into my bedroom, I took in each and every illumination which had encircled my body. Though it was chilled outside, the warmth from the light through the window made it feel as if it were the middle of summer. I loved summer, but fall always brought about a different feeling inside everyone. It always brought out a different feeling in me. To me, spring and summer was of new beginnings, and fall and winter marked an ending of something. It was a strange kind of theory, but I always believed it to be true.

By the time I reached the bottom of the stairs, the front door was closing. I looked out the front window of the house, to see mom and dad leaving one at a time. Shrugging my shoulders a little, I strolled into the kitchen to eat. I was starved. All I'd had at that diner was coffee, and my stomach was screaming for food.

I observed a note on the table.

Beth,

Since you were too tired to get up, we assumed you were too tired to eat as well. If you're hungry look through the trash, that's where we put it. Maybe next time you'll get up when I tell you to.

MOM & DAD

I balled the letter up and threw it across the room. I couldn't believe them. But most of all, I couldn't believe I thought they might've changed while I was gone. I figured they would've at least missed me enough to try to accommodate me while I was home.

Furiously I grabbed my coat and walked outside to blow off a little steam. The nerve of them, I thought, pacing back and forth on the porch. I went over and sat on the swing in the corner. I remembered when my daddy had built it, but he didn't build it for me or for Melissa. He built it for himself. His attitude was that he was more important than anybody or anything. Sometimes he acted like he did things for us, but in the end, we'd see through it all to find out it was for him all along. What a father...What a man.

Thoughts of my family weren't the most pleasant, so I substituted thoughts of Eric instead. I wondered what he was doing at that very moment, and I only hoped he was thinking of me. I guess I wasn't as hungry as I thought, because I walked into the living room, sat down, and picked up the phone. Dialing Eric's number, I smiled just at the thought of being able to talk to him. It rang once, twice, but on the third ring, someone answered.

"Hello," a woman said in a sweet sincere voice.

"Mrs. Norris," I answered nervously.

"Who is this?" she asked curiously.

"This is Beth...Beth Laney. Is Eric around by any chance? I'd really love to talk to him," I replied in an enthusiastic voice.

She laughed pleasantly and answered, "Beth. We've heard so much about you...all good I promise. Eric's outside bringing in groceries for me. I'll run get him. And Beth..."

"Yes ma'am," I answered respectfully.

"My husband and I can't wait to meet you. The way Eric talks, you were an angel sent down from heaven," Mrs. Norris continued.

Unsure of what to say, my voice shook as I answered her, "Thank you Mrs. Norris. Eric does exaggerate. But I'm glad he exaggerates about things like that."

"Here he comes dear. You take care," she said, handing Eric the phone.

Warmth filled me completely even before I heard his voice on the other end of the line I felt his presence although he wasn't there with me. Thousands of miles apart, we still connected with each breath, with each pounding of our hearts. But the true test of my love was when I heard his seductive voice again. It had only been a few days since I'd seen him, but it felt like years.

"Beth...you there?" he said anxiously.

With a tear trying to form, I quickly answered, "It's me. Is that really you? I feel like I haven't heard your voice in months."

"I know," he said sadly, "I wish you were here. I miss you so much more than I can ever say. I feel lost. In fact, last night, I started to get out of bed and just drive and drive until I found you. And since I couldn't have you there next to me, I dreamed what I only wished were true."

Silence filled the air for a moment and my heart fell. I wanted to see him and hold him, but I knew it was impossible.

"Hey, remember I told you that two weeks wouldn't be that bad. Well, I lied. I didn't think I'd feel so broken inside. Eric, my family still makes me feel like an outcast. I should never have come back. I should've gone with you. I'm sure your parents would've treated me a hell of a lot better than mine do," I said.

"Beth, I know it's hard, but it is your family. Give them a chance."

"I have given them a chance, but..."

He interrupted. "Listen, would it make things any better if I caught the next plane out to see you? I will if you want me to. I hate knowing you're so uncomfortable about where you're going to be at Christmas. Maybe if I were there you'd feel more at ease. That way, even when your parents did act crazy, or try to degrade you, we could just leave."

Flattered he would even consider doing that for me, I replied, "No, I don't want you to have to do that. You need to stay where you are. Your mom sounds like an angel herself. And I appreciate how you've built me up for them."

"Built you up, Darlin', there's nothin' to build up. You are exactly the way I described you to them. You may not be an actual angel from heaven, but you are my angel. That's all that matters to me," he said.

"I love you. I feel like I haven't told you that in a while, but I do. You are the one that's helped me even when you're not here. But I wished you were. Because if you were, I'd just tell my parents to..."

Interrupting me once more, "Wait a minute. Stop right there young lady. I refuse to hear you talk about your parents like that." he said.

"You're a nut Eric Norris. I'm in love with a nut." I laughed.

"What did you say? I couldn't hear you very well, " he said, trying to get me to repeat myself.

"I said I love you, I shouted where everyone miles around would hear me."

"Thought that's what you said. I guess I love you too." He wouldn't have been acting normal if he didn't aggravate a little.

Getting quiet once more, I somberly said, "Well, I guess I better go. If I run up their phone bill, they'll sure have somethin' to get onto me about. And Believe me, they don't need any excuses, but I don't want to give them one either. You'd just have to meet them to know what I'm talkin' about."

"Okay sweetie, but I have your number too. I'll call you tonight when I get through helpin' dad. It shouldn't be too awful late. I'll make sure I'm home early enough to call you before I go to bed. I'm gonna dream of you anyway, but if I talk to you right before I lie down, I know I'll have sweet dreams for the night," he said.

I replied enthusiastically, "Please don't forget. I need to talk to you as much as I can. That's the only way I'm gonna make it through two weeks of this hell."

"Don't worry," he assured me, "I'll call you around eight."

"I'll talk to ya then, and Eric." I said trying to catch him before he hung up.

"Yeah, I'm still here."

"Didn't you forget somethin'?" I said, as I tried to mock what he always said to me when I'd forget to tell him I loved him.

"Well, let me think."

"Eric Norris. If I were there I'd..."

"You'd what? I wanna hear this. Just kiddin' Beth. I love you. Have a good day, and don't worry so much. Everything will turn out fine. Watch and see. Have I ever told you wrong?"

Thinking for a moment, I agreed with what he'd said, "You're right. I'll do what I can to make the best of things. Now you better get going if you plan on gettin' any work done for your dad. And tell your mom it was nice talking to her."

Trying to make good-bye short and sweet, we told one another "I love you," and hung up before we had the chance to get into another long drawn out conversation. We always seemed to do that, and I just figured it would be easier to say good-bye as quickly as possible rather than to go on and on with what ifs. I already had a tear trying to fall, and I wanted to stop it before it made many more follow.

After I hung up the phone, I sat on the couch where the sun shone in on me. It warmed my chilled skin, and bright sun shining through the window, started my day out a little better. Few cars passed by the street in front of the house, but there were many children running around and playing as if they had no worries in the world.

With a smile painted from one corner of my face to the other, Eric's voice still echoed in my mind. And the way he said, "I love you," rang louder than anything else. I never doubted his love. For once I'd found someone whom I knew I didn't have to doubt at all. His loyalty to me was inconceivably true, and his presence was felt even though I was sitting alone. It lifted my spirits just talking to him, just hearing his voice. But most of all, it made me realize what I'd walked away from, and what situation I'd walked back into on my own free will. I knew then I must've been insane.

Barefooted and cold, I walked down the hallway to turn on a little more heat when I noticed all of the pictures hanging in the middle of the hall. Stopping for a moment, I gazed at them one by one. There was one picture of the family I didn't remember. Everyone was in it but me. I assumed it was because I hadn't been born yet, so I went on to the next. Then there was Melissa and myself lying beside one another asleep on my bed. We both looked so happy and peaceful. She had her arm around me and her head was leaned against mine. I only wished things could've always been that way. Although we had stayed fairly close through the years, we did grow apart enough to be noticeable.

On the other side of the wall, there was an entire row of snapshots, school photos, and football pictures of Lewis. It was like a memorial or something. I guess mom and dad thought as long as they had pictures of Lewis everywhere, they wouldn't forget him. I don't know, but it spooked me a little. In each picture of him, it looked like he was staring directly at me no matter what direction I walked. They seemed alive even though he was dead. It didn't take me long to take my eyes off the Lewis Laney memorial wall.

Heading towards my room to lie down for a minute, a knock came at the door. But before I made it half way down the stairs, the door flung open, and there stood Melissa. She dropped her bags and ran up to hug me. She seemed so full of energy and life. You could tell she was happy just by looking at her.

"Beth, how are you? How's school? Tell me what's been goin' on," she said enthusiastically.

Shaking my head with a slight grin, I replied "Slow down Sis. We have plenty of time to talk. Lets go in my room and catch up on what's been happening with both of us."

She agreed, so I helped her with her things as we walked and talked all the way back to the end of the hallway, to my room. She had gained a little weight, but she still looked wonderful. I envied her as far back as I could remember, but for once, I felt like we were equals.

"So what have you got exciting to tell me?" she asked.

"Well, " I hesitated.

"Oh no. It's a man isn't it? You met a man," she inquired.

"He's a man alright. His name's Eric Norris," I said blushing a little.

She smiled as if she were happy for me and asked, "Tell me about him Beth. Are you in love?"

So I began my story about the man I loved to talk about, "Melissa, he's wonderful. I want you to meet him. I know you will because..."

I held my hand up and the ring he'd so elegantly placed on my finger shined as it reflected in the sunlight beaming through the window.

"He asked you to marry him? What did you say?"

"I said yes. I didn't know anything else to say. You know how I never wanted a boyfriend in school, how I was scared of relationships. Well, when I met Eric, all that changed. I'm not sure what he did, but he took away the fear and replaced it with trust and more love than I know what to do with," I declared, proud to tell someone about him.

She looked at me as she leaned over and hugged me tightly. It was like old times again. Although we'd grown older, the two little girls who loved one another, were still buried deep inside of us. I was just glad we could share things as we always used to. But I knew as soon as mom and dad returned home, she'd change her attitude towards me. It really didn't matter as long as we could talk and be sisters again with no interruptions.

We talked for hours. I hold her how Eric proposed to me, and her envy was obvious. All she could say was, "All I got was a pizza, a beer and a 'Wanna get married Hun?'"

We laughed until we hurt inside. And it felt good to feel so carefree once again. Other than Eric, Amy, and Mrs. Downs, I'd had no one else to confide in. For the first time in a long time, I was sitting down with my big sister telling her everything. I didn't just talk about Eric. She wanted to know if I liked college and everything that went along with being away from home. I knew I'd gone home for a reason, and Melissa was my reason. At that point, I realized something. If nothing else good happened during my stay for the holidays, I knew it was all worth it. Because I wouldn't have given those moments away I spent with my sister for anything in the world. In fact, if it would've been possible, I would've bottled up all the laughter and love, and carried it with me everywhere. Just those few moments with her was worth all the miles I drove alone. For I didn't feel like I'd gone home to see mom and dad, I drove and drove with hopes my sister...my only sister...would be there to make me laugh. So she was, and the rest would follow.

CHAPTER 12

Spending the day with my sister was just what I needed to clear my head. We laughed and talked like we used to do when we were kids. When we left the house, we went to the old burger place we used to practically live at, and ate what we always called "the best burgers in town." I even saw a few people I knew from school. Some were home for the holidays like myself, and it was good to see folks I thought I'd never see again.

Melissa told joke after joke making me laugh until I could almost cry. I remembered her as being a jokester, but she was even funnier than before. I kinda thought it was because she'd been away from mom and dad, and could get her sense of humor back. I wondered why she didn't bring her husband with her, but she told me he had to work through the holidays and sent his love.

After we ate, we decided to go to the park and walk around. It was cold, but I always loved to go to the nearby park and admire all of it's beauty. During the summertime, I'd stare out at the water and watch the ducks gracefully go by. But winter was different. The branches were bare, but the beauty was still there. It didn't matter to me if the ducks were there. Once beautiful, always beautiful.

Sitting there on that frozen bench bundled up in three layers of clothing, I looked over at Melissa and grinned. She looked back at me perplexed. You could tell she wondered what was trampling through my mind. She always told me when we were younger, "You're a thinker Sis. You think too much." But thinking was what took me far away into a dreamland every night. I had no other outlet to free myself from unhappiness, so I'd pretend I was someone else in another place. If that's what you want to call a 'thinker,' then I guess that was exactly what I was.

"Why are you looking at me that way?" she asked raising her eyebrows and turned to face me.

Looking down and then back up at her, I answered, "I don't know. This pond reminds me of a perfect moment. It's Eric. We always meet at the pond on campus. That's just our place. I'm sure you and Shane have a special place, don't you?"

Shrugging her shoulders, she hesitated, "Well, I don't guess I've ever thought about it. I mean, we don't really go anywhere or do anything. We just sit at home after work until it's time for bed. We're not the most exciting people you've ever met."

I reached over, put my arms around her, and gave her a sisterly hug. It was the kind of hug that said "I love you, and I'll always be here." Then arm in arm we stood up and walked the rest of the way around the water until we reached our car not too far away. For a change, my thoughts were pleasant and full of hope. I didn't doubt for one moment it was because of my sister. She'd saved me from a day of depression and confusion from being in mom and dads house alone. Because if I'd stayed there all day doing nothing, I didn't know what I would've wound up doing, or where I would've gone just from pure boredom and despondency.

When we reached the car, Melissa turned the heat on full blast so our fingers and toes would have a chance of defrosting. I was shivering from one end to the other, and Melissa was as well. With chattering teeth and shaky hands, we sat there quietly until the car was warmed up enough for us to leave.

Out of nowhere Melissa asked me a question I didn't quite know how to answer. "Beth, do you want to go and visit Lewis's grave? I think we should, don't you? Neither one of us have been back there to put flowers down or anything since the funeral. What do you think?"

Revolving my head to where I was staring out my window, I uttered nothing. Her question threw me. Lewis was nowhere in my thoughts when out of the blue she brings him up. He was dead. Why go visit dirt on the ground?

Knowing I had to answer her, I glanced at her and replied, "Do you want to?"

She looked at me like I'd lost my mind. "Beth. What's wrong with you. He was our brother. That must not mean anything to you."

"Lets go. You're probably right," I agreed against my own better judgment.

"What's wrong with you. You act like you're glad he's dead," she said, waiting for a reply, but I just kept looking out my fogged up window as if she'd said nothing.

Trying to take my mind off where we were going, I began to write Eric over and over again in the fog on the window. It was like I was acting out childish behavior because I hadn't gotten my way. At times I would tend to regress back to a little girl and begin to pout. I guess that's what I was doing. But I didn't know how else to deal with what I was feeling. I didn't want to go there. I didn't want to pay any kind of respects to him. In fact, I just wished everyone would forget he ever existed. In my opinion he was horrible when he was alive, and since he died, his spirit seemed more alive than ever before.

Approaching the cemetery, I closed my eyes and relived the day he was buried. Mom, dad, Melissa, and myself, rode in the family car, and silence filled the air all around us. No one spoke a word. And no one moved an inch in their seat. Dad had no expression on his face, and mom's eyes were swollen shut from crying continuously. Melissa cried as much as mom did, but not as erratically. I was the only one who had themselves together. I never knew why I stayed so calm, but I did through the entire ordeal.

Melissa shook me as we reached the cemetery. I guess I'd let my mind wander away once again. As we parked, she got out and began to walk towards his grave, and then turned to find me still sitting in the car. With her staring at me, I finally got out and walked up to join her.

"Melissa, I don't know about this. I don't feel comfortable being here," I said peering at her with unsure eyes.

She took my hand and began to walk closer and closer to where Lewis had been placed in the ground. The eerie feeling which came over me, was unbearable. Though it was already cold, a breeze much colder than normal, cut right through me. It came from behind, so I turned around. And for a split second I could've sworn I saw my dead brother standing there with a wicked smirk on his face as if to say, "I'm alive Sis. Can't ya see me?"

I grasped onto Melissa's arm and squeezed it tightly as my eyes kept glancing back to the spot where I thought I saw Lewis standing. My heart raced as if I'd been visited by some sort of evil spirit, and my hands shook from fear, not from the cold.

"What's wrong now Beth?" she demanded, as her voiced jumped out at me in an angry way.

"I'm sorry, but I swear to you I saw him standing there."

"Saw who standing there?" she asked, confused by my words.

"Lewis. I saw Lewis standing there," I replied, pointing to where my eyes had viewed him.

Rolling her eyes as if she thought I'd lost my mind, she responded, "You're seeing things. Are you sure you're ok. I mean, you have acted a bit strange today."

I turned away from her and began to walk to the car. But with each step I took, I felt like eyes were watching me. Although no one was in sight, except for Melissa, the presence of someone else gave me the creeps. I knew I hadn't lost my mind, but there was no other way to explain what I saw. If Melissa had given me the chance I would've told her what he was wearing too. It was only for a split second, but it was more like an eternity to me. I knew it was a bad idea to visit his grave, but no one ever listened to me.

As I sat in the car and waited for Melissa to hurry so we could leave, I heard a noise in the back seat of the car. I turned and once more there he was, but just long enough for me to focus on his misery stricken grin. And then he was gone.

Frightened half to death, I swung open the car door, stepped out, and yelled at my sister, "I'm ready to get the hell out of here. I knew this was a bad idea. I don't care if he is dead. Let him stay that way."

It didn't take but a moment for her to join me in the car. At first she looked angry, but then she reached over and squeezed my hand. She had no idea what was wrong with me, but then again, she didn't ask anymore. To be honest, I think she thought I'd fell off the deep end and she just wanted to pacify me until we reached mom and dad's.

Of course, I didn't blame her for anything. She couldn't have known how much stress I'd been under, and I felt bad for snapping at her so viciously. She didn't deserve such a lashing for my own quandaries.

"Listen. I'm sorry. I..."

She interrupted saying, "Don't worry about it. It's been hard on all of us losing Lewis."

I just looked at her as if she was right, and glared at the road ahead as we drove back home. But curiosity did get the best of me. I wanted to ask Melissa something, but I just wasn't quite sure how. And after a moment of contemplation, I dove right into it with full force.

"I need to know something. And I want you to be completely honest with me," I said seriously.

"Ask away Sis," she replied, watching the road carefully.

"Well, I've been having these strange dreams lately...more like nightmares. It's happened a lot...not just once or twice, but almost every night. I was wondering if you've had dreams like that too. I know it sounds silly, but the last few have been about Lewis. I feel like he's haunting me Melissa," I said in a shaky voice.

She paused before she answered, "N...no I haven't. What kind of nightmares? I mean, are they abstract, or do they involve someone?"

Thinking back, I answered, "I'm not sure. Sometimes there's a shadow of someone reaching out to me, and sometimes it's just a grotesque atmosphere that frightens me for days. There have been times when I couldn't stop thinking about my dreams. They bother me when I'm in class, or walking down the hall. I can't seem to shake 'em. And the worst one was last night. There was a shadow in the hallway, but I know it was Lewis. I know it was."

Trying to comfort me a little, she retorted, "You know you used to dream terrible things all the time Beth. It's nothin' new. Just try to think of something positive like Eric, and they'll all disappear and leave only thoughts of him in your mind."

Laughing a little, "You sound like a therapist. You oughta be one. But psychology doesn't work on me Mel."

Leaving that conversation in a hurry, Melissa started talking non-stop about everything she could think of to change the subject. She seemed sort of freaked out when I mentioned nightmares, but I didn't give it a second thought. Anyway, I didn't figure it was worth worrying about. I had enough worries without trying to pick someone's else's brain for their thoughts. It was enough for me to pick my own.

It seemed like a long drive back, but it only took about ten minutes. I couldn't believe our day had started out so great, and ended up so frustrating. It was my fault, I knew that, but I tried not to dwell on it. The air which was so thick at one time, began to clear up to where we could talk again without arguing. Melissa and I never argued before, so it was a new experience for me.

We reached the house, but no one was there. The sun was falling little by little, and the sky was lit up burnt orange. I always loved to sit outside at dusk and admire what God had given us to view each and every night. The colors just before dark gave me a sense of accord. And once the sun would disappear, I was able to close my eyes and replay that enchanting scene of the sunset over and over again in my mind. Never getting enough of its' beauty, it seemed to be an obsession. At times, it was the only thing that would bring me out of a tunnel of ambiguous feelings.

Melissa went into the house, but I sat on the front porch swing until darkness had surrounded me completely. Crossing my arms, I tried to hide from the cold, but it was hopeless. The air rushing by was frigid enough to cut someone into, and bundling up didn't help, so I went inside.

Melissa was no where in sight. I walked up the stairs and heard the shower running, so I went back to my room to enjoy the peace and quiet until mom and dad came home from work. I knew once they returned home, there would be no more peace. I just wanted to enjoy what few moments I had left, all alone.

Startled a bit, I heard a horn honk from outside. I looked out my window and saw someone parked in front of the neighbor's home. Suddenly, the past came out at me, with no way of stopping it.

My mind was whisked away to when I was about thirteen years old. Though Melissa has always said and done as mom and dad wanted, there was once she disobeyed them totally. I remembered lying in bed one night and hearing a honk from outside. I got up, put my house shoes on, and walked to the window. Melissa's room was below mine, and I saw her crawling out her window to meet a boy she'd been told not to see. She looked around to make sure no one saw her, and then ran out to the car. I was sure she was going to be in terrible trouble, and it ate at me until I heard her coming in several hours later.

Dad knew she had left the house, and was waiting for her in her room when she stumbled back through her window and fell onto the floor. When she looked up, there he was. All I heard was screaming from below me, and there was nothing I could do about it. I wasn't sure if he had hit her, or if he just scared her when she saw him, but I knew something was strange. Because the next morning when we got ready for school, Melissa had make-up on. That was strange, because she'd never been allowed to wear make-up before. The closer I looked, I could tell she had a bruise on the side of her face which, you could tell, she desperately tried to cover. Though I knew what had happened, I said nothing. One reason was because I didn't want to get the same treatment, and another was because of Melissa. I didn't want her to feel humiliated by what my father had the audacity to bestow on her. She didn't deserve that, but I was silent. I was always silent. That was just the way we were.

As the fog cleared around my brain, I brought myself back to the moment at hand. The more I tried to keep myself out of a dreamland, the more I seemed to lose myself in the past, the present and what the future could be. For me, the past was gone, but it seemed like it wanted to resurface each time something would jog my memory. The only thing I had no doubt about was Eric. And I wished over and over again on each and every star, that he would just show up and surprise me, but I knew it was impossible. He was hundreds of miles away, but in my heart, he was sitting right next to me.

Melissa came in with a towel wrapped around her.

"Beth, lets forget about what happened this afternoon. I don't know what happened, but I'd just rather forget it"

Agreeing with her, I replied, "I think we should. I don't know what happened either, but I guess it doesn't really matter."

"Mom and dad will be home soon. How are y'all gettin' along? I know how things were before you left, and..."

Interrupting, I answered, "Just as always. Dad acts like I'm not here and mom doesn't want to hear anything I have to say. Other than that, things are fine. To be honest with you Melissa, I really thought they'd greet me with open arms, but instead, they shrug me off again. I don't know if I can do anything that'll please them. I get so frustrated. I've gotten to the point now, to where I just don't care if I please them, as long as I please myself."

She just peered at me with those sisterly sorrowful eyes and smiled. The look she gave me said something. Just by her eye contact, you could tell she was agreeing with me in her mind, but didn't want to say anything. She never liked saying anything against our parents. I didn't know why, but she never did. Even when they weren't around, she refrained from speaking against them in any way what-so-ever. Of course, I couldn't say a word. I never spoke against them either, but my thoughts were horrible. All the things I wished would happen to them were baneful and full of impure inclinations. Though I'd never admit to a single horrible thought, I knew them all in my mind, each and every one of them.

I watched Melissa as she primped in front of that tiny make-up mirror on my desk. She always had such a perfect complexion, and I never knew of her to have one hair out of place. It was funny, but even in the mornings, she seemed to wake up looking fresh and ready to walk out the door. Envy struck me for a long while until I came to the realization that everyone is special and unique in their own way. But until I met Eric, I didn't know how special and unique I was. He made me believe in myself for the first time in my life. I guess all I needed was for someone to believe in me, and he was the first. He was my first in many different ways.

I heard the front door open and close abruptly as footsteps soon followed up the stairway. It was a hollow sound, kind of eerie, but I knew who it was.

With no knock to warn us, my bedroom door flung open and my dad stood there in his suit and tie. It was like stepping back ten years in time. He had on the same suit on he always wore when we were children. And he also had that same smirk on his face as he did many years before. It seemed to be stuck in that same uncaring position after all these years.

Melissa stood up and dad met her half way to embrace her like I wished he would've embraced me, but I got nothing more than a fake smile and an uncaring attitude, as always.

"How are you Melissa? Your mother and I have called and called, but all we get is your answering machine. You must be pretty busy these days," dad said warmly.

Melissa just smiled and glanced over at me. She could tell it hurt for me to see him treat her so much better than he treated me. Her smile turned to a grim look as she realized there was nothing she could do to change his attitude. There was nothing anyone could do. He was the way he was, and I knew time wouldn't make his cold heart warm up enough to take me in as he should've done the day I was born.

"Your mother is starting supper. So wash up and we'll call you when it's ready."

I stood up and went over and pulled out a picture album out of the bottom drawer of my dresser. I flipped page after page, and tears began to appear to trickle down my face. Melissa came and sat with me for a moment, And tried to justify our father's actions towards me.

"I know you think dad treats me better than you, but Beth, you need to realize something. Dad and I were closer than y'all were when we were growing up. That's the only thing I can think of. I mean, it seems like dad would mellow a little with age, but he hasn't at all."

"You don't have to make any excuses for him. I'm not stupid. The day mom and dad treat me with respect, will be the day hell freezes over, and I don't see that happening any time soon," I said, walking off to wash up for supper.

I left her sitting on my bed staring at the floor. There was nothing either one of us could say or do to make things any better, so why try. We both knew all too well how Christmas would turn out, but staying, and proving our maturity, was more than mom or dad ever did. Sometimes I felt like I'd grown up more in four months than they had in fifty years.

When I was coming out of the bathroom, the phone rang. It was eight o'clock on the dot, and I knew who it was. Though I wanted to reach the phone before anyone else, I was too late. Dad had answered it by the time I got half way down the stairs. Then I heard him yell for me.

"Beth, phone call. It's some guy. Better make it fast. Dinner's almost done."

Ignoring his rudeness for a change, I dashed into the living room and picked up the receiver quickly.

"Hello."

"Hey good lookin'. Wanna go somewhere tonight?"

"Sure. Where'd ya have in mind?" I replied, as I played along with his silly little game.

"I don't know. You pick the place. It's your home town. I don't know where anything is."

"Quit kiddin' around Eric. I don't like it when you tease me. I miss you enough as it is."

Then from the other room, I heard my dad holler in his piercing unforgettable voice, "Off the phone young lady. Supper's ready. Be prompt or don't eat at all. You remember this mornin' don't ya girl?"

"That your dad?"

"Yeah. I better go. If I don't I'll catch hell from him."

But before I could hang up, Eric yelled, "Wait a minute Beth. I was serious about doing something."

"I told you to stop it. It's hard enough as it is without you..."

"Look out your window. There's a pay phone over on the corner one block down. Tell me who you see."

Throwing the phone down, I ran to the window and looked just where he said to look. I couldn't believe my eyes. It was really him. I didn't know how he pulled it off, but he did. He was dressed in a Santa suit with a bag over his shoulder. He was walking in my direction.

Putting mom, dad and Melissa out of my mind, I scurried out the front door and onto the lawn. By the time I reached the driveway, so had he. He put down the sack which he had thrown over his shoulder and gazed at me as though he hadn't seen me in years instead of only days. My warm hands and his hands which were cold as ice, melted into one another. And still, I thought I was having a dream sent down from heaven. But as I looked up at him, I knew he was really there. I felt warm inside. The same kind of warmth I felt when he and I embraced the day I left for home. He was there with me. My wish had come true. I was going to spend Christmas with the one I loved.

"Well, are we gonna just stand here, or are we going inside where it's warm?"

"Eric. There's something you need to know first. My dad is not a very, I mean, he's not a..."

"I don't care what he is or what he isn't. I just want them to know who I am. I want them to know the man who is going to take you away from them."

"I haven't told them yet," I said, as I lowered my chin in apology.

"Why? Why haven't you? Are they that bad? Beth, look at me. Nothing can be that bad," he said squeezing my hand to comfort me.

"I guess there's no time like the present. Lets go. I'll never know how they'll react until I tell them."

We slowly walked up the driveway, then the walkway, hand in hand. It felt good to have him there with me. I wanted Melissa to meet him because I knew she would give him a warm welcome, but I wasn't so sure about my parents. They were strange. I prayed in silence they would give him a warm welcome as well, but I knew better.

When we reached the front door, I glanced at Eric once more.

"Don't be so nervous. I can feel you shaking. If they don't respond the way you want them to, we'll leave. I have a hotel room a few miles down the road. And I sure don't mind you stayin' there with me. In fact, it'll be kinda lonely if you don't," he said, so full of concern.

As I turned the handle, the door squeaked open as it always did, and we stepped in quietly. I could hear my father stomping his feet as he got closer and closer.

"Beth. Where in the hell did you," he began to say turning the corner to see Eric standing there with me.

"Dad, this is Eric Norris. My fiancé. He asked me to marry him. Isn't that great?"

Eric reached to shake his hand, but he just stood there as his face began to turn ten shades of red. I could almost see the steam shooting from his ears.

"Married!" he screamed as loud as he could.

"Yes sir. I love your daughter," Eric continued, trying to win my dad over with his love for me. I guess he thought if my dad believed he really loved me, it would be okay.

"Get your things and leave. You are nothing but useless to me. You never were anything but useless. And before you leave, do me a favor. Go into the office and get all of those stupid poems you wrote and take 'em with you. Your mother never would let me tear 'em up or burn 'em. I don't want to see your face again."

Eric's facial expression was one I could never explain. I had told him many times how I was treated at home, but he never believed me until that moment. You could tell by the look on his face he was appalled by my father's retrogression. All he could do was hold me until he couldn't feel me shivering any longer.

"Come with me to get my things, will you Eric?" I said walking to my dad's office.

With a few tears making their way down my face, wiped them away quickly. I didn't want my father to know he'd upset me. Sometimes I wandered if that was why he said some of the things he said. It didn't matter anyway. I knew I'd tried, and that was all I could do.

Melissa caught me and Eric just as we started to search for the poetry I'd written, and left there. She got down on her knees beside me and begged my forgiveness.

"I tried to stop him so many times. I tried. But it didn't do any good."

Raising my eyebrows, I was in complete bewilderment about what she was talking about. Though I heard my father coming down the hall, I asked, "What are you talking about Melissa? What do you mean? You tried to stop who?"

Dad stuck his head in and told Melissa to go finish eating and to leave me alone. He told her to consider me dead, and that I was no longer her sister.

Though I was distracted by all of the outrage and aversion, Eric was still digging through papers trying to gather all that was mine.

But in the middle of searching, Eric stopped for a moment, as if he were reading something.

"Don't read any of that silly poetry. I wrote most of it when I was really young. It probably doesn't even make any sense," I said.

Then he turned to me and looked as though he were at a loss of words. His smile had faded, and his eyes were sagging somberly.

"What's wrong with you? My poetry's not that bad is it?"

"It's not your poetry I found Beth. I found something else."

"What? Tell me."

He didn't say a word, he just handed me some papers and walked over and sat down. The top sheet was my birth certificate. I looked it over, and noticed something I never noticed before. Where it was supposed to have the parents' names, it said "unknown."

I went and joined Eric as I continued to browse through the rest of the papers he had handed me.

"Eric, these are adoption papers. I was adopted. I was adopted," I muttered. "No. This isn't true. I wasn't adopted."

"Listen Beth. We need to get your things and leave. We'll take these with us so you'll have time to figure all this out. I know it's a shock, but you don't need to be here."

With a face that'd been striped of all it's identity, I glared at the floor without a word. I wanted to march into the kitchen and tell my father everything I'd ever thought of him, but I was afraid. I knew I shouldn't have been afraid because Eric was there to stand by me, but my father always instilled so much fear in me, that I sometimes didn't know which direction to run.

Finally agreeing with him, we went upstairs and passed Lewis's old room.

"Look. It's just like he left it. They haven't moved a thing. It's like he's still alive. They make me sick Eric."

Placing his hand on my shoulder, we walked into my room. It didn't take long to collect everything I'd brought because most of it was still packed. And Eric stayed right by my side. I could tell Melissa wanted to say good-bye, but dad kept this hold on her that made her fear him as he always did before. And those words she said to me still rang through my head like is was recorded, over and over again.

We gathered my bags and all of the things I'd found in my father's office which was mine. Eric walked ahead of me and loaded the car, giving me a moment to myself. Then moments later, I walked to the front door and went outside.

Eric had rented a car, so he pulled it in front of the house and waited for me. I shut the front door behind me and just stood there in complete astonishment. Taking one last look at the place where I grew up, I wiped a single tear away and got into my car. Backing up slowly, I could see Melissa with her hands up against the window as if she were reaching out to me. And it broke my heart to drive away and leave her there the way she left me at one time. But what was best for me, was all I needed to worry about. Realization struck me and my thoughts were erratic about the news I'd been hit with. The people I thought to be my family for years, was not my family at all. My real family was probably as caring and generous as myself, and in the back of my mind, I wanted to find them. I wanted to know who they were, where they lived, and why I was given up to such formidable people. I just couldn't help my mind from trying to put the pieces of the puzzle together. I wanted to know, and with Eric with me, I knew there was nothing I couldn't do.

I followed Eric so he could return the car he'd rented, and then we drove straight to the hotel. Feeling numb inside, I declined from saying a single word. My mind was turning faster and faster with many questions. And I had nothing to say. The way I felt was indescribable. My insides seemed twisted and torn from my shaken nerves, and the answer to those questions "why," were nowhere to be found. It was as lost as I was at that moment. And I wasn't sure I'd ever know why my life took the course it did. All I had left to do was to wait and see what happened from that point forward. As Amy once told me, "Always look forward, never look back" and that was what I had to do.

CHAPTER 13

The motel room was dimly lit and small, but the pictures and other little things sitting around, made it feel a little more like home. The curtains were green and burgundy with a touch of gold streaks down the center, and the mini blinds covering the large window by the door, were a light mauve. Decorated in modern colors and neatly arranged, I began to feel more comfortable the longer I studied the space we would be occupying for the next few days. In my mind, it was a much more pleasing place to be than where I had run from. Although it was small and the traffic was a bit noisy, I was with Eric. That alone made all of the noise and downsides, disappear. It turned into a dreamland where we would end up spending our first Christmas.

As Eric put a few of my things away, I walked around in circles in that tiny room. My skin began to form chill bumps all over and I hugged myself trying to take away the crisp air that encircled me. With my eyes not focusing on anything particular, they seemed to stare out into space. What was actually in front of me, was not what I saw. It was all a blur in my sight. And the strange thing about it, was that I saw no visions, only emptiness. No picture entered my mind as it wandered further and further away.

A hush covered the entire room as if we couldn't speak. Maybe it was because there was nothing to say. There was nothing I wanted to speak of at that time, and I think Eric knew he needed to give me some time and space to think things through completely. I didn't want to push him away, but at the same time, I needed to figure out a few things on my own.

I went into the bathroom and splashed water onto my face. In a way, I thought it might wake me from this never ending nightmare of bad news, but it didn't. But it did make me feel a little refreshed, so I decided to run some water and take a long hot bath. Lying in hot water with steam rising all around me, was always exhilarating. I knew the heat would warm my skin, and it would also help me sleep a little better. Although I was exhausted, I still had trouble sleeping. When I did sleep, shadows of the night interrupted such peace, and turned it into a night full of solicitude and grim thoughts.

I heard Eric turn on the television, and I yelled out to him I was going to take a bath. Of course, he yelled back, "Want me to join ya?" I just laughed "Just lie down. I'll be out in a minute," I replied.

Slowly trying to relax, I undressed and looked at myself in the mirror. I always hated the way I looked when I was naked. I knew I wasn't the least bit overweight, but viewing myself, revolted me for some reason. I never could look at myself. For as long as I could remember, my body disgusted me. I usually just rushed by the bathroom mirror so I wouldn't have to deal with it. I was a bit strange in that way, but I knew I couldn't be the only one who thought like that.

I crawled into the tub, and laid down resting my head at the end with my face halfway under the water. The sounds I heard were muffled, and it comforted me a little. Caressing my body as I washed from my head to my toes, made me feel like I was washing off something horrible—the past. All of my past was nothing but a fabrication. Those who pretended to be my parents weren't worth having as parents at all, and my real mom and dad were probably the most gentle human beings on the face of the earth. Of course, I'd probably never know. With my luck, I would search and search to the end of the earth, and not find one single clue as to who they were. Although I knew I'd probably never know for sure who or where they were, I wanted to try. I never was a quitter and I didn't want to give up a fight before it was started.

As the steam built up around me, I engulfed each bit of relaxation which overcame me, and it thoroughly unwound my tension. Each limb of my body was limp. Every muscle was without stress. And lying there with my eyes closed, the pores of my skin soaked in every bit of moisture out of the water and the air. Every little bit, I'd hear Eric ask me if I was alright. He was so wonderful to me. He seemed like a white knight dressed in armor when he rescued me from that dungeon of a home. I guess he knew I needed him, and he was right. I needed him more than I knew myself. Sometimes I wondered if he knew what I needed before I did.

After lying in the water long enough to shrivel, I stepped out of the tub, wrapped a towel around me, and went to get some clothes to put on. Eric was lying on the bed with his leg propped up, wearing silk boxer shorts with tiny hearts all over them. It was all I could do to keep from laughing, but after a moment of looking at him acting nutty, I busted out.

"You laughing at me?" he asked in a funny voice.

"You have officially lost your mind Eric Norris," I said, rolling onto the bed beside him.

He started tickling me furiously, and I went crazy. I never could stand to be tickled. By the time I fought enough to get away from him, my towel dropped and I stood there naked in front of him. The only sound surrounding us, was the television. All of the horse play was over. Eric seemed like an animal who had just spotted his prey, because he stood up and pressed up against me as tightly as he could. I could feel each inch of him...everything. And his hands managed to feel every single curve of my body.

When I turned to reach for something to put on, he whirled me back to him, and barely touched his lips to mine. It was purely sensual the way he expressed that one simple kiss, so sensual. Though I didn't have one thought of making love that night, his advances changed my mind instantaneously. His tenderness was too much for me to resist.

Our bodies were mashed together making one body, and our arms were wrapped around one another firmly. Every noise around us was drowned by the beating of our hearts in perfect rhythm. His touch was what I'd wanted since the day I left him, and that passion was flaming as high as ever. Being without him made me realize I needed to treasure every moment. And the moment just ahead of us was full of enrapturement. Before, I would heed my own warning of going under too quickly, but the only warning I wanted to heed at that moment, was the fear of not grasping each moment as it came. I didn't want it to pass without doing what I felt was natural—love, and making love. It had become a natural feeling to me. I couldn't believe that, for such a long time, I was scared to death of that very feeling. And then all of the sudden, I couldn't do without it.

Eric turned off the television leaving only the light above which was soft and dim. To see his face while showing one another the love we had, was like looking at a brilliant portrait—a portrait my eyes wouldn't stray away from.

Minutes turned into hours as we made love totally once again. His kiss was as passionate as it was the first time I felt it. And his touch was just as appealing as it was the first time he held my hand. Each time was like the first with him. So hard to explain, and yet, so remarkable. It was like looking out at the ocean. Each time you see it, the waves move in a different way, or the white tops are shaped contrary to the way they were the time before. Although you may have seen it many times, you peer out into the midst of it, something about it, is more exciting, more esoterical.

Once we had demolished each ounce of vigor contained within our bodies, we laid there side by side until our breathing slowly came back to a normal pace. Deep inside, I was glad my dad did what he did. If he hadn't I wouldn't have been lying next to the man I loved dearly, and I never would've found out about who I was; or who I wasn't, as the case may be.

I turned sideways, with my back facing Eric. He took the covers and covered me up until he thought I was warm enough, then pressed up against me as his hand crawled around my waist. Feeling him next to me gave me all the encouragement I needed to move forward and stop looking back.

Before sleep took us completely, I had to make sure I told him how I felt inside. I knew I had showed him, but the way I looked at things, if I were to die during the night, I wanted him to know for sure he was the man of my dreams...my true love "Eric. You awake?"

"Yeah babe. What's wrong?"

"I just wanted to tell you I love you, that's all."

He squeezed me firmly. "I love you too. Try to get a good night's sleep okay."

"I will. Goodnight," I said softly I closing my eyes and letting slumber take me away quickly. It didn't take me long to drift off because I figured sleep would help me to forget about things for the night, and I needed to forget for a little while. Remembering only hampered my ability to think straight, for my mind was confused enough.

Enjoying total relaxation of the night, my mind was clear and untarnished. For a while, I dreamed nothing, thought of nothing, and relished on harmony surrounding me, but then something began to happen to me. My cleared mind turned to short memory clips, pictures, frightening visions. And then suddenly I saw myself walking from the road beside the cemetery, towards my brother's grave. A deep thick fog entrapped me, making it almost impossible to see a foot in front of me. Blinded by vague illusions of smoke, I still continued to walk without hesitation. Unsure of why I was there, I held a bible in my hand tightly. It gave me a sense of protection from any evil which might try to manifest itself to me. I stood behind a wall built on my belief in God, sure he would be my guardian through any danger which might suddenly appear.

Then, without warning, the fog cleared, leaving only one thing for my eyes to see...Lewis's grave. With an uncaring heart, I turned to walk away, but my muscles seemed frozen...immobile. I could do nothing but stand there and wait for hell to rise and greet me. That's what I felt was happening to me. My heart began to beat faster and faster. The cold disappeared, and was replaced by so much heat I could barely stand it.

"Beth...over here Sis. Don't you want to talk to your big brother?"

Looking to my left, leaning against his head stone, my deceased brother stood there laughing in a gawking manner as he always did when life was still raging within him.

"Leave me alone you bastard," I screamed.

"Little sister's angry. What a shame. Is there anything I can do to make you feel better" he said walking closer and closer to me. Still frozen, I couldn't even flinch from the disgust I felt. I couldn't do anything.

Approaching me, I reached deep down inside of my soul, and pulled out all of the inspiration, love, and strength I'd learned from Eric, Mrs. Downs, and everyone who cared about me. That alone gave me the might to capture my faith and rid my surroundings of fear and misery. Lewis was my fear, and dwelling on what was impossible to change, was my misery.

When he reached out for me, all I saw was a large hand trying to cover my face, when I started cry aloud. The shrill of my voice turned the illusion in my mind, to darkness. He was gone, but standing motionless, I searched for a glimpse of light.

Shaking me so I would realize I was only having a bad dream, Eric woke me. I glanced at him and then buried my head in my pillow facing away from him.

"Beth, what's goin' on with you. Sometimes you're fine, but then sometimes you act like you're in a different world. I wish you'd tell me. What's happening with you, Please"

"I told you from the beginning, I don't know what's happening. It's driving me crazy and there's nothing neither you or I can do about it. It's these damned nightmares. If they'd leave me alone for one night, I might be able to restrain my sanity for a little while, but they won't. They just won't Eric," I said, starting to cry uncontrollably.

I laid across his chest and whimpered like a tiny baby. But the longer he stroked my back gently, the more relaxed I became. He almost had me asleep once again, when I sat straight up in the bed.

"I can't do it Eric. I can't fall asleep. He'll come after me again. I know he will. He wants to haunt me every chance he gets."

"Who? Who is haunting you?"

Not wanting to answer his question for fear it might trigger another nightmare inside my mind, I just curled up next to him as close as I could get without being under his skin.

"Just hold me. Please hold me and don't ever let me go. I need you to understand something. When I find out what's happening to me, I'll tell you. But until then, I can't tell you what I don't know. Besides, there are a few things I need to tell you about tomorrow. Lets just try to get some sleep. We only have a few more hours before the sun comes up anyway. Maybe things will look brighter in the morning."

Eric held me like I asked him to, and I soaked in every ounce of his affection. He didn't ask me any more questions. He just held me tight. He was so perfect. In fact, sometimes I wondered if he wasn't in a disguise, and underneath the disguise, was a real guardian angel. It was moments such as this one, when I wondered the most. Because not many people would set aside their own curiosity, for another's fear and need of reassurance. But he did, and that's what made him special to me.

The whistling of the wind and the brushing of the limbs against one another outside, filled me with serene thoughts. My tense muscles and tortured imagination were eased, leaving nothing but a few hours of true sleep, with no spirits to haunt me. But before I closed my eyes for sleep once more, I prayed to God.

Dear God,

Please take these nightmares and put them in a place far away from me. I've prayed this prayer to you many times, but the dreams keep haunting me night after night. I know I'm not supposed to fear as long as I have you to guide me, but it's hard.

Thank you for giving me Eric to love and to love me, but I'm afraid he thinks I'm lying to him. Lord, I'm not lying. I really don't know what's happening to me, but I believe you will show me when the time is right. I believe you'll help me to end this nightmare, and make things right.

Amen,

After saying my prayer to God, a kind of warmth swept through me suddenly. It was as though God was saying, "Sleep my child. I'll bring you peace. Sleep." So I put my faith in his hands, and closed my eyes. The feeling I had was right, because nothing appeared to me, but thoughts of love and splendor. And all of my apprehension was set aside for the few hours remaining for me to rest the way I needed to. I knew if I didn't recuperate from the many nights of lost sleep, nothing would keep me from fainting from sleep depravation.

The hours passed quickly. It seemed as though I woke as soon as I went to sleep, and the sun beamed down on me like a wake-up greeting from the heavens. With squinched eyes, I put my hands into a fist and when I was fully focused and all of the blur in my vision was gone, I looked around and Eric was no where to be found.

"Eric, where are you? Stop kiddin' around."

About that time, the door opened, startling me.

"Hey. I thought you might be hungry, so I went down the street and got us some breakfast. I hope you like pancakes, French toast, and last but not least a rose for the beautiful lady," he said pulling a single rose from behind his back.

"What did I do to deserve you?"

"Don't know, but ya got me baby," he replied in one of his many crazy, off the wall voices.

He sat the food on the small wooden table in the corner, then placed the rose in a glass and put it in the center. I looked at him with a loving cast on my face and rose to give him a proper "good morning" greeting.

"Thank you."

"For what? I'm just trying to make you feel better since you had such a rough night last night. You know Beth, it doesn't matter to me what your problem is. Whatever it is, we can work through it together. I have no doubt that we can do anything as long as we stay together."

Speechless, I held him until all of my foreboding was lost. And he too, held me just as steadfastly. You could tell the feeling between us, was mutual, and would never be broken into by anyone or anything.

I wasn't sure where he went for breakfast, but it hit the spot considering I had only eaten once the day before. I stuffed my face until I felt like I would get sick, then I sat back in my chair and gave a sigh of satisfaction. Eric did just the same. He ate and ate as if he hadn't eaten in days.

"What do ya want to do today?"

With a slight pause, I glanced over at the papers which were lying on the dresser beside the bed. "Well, I kinda want to see what I can find out. I want to read those papers and see if they can give me any information. A little information is better than none at all. And that's what I have right now...none."

Nodding his head in accordance, he replied, "Well, lets get to work then. If we're gonna find out who you really are Beth Laney, then we better get started."

Eric sat down with me as we both carefully looked through the documents he'd found by accident. But what made me wonder more than anything, was that the adoption papers were drawn up in the state of Arkansas. We lived in Texas. Why they would've adopted a child from another state, many hours away, didn't make any sense. Though it didn't say which town, I wanted to find out. I knew if I could find out where my real mother lived, then maybe there was a good chance I'd find her.

With revenge and hatred filling me the more I read, I had an idea.

"Eric. Will you do me a favor?" I said with a spiteful tone of voice.

"Anything."

"Take these papers down to the library and make a copy of them."

"What for? You already have these. Why another set?"

"I just do. I have an idea. And when you get back, we'll go buy some Christmas wrapping paper and a small box."

He looked at me as though he had an idea about what I was up to. But without any more questions, he went to town just as I'd asked him to. I guess he knew when I had my mind set on something, hell or high water wouldn't steer me away from it. And, in a way, that was right. It wasn't often I let something rage me until crazy thoughts started spinning around my head, but for once, I was full of tremendous animosity. I felt used and taken advantage of by the people I always believed to be, my parents. What a lie. What a distortion of truth and principle. I knew, for the first time in my life, why I had been treated so horribly. But still there was no justification for that kind of physical and mental abuse.

It didn't take long for Eric to return. The library was only about a mile away and a straight shot at that. He handed me the original copies, and placed the others on the dresser.

"What'cha plan on doin' with those Beth?"

"Well, I figure my mom and dad deserve a little Christmas present. Don't you? And I have the perfect thing to wrap up for 'em."

"You're incredible. I never would've thought of that."

Remaining still, the look on my face showed vengeance, with no sign of pity for parental imposters. Everything I'd ever wondered about, was shown to me so clearly. The reason why I wasn't treated as a member of the family, was because I wasn't. And deep in my heart, I knew it would be virtually impossible to forgive them for what hell they put me through during my childhood. I was always told forgiveness is a gift, and vengeance is baneful, but for once, I didn't care. Forgiveness was not the gift I wanted to give them, but instead I wanted to give them truth. If they knew I'd found the proof of their denial, then there'd be no way they could lie any longer. For they'd have nothing to lose. And if the truth be known, they probably never wanted me in the first place. Actions always speak louder than words, and their actions proved nothing less than having a heart of stone. In fact, I believed they didn't even know what love was, or how to show such an emotion.

Driving into town and then back to our room, the cold created more and more snow. And looking outside through the window, I felt a little sad. I guess it showed on my face because Eric walked over and put his hand on my shoulder.

"What's wrong?"

"Don't know. It's strange. I feel so lost, and yet I feel at home too."

"That's natural Beth. You were raised here. You grew up here. Don't try to punish yourself just because you have feelings about the place you spent your entire childhood. You can't change the past, but you can build on it and make the future better."

Leaning over and placing my head on his shoulder, I continued to gaze out the window. Then I began to feel bad about not being completely honest with

Eric. And decided it was time to tell him what he'd been wanting to know for a long time.

"Come over here. There's something I need to tell you. It's nothing bad, but since you're gonna be a part of my life from now on, I think you should know everything about me."

He looked at me with those gorgeous puppy dog eyes of his, and replied, "I'm listening. Whenever you're ready. You know I'll understand no matter what it is."

Taking a deep breathe, I continued, "Remember that day you ran after me and asked me where I was going?"

"Yeah. What about it?"

"I want to tell you where I was going. If you know, maybe you'll support me a little because of it."

He stared at me, and you could tell he was thinking awful things in the back of his mind.

"I'm seeing a therapist. For a while now, I've had these nightmares. Sometimes I even have horrible bits and pieces of a vision in the middle of the day. And when it got to the point to where I couldn't control them any longer, I went to Mrs. Downs."

With a slight shake of his head, Eric confessed, "I knew."

"What? How?" I muttered nervously.

"Babe, when you started to disappear for hours at a time, I got curious as to where you were. One day, I followed you. I know I shouldn't have, but I was just worried about what might happen to you when I 'm not around. I don't want to lose you. I love you."

"Did you go in and meet her?"

"No. I didn't feel it was my place to interfere with what you needed to do. As long as I knew you were okay, I was fine. And the reason I asked you that day where you were going, was because I wanted you to be able to trust me enough to tell me something like that without feeling uncomfortable. At least now I know you feel comfortable telling me."

We laid down for a moment, and I tried to describe her to him. "She's wonderful Eric. You know, besides you, I've never felt that comfortable around anyone. It's like we've known each another for years. It was strange. The first time I met her, I felt it immediately. I was scared, but not of her. I felt like I could tell her anything even though we'd only known each other a short time."

"You talk about me?" he asked with a slight grin on his face.

"Sometimes. But mostly we talk about me. She tries to dig through my mind to find out what's making me act so crazy at times. She told me I wasn't crazy, just confused. And every time I leave her, I feel like a new person again. I feel sorry for her though."

"Why is that?" he asked softly.

"She had to spend the holidays alone. She had a daughter, but she died at birth. The way she talks, she's been alone for a long time. You know Eric, it's not fair. My parents are blessed with children and treat them horribly, and those who would really be good parents end up alone. It's just not fair at all."

Wrapping both arms around me, he squeezed tenderly.

"You'll make a fine mama one day. I know it."

Fulfilling my need for understanding, I was taken once more by the only man I knew I'd ever want. And as we curled up against one another, I began to think. Even though my past was a lie, I knew my future would make up for all of the tears I'd cried. And it would also bring enough happiness, so I would forget the bad times in my life, and cover them with every tender moment from that day forward. I didn't want to let sadness drag me down where I couldn't get back up again, but instead, I wanted the future to guide me where I needed to go.

Though quiet for a moment, Eric got this energetic sound in his voice, "Know what we need?" he asked.

"What?"

"We need a Christmas tree. I bet we could find a small one somewhere, even at this late date. I mean, it wouldn't be Christmas without one."

"That's a good idea. And I know just the place. We used to go here when... never mind. Let's just go."

With no hesitation, we scrambled out of bed, and went out the door in a flash. Bundled up in a heavy coat, I clung onto him as the wind rushed by. And the spirit of Christmas was written all across his face. He was trying his best to make our first Christmas together a memorable one. And I had no doubt in my mind I'd never forget it.

I remembered exactly where we used to get trees when I was growing up. They had from tiny, two foot trees, to giant 9 foot trees, and everything in between. About a five minute drive across town, we enjoyed the Christmas music on the radio all the way there. And the tunes of the holidays created the perfect mood. Somehow it put an overcast above every disappointment, and helped me to smile.

When we arrived, there were people everywhere. It was hard to believe that many people waited until two days before Christmas to get a tree. But I was glad there were enough left to choose from. They even had a corner full of decorations.

While Eric was picking out a tree, I walked over and began to pick a few small ornaments to give the tree a little life and color. There were angels, Santa's, elves, and even a few candy canes. I picked out a few, just enough to cover the tree, and then walked on. Eric came over and was holding a small, but beautiful baby tree in his hands. I couldn't help but smile.

"We're still missing something. I don't know what, but there's something I've forgotten."

About that time, Eric handed me the tree, bent down, and stood back up with a star in his hand.

"That was what was missing...a topper. Can't have a tree without a topper, ya know."

"That's right Beth. You know what my grandmother always told me about having a star to top a Christmas tree?"

"No. What?" I said focusing on the sincere expressions on his face as he spoke.

"She used to say that if you have a star to top your tree, then you would have a special star to make a wish upon each and every night. And if you wish upon that same star enough times, be sure that wish will come true. Because, although it's silent in the night, it lights up the darkness and gives you guidance when you need it the most."

"That's beautiful. She must've been a wonderful woman."

"She was; Beautiful too. You kinda remind me of her," he said, walking over to pay for everything we'd picked out.

One by one, the clerk put the ornaments into a sack, but when he got to the star, it seemed to twinkle just a little. It was as though God was saying, "You picked the perfect star...make your wishes and believe in them."

I felt nothing but contentment as we walked out of the store. But soon, that same contentment turned to distress with no forewarning. Melissa was getting out of her car, but as I tried to keep her from seeing us, she ran over to me hurriedly.

"Beth...wait!" she yelled.

"I don't have anything to say to you."

She reached her hand out to Eric, "You must be Eric. I've heard a lot about you. Beth loves you a lot."

He shook her hand and smiled, then he looked over at me and whispered, "Why don't you tell her. This is not her fault. She had nothing to do with anything that's happened."

With a short sigh, I asked him to go to the car while I talked to her. And as soon as he walked off, I became speechless. Deep down I didn't want to throw away my big sister, but in actuality, she wasn't really my sister.

I told her about everything Eric had found while searching for my poetry, and her eyes filled with tears right away. I could tell she had no idea I was adopted, but I could also see just as much pain in her as I felt the moment I saw those documents.

"I'm so sorry," she said, as she embraced me.

Returning her affection, I replied, "It's not you I'm angry with. And I'm sorry if I've acted that way. It's just that..."

"I know what it is. I was never there when you really needed me. In fact, I was too scared to be. I was too busy protecting myself, to protect anyone else. Can you forgive me?"

It didn't take long for a tear to show in my eyes as well. And we laid on one another's shoulder until we felt that sisterly love all over again. What scared me most of all, was losing the one family link I always had to love and hope...my sister.

I told her where we were staying so she could come see me before I went back to college. I knew she would. It was hard to believe, but I think she was just as hurt by the news I gave her, as I was when I first found out. And that alone made me realize something. Even though she wasn't my sister by blood, she was my sister by love, and that was all that mattered to me. Still unsure of how the next few days would make me feel, I wanted her to be a part of them.

Christmas wouldn't be Christmas if she and I couldn't spend it together somehow. Though I loved Eric with all my heart, Melissa was also a special part of me. She was my sister for life, and nothing anybody could say or do would ever change that. But most of all, no document in the world had the power to tell me who my true family was. I had learned one thing. Family are those who love you, and wish the best for you. It has nothing to do with blood. Eric seemed like family to me already, and I wanted Melissa to join the new family I'd started. The one which I knew would make me happy. The place I spent many years of my life was not my home. I guess God made it a temporary place for me until I found out who I really was, and where I wanted to go with my life.

Getting into the car, Eric just smiled at me, as though he knew what happiness he brought to me by forcing me to talk to her.

"Think your smart, huh."

"You need her Beth. And from the look on her face, she needs you just as much. She's not the one you need to be angry with. Remember who you need to focus your energy towards, Okay."

Then our hands entwined, connecting our souls once more. Though I was still cold, he put off enough warmth for me to warm up momentarily. I felt his love drifting all around me, and it was then I knew, it had to be Christmas. Because for the first time, in a long time, I felt the true spirit of the holidays.

CHAPTER 14

The sky was white with millions of snowflakes drifting to earth so elegantly, and I sat in awe of the heavenly view. We drove slowly so we'd be able to take in each bit of splendor God had sent to us. Some large, some tiny, but the white flakes that fell upon us, turned around all sadness which lurked, and changed it into pure gratefulness of the things we were able behold at that special moment.

I was glad to be lucky enough to watch such a wonderful view with a man who appreciated it as much as I did. I could see it in his face, his handsome veneer. Then he told me of a time he remembered well.

"You know Beth, this reminds me of a time I'll never forget. I don't remember how old I was, but I remember it as if it were yesterday. It was the first time I made a snowman. I know I couldn't have been more than two or three. I'm sure it snowed enough for a snowman before then, but I guess my parents wanted to make sure I wasn't too small to get out in such weather.

Anyway, I can still see my dad running towards me. He lifted me up into the air as if I could really fly. In fact, it felt like I was flying. Times weren't always good with my mom and dad, but every time it snowed, it gave them hope that everything would turn out okay. I could see it in their eyes when they'd look out at the snow on the ground.

I had on three layers of clothes, a pair of gloves, and a winter hat, as my dad took my hand and rushed outside. I'll never forget. We ran outside so quickly that we slipped and fell face first into the snow. All we could do was laugh. My mom was always a little over-protective, because she kept yelling at my father to keep my ears covered. We'd just look back at her and continue on with what we were doing.

My dad built the bottom and the middle of the snowman, and I rolled and rolled the snow until I had a ball big enough to make the top. And as my dad placed them on top of one another, I ran inside to find something to use for the eyes, the nose, the mouth, and the buttons. It was so much fun. The best part of all, was when dad shook his head, ran inside, and came back out with one of his old pipes. Then as he stuck the pipe by the mouth of the snowman we worked so hard to make, and it looked perfect. I'll never forget that first snowman. But most of all, I won't forget that time with my father. I don't know if it was the snowman that intrigued me, or the fact that my father and I shared one of our first special moments together. That's what I see every time I'm blessed with enough snow to make a snowman. And one day I want to enjoy the same thing with my own son or daughter."

I could see it all in my mind just as he described it. He was so vivid in his expressions of what he remembered. And I was glad he had such wonderful memories to look back on.

"I bet your father is a wonderful man Eric. If you're anything alike, I know he's a wonderful man," I said, pulling into the parking lot of our hotel.

He peered at me with a loving expression on his face, squeezed my hand, then leaned over to kiss me gently on my cheek. We both hesitated to jump out into the cold weather, but we also knew the sooner we got out, the sooner we'd be able to snuggle up under warm blankets and relax. So with no more delaying, we scrambled out of the car and started running to our room. Trying to watch my step, I slipped anyway. But before I fell to the ground, Eric's strong arms caught me and pulled me back up to my feet.

Once he knew I was fine, he started to laugh at me. Feeling a little playful, I picked up a handful of snow, rolled into a ball and clobbered him with it. He got this serious look on his face, trying to make me think he was angry. Then all of the sudden, he bent down, picked up some snow of his own, and chased me all the way to our room.

We laughed until I thought we were gonna cry. But frolicking with Eric was one thing I wouldn't mind doing all day long every day.

While Eric was fumbling with the keys, I tip-toed behind him, got a little ice off the ground, and slipped it in the back of his pants about the time he turned the key in the door. He almost jumped ten foot high, but I couldn't resist such a refreshing joke. I was just glad he was one who could take a joke with no hard feelings. That was one way in which we were alike. In fact, we were alike in many ways. Maybe that was why I loved him so much.

Giggling as we entered the room, I laid the decorations on the bed, and Eric placed the tree in the center of the table.

"Well, lets get started decorating. I know we don't have many decorations, but we've got enough," I said, beginning to take out the ornaments one by one.

Eric turned on the radio, and Christmas songs were still playing, one after another. It set the perfect mood for decorating our very first tree together. We didn't buy any lights, but it didn't matter. The spirit still dwelled around us without flashing lights to remind us what season it was.

We trimmed the tree together. He decorated one side, and I the other until it looked beautiful. Though it was plain before we started, it was a sight for sore eyes afterwards. It wasn't very big, but it had a lot of meaning for it to be so small.

"Oh. We're forgetting the most important thing," I said, taking the star out of the sack.

But before we placed it on the very top of the tree, Eric had a good idea.

"Lets both focus on this star and make a wish at the same time. Maybe my grandmother was right. We'll never know unless we try. We have tonight and tomorrow night to wish upon this one special star. Ya never know Beth, maybe our wishes will come true before we know it."

Both of us held onto one end of the silvery star in front of us. Then we closed our eyes and made a wish. When we reopened our eyes, together, we placed it at the tip of the tree. For a moment, we stood there and stared at it as if it had magical powers. Of course, I'd always been told the elderly have lived enough years to know what's true. And if Eric's grandmother was right about wishing upon the same star each night, then I knew I'd have a life of security and hope. Because that was what I wished for.

Soon the light of day started to dim more and more until nothing was left but the pitch darkness of nightfall. And as I turned away from the lovely tree we'd put up together, I glanced over at the papers still sitting on the night stand beside the bed.

Eric turned off the radio and turned on the television, while I sat down and looked over the few things I missed.

"Look. Here's my old diary. I thought I'd lost it years ago. It must've been with all my poetry."

I begin to read, but was surprised and bewildered by the words on the page in front of me.

Saturday, Sept. 25th, 1982

He walks so unstoppable,
No one stands in his way.
They see only good in him,
While I seem to be his prey.
His grimace smile chills me
And his words, they cut my soul.

Tammy D. Thompson

> *I fear every man completely;*
> *Every stranger, and ones I know.*

I sat in deep thought trying to remember writing those lines of poetry, but I remembered nothing. I couldn't even imagine why I would write such a thing. But as I read it over and over again, I cringed a little. I didn't know why. It just gave me a funny feeling. "If I could only remember," I said to myself. And the more I thought about it, my insides were being eaten up by curiosity of what I should already know.

Reading on, I came to another date, with another poem:

Saturday, Nov. 6th, 1982

> *Frightened, can't seem to stop*
> *The pain he gives to me.*
> *Scared and terrified*
> *I want to be set free.*
> *He wanders in the darkness*
> *When I lie down to sleep.*
> *So many weary nights,*
> *A stranger often creeps.*
> *Fragile, yet now broken,*
> *As my bed terrifies.*
> *I cannot tell a single soul,*
> *But still at night I cry.*

Eric noticed the perplexity in my expression, and sat beside me to see what had me so puzzled.

"Look at this poetry. Babe, I don't remember writing it. I never forget my own poetry, but I don't remember this."

"Maybe Melissa wrote it," he said, trying to give me an answer to the question I was asking myself.

"No. I wrote it. It's in my handwriting, but"

"What?" he asked, a little puzzled himself.

Hesitating slightly, I answered, "I don't know. I feel connected to it somehow. Even though I don't remember writing these poems, this is my diary. And no one else's handwriting is in here. But I don't know what made me write such strange things."

"Maybe you're writing about your father. You've told me over and over about how your father wasn't nice to you in the least. Maybe you were just writing all of your sadness from your father rejecting you as a child."

"I don't know," I whispered, still not taking my eyes of the words on the yellowing pages in my diary.

"Maybe you need to talk to Mrs. Downs about it. You never know, she might be able to tell you what it means. If she's as good as you say she is, I know she can help you. I'd try, but psychology's not my major. And I'd really hate to confuse you any more than you're already confused," he said putting his tender arms around me, making me feel special once more.

Thinking so much made me feel like I needed to get refreshed somehow, so I went into the bathroom to splash a little water on my face. Then I reached and turned on hot water for a shower. Waiting until the water was just right, I leaned down into the sink once more to finish washing my face. The steam from the shower had fogged up the mirror, and as I wiped my hand across it to see myself, I jumped in dismay of the reflection of someone behind me. Quickly, Eric made sure I knew it was him.

"My God Beth. I've never seen anyone so jumpy. I just thought I'd join you in the shower."

Lowering my head, I replied in a whispering voice, "I wish I could.—I just pray that I could—I don't know...be normal for a change. I feel like I did several months ago. I feel like I'm losing my mind."

"Listen. I'm here. There's nothing you need to worry about ever again. I don't plan on doing anything to hurt you or to make you feel like your alone. Let's just enjoy being together. And everything else can be set aside until it has to be dealt with."

Then his hands slithered around my waist like a snake on the prowl, and I laid my head back until it rested on his shoulder. Rocking back and forth, left and right, he made me feel like a tiny baby again. He seemed to be rocking me out of my frustration, and into his love. Nothing was more soothing than knowing someone's there for you. And I knew positively he would never leave me. I just couldn't wait until I became Mrs. Eric Lee Norris.

The shower continued to run. Turning to him, I slipped off my clothes and started undressing him.

"Still wanna join me you sexy man?"

He didn't answer me vocally, but physically he answered my question with no doubt of what his answer was. Our lips seemed magnetically drawn together, and our bodies, once again, were as close as they could get without transforming into one existence. And as we stood there naked and groping one another, every other thought which was prominent moments earlier, were replaced by only thoughts of Eric.

We stepped into the shower and closed the curtains. Caressing one another all over, as the warm water rolled off our backs, was exhilarating. And his flesh pressed up against mine created more steam from our bodies than from the hot water which was pounding on us.

The warm kisses from my neck all the way down, made me tingle all over. And the touch from his fingertips in every curve of my body, made me feel sexy and wanted. His touch let me know he wanted me. And I wanted my touch on his flesh, to let him know how much I wanted him as well.

He took a bar of soap and begin to lather my back, from the top of my neck, all the way down to my hips. It felt wonderful. It reminded me of when I was a little girl. Me and my sister used to take a bath together, and she would always soap up my back, then write on it. I'd have to try and guess what she wrote. It was relaxing and innocent then, but with Eric, it was stimulating to my entire being. Just his touch made me focus on nothing but good things, and it taught me to sift out all the bad.

Then I tried to relax him as much as he'd relaxed me. So I did the same for him. With his back to me, I massaged his shoulders, then down his arms. The muscles which protruded distinctively were seductive, and firm to the touch. Looking at him enticed my appetite and my craving for each inch of his body. He was my desire. He was what I needed for me to feel cherished, but at the same time, I wanted to give him the secure feeling I would never leave him.

As the water began to lose its' heat, and the cold started pounding on us, we scrambled out quickly. I lunged for a towel, but before I could get it in my grasp, Eric jerked it away and tried to pop me with it, again being playful.

"You sure are in a good mood."

"Well, what can I say. I'm in a hotel room with a beautiful woman who wants me. Why not be anything but happy," he said with his eyes shimmering as bright as any star I'd ever seen.

Blushing a little, "Flattery will get you everywhere. Of course, it looks like you already know that."

And still, he continued to rough house until I was tired of fighting him off. It wasn't that I didn't enjoy his attention, but exhaustion had taken a bigger bite out of me than I thought, and I just wanted to sleep.

Once I talked him into leaving me alone for a few minutes, I went over and got a bottle of pills out of my purse.

"What's that?" he asked, very concerned.

"Oh, it's just something Mrs. Downs gave me to help me sleep. You know how much trouble I've had lately. I just need a little something to clear my head at night. I'm tired of facing all sorts of crazy hallucinations when I'm sleeping."

With a slight pause, he turned around and started watching television. I could tell he disapproved of me taking anything, but he didn't say a word. So while I fixed me a glass of water, I glanced over at him a time or two. I didn't want to do anything he didn't want me doing, but if he only knew what I'd gone through with my thoughts, vision, and nightmares, he would insist on me taking something.

Considering we hadn't eaten much of anything all day long, Eric suggested he go and pick up something before we laid down for the night. My stomach had made a few loud noises, so I didn't think it was a bad idea at all. I guess, with all the commotion, eating was the last thing on my mind.

After he put on his coat and walked out the door, I slipped under the covers, grabbed my diary, and began to read a few more pages. One date rang clear in my mind for some reason. It was January 7th, 1983. I probably wouldn't have remembered anything at all, but the poem I wrote on that day, made things all too clear. It read:

> *This corner remains my friend*
> *As I often greet it every night.*
> *When I'm hiding from what fears me,*

And fills me full of fright.
I sit huddled quietly
Hoping not to be seen
As I watch the light outside my window,
But I dare not to scream.
Only sounds of breathing
As quiet as I can,
I sit alone once more
Cause no one understands.

I stared at the wall, in a daze, as I laid the diary down on my lap. I saw it in my mind precisely as it happened that day. My father and mother had been arguing, so, I did what I normally did. I went out on the front porch as the sun started to fall, and swung back and forth, trying to muffle the sounds of screaming. When I heard a thump, I glared through the curtains, and saw my mother on the floor. As far as I could remember, she hadn't done anything horrible enough to deserve that. Though not normally one to get involved, I ran inside and tried to help her up. In turn, my father pushed me aside roughly. But when I tried to help her again, he tried to abuse me as well. I ran up the stairs as he chased me. A little ahead of him, I ran in my room, opened the closed door, and huddled up in the corner quietly. I remember being scared to breath for fear he'd find me and beat me the same as he was doing my mother already. When I finally came to the conclusion I was safe to come out, I tip-toed softly to my door and checked down the hallway making no noise. Then I went and sat at my desk. Finding a pen and a piece of paper, I began to write. Each bit of emotion I felt inside, I condensed into a short poem. I guess to someone else it might not have any meaning at all, but to me, it was my past; but only one glimpse. The rest remains in bits and pieces.

I was startled a little as Eric turned the key to let himself back in, but I was glad he was back so soon. It seemed like the longer he stayed gone, the more paranoid I became.

With a star in his eyes, he made a wonderful statement, "Tomorrow's Christmas Eve, and look who I'm spending it with. I'm gonna be with the most beautiful, the sweetest, and the most loved woman I know. Well at least I love you the most."

"Stop it. You're crazy. What's so special about spending Christmas with a confused, erratic, nut case psycho, that doesn't even know why she's gone crazy."

He replied, "That's why I love you. You have a sense of humor that makes me laugh."

"I was being serious," I said, trying to act upset, but let a hint of a smile show through.

"Come on Beth. You know you're not crazy, and I know it too. So let's cut to the chase. You need to finish your counseling with Mrs. Downs, restart your life with me, find your real parents, and then you might be able to sleep at night. And I intend on helping you do every one of those things." Tilting my head to the side in an unsure manor, he placed his hands on my face, "I love you, and there's nothing you can do to change that. Crazy or not, you'll be my wife one day."

"Yes I will. And I want to be the best wife you've ever seen. You deserve the best Eric. I just hope I'm capable of giving you the best, when mediocre is all I've ever been."

Trying the break a moment which had gotten way too serious, I opened up the sack he'd brought in, and we ate quietly. He kept staring at me with those penetrating eyes, and I was lit up inside. He tried his best to make me feel as if I was as normal as any one else, but I knew I would have to be the one who proved that to myself. No one could do it for me.

By the time we'd finished eating, the sleeping pill I'd taken, was making my eyelids very heavy. In fact, it was almost impossible for me to hold them open any longer. Eric could see I just about to pass out, so he tucked me in warmly, and turned off the lights. Then the night was gone. About the time I went to sleep, I awoke. Nothing interrupted my good night's sleep for a change, and I felt more refreshed than I'd felt in a long time. I didn't even remember Eric getting into bed. I hoped he didn't think I was ignoring him, but I was glad, for once, I had no fears to drag me down. It was only for one night, but that one night made a difference in my attitude.

Lying there for a while just watching my sweet Eric sleeping. He looked so peaceful. And I was sure he was dreaming of me. Every once in a while, he'd grin a little. I could tell he was having a pleasant dream.

Trying not to wake him, I scooted up to him as close as I could get, and rubbed his chest slowly. His sex appeal was too much for me to handle. Just the thought of him, made me want to scream out to everyone, "I love Eric Lee Norris, and he loves me too." And I knew he and I would always have each other to lean on.

After a few moments, he began to move around.

"Wake up sleepy head," I whispered, gently kissing his cheek.

"'Mornin. How long you been awake?"

"Not long. I've just been sittin' here watching you."

"I bet that was exciting."

"Well, it made me realize something."

"And what was that?"

"I realized how happy I'm going to be each and every morning waking up with you."

"I'm glad you feel that way because I'm not letting you go anywhere."

Lying still and quiet for a while, the devotion we had for one another consumed us completely. There was no question in my mind I had made the right decision about marrying him. In fact, it was probably the only decision I ever made which I had no doubts about. I didn't want to get out of that warm bed or out of his arms, but the day had shown itself it us.

"Lets get dressed and go outside and play."

"Play. We're not kids anymore."

"Yeah, well, we can act like it for one day can't we? There's a park across the street. Why don't we walk over and see who can win at a snowball fight."

Both of us briskly ran to put on some warm clothes. But it didn't take long. Of course, I was always slower at getting ready than he was. By the time I had gotten my shoes on, he was waiting at the door excited and ready to make the best of the beautiful snow on the ground outside. I could tell he wanted to take advantage of the snow.

We raced all the way to the park, and Eric stayed a step ahead of me the entire way. There were children all over the place. They looked like they were having a contest for building the best snowman. We stood there for a few moments and watched. The smiles on every child's face was enough to make me smile too. You could tell they were having the time of their life. Some of the kids acted like they'd never seen snow before. They were running around throwing snowballs while their parents stood and gazed at them having such a wonderful time.

Wanting to surprise Eric, I picked up a handful of snow when he wasn't looking, and threw it at him when he turned back around. Then the fight was on. We acted like the children surrounding us. We must've run a hundred miles in the snow chasing one another. And Eric kept on trying to get the last hit, but I wouldn't let him. I didn't like losing any game, so I kept on and on until we were both too tired to run or throw snowballs any longer.

We found a picnic table which was unoccupied, sat down, and caught our breathe. I'd forgotten how out of shape I was, and running around like I was still six years old again, drained all of my energy. But the enthusiasm I felt when Eric was around, was extraordinary. He gave me new bursts of energy with a single touch. And that energy transferred through every muscle, bone and nerve in my body.

Noticing how much time had slipped away from us, we walked over to a little hot dog stand on the corner. It was hard to believe someone had the nerve to be out in such cold weather just to sell hot dogs, but the line was long. The park was full of folks who loved Christmas weather, so I guess the guy had the right idea.

When it was finally our turn in line Eric ordered two hot dogs.

"Hot Chocolate too sir?" the man asked.

He looked over at me, and I shook my head in an agreeing manor.

"Sure. Make that two hot chocolates too." Eric replied to the man.

Holding onto one another, waiting, we got our food and went back over to our table and sat down.

"Oh Eric, this hot chocolate hits the spot, but I'm freezing."

"Me too. When we finish eating, we'll go in. I'm feel frost bit myself."

Eating hot dogs, and sipping on the hot chocolate, I studied everyone around me. Sometimes it was like I could tell what was going on in someone's life without even knowing that person. There was one woman leaning against a tree looking out at her daughter playing. Every little bit she'd run up and hug her mommy, then run back and play. The look on that woman's face was happiness, in a way, but sadness for the most part. It looked like she might've been divorced, or without her husband, and she seemed to put forth all her energy into that precious little girl.

"What'cha thinkin'?"

"Nothin' really. I was just lookin' around at all the people."

"Yeah, me too. Everybody looks so inspired by the holidays, don't they?"

"Some do," I replied shortly.

"What do you mean?"

"Some look like they're trying to be happy, but seem to fall a little short."

"Well, I guess we fit into that category."

I just looked over at him and smiled grimly, "But I'm glad to be with you. I can't think of anyone else I'd rather wake up Christmas morning with."

Eric took my hand, leaned over, and kissed me on the forehead like a father would his child. Then we carefully made our way back to the room where we had practically lived for the past several days. The roads were icy, and a time or two we almost slipped and fell, but we kept our balance enough to stay on our feet. A couple of times Eric acted like he was gonna make me fall, but then he'd just laugh. He was such a jokester.

Falling onto the bed as we walked in the room, I yawned. My body was tired. My feet were sore; And I felt like sleeping. In fact, if Eric had left me alone long enough, I would've been out like a light, but he didn't. He lifted up my layers of clothing, and began tickling me until I fought back enough to get him off of me. Though he was strong, I tried to do him the same; But his strength went way beyond what I could hold down. His arms were like iron rods, and the grip he had on me with his hands, was almost impossible to unclutch. Finally, after wrestling, tickling, and aggravating one another to no end, we slowed down until all of the energy left over from the day, was demolished.

"Beth, I know it's early, but I'm really tired. Anyway, you know who comes tonight." He chuckled a little.

"Good Ole St. Nick."

"That's right. And he's probably watching us right now."

I laughed and replied, "Well, if he's watching, maybe we should give something good to watch."

I rolled over on top of him quickly. The surprise in his eyes was obvious. Most of the time I pretty much let him be the aggressor, but just to shock him, I thought I'd role play and be him for a moment. It was interesting to be the one in control. Although I knew I wanted him to be the leader, I thought a change of pace might make things a little more interesting.

But just before we got heavily involved in what we were doing, I thought of something I had to do. Jumping up, Eric laid there with a disappointed look painted all over his face.

"I forgot something."

"What? I'll go get it."

"No. It's nothing you can get. It's something you've already gotten for me."

Bewildered he sat there waiting to see exactly what I was talking about. I went over and pulled out the papers he had copied for me. Then I took out the box and wrapping paper. I placed the papers in the box, taped it up, and then wrapped it beautifully. Tearing a small piece of wrapping paper off the roll, I bent it half into and wrote, "To: Mom and Dad From: Beth Have a Merry Christmas."

Eric strolled over to me and looked at the present I wrapped.

"That's cruel Beth. Why don't you just tell them?"

"I am. This is how I'm telling them. They deserve to get the news in this way. They ruined my Christmas Eric. Do you really think I want to let them have a good Christmas after sabotaging mine. No. They need to feel what I feel—disappointment."

He stared at me in neither an approving or disapproving manner, but somewhere in between. I knew what I had to do to make myself feel gratified. And putting my so-called mom and dad through hell and back, was exactly what needed to be done. I intended on telling them everything I ever wanted to say, but always afraid to—from the first time my father hit me, until the time he kicked me out of the house just days ago. I didn't want to leave out a single detail. So much pain had welled up inside of me for such a long time, and something told me it was time to release it before it ate me alive.

With Eric still peering at me, I got out my night shirt, and slipped it on.

"I guess you're ready for bed now," he said in a low voice.

"I need to take my pill first." I replied, reaching into my purse and pulled out the bottle of pills that turned out to be my nightmare cure.

"Are you sure..."

"Yes Eric. I need to take something. Otherwise..."

"Okay." he said, trying to keep me from getting upset.

I got a glass of water, popped the pills in my mouth, and took a drink to wash them down quickly. As before, Eric didn't approve, but there was nothing I could do about it. He wasn't the one having such terrible nightmares. And he sure as hell wasn't the one having to live with some enigmatic fear day after day.

When I got in bed, he had his back turned to me. I felt like an outcast all over again. And I never thought he would be the one to make me feel that way. I searched for the right words to say to make him understand why I had to take sleeping pills, but nothing came to mind. Lying there with my fingers entwined on my stomach, I took a deep breath trying to get his attention so he'd turn around. But still he kept his back to me and made no noise. It was hard to tell if he had fallen asleep immediately, or if he was only trying to refrain from talking to me because of his slight anger about what I was doing.

"Eric." I said, as I shook him delicately.

Gradually turning towards me, he replied, "What?"

"I don't want you to be mad. I don't need to explain this to you all over again, do I? I mean, the reason I need to take these pills."

"Beth. How are you ever gonna be able to get past these nightmares, if you don't face them. I know you don't want to have to take those pills every night from now on just because you're afraid you'll have a dream. If that was the case, there's probably a lot of people who'd be hooked on sleeping pills."

"Okay. Tonight's the last night. But if I feel like I need them again, I mean, really need them, will you not argue. Will you take my word for it, and stand behind me?"

The smile on his face said yes, and I felt relieved. The last thing I wanted was for him to turn against me. I needed him beside me more than anyone else. It was hard to describe to anyone what I was going through, but I had to try to make him see, because he was all I worried about. If he didn't understand, then in actuality, I had no one besides Mrs. Downs, who really understood me.

"Just hold me. That's all I need. Just hold me until I fall asleep. Then I know I'll sleep well."

He did just that. His arms were warmer than the blankets which covered me, and the rhythm of his heart, beat after beat, slowly put me to sleep. And as my eyes got heavier and heavier, I heard him whispering to me, "It's gonna okay sweet Beth. No one will hurt you. Go to sleep. Go to sleep."

Those words replayed in my mind over and over again until my worries were gone, and absolute contentment filled my soul. I believed every word because they were spoken from within his heart. I knew his heart better than I knew my own. It was kind, generous, caring, and most of all, it was mine. He gave it to me completely, holding nothing back, but instead, giving all he had.

Sleep brought a few thoughts which were unsettling. I knew when I woke, I'd have to confront my mom and dad. The reluctance I had was immense, but the rewards would be great. Facing them would help me to pull together what time had torn into many tiny pieces. I needed to heal; But healing had to start from the inside out. I had to heal my heart and my soul before my mind would ever be right again. I just had to wait and see what Christmas day would bring to me...joy of new beginnings, or the destruction of the past.

CHAPTER 15

The light of the morning sun beamed through the small opening in the curtains, and I pulled the covers over my head to try and sneak a few more moments of sleep away from the day. I guess I didn't move a muscle all night long because the spot where I was lying, was still very warm. Eric's arm was still draped around me securely, and our legs were interlocked, crossing one another. Nothing, not even a glimpse of a dream, interrupted my slumber the night before, and the refreshing feeling I had all over, filled every inch of me...from the top of my head to the tips of my toes.

Moaning and groaning, Eric stretched his arms and twisted his body, making his bones pop like fire crackers, one after another. I snickered at him because of the face he was making, then I used his chest as a pillow once again. I felt like lying there forever. I didn't want to crawl out from under those warm covers, but I also knew sleeping all day long wouldn't do any good. So I stretched as Eric did, rolled over, and stumbled out of bed clumsily. Only half awake, things were blurry, but there was one thing I saw clearly—the star.

Standing in front of the small, lightly decorated tree, I smiled. Although it was daylight, the silvery star resting on top of the insignificant tree in our room, still shined in my eyes. It had something special. Maybe it was all because of the little story Eric told me, but still, it was special. I never wanted to be without it. The way I looked at it, if Eric and I were to use that same star every year at Christmas, we would never stop having a star to wish upon. I believed what he told me, because I believed in him.

Still thinking I was the only one fully awake, I heard footsteps behind me. But before I could turn to see, Eric began to ravish the back of my neck. He swung my hair around and smothered me with gentle kisses.

"Stop it. It's too early for that kind of behavior," I said kiddingly.

"It's never too early," he replied, giving me an enthusiastic good-morning greeting.

Pushing him away, I remembered the card he'd given me before I left him at college.

"I almost forgot about my card."

"Beth. I wrote that thinking I wouldn't see you for Christmas."

"That's ok. I still want to read it."

I walked over and opened my purse. Sliding it out carefully, I glanced back at him with the spirit of Christmas running through my entire body.

Slowly opening the card, it read:

On this Christmas day
    Though I cannot be with you,
I still wish the spirit of Christmas,
    And hopes to start anew.
Though God may be your guardian,
    I, too, guard your heart.
And for the many Christmas's to come,
    I never again want to be apart.
So as you wake on Christmas morn'
    Know my mind is filled with you.
And just knowing that your happy,
    Makes my greatest wish come true.

HAVE A WONDERFUL CHRISTMAS & I LOVE YOU
    ERIC

Lowering the card slowly, I looked at Eric with eyes which were filled with nothing but happiness. Every word I read gave me the reassurance he wanted to be with me, and the fact he flew hundreds of miles, showed me his determination. I was completely overtaken. I used to think that nothing could ever stay good forever, but every day, he seemed to give me a sign that things would always be the same.

"Oh Eric. If you hadn't been here to make my Christmas worth while, then this card would've done it all by itself. Thank you."

"I just couldn't imagine being without you, and when I told my parents how I felt, they told me to follow my heart. And since you have my heart, I had to come to you. I didn't have a choice. It was either be miserable, or jump on the next plane out and play Santa for the most beautiful woman I know."

"You're somethin' else Eric Norris. I'm not glad you had to spent this holiday without your family, but I am glad you're here with me."

"Beth, you are my family. You will be my wife. That's all the reason I need."

I ran my fingers through his hair, and we just stared into each other's eyes until I felt my soul was melting into his. Then we held each other tightly. I didn't want to let go of the moment. His arms were the blanket I needed to keep me warm through the cold. And I had a feeling the cold weather was just beginning.

"We need to get dressed. There is one stop we need to make before we leave. I'm just glad you're here with me. I'm not sure I can do it without you."

"Don't worry. I wouldn't want to be anywhere else."

He went in the bathroom and began taking a shower while I gathered our things. Eric didn't have much, but my clothes, and odds and ends, were scattered all over the place. Picking them up one by one off the floor, I was startled by the phone. I couldn't imagine would be calling, then I remembered giving my number to Melissa.

I sat down on the bed, and answered softly, "Hello."

"Merry Christmas Sis." Melissa said kindly.

Not sure what to say to her, I replied, "Merry Christmas."

"Listen, I wasn't sure if I'd see you today, so I just wanted to..."

"You'll see me." I responded quickly.

"What do you mean. You're not coming here, are you?"

"I have something for mom and dad. Anyway, I have a few things I need to say. You know, the things I was always too afraid to say before."

"Are you sure you want to put yourself in that situation. You know how dad is."

"Yes, I know how he is! I want him to know how I am. I'll see you in a few hours," I said. I hung up because I didn't want to give her the chance to try and talk me out of doing what I knew I had to do. If I had stayed on the phone for one more minute, she would've lectured me until my anger shadowed me all over again.

Sitting there, my thoughts were running rampant like wild animals in a secluded forest. The tone in her voice seemed one of worry. I guess she thought I'd be the one to end up hurting, but I knew different. My reasoning for wanting to see my parents one more time, was not for revenge, but instead, for bringing out the truth-what I thought of them, and what they really thought of me. A part of me told me not to go, but just a small part. The rest of me, told me to face the facts and put them behind me as quickly as I knew how. And the quickest way, was for me to deal with them face to face, then turn and walk away.

I heard Eric turn off the water and step out of the shower to dry off. I started putting the clothes I was going to wear, on the bed. It was Christmas, and I wanted to dress appropriately. Even though this particular Christmas wouldn't be the best, I always said, "If I look good, I feel good." And looking as good as possible was always very important to me.

I was walking towards the bathroom, and Eric turned the corner with nothing but a towel wrapped around him. Giving him a playful look, I brushed by him slowly, yanked his towel off, then ran into the bathroom. Horseplay with him was such a diversion for me. It sometimes helped make me forget things I'd rather forget. But it also released my frustration, and transformed it into unconscious denial.

Time had flown by as Eric and I played around. The laughter did me good, but realizing how late it was getting, I hurried along much faster than usual. We had to be checked out at a certain time, and that time was nearing quickly. But Eric didn't rush me at all. He had such patience, unlike myself. As long as I could remember, my fuse was always short, and my patience was always thin. In so many ways, we were such opposites, but in others, we were exactly the same.

None the less, I was dressed and ready in no time at all. And Eric had taken the liberty of packing the rest of our things and putting them in the car.

"Ready to go?" he asked as a smile was melted across his handsome face.

"Guess so. Now is as good a time as any." I replied in a nervous, shaky voice.

"You know, we don't have to go over there. We can just leave town and you can leave them behind. It'll save you a lot of pain in the end."

"Yeah, but what about all of my unanswered questions. I deserve answers don't I? I deserve an explanation for everything. Why they didn't tell me? And most of all, why they even wanted another child. It just doesn't make any sense."

He rubbed my face gently, then kissed my forehead, "Babe, sometimes nothing ever makes any sense, but it's just like riding a tide. If you can bare riding a horrible, terrifying wave, then you know that calm waters are near. You can't let yourself go under. If you do, the tide wins and you'll never get the chance to enjoy still waters at all. I'll have to admit, what you're going through now, is a ten foot tall wave, but if you let me help you, I promise it'll all smooth out in the end."

"Thanks. You always know exactly what to say."

Arm in arm, we walked out of the room which we had stayed for several nights. Then stopping for a moment, Eric turned to take one last look.

"I'll never forget this first Christmas with you. I know we'll have many more together, but this first one"

"Yeah, me too," I added, then we strolled slowly to the car.

The wind had gradually come to a halt, leaving only a dry cold atmosphere. The children which were playing so enthusiastically the day before, no longer occupied the park across the street. And only few cars were on the slippery roads. Careful not to slip on ice, I braced myself by clutching onto the car door handle. And as he unlocked the doors, I didn't hesitate one minute to hop in. The cold was too much for me to handle. I was always a spring and summer kind of girl. The cold never agreed with me at all.

"Where ya wanna go first? How 'bout somethin' to eat?"

"I am a little hungry," I answered in a shivering voice.

We sat there for a moment waiting for the car to warm up, discussing where to eat. Although eating wasn't the most important thing to me at that moment, I knew I needed my strength and energy.

There was this small cafe' a few blocks away where my sister and I used to go.

I told Eric about their home cooked food, and that was all it took. He backed up swiftly and headed in that direction. Looking around, the town looked deserted. There were only a few people in sight, and I saw no children playing in the snow like the day before. But then I realized, everyone was more than likely enjoying their time with their families. There were probably hundreds of families sitting down for Christmas dinner, bowing their heads and giving thanks. But I felt lucky to be able to have my Christmas dinner with the man I loved dearly. I was more thankful than I'd ever been about anything. Even though we wouldn't be sitting down in a warm home, at least we were going to be together. It didn't matter to me as long as we were together.

Pulling in to park, I noticed only a few people inside eating. I was sure we weren't the only ones who had nowhere to go on such an important day. Maybe the others didn't have a place to call home either, or maybe they just didn't think of it as home, like me.

"Come on," Eric said, opening my door, taking my hand, and helping me out of the car.

I followed behind him, gripping tightly onto his large, warm hand. And I'm sure those who saw us, knew we were completely in love. Touching was always a big thing with us. Neither of us were afraid to show affection in public. And maybe that was why we fit together so perfectly.

We wandered in and the waitress came over and seated us right behind an old couple. I looked at them with envy. You could tell they'd been together for many years. And the happiness which showed on their faces, was distinct. From what I saw, the years they'd probably spent together only made them stronger in the way they felt about one another. Every little bit she would reach over and squeeze his hand. And he'd just grin and look at her with love.

"What'cha thinkin'?" Eric asked, trying to pull me out of the daze which I'd fallen into.

"Oh, I don't know. I was just looking at that couple over there."

"The elderly couple?"

"Yeah. Just look at 'em. I want that when I'm old. I don't want the fire to leave us. Just like them, you can tell they still burn for each other. You think we'll feel the same about each other in fifty years?"

"No."

With a disappointed look on my face, I started to say something, when he finished, "No. I think I'll love you even more. Beth, nothing stays the same, but things do get better."

Then I did just as the old woman did. I reached over and squeezed his hand as if to say "Thank you." He just grinned and looked at me. That was all I needed. He didn't have to say a word. Just as many other times before, I knew what he was thinking. He was so easy to read. And I'm sure, to him, I was an open book as well.

The waitress came over, but she was nothing like Belle. She talked as if she wasn't the least bit country. Her language held no slang, and her walk was proper. Eric ordered for both of us and handed the menus back to her. He continued smiling at me.

"Why are you so happy?" I asked, knowing where we were going after we ate.

He reached over, stoked my hair once or twice, and answered, "Just having you here with me on such a wonderful day makes me want to thank God. I never thought I'd be this lucky Beth. You may have never thought of yourself as 'special,' but to me you are my life. I'm proud to be anywhere with you, whether it's in a restaurant or any where else. I'm proud of you. You're a lot stronger than I thought you were."

"Well, sometimes you have to face reality, no matter how horrible or fearful it might be. And I know that if I don't face things head on, then I'll be caught up in a war inside myself. And to be honest, I'm tired of fighting my feelings. You taught me to let them go, to show them. And that's what I'm gonna do. It might make me feel lousy at first, but in the end, I'll be a better person for it."

It was only a few minutes before the waitress brought over our food. It looked delicious. It probably wasn't as extravagant as most people were having, but the food wasn't the only factor. Who you spend time with, is most important. And I couldn't have been with anyone better, or anyone who loved me any more than Eric. One by one, the tables were emptying slowly, leaving only me, Eric, and the old couple who were sitting near us. You could tell the people who were working there, were ready to leave. Their families were probably waiting for them to come home. But, deep down, I wanted to stay there as long as I possibly could. I wanted to stall as long as possible. Because once Eric and I drive to my parent's house, the rest of the day would be ruined. And I wanted to enjoy what peaceful, and enjoyable time I had with the love of my life.

Taking tiny bites, he began to stare at me. His plate was cleaned ten minutes before, and mine was still half full. Twirling my fork around and around each noodle carefully, Eric looked at me, grabbed my arm, and asked, "You nervous? You look more nervous than I've ever seen you."

"I'm fine. I'm trying to enjoy my food. Anything wrong with that?"

"No. Listen, I'll go pay the check, and I'll be right back."

I nodded then looked back down at what remained on my plate.

"I don't want this." I said.

I pushed my plate aside, put a few dollars on the table for the tip, and went to joined Eric at the register. By the time I reached him, he was turning towards me.

"Ready? I'm ready. There's no time like the present, right?"

"No time like the present." he replied, taking my hand firmly.

Walking out the double doors of the restaurant, we wrapped our arms around one another, trying to stay warm. His arms was still the warmest blanket I'd ever had around me, and his heart, the warmest as well. Then Eric ran ahead to open the doors, and start the car. By the time I got in, the cool air started to warm up. Still shivering, I draped my arms around myself.

In an improbable tone of voice, I said, "Well, lets go. You know the way. I hope we don't interrupt their dinner."

Eric did just as I said. He backed up, smiled an admirable smile, then headed towards my parent's house. It was as quiet as it could be. The radio was off, and the only sound surrounding us, was the sound of a slight wind outside. Taking a deep breathe, I reached into the back seat and grabbed the present I'd wrapped. My hands were fiddling around like I had no control over them until Eric grasped onto them.

"Everything will be fine. Just say what's in your heart and everything will be fine. Be honest, that's all you have to do. Say everything you've ever wanted to say. And maybe that'll be the key to releasing yourself from the past. Beth, if you don't confront them totally, they'll always be the ones binding your heart and your soul. You'll always be in captivity if you don't take a stand right now. I'll be right there with you."

"I'll try to remember that."

Then, only a block away, my heart began to race faster and faster. I tried to take deep breathes, but it didn't seem to work. My fear started taking over what calmness had prevailed. I didn't fear being hurt physically, I feared being hurt mentally. I knew there was nothing my father wouldn't say to me. It didn't matter to him how abandoned I felt, being kind never crossed his mind. He was the only person he ever cared about. The way he looked at things, as long as he was happy, that was all that mattered.

The car made a whistling sound as we casually pulled up into their driveway. Smoke poured from the exhaust, and we sat there quietly for just a moment. I had to gather my thoughts before I barged in on their perfect little Christmas dinner. I didn't want to ruin Melissa's day, but I knew what I was about to do, wouldn't exactly make it the most wonderful Christmas she'd ever had. She was important to me, but my sanity was more important. When I had my mind clear enough, I started to get out, but as I pulled the handle to open the car door, Eric pulled me to him suddenly. He kissed me with such passion, that all of my nervousness was withdrawn. His lips, warm and soft, sent electric shocks throughout my body. It was as though he knew his kiss alone, would ease my mind, and help me to pull myself together completely and without fail. He was right. When our lips ceased to touch, in a way, I still felt them. And the look in his eyes was a look of concern and consideration of my feelings. I could tell he didn't want me to be hurt, but he also wanted me to do, what I believed in my heart, I needed to do.

"Come on," I said, stepping out of the car, and glaring towards that old, two story, imposter of a home.

Making my way around to Eric, I was careful not to slip on what little ice was left on the concrete driveway. We started to walk towards the porch, taking each step in perfect unison. His hands were warm, making me feel warm as well. But I was still shaking inside. Still unsure of what I was going to say, I figured it would come to me when the moment arrived.

Climbing the few steps up to the large porch, one after another, I heard laughter inside. It was strange. I'd never really heard much laughter in that house. Mostly it was screaming, sometimes just pure silence, but seldom laughter. I heard it even louder as I stood by the front door. In slow motion, I raised my finger up to the doorbell. Quickly pushing the tiny button, I turned with my back to the door, but facing Eric. The tension throughout my body was not only felt, but Eric could see it by looking into my bloodshot eyes.

But as Eric started giving me a few words of consolement, the door opened. There stood my mother, and her eyes begin to fill with tears. But before I could say a word to her, my father pushed her out of the way, and saw me.

"What in the hell..."

"Dad, I need to talk to you. I have something for you."

Giving me a look of disbelief, he raised his eyebrows, keeping that growling expression he always had painted across his face. "Something for me?"

"Can I come in?" I asked in a halfway considerate tone of voice.

"Suit yourself." he said stepping aside.

Eric and I held onto one another as we took a few steps into the house. All of the laughter had ceased, leaving silence as I remembered it. Melissa was sitting in the living room not saying a word, and mom stood behind my father as if to be submissive once again.

I handed my father the small Christmas wrapped box. He stood there staring at it for a few seconds, probably in bewilderment of why I was giving him anything.

"Open it!" I said, raising my voice to him.

"You think you can tell me what to do? You think you can use that tone of voice with me, with your father."

"You're not my father," I screamed as loud as I possibly could.

Shock covered his face. It was the first time I'd ever seen him at a loss of words.

"And you're not my mother," I continued, glaring at my mom.

Without any more hesitation, he ripped open the package, finding the papers of my adoption and birth certificate. Mom looked over his shoulder to see what was in the box.

"Oh my God! Oh my God," she said, turning her back to me.

"I never meant for you to find out this way. I wanted to tell you so many times Beth. I just never found the courage to tell you that you weren't my real daughter."

Filling with anger, I lashed out, "I wasn't your daughter at all. You and dad both treated me like I was a stranger. I don't think I ever remember either one of you telling me I was special, or that you loved me. No. I don't remember any kind of affection at all from you.

I just want to know one thing. Why? Why did you want another child." I asked, beginning to sob. "You already had two perfect kids. Why another. Tell me!"

Mom wiped a few tears away, then answered, "I don't know Beth. I always loved little girls. And I used to tell your father.."

"He's not my father! "I yelled.

"I used to tell your...I mean, David how much I wanted another daughter. Oh Beth, I had such dreams for us. I had such plans for our family."

Shaking my head in a quandary, I lowered my voice and tried to continue calmly. "What plans?"

Then dad jumped in abruptly, "Listen little girl, if we hadn't gotten ya, somebody else would've. Your real mama didn't want ya, so we took on her responsibilities."

"How do you know my real mom didn't want me. Maybe she was forced to give me up. Maybe she had no other choice!"

Mom cut in so she could continue her explanation, "Beth, I wanted another child, but your father...David...he didn't...I mean."

"What are you saying. He didn't want another child, but he signed the adoption papers anyway. You both intentionally put my life through hell because one of you wanted another girl, and the other didn't. My God. What is wrong with you? Do you think I had a wonderful childhood? Do you think I had a fairy tale childhood to tell wonderful stories about? hell no. I didn't. And it was all because of you.

For all these years I had a sister, a real sister. For all these years, I just thought there was something wrong with me. I thought that maybe if I had acted better, you would've treated me better. Now I have no family at all. At least before I had a bad family. My sister was a fake, and you and dad were playing mommy and daddy to someone else's kid."

Then dad's face turned red and filled with rage, "You didn't even mention Lewis. He was your brother just as Melissa is your sister."

Taking a chance of being slapped around, I slowly stepped in front of him and got right in his face, "Lewis, Lewis, Lewis. I hated Lewis. But he was perfect wasn't he. He was the most perfect child wasn't he dad. Is that why he humiliated me over and over again in front of my friends? Is that why he slapped me around like a rag doll, or did he get that from you?"

About that time, dad raised his hand as if he were going to knock me down, but Eric jumped in and grabbed him.

"Sir, I'm sorry, but no one will ever lay a hand on her again...not even you. Real men don't hit women, and from what I can tell, you must not be a real man at all."

Eric released his arm and dad flung it back down to his side. I wasn't sure if Eric startled him, or if he just couldn't believe what he'd just said, but he didn't say a word.

Mom couldn't speak anymore. She was too busy crying. I think the only reason she cried at all, was because she was upset I found out, and not sorry she didn't tell me herself. And me, I was out of words. My anger ran wild just long enough for me to get all of my horrible memories off my chest, but stopped before I went too far.

And still, there she sat in the living room., my dearest sister, never saying a word through it all. Her eyes were sunk deep in her head, and she clutched her hands tightly.

She seemed to be glued where she sat. And I couldn't believe she didn't get up to say a word about anything anybody said. She looked like a little girl again. But instead of hiding away in a dark corner, she was hiding away in herself.

When I thought I'd said enough, I told them good-bye rudely, "Have a nice life. And by the way, I will find out who my real mom and dad are." Then glaring straight into my father's eyes, I said, "As far as I'm concerned, both of you are dead, just like Lewis."

Hate dwelled in his eyes as it did mine, and fire seemed to fly from his heart. But mom just walked off, whimpering the whole way. I guess she knew she'd never see me again. And I didn't ever want to come back.

Giving me a hug, Eric wheeled me around and we began to walk towards the door. Dad had already left the room, and I glanced back. For a moment, I saw everything in black and white, as if it were long ago. I could still see Lewis, Melissa and myself, running up and down, up and down, until we'd get in trouble. But then the black and white turned to color and I had found myself once more.

Eric turned the handle, when I heard Melissa running up to me.

"Beth," she said, embracing me tightly, "I love you Sis. You are my sister. Don't ever doubt that."

Tears began flowing down my cheeks like rain, and I held her as firm as I could.

"I know. I don't want to lose you Mel. You'll always be my sister no matter what happens."

When we released one another, wiped our eyes, and looked at each other oppressively. I didn't want to lose contact with her. I wanted her to remain my friend as well as the sister I grew up with.

Laughing slightly, she muttered, "We're a sight, aren't we?"

With a slight grin, I replied, "Yeah, we are."

Then Eric interrupted by taking Melissa's hand, "I'm glad she has you. She's never said anything but good things about you."

Although they didn't really know each other, she leaned over and hugged him gently as if to say "Thank you."

Knowing we needed to leave, I turned to tell Melissa good-bye, but she had walked into the other room. Eric opened the door, and we started out towards the car, when Melissa came running outside.

"Wait!"

I stopped, and when she reached me, she handed me a small boxed which was wrapped up beautifully.

"This is for you. I love you Beth. And Eric, it's wonderful knowing she's got such a terrific man to take care of her."

Holding that tiny present in my hand, Eric guided me to the other side of the car, then helped me in. My heart had dropped, and it seemed so out of sight. Though I wanted to rid myself of unwanted parents, I didn't intend on hurting someone like Melissa, in the process.

The engine roared as he started the car, reminding me I was leaving behind my past. And as we drove off slowly, I carefully opened the package my sister had handed me just before we left. The paper was beautiful. It was a wintery scene, and on top, was a bright red bow. Trying not to tear the paper too badly, I slid it off the box. I folded the wrap and placed it on the seat beside me. Then lifting the top off that small box, my face lit up. It was a locket. And when I turned it over, it had an inscription on back. It said, "To my Sis, with love." Admiring it with every breath, I opened it. Once again, I was overtaken by her surprises. Inside the locket, was an old picture in black and white, of she and I when we were small children. It was a picture of us sleeping together. We were asleep, and I had my head rested on her shoulder. I remembered how much I used to love that picture. Sometimes I would get that one picture out of the album and place it beside my bed. I used to think it would fight off any evil, I guess because we loved each other so much.

"Look Eric."

He pulled over at the nearest stop, and took the locket from me.

"She must really be your sister...not by blood, but by heart."

"She must be." I agreed, taking back the locket which I knew I would cherish from that day forward.

Eric had a confused look on his face as he asked, "Where to now?"

"Home," I replied.

Though I did feel a little pain from all of the lashing of words between my mother, my father, and myself, I felt like I'd done something worthwhile. Like Eric said often, "You've got courage, Beth Laney." And I guess he was right. It took a lot of courage to face my parents the way I did, and for a change, I was proud of myself for something. I didn't back down and let fear take the place of truth. I let the truth roar louder and louder until it was heard.

"What a Christmas Eric."

"But Beth, it was our first Christmas together. Like my grandmother always told me, 'Something good can come out of everything.' And I believe it."

Holding the locket Melissa gave me, in the palm of my hand, I had only good thoughts. For when bad thoughts come into play, happiness is so very far away.

So, as peace covered me, I reached for the pen and notepad in the back seat, and wrote my thoughts for the day:

December 25,

Today I realized something. Family is not just those who are related by blood, they are also those who love you as if they were related by blood. And the ones who claim to be family, that show no love at all, were never your true family to start with. Though Christmas could've been better in the family state of mind, it couldn't have been any better in the regards of love. Because this is the first Christmas in which I felt like I was being ravished with love. And I owe it all to the man that will one day be my husband. I owe it to Eric Norris...my love...my life...my friend.

BETH LANEY (NORRIS)

CHAPTER 16

After writing down my thoughts for the day, I yawned. I knew needed a little rest, so I laid my head back, and closed my eyes, still holding that beautiful locket in my palm tightly. I was afraid to release it.

"Get some sleep babe. We'll be on the road for a while." Eric whispered.

I just nodded in agreement, then twisted and turned until I was comfortable. Though we didn't get up early, I felt like I hadn't slept. And it didn't take long for my eyes to droop more and more until I fell asleep.

For a while, it was only sleep, but then I relived a beautiful moment in a dream. I must've been smiling, because there was nothing about what I envisioned that could've made me feel anything but contentment. It was a remembrance of my sister and I when we were little. In fact, it reminded me of the picture in the locket. I couldn't have been any older than five or six. Mom and dad had been arguing, but we blocked it out completely. She sat with me on my bed brushing my hair. She acted like she was trying to play mommy or something, but I didn't mind. I was glad someone cared enough to do those things for me.

After brushing my hair for the longest time, we went over to the window and stared up at the stars.

"Do you think there's a heaven Beth?" she asked.

"I don't know, I guess."

"Well, I think there's a heaven. I think God gives us love through flowers and trees and every other beautiful thing."

"What about the devil Melissa? Is he real?"

She hesitated, then answered, "Well Sis, I guess if you let yourself be afraid, there's a devil. I don't know. I never really thought of it."

"Well I think of it all the time. Sometimes I think the shadows on the wall are the devil comin' after me. That's when I run and get in bed with you."

She just laughed and replied, "I don't think the devil bothers anybody who believes in God. Do you believe in God Beth?"

With an indecisive look on my face, I answered "Sometimes I do, but sometimes..."

"What?"

"Sometimes I think the devil is the one who watches over me, not God."

She hugged me and patted my back as if to say "I'm here."

We laid down together, and she stroked my hair until I fell asleep. I felt so safe with her. And the image of sisterly love was very powerful.

I began to toss in my seat, when Eric shook me.

"You alright?"

"I'm fine. Why?"

"You were just mumbling something, but I couldn't understand you. I wanted to make sure you weren't having one of your strange dreams."

"No. Nothing like that. In fact, it was a good one for a change." I said with a slight grin on my face.

The sun was gradually going out of sight, and I watched it attentively. The blue, gray and orange streaks of light seemed to fade into one another creating a kind of rainbow in the skyline darkness. The colors were amazing. You never see colors such as those in the sky, until the light gives in to the night. But the view which only lasted moments, is the view that makes some dreams come true.

It took me in until all of the light was gone, and there was nothing but a pale moon, and a few scattered stars left in the atmosphere above. Another galaxy, another world was probably out there waiting to be discovered. But we were occupying the only world we knew. And sometimes I wondered if things would turn around for people like myself. It made me feel a little unwanted just knowing my mother gave me away, but what made me feel even worse, was the fact that my adoptive parents didn't want me either.

The longer I thought of hurtful things, the worse I became, so I put my mind into a different gear. I gazed at Eric solemnly driving, as if he had no worries in the world, and I wished to God I was more like him. I wanted his loving attitude, caring heart, and consideration, to rub off on me. And I knew only time would help me to turn my life in that direction. But it did feel good being next to him. Although it was quiet, he and I were together, inseparable.

I noticed him trying to nod off a few times, and I began to worry.

"Eric, do you want to stop at the next town and stay there for the night?"

Rubbing his eyes, he replied, "That's probably not a bad idea. I'm getting pretty tired. Driving always exhausts me faster than anything."

We passed a sign that said "Texarkana-23 miles." I didn't remember going through Texarkana on my way home, but then again, it was late when I was traveling. I hurried through every town without looking at names at all.

"Ever heard of Texarkana Eric?"

"Sure. I've got a friend who lives near there. They call it the 'Twin cities.' They call it that because half of it is in Texas, and the other half is in Arkansas. There's a boundary between the two called 'State Line.' Neat huh. You learn somethin' new every day."

"Is it very big?"

"About average I guess. It's not real small, but it's not like Dallas either. I guess there's somethin' to be said about smaller towns."

I glared back at the road ahead of us. It was clear, not icy at all, and not many cars on the road. As we got closer to Texarkana, I noticed a billboard on the side of the road. It said "Cuff & Collar for Tall and Big Men." And I had to make an aggravating remark to Eric. The moment needed a little humor. Things had gotten too quiet for me.

"Hey, maybe we should go visit that store in the mornin'," I laughed.

"I'm not big," he said with a smirk.

"Well, you never know. It does say tall. And you're pretty tall."

He glanced at me once more then back to the road. I guess he didn't think it was funny. He normally took aggravation quite well, but he was tired. That was all I could figure. What got me, was that I didn't even get a half smile out of him.

Making it to town, we couldn't make up our minds where to stay. Most of the hotels seemed full, so we stopped and asked someone for help. We pulled into a gas station and the attendant walked over. He was wearing greasy overalls with a T-shirt on under it, that I suppose, used to be white. His jaw was full of tobacco, and he had on a cap that looked like it had been through the ringer.

"Excuse me sir. Could you tell us where would be a good place to stay in this town?"

He looked over to the side, scratched himself, and said, "You two newlyweds?"

"Well, not yet, but..."

"I got the perfect place for ya. It's an old mansion over on Main. It's a bed and breakfast now. I hear it's quite a place. All them antique things everywhere. I bet you and the misses would love it, bein' newly weds and all."

We looked at one another, then Eric asked for directions to the place the man had described. Although he looked half-witted, his directions were simple and clear. Eric wrote them down, so we wouldn't get lost or confused. We were both tired, and neither one of us felt like driving around in circles.

Taking the stranger's advice, we followed the directions he'd given us. And after making the last turn, sitting on the corner, was a sight like none I'd ever seen before. The sign read "Mansion on Main." And it was a mansion, no doubt. It had big beautiful ionic columns which accented the forest green trim. And the garland which swagged down from each balcony, gave it the glorious touch of Christmas. Flowers were set in the garland, adding color, and the feeling of being at home.

As we stepped out of the car, Eric took my hand. For a second, I felt like Dorothy in the <u>Wizard of Oz.</u> The walkway seemed like a yellow brick road that would lead to wonderful gifts and treasures.

The closer we came to that exquisite home from the past, I felt all of the cold feelings inside of me turn into warm soothing expectations. The character it had was amazing. It had something special.

When we made it up the steps, I started reading a plaque which was elegantly placed on the right side of the door. It read:

Moores-Burke
Ragland Home

The residence was erected in 1895 for Rachel Perry Godbold-Moores (1830-1904). Her husband David (1827-1892), was a member of the Pioneer Moores family. Henry Koerner designed the neo-classical house with decorative fish-scale shingling. The interior has elegant Parquet flooring. Robert Emmet Burk bought the old house in 1904. It was occupied from 1920 to 1965 by the S.M. Ragland family.

Recorded Texas Historic Landmark 1978

After reading the plaque, Eric squeezed me tightly then rang the doorbell. We both feared there would be no rooms left to rent because it was Christmas night. Everything was very still, but after a moment or two, we heard footsteps. The door slowly opened, and there stood a woman with a friendly essence about her. She seemed to glow with vivacity, and her smile alone was a welcome change to what I was used to.

"Don't stay out there in the cold. Come on in," the woman said in a soothing voice.

We stepped inside, and what I saw was completely amazing. I couldn't seem to take my eyes off all the beauty surrounding me. With Eric still holding my hand, I looked up at him briefly, then back at the innkeeper. It didn't seem to make any difference what day it was. I got the feeling we would've been welcome any time.

"Come in and make yourselves at home. My name is Inez, and my husband's name is Lee. We take care of the place. Come and sit in the dining room you two, and I'll make you some coffee, she said politely.

We followed her into the dining room and sat down. The atmosphere was of a comfortable nature. I could tell Eric felt the same. He had such a satisfied look on his face. It felt good to be in a place where being friendly and courteous meant something. For a long time, being friendly and courteous only got me into trouble. My father used to tell me, "Don't be too nice Beth. People will think you're a pushover." And for the longest time, that was exactly how I thought.

When Inez came back with our coffee, she began talking to us as if she'd known us forever. And the strange thing about it, was that I felt like I'd known her forever too. She was just that kind of person.

As Eric and I admired all of the things in the house, Inez asked, "You want to take a look around? I don't mind at all. And if you're thinkin' of stayin', after you see all the rooms, you can decide which one you want to stay in for the night. They're all lovely, but everybody that passes though, has a preference. And I'm sure you will too."

Eric turned to me as if he were waiting for me to say something, but he could see in my eyes just what I wanted. We nodded our heads, and followed her once again. It was a unique experience to be able to see such a wonderful piece of history, and just the thought of how much things had changed over the years, astonished me. Just by seeing the old trinkets from the past, I knew there was once a "simple life." But when chaos and destruction took over, simplicity was gone.

Entering the first room, Inez began to tell about its' history in detail.

"This is called the governor's sweet. The home is a hundred years old. It was built in 1895, and this old piano they found, happens to be a hundred years old as well. The flooring is made of pine, and the bed in this room is an antique canopy bed. It's very unique. In fact, this room was originally used as a music room. See the treble clef archway here? That's why it was put there."

Out of curiosity, I stared at this couch looking, velvet covered piece of furniture in the corner, "What's this?"

She laughed and replied, "Oh my dear, that's what'cha call a 'fainting couch.' Back in the old days, the women used to wear corsets so tight, that they would actually faint from not being able to breath. It's quite funny, but it's true."

Looking over at Eric, I laughed with her and remarked, "Can you imagine that? Things have changed haven't they?"

"Yes they have my dear, "she replied, walking out of the "Governors Suite."

We continued on our tour of that beautiful mansion. But as we approached the stairway, something else caught my eye. On the wall, from the bottom, all the way to the top, were old, black and white photographs of families which used to live in the home. And just looking at such photographs, made me envy what innocence used to dwell, so unlike how things turned out after time had taken its' toll.

At the bottom of the stairway, a large, stain-glass window took me in. It contained every color of the rainbow blending into one another exquisitely. In a way, it seemed as though, if you were to stare at it long enough, it could hypnotize you. That was just how beautiful it was. It was nothing short of breathtaking.

Eric and Inez had reached the top before I could stop peering at such a wonderful vision.

So I carefully went up the stairs to join them. Then Inez started towards another room of the house which was quite interesting.

"This room is called 'The Butler's Garrett."

"Why? Did the Butler really sleep here?" I asked.

She grinned, "Yes dear. This is the smallest room of the house, so the Moore's put the butler here. They wanted to save the larger rooms for guests, if they should ever have any."

"That was a dumb question, wasn't it?" I said as my face began to flush a little.

"No. There's no dumb questions, only dumb answers."

She went further down the hallway, and stopped at another room, but the door was closed. It read "Rachel's Bed Chamber."

"What is this room?" I asked curiously.

She shook her head and replied, "We have one rule here. If a door is closed, we assume someone is occupying it. We are here to give a home-like environment, and we sure wouldn't want to invade anyone's privacy while they're staying with us. Come on, I saved the best for last."

My anticipation was great as we followed her to the last room. I looked at Eric as if I were a kid in a candy store. Everything she said, I absorbed completely. And I couldn't wait to see what was next on the agenda for us to behold.

She stopped for a moment, and pointed out a beautiful oblong table in the middle of the hallway by the top of the stairs.

"We do our best to make our guest feel welcome, so we try and make them feel more at home with little things such as this. We keep hot coffee and refreshments here just in case someone doesn't feel like going downstairs. It makes it convenient for everyone."

Then, stepping up a small step, we entered the corner room. I knew right away that was the room I wanted.

"This is the 'Penthouse Suite.' It wasn't originally a part of the house. It used to be a sunroom before the house was restored several years ago. Most people pick this room above any of the others. It's understandable. It is the most modern, but it does have a few small touches of the past here and there. See these pictures of roses. These pictures were taken right in the front yard, in the rose garden, in the spring of course. Like I said, most people like this room the best."

We wandered around the room admiring every little detail of elegance it had to offer. And as we walked to the entrance way of the bathroom, I was amazed at what I saw. There were two claw-footed bathtubs toe to toe. They were dark green and very different from anything I'd ever seen before.

"Oh yes, the famous toe to toe tubs. If you look closely, one is longer than the other. One is for the man and the other for the woman. And they both have shell shaped pillows at the end of each one for comfort."

Eric rubbed up against me, and commented, "Two? Why do we need two?"

I tried to keep Inez from hearing him, although he wasn't being very quiet with his sensual remarks. And by the time she came to where we were standing, I had convinced Eric to refrain from any more personal commentary.

There were two gowns hanging on the wall in the oblong bathroom. As I picked them up, Inez explained what they were, and why they were there.

"You know, back years ago, this is what people used to wear to bed. And we provide these for our guests. We think it helps to take you back in time a little better if you're wearing what people wore a century ago. It makes it fun anyway."

Then from downstairs, a voice called for Inez.

"Excuse me for a minute. I'll be right back. Look around if you like. There's a lot to look at." she said as she walked out of the room.

With a huge sigh, I couldn't help thinking how beautiful everything was. Until we were blessed by such a wonderful view of the past, I didn't think anything would've been able to take my mind off of all that had happened to me, but the old restored home, also restored my faith as well. If something which was in such horrible shape, could be replenished to perfection, then I knew there had to be hope for me. Although I felt crushed inside, at some point in my life, I knew I'd either crumble and fall, or come out on top and be a winner. And if I had my choice, I knew which one I wanted to happen. For once, I felt like hanging on until everything was put back into place.

The natural colored blinds on the endless windows, were open, and the head lights from all of the cars which passed were streaking by, one after another. So, I casually stepped over beside the bed, and near the windows. There were a few people walking on the sidewalks below, holding hands. And my eyes illuminated when I noticed a horse-drawn carriage on the other side of the street. The horses had long flowing manes, and the top of the carriage was black and gold. It looked so romantic.

"Look Eric. Look down there. Isn't it fascinating."

"You want to go see about taking a ride around town in a carriage?" he said, as his eyes gleamed tremendously.

"You mean it?"

"I wouldn't ask if I didn't mean it. Come on, let's go tell Inez that we'll be right back."

Without hesitation, hand in hand, we hurried down the stairway and found Inez, the Innkeeper, just about to walk back up to where we were.

"We're gonna see if we can catch a ride from that old carriage outside." Eric said, thrilled with the anticipation of another first together.

She smiled, shook her head, and opened the door for us. She could tell how much in love we were. It was far too much to hide. I guess the looks on our faces said it all. And awaiting to take a fantastic ride on a dazzling, but simple old-fashioned carriage, was like a dream come true. A wonderful dream. I wanted to be able to share unusual, and memorable romantic things with Eric. All my dreams were becoming reality, one by one.

We carefully walked up to the horses, cautious not to frighten them. Then the old man guiding them, spoke to us in a country, but friendly voice.

"Bet you two wanna tour of our little town. We only make a block, but if you've never rode in a carriage, it'll be quite an experience."

"Yes sir, we do. Is it too late?"

"It's never too late. Hop in and I'll try not to go too awful fast."

Eric took my hand and helped me in before he got in himself. I felt like I should've had on a long dress and a bonnet, like women used to wear long ago. And as Eric crawled in beside me, I pictured him in a suit, bow tie and a top hat. Then I laughed at myself for being so silly.

"What's so funny?" Eric asked, looking at me out of the corner of his eye.

"Oh nothing. You know me. I think too much."

He just shook his head and focused on the scenery which surrounded us. Although we weren't in a wooded area, or even near a pond or stream, things were different. The people seemed friendlier than where I grew up. And the moon reflected down on us like a spotlight in a Broadway show.

The wind gently caressed my neck and whisked through my hair at a slow, but steady pace. It didn't seem as cold, for some reason, as it did when we first arrived. Maybe it was because Eric was blanketing me with his warm, compassionate arms. In my eyes, just that, would remove any ounce of cold which may linger. It never took much for him to make me feel secure. The way about him made all the difference in the world.

After slowly turning several corners, and enjoying the peacefulness of the night, we made one last turn which took us back to where we started. The old man pulled on the rains, and the horses halted immediately.

"Well kids, ya enjoy the ride. I know it ain't much, but I promise you'll never forget the buggy ride you took in Texarkana."

"Thank you sir." we said, as we paid him and walked back across the street to the old mansion.

But before we even reached the door, it opened, and there stood Inez.

"How'd ya like it? From those smiles, I bet you've never done that before."

I blushed a little, scooted next to Eric, and replied, "No we haven't, but I'm glad we had the chance."

She shut the door behind us, and pointed out one last thing.

"Y'all do want to stay don't you?"

I almost answered her before she could get the question out of her mouth, "Yes we do."

"Well then, I thought I'd tell you about one thing that makes the stay here special and unique." she said, as she walked over to a hat rack sitting in the corner. "See these old-fashioned hats here. There's some for the men and some for the women. Pick whichever one you like. And when it's breakfast time, put it on. We all kinda act like we're back in the old days. And by putting on a hat from that time period, it makes you feel that way. You don't have to if you don't want to, but it's fun for those who do."

Eric stepped over to the hat rack, picked one, and walked around in a circle modeling it for me. I couldn't help but laugh. He was such a joker sometimes. Inez indulged in his humor, and laughed along with me.

"You've got quite a man there." she said.

Wiping away a few tears of laughter, I replied, "I know...I know."

"Well kids, let me get Lee down here to help you with your things, and then you can get settled in."

"Thanks, but I think we can handle it. We've taken up enough of your time."

Carefully walking up the stairway with our bags, we heard Inez tell us goodnight from down below. And Eric and I were taken in by her friendly hospitality. Deciding to stay in such a wonderful place, filled me with bliss. And I looked forward to being in such historical locale for the night. It was different, but in a good kind of way. At least it reminded us there was still many types of romance lingering all around.

We put our things in the splendid room which we had chosen to spend one memorable night, and I danced around and around in circles displaying my excitement. He glanced at me and shook his head with a slight bit of a grin spread across his masculine veneer. I couldn't help it. It felt as though we were far away from the rest of the world I couldn't have been any happier. I was with the man I loved dearly, staying in a beautifully untarnished historical home. I didn't think anything could get any better.

I walked over to the bed which was covered in a hand knitted comforter, and noticed something lying on the pillow. It was some kind of prayer the Innkeepers provided for all who stayed in their home. It read:

Tammy D. Thompson

—To Our Guests—

"A Prayer For The Stranger Within Our Gates"

We pray that God will grant you peace and rest while you are under our roof.

May this be your "second" home. May those you love be near you in thoughts and dreams. May you be comfortable and happy in our house, and when you leave, may the guardian angel, share your journey home.

We are all travelers. From birth till death, we travel until we reach our destination in eternity. May these days be pleasant for you and profitable for society, helpful for those you meet, and joy to those who know and love you best. May the blessings that come from Jesus Christ abide in your hearts always.

Mansion on Main,
Texarkana, USA

I sat it down on the nightstand in front of me, and when I turned around, Eric was standing there with one of those old gowns on. He looked so silly, but cute at the same time.

"Go ahead, put yours on. I bet you'd look gorgeous in it, he said in a playful voice.

So I went into the bathroom, took the gown off the hanger, and slipped it on. I looked into the mirror, and Eric walked up behind me. We looked as though we had stepped out of a 1920's movie, but it was fun. Eric had on a long, striped nightshirt which buttoned all the way up, and mine touched the floor. It had a little lace, but other than that, it wasn't fancy at all. For a moment, I felt like we were portraying a role in an old movie. For a change, it was nice to be someone else. It was nice to forget about the terrible world around us and step back and smell the roses. For way too long, our serious side had taken over, but the humorous side was beginning to show through.

While in the bathroom, we turned to admire the way the bathtubs were placed, toe to toe. It was so unique. Then his hands began to roam. I thought he was trying to nudge me towards the bed, but he wasn't. Instead, he started tickling me. Curled up in a ball trying to free myself from his grips, I laughed continuously until he stopped. I couldn't stand to be tickled, and he knew that.

"Would you stop?" I told him abruptly, but kidding at the same time.

He took off his old nightshirt, and went over to the oval shaped bathtubs. Turning on the water in both of them, he glanced back at me with a smirk on his face.

"Come on baby, lets take a bath. This one's yours, and this one's mine."

Playing along with his little game, I agreed. I took off my gown and waited for the tubs to fill. There was a little yellow rubber ducky on the table in between the two bathtubs. Eric picked it up and squeezed it once or twice. His boisterous attitude was refreshing and comely. I liked seeing him have a good time. And he was having a great time. The look on his face told me how much he was enjoying our stay so far.

Once the tubs were full enough, we carefully crawled in and laid our heads back on the shell shaped, air filled pillow at the end of each tub. We were facing one another, and Eric kept flipping water on me. The difference in my bath and his, was that he had put bubbles in mine. Bubbles covered me up to my neck, and it felt remarkable. Those tiny air pockets bursting all around my face gave me a tingling feeling. For a while, it was as though I was a Queen being pampered. But instead, I wanted to be the one doing the pampering. It gave me a sense of worth knowing I could fulfil his needs, and before the night was over, I knew I would fulfil any need he had, thoroughly. His needs came before mine. And since I'd found someone to care for, I didn't want to hold back anything. My love was unconditional, and his was exceptional.

After a while, I felt like I was going to shrivel up, so I got out and wrapped one of their soft, thick towels around me. Then I threw one over to Eric as he stumbled out as well. After drying off, we put the old gowns back on. I was still shivering, so I huddled under the covers in bed while Eric turned on the television.

He joined me, snuggling up close and tight. It took a while for us to regain any warmth, but we were still having a wonderful time. We watched a little T.V., then decided to turn in for the night. The day had been adventurous to say the least, and I was worn out. But the warm water from the bath had relaxed every muscle in my body. Nothing felt tense or disturbed.

Eric got up, turned the T.V. and the light off, and wandered back to bed. And in the process, he almost knocked over a radiant poinsettia. I giggled a little, but I didn't think he heard me. He just fell back into the spot I saved for him, right next to me. Arm in arm, we were wrapped up into one another. No other position could've been more comfortable. That was exactly where I wanted to be...in his arms.

Though we wanted to make love, out of respect of Inez and her husband, we sustained. At times, we would get loud, and I sure didn't want to disturb anyone who might be anywhere near us. Besides, being there was enough. I didn't need to make love to him to feel his love. I felt it whether we were making love, or just lying next to one another. It made no difference to me.

Lying there in the darkness, we could hear the cars passing every little bit, and from afar, the noise from a train, was faint, but distinguishable. The noises didn't bother me, but instead, it put me to sleep. To me, it was the sounds of a peaceful, kind town.

And I wanted to cherish the moments there in that place. For there would only be another set of pictures in my mind of Eric and I. They would be memorable pictures which would soon represent the past. Although I treasured the moment at hand, I knew how quickly time would engulf such precious moments. So I held onto him tight and took in each breath, each noise, and each vision entirely.

I closed my eyes and embraced what silence there was in between the dull discord outside. There was no doubt in my mind I would have a more peaceful slumber than I'd had in a long time, and I had a feeling the morning would bring a magnificent new day. I couldn't imagine what else it would bring. For being in a place as lovely as this, the following day had to be incredible. And there was no doubt in my mind this would be a memory I'd cherish until the day I expired from this earth.

I took a deep breath, and the smell around the room filled my senses with tranquility. It was unforgettable, and the feeling of love entrapped me. That was one thing I didn't mind being imprisoned by…love.

I nestled my body closely to Eric's as I fell off into a wonderful, not frightening, dreamland. He and I were running through an open field dressed in old time clothing. Eventually, we fell down onto the caressing, green grass which swayed back and forth, almost hypnotizing. And the sun shined on us like a spotlight from heaven. Like two stars in a Broadway show, we took the spotlight, and danced around and around, laughing all the while.

A smile appeared on my face as I slept. For once, I didn't have to run from monsters. For once, I didn't have to fight the night for serenity because it had become my friend. I was consuming every ounce of happiness my visions of the night, had to show me, and grasping onto them fastly. Though they were only visions, ones which would fade as morning approached, I didn't care. Because while sleeping, they were mine to indulge upon. And I wouldn't have given that up for anything.

The darkness of the night soon turned to dawn before I knew it, and as I opened my eyes, the only feeling I had, was a feeling of being totally refreshed. Eric was still lying there asleep, breathing slowly...in and out, calm breathes of relaxation. I wanted to touch him, but I didn't want to disturb his peaceful sleep. He looked like a tiny baby as he rested placidly. And I dared not to interrupt such an innocence. It would've been a crime to wake him, so I carefully eased out of bed and put on my new delicate satin robe. It felt like rose petals against my skin, so sensual. But another reason I loved it so, was because Eric had gotten it for me right after the first time he and I made love.

Startling both of us, the phone rang. I quickly ran over and answered it.

"Hello."

"Good morning. This is Lee, Inez's husband. I just called to make sure you two had a good night's sleep, and to make sure you were enjoying your stay so far."

"Yes sir, we are. It's beautiful here." I replied in a sleepy voice.

"Well, breakfast will be ready in fifteen minutes, if you want to join us. And remember, pick a hat before you come down. It might sound silly, but it's a lot of fun."

"We'll be down shortly. Thank you for calling." I said, hanging up the phone.

Eric tossed and turned as if he didn't want to rise to greet the beautiful new day, so I crawled in beside him and kissed him gently on his cheek.

"Wake up sleepy head. Throw some clothes on so we can go eat breakfast. Remember, Inez claims to be a wonderful cook. And I've never heard of you turning down good home cooked food."

He rubbed his eyes and sat up on the side of the bed. Stretching left and right, I heard every bone in his body crack. It was his usual routine. I handed him his robe and we both went into the bathroom to run a brush through our hair. I didn't dare go downstairs with my hair flying in ten different directions. If anything, I was particular about that.

Once we made ourselves look presentable, we walked out into the hallway. Eric started to go down the stairs when I stopped him.

"Hey, you forgot to pick a hat."

He just laughed and replied, "I'm not wearing a hat."

"Yes you are."

"No I'm not." he replied once more.

Then I put on one of my best sad faces until he agreed to play along. As Inez had said, it makes the stay more interesting. And I believed her, so I picked up one of the large hats on the top of the rack.

"How about this one. You like it?"

With a bit of a snicker, he shook his head then reached for one himself. He picked a black hat which kinda looked like a top hat, but not so tall. He looked whimsical, but I didn't say a word. If I had, he would've taken it off, and I wanted to role play for a while. In fact, I felt like I'd been role playing all night long already, and it was great.

We looked at one another and tried not to laugh, but it was hard. We both looked like we had gone back in time, but so did everyone else. Another couple headed down the stairway with hats on as well, so we didn't feel near as stupid. As long as we weren't the only ones playing along, it didn't make us feel the least bit funny.

We went down to join everyone at the breakfast table, and to my surprise, it was like being in grandma's kitchen. Everyone was talking to one another as if they were all family, and Inez and her husband Lee, acted like grandparents fixing an old-fashioned breakfast.

We sat down and tried to make ourselves comfortable. It wasn't hard to do because everyone acted as though they knew one another. And that alone, put us more at ease.

Peering around the room, I noticed several things. The centerpiece on the table was what I noticed the most. It was an arrangement of many different flowers combined into one large, hourglass shaped vase. There were roses, carnations, daises and many more kinds of flowers, giving the room an aroma which was breathtaking. I wouldn't have minded staying there forever. It bestowed that much pleasure.

Then, almost exactly seven o'clock, they begin to bring breakfast to us.

"I hope you all enjoy what I've cooked today. We have shirred eggs with honey cured ham, orange pecan French toast with vermong maple syrup, cheese blintz with fresh seasonal fruit, healthy parfait with yogurt, granola and fresh fruit, and chicken a la Mansion with sourdough biscuits." she said so elegantly. "Enjoy, and if there's anything else I can get for anyone, please don't hesitate to tell me."

Looking at such an appetizing spread, my stomach started screaming. Eric didn't wait one minute before digging in. He acted as though he hadn't eaten in weeks. I was a bit embarrassed by the way he shoveled down his food, but it was also funny in a way. Inez walked over to him, put her hand on his shoulder, and laughed.

"It must be as good as I intended it to be."

"Yes ma'am," he said with his mouth full.

It was delicious. The flavor of each dish was so satisfying. I hadn't eaten a meal like that in a long time. In fact, I didn't remember ever having such a wonderful breakfast. Like she told us the night before, they did their best to satisfy the needs of everyone who stayed there, and she was right. We were more than pleased by the way we were treated. It did feel like home, a real home.

Savoring each and every bite, we took our time eating. Inez and her husband Lee, came into the dining room and joined us. They were both interesting, but in different ways. Inez told us about the Cajun restaurant they owned in New Orleans at one time, and their story was fascinating. She did most of the talking. Lee just nodded his head in agreement at everything she said. It wasn't as though he was being lead around by the tail or anything. I think he just liked letting her have the spotlight. And you could tell she loved to talk. But it didn't bother Eric and I. For the most part, it was refreshing hearing about the successes of someone so delightful to be around. I was glad they were doing so good. Although I didn't know them very well, I knew them enough to know they deserved the best. Anyone who was caring enough to let a us stay on Christmas day, and treat us like family, had to be exceptional people. And I had no doubt they were extremely exceptional.

We pushed our chairs away from the table, thanked the Innkeepers for their hospitality, and walked back up to our room to get bathed and dressed for the day. The smile on my face seemed to grow more and more the longer we remained in such a soothing atmosphere. I didn't want to leave. I felt as though I had gained a few new friends which I didn't even know the day before. And I knew anytime we were to come back through that small town of Texarkana, we would be welcome by Inez and her husband Lee, with open arms.

Eric went to take a bath and I was right behind him until I noticed a small tapestry covered book lying on the white wicker table, in front of the small couch in the corner. I flipped through it and realized it was diary entries of all of the people who had stayed in that room. They all wrote of their stay. Some were pages long, others were only a few paragraphs, but they all wrote what a wonderful and unique time they had there.

Making Eric wait for me, I picked up a pen lying on the table. I sat down and begin to write down my thoughts and feeling about our stay:

> *I never thought I could feel so comfortable around people I barely knew, but I did. Eric and I needed the time away from the world which was cruel and uncontrollable. And when we saw this beautiful house on the corner, it was a vision.*
>
> *Inez portrayed such a mothering attitude that I felt I was really at home. In fact, the stay here was much more pleasant than my stay at home.*
>
> *What took me in most, was the old pictures all around. Everyone looked peaceful in each photo. Staying here gave me a new sense of hope. It made me realize that some things do stay the same. Although years may have passed, this old house remained the same.*
>
> *We were proud to be able to spend time in the company of such wonderful people, and we thank them more than they could ever know.*
>
> *We'll never forget this place, or at least I know I won't. Each picture, each antique sat neatly around, and all of the love shown here, will remain with me forever. It was an experience that I was glad I had the chance of having.*
>
> *Thank you Inez for showing me things can stay simple and carefree. I almost forgot that until you reminded me by opening up your heart and home.*
>
> *Beth Laney(Norris)*

Placing the book carefully back where I had found it, I heard Eric calling for me, "You comin'? What are you doing in there?"

"Nothing. I'll be right there." I replied.

This time when I joined Eric, we shared the same tub. It was a tight fit, but it was interesting. We flipped and flopped until most of the water was on the floor instead of in the bathtub. Then we figured we'd better try and clean up our mess a little before we left. So we got out, dried the floor and ourselves.

Though we had plenty of time until noon, which was check-out time, we decided we needed to get back home as soon as possible. The campus would be peaceful because there was probably no one back yet. We still had more than a week before we officially had to return, but things just didn't turn out that way. Anyway, I felt like I needed to see Mrs. Downs as soon as possible. I wanted to share the things I'd found out, with her. I thought she might be able to make some sense out of the whole thing. I doubted it, but it was worth a shot. Anything I thought I could do to put the many jumbled pieces in place, I wanted to try. Because I knew I would never be able to go on with my life as long as there were a few missing links. And at the time, there were a few links I had to find before anything in my life seemed right again.

We casually got dressed, pulled out our suitcases, and packed our things. But the entire time I kept wishing I didn't have to leave. What a wonderful place that would be to live. And as Eric placed the last few things we had, in our bags, he leaned his forehead against mine and muttered, "I hope all of this made you feel better. But I can tell by just looking at you, that it did. I love you babe. And it doesn't matter if we ever see this place again, at least we'll always be able to carry it in our hearts."

I nodded my head in agreement and flipped our suitcases shut. Eric took most of the bags down ahead of me, leaving only one small, over the shoulder carrying case. I flung it over my left shoulder and stepped slowly towards the door. But before I left, I went over to where I had laid that little prayer which was lying the night stand the night before. I picked it up, folded it into, and I placed it into my purse for safe keeping. It would soon be put into my scrapbook of memories, for the adventure of staying at the "Mansion on Main," was one adventure nor I or Eric would never forget.

All of the old pictures hanging all around me as I stepped down the stairway, seemed to follow me as if they didn't want me to leave. It sounds silly, but our stay there, gave me such a passionate attitude towards the future. For a short while, everything appeared so perfect, and although I knew things would eventually turn to normal again, it didn't matter. My heart was softened by Inez and her husband Lee, and my views about the past were transformed. Although I still didn't know exactly how people lived decades ago, or even a century ago, I did know they were happy with simple things. I guess that's how everyone should still be. Simple things sometimes mean more than anything else.

When I reached the front door, I noticed our bags sitting by the coat rack in the corner, but I didn't see Eric anywhere. Then as I glanced out the window, I saw him on the verandah. The look on his face was dignified, but sad. So I stepped out the door to join him. He was sitting on the swing swaying repeatedly back and forth. I walked up to him and placed my hand on his shoulder. His feelings were generated from his heart through my fingertips compelling me to experience the depth of his emotions. And as the chilling brisk zephyr whisked by, chill bumps arose all over each inch of my flesh. But Eric seemed to refrain from letting the cold torture him. He seemed to ignore it. Then I knew I had to find out what was wrong. It wasn't like him to be gloomy. He was the most vital and optimistic person I knew. It wasn't often he let himself be drug down by worries or sorrows.

When I sat down beside him, his eyes cast a spell on me when he gave a short glance in my direction. It was like we were sharing the same heart, mind and soul. In a way, I felt like I knew what he was thinking and feeling. But to be completely sure, I tried to talk to him.

"Eric," I whispered lightly, "What's wrong?"

He just shook his head and replied solemnly, "I don't want to leave, do you?"

"No, but you know we have to. We can't stay here forever."

"But wouldn't it be nice. Wouldn't it be wonderful to be able to set ourselves aside from the craziness in our lives and just stay here."

I smiled in agreement, then tried to reassure him, "Eric, we don't need to be here to set ourselves aside from anything. You know why? Because like you told me before, you have to ride the tides before you can enjoy calm and peaceful waters."

Chuckling, he shook his head, "Yeah. How'd you get to be so damned smart?"

"I guess I learned from the best," I replied.

Sitting there for another moment or two, he stood, took my hand, and led me back inside to get our things. As we opened the door, there stood the Innkeepers, Inez and Lee, still with a smile on their faces. I don't think I ever saw them when they weren't smiling. But after staying there only one night, I knew why they never frowned. If Eric and I lived there, I knew we'd feel nothing but pure and untainted happiness.

"Well kids, I guess this is where we say good-bye."

With melancholy expressions on our faces, we nodded, "Yeah, we need to get on the road. We still have a few hours of driving before we make it back home."

Inez walked up and embraced me as if she'd known me all her life. And as strange as it may seem, I felt the same. I guess because of the generous hospitality she offered to us. I knew I'd miss her.

Lee reached over and firmly shook Eric's hand. It was like departing from a loving family, even though they weren't family at all. But then I remembered what Mrs. Downs had told me right before I left for home. She told me that family is a feeling of love from one person to another. It doesn't have to be a blood relative to feel a sense of family. And she was right. I felt a connection that I hoped would never be broken. And in the back of my mind, I knew I'd travel back to the "Mansion on Main," just to see them.

CHAPTER 17

After loading the car, we got in and tried to get as comfortable as we possibly could considering we still had several hours of driving left before we made it to our destination. And for a change, I wasn't the least bit tired. I had gotten such a wonderful sleep the night before that my entire body felt rejuvenated and full of energy. I hadn't felt that rested in long time. But I knew one day we would go back to that beautifully restored, full of life, unforgettable home on the corner of Main, in the small town of Texarkana.

Trying to lift my spirits, Eric suggested we go shopping. Even though we didn't know the town very well, he told me we'd find a nice little shop where he could buy me something to raise my spirits. He intrigued me with the gestures which went along with what he said. The way he raised his eyebrows when he was enthusiastic, or the quiver in his lip when he talked, were a few things I cherished about him. And it wasn't often that I'd turn him down for anything, so I conformed to his offer immediately. There was no reason for me not to want to.

Hurriedly we backed out and followed the signs pointing to downtown, the main part of town which had everything from jewelry to clothes, and much more. And as we drove, I felt more at ease about leaving such a magnificent place. Besides, I didn't want to leave Texarkana until I'd at least seen a little of what it had to offer.

Entering the heavy traffic on the narrow streets of the downtown area, I watched all of the people going from one store to the next. Everyone seemed so happy. From what I gathered, everyone knew everyone. It was like one big happy family. Men were tipping their hats to the ladies, and the ladies would just blush from embarrassment. It was like taking a courtesy trip back into the past.

After scrambling for a parking spot, we got out and walked several blocks going in and out of all kinds of stores. The sidewalk was crowded, but not enough to where we couldn't get through. We didn't have much money, but when we found this little jewelry store on the corner, Eric found something that caught his eye. It was a tri-tone, gold, diamond cut bracelet. It was small, but elegant. And when we saw the diminutive tag which said "sale," our eyes stared even more intensely.

About that time, a lady walked up, "Would you like to look at it? It is beautiful isn't it?"

Nodding my head, I replied, "Yes, please."

The lady took out a key, opened the case, and handed it to me carefully. My eyes were affixed on that shiny piece as Eric took my wrist and put it on me. I was in a trans. I'd never been treated with such respect and love. And I could tell he wanted to buy it for me.

I unhooked it and let it slide off onto the counter, "It is lovely. Thank you for letting us look." I said taking Eric's hand to walk out the door.

But before I could take many steps, he stopped me, "I want you to have it. I can afford it Beth. I told you once before, I want you to feel like a queen."

Staring into his passionate eyes, I replied, "Eric, you don't have to buy me things to make me feel like a queen. I feel like a queen every time I'm with you. Jewelry won't make me care for you any more."

"None the less, it's yours," he said turning to the lady and requested, "We'll take it."

Though hard-headed, he was sweet and generous. He was just about as stubborn as I was when it came to something he wanted to do. But I couldn't object to such a impressionable gesture, but instead make him feel like he was my prince charming or my night in shining armor.

He paid for it gallantly and came over to me, "This is yours, I think."

The lady behind the counter looked at us as if she was envious of what we had. There was no doubt to anyone around us, that Eric and I were very much in love. And to be envied by others was something I wasn't used to, but also something I could learn to like.

As we strolled a little further down the road, the sun put a spotlight on us. It took away from the cold enough for us to enjoy our serene visit to a compelling town. Though the wind was cold, the rays from above warmed our skin a little. And there were still a few more stores to make before finishing the circle which took us back to our car.

Going in and out of a couple more shops, we didn't buy anything, but it was interesting. It was a good change for me anyway. My body felt relaxed and vivacious at the same time. Just the atmosphere created an inspiring mood for the both of us. And the many memories we had made at the old mansion was enough to inspire us for a long time. In fact, I didn't think I would ever be able to get the picture of that place out of my mind. It was etched deeply and significantly inside of me.

Hand in hand, we watched the cars as we ran across the street. There was so much traffic, it was very difficult to find a break in the line of cars to where we could make it across, but we made it safely.

After waiting for a good while, we finally had the chance to back out. For it to be such a small town, there were people everywhere. And as we got back on the road, the peace of the stillness filled me completely. There was no radio playing, no loud noises to startle me, or not even a flash of fear to control me. My dreams had come true for a short time. I just wondered how long things would stay that way.

After a while, Eric reached for the radio, he turned it on very low. The music was mellow and hypnotizing. It didn't bother me at all. In fact, it comforted me. The treble, the bass and the mesmerizing sound of the saxophone in the melody playing, consumed my soul. Even though I'd never been one to listen to that kind of music, at the time, it was soothing. It wasn't tainted by sad or discomforting lyrics, instead it contained only a melody, a beautiful melody. And I watched the few clouds above us clear out until the sky was as blue as God meant for it to be.

We didn't talk for a long time, but we didn't have to. We were both enjoying our time together. But in the back of my mind, I couldn't help but think of my sister, what she was doing and how she was feeling. I tried not to worry myself with such useless thoughts, because there was nothing I could do about it. Even if she was mournful of what took place, she had to do exactly what I planned on doing. I had to let time take care of it. For time was the only thing that could make each and every pain dissipate eventually. It wouldn't happen overnight, but it would happen.

Just that thought reminded me of a poem I had written. It was about time and the way it is spent. The words were taken from my heart after I met Eric. It rang through my head over and over again:

THE FIRST THING TAKEN AWAY

Each minute, each hour, passes like a flash of lightning
And so never to look back.
For the way each second is spent
Means more than all the stars which hover above,
And the more we spend loving,
Is only more for us to look back on and smile.
Instead of seeing what could've been done
And what hours could've been filled with laughter,
Instead of the overflowing tears of pain.
A year can flash as if were never here at all,

> And a lifetime is seldom seen,
>
> Until we slip and take a fall.
>
> So cherish the light that awakens you
>
> In the midst of the early dawn.
>
> And remember the light that was there one minute,
>
> Is soon taken away the next.
>
> Never take for granted tomorrow will bring
>
> New flowers and beautiful skies.
>
> Never wait to tell someone how you really feel in your heart,
>
> For when you think time is all you have,
>
> Sometimes it's the first thing taken away.

I always cherished that poem because it was all too true. But most don't realize it until it's far too late. But I knew it in my heart, and wished others would see it before it was too late.

After letting my mind wander, I begin to feel my stomach rumbling. We had been on the road for a little while, and I was beginning to get a bit hungry. I recognized where we were. It was only a few miles away from that small cafe' where I stopped at, on my way in.

"You hungry Eric?"

"I could eat, but there's nothing in sight."

"There's a little place a few miles ahead."

"Okay. We'll stop there and eat. Breakfast was good, but that was a while ago."

I grinned at him and glanced back up at the road. Everything was so still. Only a few cars occupied the roads, and the sky was baby blue. Nothing seemed more peaceful than that moment.

It didn't take long to reach the small cafe'. And to my surprise, there sat that old, faded red pick-up truck. I thought to myself, "She must work all the time."

We pulled into the half paved parking lot and quickly got out. You could tell we were both starving. And although I only had coffee when I had gone there before, I was sure the food was good. You could tell by the country atmosphere that it had to be. And I was ready for something that would hit the spot.

The tiny bell rang as we opened the door. And standing behind the counter, was none other than Belle. She was serving someone, and the swing she put in her hips as she walked over to them could've knocked someone's eye out. It was all attitude.

We found a seat, sat down, and searched the menu for something which sounded appetizing. It wasn't a minute before I saw Belle walking towards us. You could tell Eric was amazed by her, but I made sure his focus stayed on me.

We were still looking at the menu when she walked up, "I know you Hun. Didn't 'cha come in here a couple a days ago?"

"Yeah. We're heading back home."

"Well, well, well. Who's the fella?" she said, as her faced showed a glimpse of wanting.

I took his hand and replied, "This is Eric, my fiancé."

She looked off to the side and back over at us, "Hang on to 'im sugar. Ya know there's some women out'er who'd try and steal him, no time at all. Ya hear me."

"Thanks for the advice. I think we're ready to order." I replied, handing her our menus.

"Ready when y'all are, but don't go too fast. I'm slow with a pen, but quick with the men. If y'all know what I mean."

Eric couldn't believe she was so straight forward. In fact, I was surprised she didn't sit on his lap. The look she gave him was one of interest, but she declined from acting on it because I was sitting there hovering over him. It wasn't like she wanted to take him, I think she just wanted to flirt. She seemed like the type to flirt with anyone, attractive or not.

We placed our orders and as she walked off I couldn't help but laugh.

"What?" Eric said.

"I don't know. There's something about her I like. I'm not sure what it is, but I like her."

With a smirk, he replied, "She acts like a down-home, hillbilly girl, who wouldn't know good manners if they hit her in the face. And you like her."

"Well, maybe she raised my spirits a little at one time, a time I really needed it."

Peering questionably at me, he said nothing more. He had no idea what I was talking about, but it didn't matter. At least I knew. Although I'd only met her once before, I knew what she'd done for me.

Belle pranced back up to our table with our orders, sat them down abruptly, and scurried back to the kitchen. It wasn't as though the place was packed, it wasn't, but she tried to keep herself busy. I guess it made her long working days go by much faster. But still Eric couldn't see what interested me about her. He saw the same thing I saw at my first impressions of her, but if we stayed there long enough, I was sure he'd see the side that wasn't so rude, but half-way friendly. It was there, it just needed a little help to surface.

The food was wonderful. It was exactly like I imagined it would be. It was good in a home-cookin' kind of way. Each dish was perfectly prepared, only without all the frill of the little pretties other restaurants usually put on your plate. Who needs all that frill when the food is superlative. And a waitresses charm is as deep as her interest in those she serves. Although Belle seemed to lack much charm, she made up for it by her zingy attitude towards life.

After we ravished our plates until there was nothing left, we waited for the check. But Belle kept on leaning against the counter chewing her gum continuously with not even a glance in our direction. So I took the initiative and went over to her.

"Excuse me, Mrs. Belle," I said.

"It's Ms., and my last name's Carter. So if ya gonna address me atol, then call me Ms. Carter," she said in a snappy voice.

"I'm sorry, but we..."

"Yeah, yeah, ya want your check. Comin right up. Keep your drawers on honey."

Thinking she'd be friendly to me, I was surprised. But as before, she had a heavy guard up. It seemed she didn't want to get to know anyone. And the way she was acting, she was doing a damn good job.

I went back over and sat down, and Belle followed almost directly behind me.

"Here's ya check. Y'all have a nice day," she said looking at me and slightly grinning.

Eric still thought she was strangely rude, but I knew her even though I didn't know her very well. In a way, she reminded me of myself. For the longest, I tried to keep away from people for fear I'd get hurt. And I hoped she'd meet someone like Eric to change her attitude as he changed mine.

Throwing a few dollars on the table after paying the check, we walked towards the door. And to my surprise, I heard her call to me.

"Beth. That's your name isn't it?"

"Yes," I replied slowly pivoting towards her.

"Congrats. You seem like a sweet gal," she said reaching out her hand confirming my thoughts of having a new friend..

CHAPTER 18

After leaving that small cafe, I felt like I had made a difference in someone's life. My only hope was that Belle knew I liked her even though she was imprudent. Everyone has their faults, but even with those faults, they should be given a chance.

Eric continued to shake his head. The look on his face was one of disbelief that I was so nice to her. And his attitude surprised me. I always thought of him as one person who gave everyone a chance without judging them. But I put the cafe, and what happened in the back corners of my mind and looked ahead.

Since we still had a while to drive, I reached into the back seat and got my childhood diary. I wanted to read a few more entries because I thought it might accidentally jog my memory about why I wrote them. So I opened it and began to read once again. I came to one which put me into a quandary. It was written on January 6th, 1983. And it read:

> Reflections in the mirror,
> > But who is standing there?
> I no longer know that face,
> > As I continue so to stare,
> I'm saddened by such terror,
> > But with nothing left to do.
> Crying only makes things worse
> > As I search for the truth.
> His face is like the devil's.
> > His hands are cold as ice.
> Taking part in a service,

Tammy D. Thompson

> As I am sacrificed.
> My screams no longer heard.
> Like padded walls surround me still.
> To smile with all my fear inside,
> Is impossible to feel.

Squinting my eyes, I try harder and harder to remember why I wrote such horrible things. But I had no idea what possessed me to write in such a grim manner. Although I didn't have the most wonderful childhood. The only thing I could think of, was maybe those times when my father's temper flew out of control. He never could control his temper, and it always scared me. But other than that, I was blank. It ate me up inside, not knowing. I would much rather know the truth, than to be haunted by unclear memories from the past. And then I realized, I wouldn't live like that forever. I was willing to do whatever I had to do, to find the answer. And Mrs. Downs was the key. I was hoping she'd be able to unlock the door which had been closed within my mind for such a long time.

With time slipping away swiftly, glaring out ahead, and I noticed something. There was a bell tower in the center of our college campus, and from a distance, I saw it clearly. Once I saw that, I knew we were almost back. The closer we came, the more at peace I felt. And when we pulled onto University Dr., the place looked like an old, deserted, western scene. No one was in sight. There were a couple of cars here and there, but I figured they were the cars of the janitors, or maybe a few teachers who had unfinished work to do. I wasn't sure, but there was one thing I was sure about. There'd be no one in the dorms to disturb us. I was positive no one was crazy enough to return back to college with more than a week left of Christmas vacation. Only Eric and I were put in that situation. We had no other choice, and no where else to go. But we tried to make the best of a bad situation.

Since there was no fighting for parking places, we pulled up directly in front of my dorm, and parked. We stumbled out and unloaded our things on the sidewalk. It was kind of spooky. The leaves were being blown around in circles all over the frozen ground like tiny tornadoes, and the trees around us, were like wooden skeletons leaning in our direction. I tried not to let my imagination go too far off, but that was just the way I saw things—empty, abandoned, and uninhabited. Everything was peaceful, but eerie at the same time.

We made our way up the walk, reached the door, and I pulled out my keys. Opening the door, there was dead silence. It was strange, because normally there were people everywhere, the TV. was usually blaring, and the hall monitor was always standing around making sure there was no trouble. But no one was around but Eric and myself.

"Beth, go on. These bags are heavy. What'cha got in here...bricks?" he said nudging me out of his way and opening the double doors leading to my room.

Passing the bathroom, I heard water dripping slowly, one after another. But that was the only sound consuming those deserted halls. And when I opened the door to my room, Eric rushed in, dropped the bags, and gave a sigh of relief. The smell floating around us was faintly stale. It smelled just like it did the first day I moved in. So I opened a window to circulate enough fresh air to overcome the odor which still lingered.

Immediately I unpacked my things. I didn't want to spend all night putting up my things, so I hurried the best I could. Eric just laid back on my bed, closed his eyes, and started breathing heavily. He had told me driving always tired him, and he was telling the truth. At least I was able to lie back and relax; he had to watch the road for all them hours.

After putting the very last thing in its' place, I reached into my purse and pulled out the phone number Mrs. Downs had given me before I left. It was her home number, and I felt like I needed to talk to her. So while Eric was resting, I picked up the phone, sat down in the floor, and dialed her number.

"Hello," she said in a sweet voice.

"Mrs. Downs, this is Beth. I just got back."

"So soon?" she questioned.

With a slight hesitation, I replied, "Well, things didn't go that great. In fact, I have a lot I need to tell you."

"Why didn't you call me dear. I told you if you needed to talk to call."

"I know, but I didn't want to ruin your Christmas just because mine was destroyed."

She was silent for a minute, then she replied, "Beth, if anything, you would've made my Christmas worth while. I spent Christmas by myself."

My heart dropped from compassion for her. And I had nothing to say. What could I say to someone who had to spend Christmas alone.

"I'm sorry," I said sincerely.

"Oh, I'm used to it by now. Since my husband Jerry died five years ago, it's kind of become force of habit. You know, I like my own company, but it took me a long time to come to that conclusion."

She had no sadness in her voice, in fact, it was quite cheerful. It amazed me, but it also made me envy her. It was hard to believe someone could be happy alone, but she seemed to be very content.

"Mrs. Downs, can I see you tomorrow? I really need to talk to you. There's a lot that happened at home that may be able to help you to help me."

"How could I say no. Why don't you come around one o'clock. That'll give me a chance to eat lunch and make it to the office."

"Thank you so much."

"Anything for you Beth. I'll see you tomorrow dear," she said softly hanging up the phone.

I hung up and then peered over at Eric. He looked exhausted. I didn't want to wake him, so I took Amy's bed for the night. I undressed quietly, slipped on an old T-shirt, and turned out the lights. With the moon shining through the window on Eric's face, it presented a perfect silhouette of a remarkable man. It was like viewing an expensive painting. The curves of his cheeks and the smoothness of his hair, was a flawless vision.

I turned facing the wall, covered myself entirely, and closed my eyes without even an ounce of uncertainty. My body felt worn and shattered from the days activities. And I knew a decent slumber would restore my energy for the following day. I couldn't wait to see Mrs. Downs. I missed her a lot. I guess you could say she'd become a part of me. After telling her many things about myself, sometimes I wondered if she knew me better than I knew myself.

I focused on blissful thoughts as I let my body completely relax. And once I'd let every muscle in my body conform to nothing but relaxation, I drifted peacefully off into never-never land. I wasn't surprised how it was easy to fall asleep. Other than the fact that I was desperately tired, Eric was across the room from me. And I thought, how could I ever be frightened of anything with him so near?

For a while, nothing entered my mind, but instantaneously I was relocated. Once again, as many other times, I traveled far, far away. I saw myself as a child lying in my bed, in my old room, with only a small night light in the corner, which created tiny shadows surrounding me. Pulling the covers all the way up to my neck, I gripped onto them tightly. Then suddenly, my door began to open very slowly. I squinted inch by inch until my eyes could view the person standing there who wanted so desperately to frighten me. At first it was just a figure as it had been in many other dreams, but this one was completely different.

This time, the unknown had enough courage to show its' face. One step then another it took until I saw the face of the one who had been haunting me-my brother. It was Lewis. He stood there laughing his horrible, ghostly laugh. And the look in his eyes was one of revenge. His pupils were fire red, and smoke encircled his deathlike being. For a second, I stared as if he were real, but I knew he wasn't real at all. I had created every vision out of an imaginary fear...a fear I needed to get a grip on.

Trying to make him leave me alone, I cried out, "What do you want? I never did anything to you? Please let me live my life while you enjoy your death."

Again he laughed, but this time it was even more extreme. His appalling laughter became louder and louder until he burst into flames and disappeared. In my dream, I sprang to my feet, but when I woke, I was running out my door and down the hallway. I heard footsteps running after me so I ran even harder. My heart pounded to where I felt it all over each inch of me. But when I reached the front door of the dorm, it was locked. I turned and saw Eric standing there trying to talk to me, but I could barely hear him. It was like he was in a tunnel and every word he muttered was muffled drastically. I slid to the floor and pulled my knees up to my chest for security. And as his voice came to me more clearly, I just kept shaking my head furiously.

"I can't take it anymore! I can't live like this. I feel like an animal trapped in a cage, unable to escape. You can't help me, and I've tried to help myself, but nothing seems to work."

Thinking he would ask me I had dreamed, I waited, but he never said a word. He picked me up in his arms like a tiny baby and carried me back to bed. All the way back to the room, I buried my head into him, scared to look up. Then as he laid me down, covered me up, and kissed me on my forehead, still he said nothing. I guess because there was nothing he could say to make things any better. He was speechless, but his heart was heard loud and clear. He pulled up a chair beside my bed and stroked my hair gently. It calmed me, and once or twice I almost drifted off to sleep again. But each time I felt like my eyes were closing, I'd jump. It frightened me to enter that world again. There was a chance I wouldn't have any visions at all, but there was also the chance I might. Time after time Eric assured me of my safety, and after a while, he walked over, reached into my purse and pulled out the bottle of pills which he disapproved of at one time. He got me a glass of water, then handed me the capsule which would solve my problems for the night. I took it quickly, and looked at him confusingly.

"Eric, promise me something."

With the pale moon shining on his face, he answered, "Anything."

"If I start to toss and turn, please wake me."

He nodded in agreement and continued to caress my hair. At last, I released myself to him and sailed away into another time of uncertain sleep. So ashamed of my actions, my mind wandered as my eyes slowly closed.

Many thoughts trampled through my head, one after another. One, was that I thought Eric might think I was completely deranged. And another was something I thought of myself. As hard as I tried to run from such enigmas, they seemed to follow me everywhere I went. And I'd come to the point to where I was at a dead end street. My only direction left to run was directly into what was entrapping me. I tried it once before, and for a while, everything seemed to stop, but it only came back when I pretended it was gone for good.

It took me a while, but lying there in the in the stillness of the night, I cleared my mind and tried to think of nothing but joyous and soothing thoughts. It seemed to work, because when I opened my eyes the following morning, I glanced over to find Eric asleep in the chair beside me. I guess he'd slept there all night long. It made me feel special that he didn't leave my side. And even in his sleep, the expression on his face, was one of worry. I felt guilty for making him fidget, but I needed him to understand.

I reached over and touched his hand which was ice cold. He was a little startled, but I only woke him so he could lie with me, if only for a short while. We really had nothing to do, so he stood up, stretched as he always did, and nudged up against me and covered us both entirely with warm, soft blankets. All of the windows gave the cool air a means to slither its' way in, and he was trying to guard us from the frost of the morning. Feeling his warm breath up against the curve of my neck, gave me chill bumps all over, but it also scared away the numbness I felt. His flesh was temperate and manly. It felt good to have his body lying that close to me. I wouldn't have wanted it any other way.

Before I knew it, we had both fallen asleep once more, and when I opened my eyes, it was already noon. I uncovered very slowly, trying to make sure I didn't wake prince charming lying beside me, and then I went over to get some clothes to wear out of my closet.

"Come back to bed," Eric said in a slow, almost distorted, voice.

I walked back over to him, kissed him lightly, then grabbed a towel and headed for to the bathroom to shower. It was so quiet down the halls. It was unusual to walk in the dorms without having a million people running into you, or even seeing a handyman coming out of nowhere with no forewarning. But it was kind of nice having such peace surrounding me.

Barefooted and with hair sticking up like Pippi Long Stocking, I stepped into the largest shower in the corner. Turning on the water, I was drenched by the soothing, hot, steamy, and massaging jets falling down on me. The fastness of the water always energized me, but at the same time, it made me feel relaxed. At times I didn't know whether to go back to bed, or to jump into the day enthusiastically.

Then when I felt the water trying to turn from hot to warm, I knew I didn't have long before the cold would force its' way in. Trying not to slip, I carefully stepped out of the shower, wrapped up in my robe, and hurried down the hallway to my room. When I walked up to my door and went in, Eric was gone, but there was a note lying on the bed.

My darling Beth:

Good luck today with Mrs. Downs. I needed to unpack my things, and I also had a few more things to take care of, so I thought I'd give you a little time to yourself. I figured you might be getting tired of me by now.

You know where to find me when you're done today. Remember I love you. I'll see ya later.

Love,
Eric

Laying the note down on my desk, a warm feeling of contentment trickled through every vein of my body. It was strange, but even though I read his note, I could hear him saying those words in the back of my mind. I was glad he took it upon himself to leave me alone for a while because I needed the time to think. And I knew if he was there I wouldn't be able to do anything except focus on him and only him. It was as though he read my mind. I didn't say a word, but as before, he knew what I needed without me having to say a anything.

Before getting dressed, I walked over to the few blinds which closed, and opened them, letting in more light. I always had a feeling of freshness and safety when the room was fully lit. In a sense, it was a symbol of taking in God's warmth, and letting his light fill whatever darkness lingered. It always seemed to work. My view on life was "As long as God is gracious enough to give such a guiding light to me, I will be gracious enough to accept it with love and adoration."

Combing my long, shiny hair, I caressed it like you would a pet. Most of my pride was captured within my looks. Although I never considered myself one of the most beautiful women in the world, at least I could try to be one. And in such frustrating times, I needed something to give me a little courage. I wasn't quite sure, but from what I'd been told, the greatest courage comes from within, and the greatest fear can be freed by those who hold enough courage for everyone. I wasn't sure how much courage was within this fragile body of mine, but I had a feeling it was far more powerful than I ever gave it credit for. That was what I needed to focus on. And for those who hold courage in the palm of one hand, they hold their happiness in the other.

Looking in my closet for something comfortable to wear, I searched and searched for my favorite sweat shirt, but I couldn't find it anywhere. I assumed Amy borrowed it when she left. She always borrowed my things, but I didn't mind. I felt like I owed her for all of the support she'd given me.

Finally I found something to wear, got dressed, and began to put on my make-up, a daily, morning ritual. I didn't dare walk out of my room without my fake mask on. In fact, the only people who had seen me as God created me, was my family, Amy, and Eric. Other than that, no one had any idea what I looked like under so much of a disguise.

I glanced up at the clock, and the time had slipped away even more. It was a quarter till one. I only had a few minutes before my appointment, and I was rushing to get my things together, make my bed, and think of some of the things I wanted to tell my psychology friend. I knew what I wanted to tell her, but I didn't know in what exact sequence. I didn't know whether to start from the moment Eric asked me to marry him and work my way to the present, or skip around and just tell her of all of the bad things. But I tried not to dwell on boggling thoughts because my mind was boggled enough as it was.

Almost ready to go, I grabbed my purse and threw it over my shoulder. But as I was almost out the door, something stopped me. Then I turned around and remembered my childhood diary which I had laid on my desk against the wall. Slowly walking over to it, I picked it up and slipped it in my purse. That was one thing Mrs. Downs had to see. If she was able to make anything out of it, then she was better than me, because I was completely bewildered by each and every line. Even though it was in my handwriting, I wanted to remember why I wrote such horrible and unsettling things. And even though she might not be able to tell me, at least it would give her a little more insight on my problems and where the core of my uncertainties lie. It was very possible all of those childish, but harsh words, were a few of the missing pieces of the unsolved mystery puzzle I'd been searching for. There was such a large gap in my life I was unsure about, and I was ready to go to any lengths to find out what those gaps consisted of.

With a smile on my face and with my heart full of determination, I was ready to meet with the lady who had changed the way I looked at many things. Since I'd been seeing her, I felt better about myself. But most of all, I was beginning to get to know the person I was inside. For a long time I had no idea who I was, but she helped me find my true self hiding back in the corners of my mind.

Leaving the dorm, I looked all around trying to find a glimpse of someone else besides myself. It wasn't that I was frightened. How could I be frightened? The sun was shining down on me with such brilliant light, and the weather was pretending to be springtime. Although it wasn't, it seemed like it.

My car was parked in front, so I took my time walking over to it. I wanted to absorb every ounce of pleasure out of the day. I wanted to let the warmth from the eye of God seep through every pore of my skin, and I needed to "stop, and smell the roses," as many people would say. I was never one to take many things for granted. If I ever had the chance to watch a flower bloom, or to stare at the stars on a clear beautiful night, I never passed up such chances, instead, took them in totally.

When I reached my car, one of my professors was crossing the street as if he were going to the dorms.

"Beth, what are you doing here. I figured everyone would be at home with their families." he said.

"Well, I just decided to come back. I love it here, and it's so quiet."

"It is that...well, you have a nice day," he said walking off.

I had a weird feeling about talking to him. He was a wonderful teacher, but he never talked to me outside of class. Sometimes he seemed like a loner, but as long as he did his job, it didn't matter. As long as he passed me, it didn't matter at all.

I got into my car in a very cheerful mood. I kept humming to myself as if I had no worries what-so-ever. And at the moment, I didn't. I was taking things one moment at a time, instead of one day at time. Because as long as I took it moment by moment, then all of those moments would turn into hours, and hours into days. That was the only way I knew how to deal with everything.

I circled the campus to see if Eric was anywhere in sight, but I didn't see him, so I started towards Mrs. Down's office. The closer I got, the more I believed she would find a breakthrough in my dreams and visions. I had no doubt in my mind she would reach what was really bothering me, and as I pulled up into the parking lot of her office, I felt relieved. I'd missed her even though she wasn't family, and even though I'd only known her a short while. She seemed to have become a big part of me, the part which continually told me I wasn't crazy, but instead she told me how special I was.

Walking to the door, I saw her step into her office. Her hair was pulled up and she was dressed very casually. And I knew the next few hours could possibly bring out something I'd been wanting to know for a long time. I'd made my mind up I was ready to let go of myself completely and let her do what she had to do to make it happen. I set my fear aside and replaced it with hope. Because if hope wasn't a major factor, then I was only wasting my time and hers as well.

I let myself in and looked around the office. It too, looked abandoned except for Mrs. Downs being there. The only light on was the one in her office, and there was a radio playing very low.

When I reached the doorway to her office, she looked up from her desk and smiled at me so sincerely. And before either one of us had the chance to say a single word, the feeling I had inside was one of acceptance. She accepted me as a client and a friend with no pre-judgments, or speculations. She took me in as I was, nothing less, nothing more.

"Beth, come in, sit down, and lets get started. I'm anxious to talk to you about your Christmas holiday, but more than that, I'm delighted to see you."

"Me too, Mrs. Downs."

"Why don't you start calling me Penny. I think we've reached that point don't you?" she said sweetly.

"Penny, I like that. Okay...Penny."

She just shook her head and grinned. Although I knew this particular session would probably be harder than any of the others, I was ready. So I closed my eyes and let her do her job...dig into my mind until she struck oil...my memory.

CHAPTER 19

Sitting in that cushioned chair studying everything around me, I realized something. I felt so much more comfortable with her than I did the very first time I walked into her office. The first time was awkward for me, but after several sessions with such a tender hearted woman, my nerves stopped shaking quite so much, and I felt more at home. It was strange, but looking at her was like looking at still waters. She was so calm about everything. It didn't matter what was happening, she always had a calm attitude through it all. I only wished I could do the same. If anything, it cut my anxieties in half, and improved my self-esteem more and more. And God only knows how much I needed that.

She put on her petite, wire framed glasses and leaned on her desk. And the light from the sun shining through the large windows, instilled more and more peace inside of me the longer I sat there. But after a moment of nothing being said, she began.

"What's this you said about having a lot to tell me Beth?"

"Remember you told me what the difference was between a home and a house? Well, all those years as I was growing up, I was only staying in an uncaring and unloving house full of strangers."

She raised her eyebrows in puzzlement, "What do you mean? What happened?"

"I'm not even their daughter. They adopted me, but why? That question has been storming across my mind ever since the moment I found out. The weird thing was how my father acted. Of course, it came as no shock, but he treated me like a stranger on the street, as if he could care less how I felt, where I went, or what happened to me."

"How did you find out? They didn't tell you, did they?"

"No. Eric found the papers by accident after my father told me to get out of his house."

In more of a quandary, she asked, "Eric, what was he doing there? I thought he lived in Carolina?"

"It's a long story, but I'll try to make it a short one. I had talked to Eric a couple of times on the phone, but I didn't realize he could hear the unhappiness in my voice. Anyway, he took it upon himself to come down to where I was. He left his family to be with me."

She took her pen and wrote down a few things, then looked back up at me. "Then what?"

"I guess you could say, Eric and I were each other's company for Christmas. But nothing could've made me any happier than to spend such a wonderful holiday with the man I love."

Turning her head sideways, she got a hint of a gleam in her eye. "You're not telling me everything are you Beth? I mean about Eric. What's going on in that situation?"

Smiling from ear to ear, I told her, "He asked me to marry him Penny. I was so surprised, but after I got over the shock, I was more excited than I had ever been. I told him yes...no doubt in my mind. You know, he makes me feel like a queen, even though I feel like a useless peasant. It's funny, but I feel important when I'm with him. That's just the way he makes me feel."

I held up my hand and showed her my ring. It was shining even brighter because of the glare of the sun beaming down on it.

"It's lovely Beth. I'm happy for you. You deserve a man who wants to be good to you. I wouldn't want any less for you."

"Thanks. I just couldn't wait to tell you. But I still ponder how Eric thinks of me. I'm not saying I doubt his love, but last night I really went crazy and he may think I am."

"Was it another dream sweetie?" she said in a very sincere voice.

With a deep breath in and out, I replied, "Yes, but this time I saw the shadow's face. It was Lewis."

"Your brother Lewis? The one who died?"

"Yeah. Strange, huh. I can't explain it. But I do have something that might be able to help you understand a few things," I said, pulling the diary out of my purse.

"What's this?" she asked flipping through it careful not to tear any of the pages which were already worn.

"I found it with all of my poetry I used to write as a little girl. I read a few entries, but I don't remember writing them. I even dated every single one, but still I don't remember. Wouldn't it seem like I'd never forget something I'd written?"

"Well Beth, not if you put it so far in the back of your mind. Sometimes people forget things because it's too painful to remember. But since you brought this to me, I think it can be beneficial to you. I have an idea, but you have to agree to do it."

"What? I'll do anything. I'm ready to go on with my life, and I can't as long as I have this unknown solicitude chaining me down. I have to know. What do you want me to do?"

She looked me directly in the eye and said, "I want to hypnotize you. If I can put you under hypnosis, and use these dates you have written down, maybe we can find out why you wrote them. Many psychiatrists use hypnosis. I've done it a few times when there was nothing left to do. Would you like to try it?"

I stood up, walked around the room slowly and thought for a moment. I know I told her I'd do anything, but being hypnotized scared me. I guess because I knew it would fill in all of the blank spaces of my life. With many thoughts in my head going around and around in circles, I went over to her. "I'll try it Penny. It can't hurt right?"

She leaned over and squeezed my hand. Her skin was as soft as a rose petal and just her affection made me trust her decision. If she thought it was the best thing to do, then I had no hesitation in doing as she asked. She knew what she was doing, even though I had no idea what the outcome would be.

"Alright," she said softly, "We'll have to wait until next time. It takes a lot of preparation on my part, and a lot of thought on yours. I want to make sure you're ready for something so drastic. I can't tell you that you won't see something frightening. And I can't tell you that you won't be terrified of what you've hidden from yourself. But I will tell you this, I'll be right beside you. And the moment I feel you've taken in too much, I'll wake you. So there's nothing to worry about."

"Okay. I'll do it for you. I trust you."

She walked around her desk and kneeled down in front of me, "You know I envy you dear."

Curious, I asked, "Me, why me?"

"My sweet Beth, you are so full of spirit. Many people would be scared to death about what they might see, but you're ready to face the darkness. I was always scared of everything, especially after Jerry died. When I lost our baby, then I lost him, I had nothing left to hang onto except for myself. And for a while I thought I'd lost myself too. I did as you used to. I hid away for a long time, but then one night, my whole attitude changed. I was in bed asleep, when I woke to see a tiny spirit floating around my bed. The tiny voice kept saying "We'll be back together one day mommy. We'll be back together." And it made me feel warm all over. It was my baby. At first I thought she was trying to tell me she was still alive, but then I realized what she was really saying. My husband is taking care of her, and they're waiting until I reunite with them. And just that thought alone made me realized I'd be fine."

A tear formed in my eye as she talked. I couldn't help it. I felt sorry for her. I didn't want to pity her, but she seemed so alone.

"What's the matter dear?" she asked.

"It's you...It's not fair you know."

"What's not fair?"

"You're such a wonderful person. Why did God have to take your family away? Why didn't he let you keep your family, and destroy my mom and dad's life instead. They're horrible people. They didn't deserve three kids when you couldn't even have the chance to love just one. It just doesn't seem fair at all," I continued, with a tear rolling down my cheeks.

Smiling that tender smile of hers, she reached over and wiped each tear away which was trickling down my face. She didn't have anything to say. She was as speechless as I was. I didn't have any answers, and to my surprise, she didn't either.

"Come on Beth. You're a lot prettier when you're not crying."

Giving her a slight grin, and as she stood up, so did I. "When do you want to come back? Is tomorrow too soon?"

"No, that's not too soon. The sooner the better," I replied.

She walked me to the door, and hugged me. "You relax and don't worry about anything. I'll take care of everything. And if you'd feel more comfortable, we can do our next session at my house. I can fix dinner and you can bring Eric. You might need him there for a someone to hold your hand. And I know you don't want anyone but Eric, holding your hand."

I laughed and replied, "That sounds good. What time?"

"Tomorrow, say around seven o'clock."

As I walked away, I replied, "See ya then Penny."

After talking with her, I felt an unexplainable urge to find Eric and hold him as close to me as God would allow me to. Hearing her sad story, made me appreciate what I had and what could be taken away from me if I wasn't careful. And even though she wasn't sad, I was dispirited enough for the both of us. I looked up to her. And just knowing what horrible things she'd been through in her life, it made me wonder if what was happening to me, was worth worrying over.

With hundreds of thoughts crossing my mind, I got into my car and drove straight back to school. And the first place I went was Eric's room. After parking abruptly, I sprung out, and ran to his door, knocking loudly, but there was no answer. I didn't even think to look and see if his truck was parked out front, so I went back out. I looked everywhere, but his truck was nowhere in sight. And the creases on my face which were obvious each time I'd smile, were no longer seen. They had disappeared instantaneously.

So I drove back and parked in front of my dorm and walked in very slowly. Still no one occupied that three story dorm but me, and being alone was something I didn't want at that time. I wanted to be able to reach out and touch the one person whom I was going to spend the rest of my life with...Eric. I needed him. In a way, after talking to Mrs. Downs, I needed reassurance of how he felt about me. Even though I had no doubt he loved me, I still needed him to assure me of that over and over again.

After going back into my room, turning on the TV and staring out the window for a long time, a knock came at my door. But before I has the chance to get up, the door opened. Eric stood there with a huge folder in his hands. It struck me as odd. We had no homework, and school wasn't starting again for another week or so.

"What's all this." I asked curiously.

Cutting his eyes timidly, he answered, "Promise you won't get mad?"

A little scared of what he was about to say, I replied, "What is it Eric Norris? I won't get mad as long as you tell me the truth."

"Okay. Sit down."

We went over to my bed, and sat as he placed the folder between us. I was still baffled a bit about what he was going to say, but I sat there patiently and waited.

He opened the folder and handed me some papers. "What are these?"

"I've been doing some research today. And I found out a few things about how we can find your real parents. It's easy if you know the right people. That's what I'm working on now."

"Who do you know that's important enough to help us?" I stated as I shook my head in disbelief.

"Believe it or not, I'm close, but it is a bit hard to trace."

I read through a few of the papers he'd placed in my hands, but none of them told me anything. In fact, I wasn't even sure Eric knew where to start when it came to finding my maternal mother and father.

"Eric, this is really sweet of you, but you know it's impossible. Those records were probably sealed many years ago, maybe even thrown away. It's a lost cause. There's no chance I'll ever know who they are. And if there were a chance, we'd probably never know how to go about doing it."

Placing his hand on top of mine, he smiled at me. His brilliant white teeth were like the many bright stars above. "Beth, we have to try. Like you said, you'll never be completely happy until you know the truth. I'm trying to help you. That's all I'm doing. Don't you understand that."

"Yes I do, but Eric, you think you can do anything. The way you act, you probably think if you jumped off a mountain, you'd land on your feet. Life's not that simple. It's just not."

"Ok. I won't say another word about it for now. But I will find them. For you, I'll find them. That's how much I love you. You can't be completely happy until you find the people who brought you into this world, and we can't live like that. Just leave it all to me. I'll take care of it. I'll find 'em. And ya know what?"

"What?"

"They're gonna love you baby, just as much as I do. And they'll see what they gave up. They'll see what a beautiful daughter they could've had the privilege of raising. But most of all, they'll have the chance to make it all up to you. And maybe for once in your life, you'll have parents you want to talk about and go see. That's what I want to happen. Of course things don't always work out the way you want them to, but if I have anything to do with it, you're gonna end up the happiest and most loved woman I know."

I know I've said it a million times, but he overwhelmed me once again. I'd never known someone who always knew what to say and when to say it. He seemed perfect even though I knew no one was perfect except for God. But he was the closest to perfect than I'd ever seen before. It was hard to express to him my appreciation, but I tried. I leaned over to him and placed my head on his chest. Then one after another, he stroked my hair which draped down my back. Saying "thank you," wouldn't have been enough, so I didn't say anything. It was enough to be close to him. He knew how I felt, and there was no sense in ruining the moment with a bunch of unnecessary words and explanations.

We sat there for the longest time. And the only sound I heard was the sound of both of us breathing in and out, over and over again. It was faint, but unmistakable. At times I felt out of control, but moments such as this one, made me wonder if I was missing something, overlooking something very important.

Then, out of the blue, Eric stands, takes my hands, and heads for the door.

"What are you doing? You're always up to something Eric."

With his dimples shining, he replied, "I just had a great idea. We don't need to sit around here all day long. Lets go somewhere. How about a drive. We can drive and drive until we come to a place we find interesting. I don't want to waste all our time sleeping or doing nothing at all. We've got time which we can spend creatively. And that's what I intend on doing."

So I took him up on his spur of the moment idea. A drive might do both of us some good. It didn't take me but a few seconds to snatch up my purse, lock my door, and run after that maniac of a man, to his truck which he'd parked right beside me. We did just as he said. We took off down the road, in no particular direction, and watched every bit of scenery surrounding us. It was that simple. And since we were both writers, we exchanged view points on how to describe a certain tree, or an old house. It was interesting to say the least. He was always full of surprises. But that was what made him who he was. His spontaneity, his joy of life, and his adequate mood for laughter combined, made him the man I fell in love with.

We drove for over an hour, and I felt like we had been driving in circles, until we reached a most heavenly place. There was this open field in the middle of nowhere. There wasn't a soul around, and the only sound was the swaying of the trees and the whistling of the wind. As we got out, a flock of birds rose from one of the trees nearest to us, and they all flew away in perfect form. When one would turn, another would do the same, until they all seemed to be playing a game of follow the leader. It was astounding to watch.

We walked towards the field, and I noticed how the grass swayed back and forth so elegantly. And although a heavy wooded area surrounded that open field, I felt like God had left that open for a reason. It was too beautiful to be covered by anything but grass and flowers during the spring and summer.

Throwing my arms up, I ran into it, feeling more free with each step I took. And Eric stayed behind watching me. But when I turned facing him, he began to run towards me. Without a thought going through my mind, I started running too. It was like reliving a scene from one of the old 'Little House on the Prairie,' shows. Although we were running, everything seemed to move in slow motion. And my hair swung back and forth as the cool wind whisked through it, making it dance around.

When we reached one another, he picked me up as high as he could lift me, and twirled me around and around. We both held such a feeling of freedom from worries in that place. And when he let me down, I refused to release him. I didn't want to. I just ran my fingers through his soft, almost perfect, hair, as the breeze sneaking by us, twirled his around as well. It looked as though a tornado had landed on our heads, but we didn't care. Everything around me, made me forget for a while, about all my discouragements.

I was tired of being discouraged. Just feeling free for a little while was better than keeping myself cooped up all the time and never feeling that way. It was worth it. I was glad Eric took it upon himself to drag me out of that small, dull, dungeon of a room, and exposed me to a few things God meant for everyone to see at least once in a lifetime.

We played outside for hours acting like two small children. Running around and around, we enjoyed every second, every minute. But soon the sky started to lose its light, and we hurried back to his truck. Laughing the entire way, I looked inside myself and saw the person I always wanted to be, carefree and full of life. Not sure how long it would last, I engulfed each ounce of that feeling.

We quickly drove back to that empty campus which only he and I were occupying at the time, and went to my room. And after watching a little TV, I yawned, went to my purse, and took another pill to make me sleep peacefully. This time Eric said nothing. I guess he didn't want me to replay what happened the night before, so he didn't say a word. Snuggling up next to him, sex didn't enter either one of our minds. We were just glad to be together. With his arms blanketing me, I closed my eyes and let no uneasiness enter my mind. My only thoughts were of the wonderful afternoon I'd spent with the man I loved more than anything or anybody.

The night flew by. It seemed like I woke up right after I'd drifted off to sleep, but I felt rested. I looked over at the clock to see what time it was. It was only seven o'clock in the morning. It surprised me because I was never one to wake so early. If anything, I was the one who wanted to stay in bed all day long. So I closed my eyes once more and went back to sleep. And my twisting and turning in bed didn't even half way disturb that handsome man lying beside me. He just kept on snoring as if no one was there but himself. And his arm was still around my waist, as it was when we laid down the night before.

Three or four hours passed quickly before I woke once more. And once again, the sun was glaring in at me through the large window beside my bed. I sat up and closed the blinds so I could steal a few extra moments from the day, and fell back into his arms. It wasn't that I wanted to go back to sleep, I just wanted to lie with him as long as I possibly could before we were forced to get up and greet the day. And since we had no reason to get up early, I saw no sense in rising.

Playing the lazy dog for a while longer, I finally forced myself crawl out of such a warm embracing bed. I shook Eric, but I knew he was just acting like he was still sleeping.

"Open your eyes. I know you're awake. You can't fool me."

Snickering with his eyes closed, he cracked one eye open. "Why do we have to get up. We don't have to do anything but lie here all day long, if we ant to."

"Remember, tonight we have to go over to Mrs. Down's house. She wants you to come too. Didn't I tell you?"

"Tell me what?"

"She wants to hypnotize me. She says it'll help me to remember. And she also told me that if you were there, I'd feel a little more comfortable with it. Please come. She's fixing dinner."

"Alright, I'll go."

"I knew that dinner part would get'cha."

Pushing me away from him jokingly, he sneered at me, "Well, a free meal can't hurt anything."

I pushed him back and got out of bed. And while he laid there being lazy, I went ahead and took a shower and got dressed. Of course, it didn't take him but fifteen minutes to do exactly the same thing that took me an hour to do. He always aggravated me about that. I couldn't help it if I was concerned about the way I looked. But he always told me I was beautiful with or without all that make-up. If I believed him, I would've gone without it all the time, but he was too much of a sweet talker for me to believe something that corny, so I continued to do my daily routine.

We spent the day together doing everything from shopping to walking by the pond. In fact, I almost lost myself in all of the happiness he gave to me. Each time I looked at him, he was smiling. And every time he touched me, it made me smile right back. But in the back of my mind I was worried about what would happen at Mrs. Down's. I was sure she wouldn't do anything that would hurt me, but at the same time, I was terrified to be hypnotized. I always heard of people doing that, but I never believed in such things. To me, it seemed weird. I never believed it would work. It was hard to understand how someone could be taken back in time and made to remember something that happened so long ago. Whether it be happy memories or horrible ones, the way I looked at it, if you couldn't remember it before, how could you recall it just by someone asking you to close you eyes and remember. It didn't seem possible, but I was willing to try it because I trusted her.

The day flew by way too fast, and it was almost time to go and meet with Mrs. Downs. We went back to my room and I called her to make sure I knew how to get to her house. Eric wrote down the directions and we got in his truck and headed that way. We had only eaten a little that day, so we were starved. I couldn't wait to eat a home cooked meal. Other than the bed and breakfast, and the dinner at that little cafe; I hadn't had a home cooked meal in a while. I was looking forward to it, and I think Eric was too.

On the way to her house, we talked about her.

"Beth, are you sure this is a good idea. I mean, hypnotism. Sounds crazy to me. I think it's just a bunch of mumbo jumbo."

"I've got to try it. If nothing else, at least I can say I tried it."

Cutting his eyes over to me, he replied, "Yeah, I guess anything's worth trying. If it'll help you at all, I guess it's worth it."

We found her house easy enough. It was an old, two story, framed home sitting on the corner, almost in the center of town. It looked as though she'd been there for so long, that everything was built around her home. In fact, I think that was what she had told me. It was hard to imagine this town any smaller.

We pulled into her two car garage containing only one car sat, and got out. But before we could even make it half way up the walk, she stepped out onto the front porch. Her partially silver hair was shining almost as much as her smile, and she came down to greet us.

"Beth, this must be the famous Eric," she said, reaching out and shaking his hand.

"It's nice to meet you Mrs. Downs."

"Call me Penny. I feel like I already know you. I've heard so much about you from Beth," she said, walking us into the house.

The interior of her house was decorated beautifully. She had two elegant hunter green wing-back chairs, and her coffee table was oval with old-fashioned carved legs. The colors were all modern, but the style was sort of antique. Everything looked like a collector's item. My eyes wandered all around focusing on the most interesting things. I went over to a small table up against the wall, and there was a picture of her when she was pregnant. And beside her stood a most handsome man.

"Was this your husband," I asked.

She lowered her head and answered, "Yes. And that's the way I remember him. He always had his arms around me, so loving, so caring. I wouldn't want to remember him in any other way."

I put down the picture and joined Eric on the couch. And as we sat there, a most appetizing aroma floated around us. I remembered she told me she was going to fix spaghetti, but the smell was like something homemade. With each breath I took in, I couldn't get over the comfortable feeling I had. Although I'd never been there before, the atmosphere in the room was one of hospitality.

"You two hungry. Dinner's ready. Just let me set the table and we can eat." she said hurrying into the kitchen.

"Can I help?" I yelled to her.

I heard a faint laugh, "No dear, you are guests. I like my guests to just sit back and enjoy."

I looked at Eric then browsed around the room once again. There were many old photos hanging on the walls. Most of them were of her husband. I thought she must've loved him an awful lot. About that time, I heard her call for us to come and eat. We made our way into the kitchen, and as I started to sit down, Eric came up behind me and helped me with my chair.

"What a sweetheart," Penny said, peering as both of us.

After we all got comfortable, she suggested we bow our heads and thank the Lord above for the food. And so we did. She said an eloquent prayer, and I kept thinking how wonderful it would've been to grow up in such a place.

"Well kids, what are you waiting on? It's gonna get cold. And don't worry about there being enough. I've got plenty to go around. Eat all you want." she said passing each dish down to us.

Eric piled his plate high. He acted as though he was just as comfortable being there as I was, and that made me feel good. I was glad he liked her. And the look in her eyes told me how impressed she was by him. His politeness overwhelmed her. And at times it overwhelmed me as well. Most guys his age weren't as sensitive and caring as he, and that was obvious.

We ate several helpings, then I got up to help clear the table.

"Just leave them dear. I'll do them later. Why don't you two come into the living room and make yourselves at home."

Following her, we went back and sat on that beautiful green and burgundy velvet, high backed couch. It did wonders for my back. Even though it looked old, it was massaging each muscle as I rested on it. Eric placed his arm around me and squeezed my shoulder. I guess he knew I was nervous about what she was going to do. Neither one of us knew what to expect, so we were both a little shaky.

Penny went over and dimmed the lights a little, then returned back to her chair.

"Beth, are you ready to get started?"

Taking a deep breath, I replied, "I'm ready when you are."

I glanced over at Eric one last time before I was taken into another place and time in my life. Like she had told me the day before, maybe I'd forgotten certain times in my life for a reason. Maybe they were just too painful to remember, but I had to find out. So I sat there still and quiet and waited for her to tell me what to do next.

CHAPTER 20

After a moment or two, she broke the silence which had consumed me. And I listened to her instructions carefully.

"Okay Beth. Sit back. And remember, Eric and I are both here with you, so there's no reason to be afraid."

I did as she said. I sat back and let my whole body relax entirely. It was hard, but as she said, they were there for me. All I had to do was reach out, and Eric would be right there.

"Now close your eyes and breath deeply, in and out, over and over again until you feel yourself drifting far, far away."

I closed my eyes and did as she asked. And with each breath my mind wandered further and further away.

"Now, as I count backwards from ten to one, you'll feel yourself becoming very sleepy. Ten, nine, eight...breath slowly...seven, six, five, four...in and out. Feel each inch of your body relaxing. Three, two...deeper and deeper...one."

It was strange. I felt like I was placed somewhere in the clouds above. I had no emotions surrounding me, none at all. But then I heard her voice once again.

"Now Beth, open your eyes. Do you feel relaxed?"

"Yes." I replied in a dazed state.

"Good, good. Now listen to my instructions, and at any time during our session I feel you need to be awakened, I will snap my fingers and you will wake feeling refreshed and revived."

Staring blankly ahead of me, I could see Penny, and her voice was clear as she continued on.

"I want you to travel back in time to when you were eight years old, on a Friday, January 7th. Tell me what happened that day."

Suddenly I was taken back quickly to my youth. But the strange thing was that I was reliving that day exactly as it happened.

Again she asked, "Beth, what happened that day. Just take your time. We're in no hurry."

As that day showed itself clear to me, I answered, "Mom and dad are fighting again. I'm scared to leave my room."

"Is it morning?"

"Yes, and they keep on yelling so loud. Why can't I make them stop?" I replied, as my voice transformed into the voice of a small child.

"Okay. Lets go further into the day. Now tell me what's going on."

"I'm walking home from school by myself. There's a couple of kids walking behind me laughing at me. I wish they'd stop. I'm so tired of getting made fun of. They just keep on and on."

"Then what Beth? Just stay calm. Keep breathing in and out."

"I'm walking in the house. Dad's sitting on the couch watching TV."

"Does he say anything to you?"

"No. He's just sitting there with his feet propped up on the coffee table."

Pausing for a moment, I wait to see what happens next.

"Oh my God, no more. Please make him stop." I cried out.

"What Beth? Tell me what's going on."

"He's come upstairs. He's hitting me with his belt. Over and over again, he just won't stop. I hate you! I hate you!"

"Who are you talking to?"

"My father."

"Okay Beth, go a little further into the day. It's after supper. Tell me what you see."

"It's like always. Melissa's sitting there not saying a word, and Lewis is making ugly faces at me." I said calmly.

"Is anything strange about this particular night Beth?"

"Mom's acting funny. In fact, she hasn't said a word all night. I don't know, but I don't care either.

"Oh no..oh no..."

"Tell me."

"My father just went into the kitchen. He's hitting her. Stop hitting her! Stop it...stop it!"

"It's alright Beth. I'm here with you."

"He won't stop. I'm running towards him and pounding on his back trying to make him stop. He's looking at me. Please God don't let him come after me. Please."

"What's he doing?"

"He's running after me. I'm so scared. Why does he do this to me. I don't deserve it. I don't deserve it," screaming to the top of my lungs.

"Where are you running to Beth."

Feeling shaky and unsure, I answered, "My room. I'm going to my room. I've got to hide. Where can I hide?"

As tears began to flow down my cheeks, I started rocking to and fro hysterically. The memory of my father frazzled my mind and bruised my heart all over again. But before it completely tore me into, Penny snapped her fingers and I woke from a nightmare that happened years earlier. Sweat was dripping from my forehead, and my hands were clutched so tightly I could barely open them myself.

Penny leaned over to me and asked, "Are you alright?"

"I'm fine, just a little uneasy."

Eric put his arms around me gently and hugged me. "You did great babe. Are you sure you're alright with all of this. I mean, if you don't want to do this again, you don't have to."

"That's right," Penny said, "If you don't feel comfortable with any of this, you just say the word and we'll stop."

Shaking my head, I replied, "No. I want to do this. I feel it's something I need to do."

After writing a couple of things down on her small note pad, she looked up at me with caring eyes. It was almost as if she had tears filling them, but I could've been mistaken.

"Why don't we call it a night? We can continue tomorrow. Is tomorrow alright Beth?"

"Tomorrow's fine. This is all strange to me, but then again, I never thought I could be hypnotized."

Penny laughed lightly as she stood up and came over to me. "I'm proud of you dear. You did very well for your first time. It'll get harder, but I know you're strong. And believe me, you'll be a much stronger person after you know the whole truth."

"But none of that stuff I remembered was really forgotten, I just don't think about it. There's no sense in it. That can't be what's holding me back. I've always known what a cruel and horrible person my father was. That was never a secret. Eric saw that for himself. He can tell you first hand about my father's son-of-a-bitch attitude."

"Well, you may already know he treated you badly, but some of those memories are locked away deep inside of you. And if we pull them all out, then you'll be able to better deal with them one after another. If you only know a few incidents in your life, then you'll be stuck forever trying to figure out the rest. That's what I'm trying to do. I'm hoping we can figure out the rest."

With my heartbeat returning to normal, I thanked her and took Eric's arm as we went to the door. Penny ran ahead of us and politely let us outside.

"Let's make it the same time tomorrow. I'm sure you kids could use another good meal. If I were you, I'd get tired of eating at those fast food joints in town. And besides, I'm delighted to be able to cook for someone for a change. As long as I'm making someone happy, I feel like I'm doing my job." she said patting both of us on the back. She was sincere. There was no doubt in my mind about that.

The scene I encountered was replayed over and over in my mind. It wasn't that it bothered me, I just couldn't believe I had forgotten, or misplaced it, in my memory. But most importantly, I knew there was something else buried far deeper than what Penny had brought to the surface. Because like I said before, the mean way my father treated me, was no shock. And the dilemma consuming my broken memory, was still hidden, still there to discover.

After driving back, I couldn't help but think about what our next session might be like. I didn't know if it would be scary, or if it would be something I already knew in my subconscious. But however it should turn out, it had to be helpful. Anything that would make me remember even a little bit of my past, would get me that much closer to opening the door of sanity.

The anticipation of the following day drug each second, each minute, by slower and slower. But soon enough the night came and went. And once more, I took a sleeping pill for reassurance of a good nights sleep. The whole night through I didn't move an inch. As the night before, I cuddled next to Eric and used him as my security blanket.

Then the sun created a brilliant light letting us know it was time to start a new day. But instead of getting up, we laid there for hours watching old movies made in black and white. Those kinds of movies always gave me the feeling everything would be that simple forever. Although I knew things were complicated in my life at that point and time, I was still able to close my eyes and imagine those comical characters on that black and white movie screen, and it would uncomplicate my life for a little while.

Lying there half the day, I noticed the stillness lingering around us. The halls were completely quiet, and I seldom heard a car pass in front of the dorm. And for the first time, I looked at it as more of contentment, instead of being an eerie feeling floating and hovering over us. My pessimistic side was being worn down by a roar of optimism, with still a hint of fear somewhere in between.

Hour after hour, time flew by. It was the middle of the day and we were still in bed. Of course there was no reason for us to get up, so we didn't move. I enjoyed the peace I felt lying there with him. Even though we hadn't talked much, it didn't matter. His touch spoke to me each time his flesh would encounter mine. And his touch said more to me than any words could ever say. Each time he caressed my skin, he seemed to say "I love you," without moving his lips. And my touch on his skin told him the same thing. It was understood.

Finally we stumbled out of bed and raced to the showers. We figured it would save a little time if we showered together, but all it did was make us take much longer.

Standing on that cold bathroom floor, I threw off my clothes and dropped them. And looking up, I began to laugh. Eric was standing there in his hang ten, purple, bikini underwear. He always loved that sexy kind of underwear. He started posing like a body builder would, flexing his masculine, irresistible muscles. I just wanted to reach out and feel his hard, perfectly shaped biceps. But before I could, he bent over and took off the remainder of his clothes as well.

Following me into the shower, he turned on the water. Those hot jets pounding down on both of us as we clung onto one another, were nothing short of heavenly. Then he reached for the soap in the corner and began to massage my entire body with it. He washed my back in a circular motion. And my skin flinched with every touch as sensations rapidly scurried through me. He began to kiss the curve of my neck over and over again. At first it tickled, but then it excited the sensual part of me. With each lashing of his tongue on my warm pale skin, I wanted him more and more as I begin to get hotter and hotter for luscious sweating body.

His fingers crawled around my waist, then lower and lower, until he touched the perfect spot. I couldn't help but arch my back from his erotic caresses. Twirling around, I grabbed him. Starting at his lips and making my way further down, he ran his big rough hands through my hair the whole time. I wanted to stay pressed up against him forever.

And as we made out way to the bottom of the shower, we became one being. He thrust his love upon me time after time until I had reached a tremendous peak of pleasure. And since I had no reason to hold my tongue, I burst out a shriek of ecstasy. No one heard my screams. And for once, I was able to let it all out without holding in one ounce of my happiness. For once I didn't have to lock away my excitement, but instead, I released it with all the strength I had inside of me. It seemed like it had been a lifetime since I'd felt his love in that way. Even though it had only been days, I still felt like it had been much longer.

Then as our breathing slowed down, we sat in the corner of the shower letting the water trickle down on us. It was still warm, so we finished washing, got out and hurried back to my room just in case someone else might accidentally be roaming the halls. Eric acted like we were running a race. He jetted ahead of me and landed on my bed with his towel still neatly wrapped around him.

"You better not go back to sleep. We've gotta get ready in a hurry."

He laughed and replied, "You're talking about dressing in a hurry. It takes you two hours just to put on your make-up."

Squinting my eyes, I reached for a small pillow lying on Amy's bed beside me. And before he could protect himself, I clobbered him with it. Then the fight was on. I knew he wouldn't let me get the last hit, so he rushed me. Falling backwards, we both tumbled to the floor laughing.

"Come on now, we've gotta get ready. Do you ever stop playing around?" I said, trying to act mad at him.

With a strange look on his face, he replied in one of his funny voices, "You started it sweetheart. You started it."

I pushed him off of me and went to the mirror to fix my hair. And it seemed like every five minutes he would make fun the way I was doing something. Either I was making funny faces as I put my make-up on, or he'd laugh at the way I was teasing my hair. He was so crazy. If the truth be known, there was never a dull moment with Eric Lee Norris. In fact, he was like a barrel of monkeys. You couldn't help but laugh at him.

As we were just about ready to go, my stomach made the most awful noise. It was then I realized how hungry I was. Eric and I had been so busy sleeping and being lazy all day, we didn't even think to eat. But we both knew Penny would have something hot and delicious waiting for us. I liked being waited on as she did, but it was also something I could get used to, far too easily. So I didn't want to make a habit out of it.

Hurrying to her house, we didn't make one wrong turn. He remembered exactly where it was. And once again, as we pulled up into her driveway, she met us on the porch. And still, she had that happy look on her face. I wondered sometimes if she ever frowned at all. I'd never seen her in nothing but a smile, so I wasn't sure.

Walking up to her, I hugged her as if it were second nature to me. And to my surprise, Eric did the same. He embraced her firmly as if he were hugging his own mother. Then hand in hand, Eric and I walked into her home which was so welcoming to us.

"I bet your hungry."

Almost before she could finish her sentence, Eric answered, "Yes ma'am."

"We'll have to do something about that. It's all ready. All you have to do is fill your plates to your hearts content." she said taking off her apron and leading us into her dining room.

"This is great Mrs. Downs." Eric said with a mouth full of food.

"It's Penny dear. Please call me Penny. It makes me feel old when people call me Mrs." she said.

"I'm sorry ma'am. This is great Penny."

She just smiled and continued to take bird like bites of her food.

"Penny, what are we gonna do tonight. I mean, have you got a plan on where in my past I need to go?" I said curiously.

"I have an idea dear, but I can't be sure until we put you back into that time capsule of hypnotism again. It's hard to tell. It is true you relived a horrible memory last night when you were under, but it's not the core of your problems. We have to reach the core, not just touch on the surface. Do you understand?"

Nodding, I replied, "I understand, but all of this is weird for me. How is it possible to remember something that you chose to forget for so many years."

"You see dear, the mind is very complicated. There are many places your memories can go. Some memories are easily reached because you want to remember every second of that particular time, but others are locked away. It's hard to explain, but your mind seems to know which memories you want to remember, and which ones you'd rather forget. And what we're trying to do, is to bring out all of those times which have been locked away." she explained.

"Hmm, makes sense I guess. So what you're saying is that some memories we put on a shelf, where they're easy to reach, and others we put in a safe, locked away," I said with a bewildered look on my face.

"That's a good way of putting it Beth. I'll have to remember that explanation. I may need it sometime."

Penny Looked at me with eyes of concern, and for a moment, I thought I saw a star shimmering in the midst of them. Almost like the star on the top of our Christmas tree in that small hotel room in Dallas. But when I looked back at her, the star was gone. I must've been letting my imagination run away again. But it didn't seem like my imagination at all. It was real. Maybe she was my guiding light. Maybe God had sent her to lead me to the right pathway. And if he did, I had no doubt where my life was headed...towards happiness and love.

"Beth, you're not eating and Eric's already had two plates. Something wrong?" she asked.

"No, I'm fine. I'm just tired." I replied, trying to cover up all of my worry.

After dinner, I went against what Penny had said the night before, and I began to pick up the dishes and take them into the kitchen. And the whole time, she kept on insisting I go sit down.

"I want to help you. You told me that it's not often you get to cook for anyone, well, it's not very often I get to help someone who's been so terribly nice to me. Please let me do this. I'd feel much better if you did."

With a slight pause, she replied, "Oh, alright. You're about as hard-headed as my husband was. In fact, you remind me of him, in a way."

"What do you mean?"

"It's strange, but the expression on your face sometimes. It's almost like...oh, listen to me. I'm just going on and on. Maybe I'm the one who needs to be hypnotized."

Her words clung to my mind. I was glad I reminded her of the man she devoted her life to. Maybe if she saw his expressions in my face, then she would be truly happy. I know it sounds funny, but I wanted to make her happy. She deserved it far more than my mom and dad ever did. And, in a way, I wished I could adopt her as being my mother figure. But I didn't have to. I looked up to her so much already, and I didn't think it was possible to think any more of her than I already did.

After helping her with the dishes, I glanced into the living room to see what Eric was doing.

"He's fine dear. He's probably just browsing around this old house. Besides, I'm glad I have a moment alone with you. I wanted the chance to tell you what a wonderful young man he is. He seems to really care for you. In fact, I haven't seen two people that in love since Jerry and I. We were just like y'all are now. We couldn't seem to get enough of one another. And when I was by myself, I thought of him constantly. I don't know. It was like we were a part of each another. When he would feel pain, I'd feel it. And when I'd feel happiness, he'd smile just as enthusiastically as I did." she said as the smile faded the longer she talked.

"Penny, it's alright. He's probably watching over you every day making sure you're alright. And by the look in his eyes in all of those pictures, he's probably even got his arm around you right now, but you just don't know it."

Taking a huge sigh, she replied "You're right. There's no sense in being sad. I was sad for way too long. I know he and I will be together again one day, and that's what I should focus on. It might be forty years away, but I'll still love him just as much then, if not more."

Reaching for her hand, she grasped firmly onto me. "Thank you Beth. I needed that talk. Sometimes it gets awfully lonely here in this big house. And it's nice to have you here, both of you."

"Come on, let's get started. The sooner the better right?"

Smiling at me, she replied, "You learn fast. Come on. Eric probably thinks we got caught up in girl talk and forgot about him."

"Penny, I'd never forget about him." I said strolling into the living room.

Eric was sitting on the couch with his head propped up, and his eyes closed. And since I loved to aggravate him, I tip-toed over to him and yelled as loud as I could, "Wake up!"

He jumped so quickly I think his heart may have skipped a beat, and Penny and I stood there laughing at him. Then he rubbed his eyes and glared at me as if he were trying to act mad.

"Sorry babe. I know how hard you are to wake, so I thought I'd do it the best way I knew how."

"You've woke me up in better ways than that," he said chuckling a little.

"Eric!" I sternly said, "Don't say stuff like that in front of..."

"It's alright dear. I'm middle aged, not dead," she said, grinning from ear to ear then sitting down directly in front of me.

Blushing a little, I lowered my head in embarrassment. I guess it didn't bother Eric talking like that in front of her, but it sure bothered me. I respected her, and I felt talking that way in front of her was doing nothing less than disrespecting her. Although I was probably over-reacting, I still felt strongly about it. Our personal life was between he and I, not the rest of the world too, especially Penny.

And as my frustration from the prior moment ran through me, Penny got up and dimmed the lights as she did the night before. That's when I scooted closer to Eric. Even though I knew she would wake me before I felt at risk of being hurt, I was still concerned about what I would see. Although I trusted her, I didn't trust myself enough to know I wouldn't dream exactly what I was going to see. That was the thought which scared me the most.

While Penny came back and sat down, I closed my eyes and begin to relax. I started breathing in and out, over and over again until I started feeling free from worry, frustration, and fear. And with each breath, it seemed to work. In and out, in and out, I felt myself drifting further and further inside my subconscious. Then I heard her voice.

"Beth. Listen closely. This time I'm going to take you to a different time. And remember, if I snap my fingers, you will wake feeling refreshed and calm."

Listening to her words, I waited for her next command. My mind traveled nowhere, instead, it just floated around and around, waiting...just waiting.

CHAPTER 21

With nervousness consuming me, Penny began to talk to me in a low and tender voice. It was like hearing an angel talk to me from above.

"Okay Beth. I'm going to ask you to search your mind, far back in your mind. Can you tell me about what happened on January 9th, when you were eight years old? Take your time and scan through the day."

Thinking and thinking, as before, a picture came clear to me. "I'm walking down the hallway to my room. Mom and dad are yelling again. I can't stand hearing them yell at each other. I just want to scream."

"Is there anyone else in the house?"

"Yes. Lewis is home. He's in his room playing his music really loud. I keep telling him to turn it down, but he won't listen to me. He never listens to me. He acts like just I'm someone to make fun of, but no one stops him. He just keeps on and on until I feel myself drifting off into a dreamland."

After a short pause, Penny continued, "Go a little further in the day. And continue whenever you're ready."

"The yelling just stopped. I don't know, but I think mom just left. The front door slammed loud enough for me to hear. I think it was mom that left," I said, unsure of what was happening.

"Is it still loud from Lewis's music?"

"No. It's strange, but I think he turned it off. I don't know why. He never does anything I ask him too. And I don't hear dad either. I'm not sure what's going on. I sure wish Melissa was here. She went to spend the night with a friend. And I can't stand being here without her."

"Why Beth?"

"She protects me."

"What does she protect you from?"

"From him. She protects me from him. And when she's not here..."

Feeling Penny's hand touch mine, she asked, "Are you ok?"

"Fine...just fine." I replied calmly.

"Good, good. Now tell me what you hear."

"Nothing. Nothing at all. I guess I might as well get ready for bed. Let me see, here's my night shirt and robe-oh no! Not again. I've got to hide. I've got to do something. He can't find me tonight. I don't think I can take it again. Please God don't let him find me. Please!"

Reminding me I was in a safe environment, I was soothed by her words until the rest of the picture in my mind, showed itself to me.

"I'm in bed now. But I know he'll come for me. I know he doesn't care about how I feel."

"Who Beth? Who?"

"Oh God, my door is opening. I'm trying to clinch my eyes shut, but it doesn't help. Now I hear his footsteps coming closer to me. Don't let him do it to me again. Don't let him touch me.

It's too late...It's too late. His hands, his cold hands are shaking me, but I'm pretending to be asleep. Sometimes I pretend to be asleep because I think he might leave me alone, but this time he doesn't care."

In a caring, but curious tone of voice, Penny asked, "Can you tell me who is there? Can you tell me Beth?"

"No, I'm ashamed. I'm ashamed," I said in a horrified voice.

"There's nothing to be ashamed of. Who's hurting you?"

"NO...NO, he's on top of me. God make him stop. It hurts...It hurts...I want to die. I just want to die."

With Eric's arm draped around me, I was being held tightly as those horrifying visions from the past showed themselves to me as clearly as if it were happening at that moment.

A bit shaken, I continued, "I hear footsteps coming down the hallway. I hear someone coming. 'Help...Help' I yelled. The door's opening...wider and wider. It's my daddy. Daddy...make him stop. Make him stop. Oh No, don't leave me. Please don't leave me," I cried out loud.

"Beth tell me what's happening. I can't help you if you don't tell me what you see. I know it's painful, but you have to tell me what you remember," she said sternly.

"Oh my God. Oh my God. Why did he let this happen to me. I'm bleeding again. I bleed every time he does this to me. But he's gone now. I'm alone now, even without God. Because God wouldn't let this happen to someone he loves. He just wouldn't."

"Who just left? Who did this to you?"

"It was Lewis. He does it all the time. But this time Daddy let him. Daddy didn't even stop him. He let Lewis violate me. Why?" I said, beginning to scream as loud as I possibly could.

"Beth, can you continue? Do you want to stop?"

"No. I want to finish. I'm writing now. I'm writing everything I feel on paper. I have to. I have to have a way out of this hell."

Whispering, Penny asked, "What are you writing?"

"Like a God shadowing me,
I'm covered with loss of voice.
Fighting demands are whispered
With no feeling of remorse.
Shadowed, feeling helpless,

Knowing no one will care.
So I remain still and silent.
As I continue to say a prayer.
"Please God take me from this fear
Please help me passed this scorn.
Give me lord, one answer,
Why was I ever born."

Stillness filled the room after reciting what words I'd written as a little girl.

Neither Penny or Eric said a word. They must've been as overwhelmed at what they heard, as I was for remembering it.

Trembling inside, the visions kept coming and coming until I heard Penny counting down once more to open my eyes. And when she reached one, then snapped her fingers, I came back to reality with a sick sense of shame about myself. My mind was boggled by every appalling scene which swept through my mind as I was taken back into my wretched past. Reliving those moments once more after I was awakened, I began to shout. And without thinking, I jumped up and ran towards the front door. Then slinging the door wide open, I stumbled out onto the front porch. And Lewis's sickening voice seemed to whisper to me in a dreadful and ghastly voice. Echoing all around me, a combination of the whistling wind and the voices in my head, convinced me I was losing my mind completely.

And as I heard footsteps walking up to me, I was distraught once more. In my mind, I kept seeing that face...that frightful and ambiguous face of the person who had ruined my life from the time I was a child. And although I wanted to erase it from my mind, I didn't think it possible to erase a part of my past which had such influence on my life. But until then, I didn't know how much of an influence it had. Until then, I didn't know what was turning my life upside down.

"Beth." Penny said tenderly.

"I don't want to talk. I think I've said enough, haven't I?" I said in a agitated tone of voice.

Placing her hand on my shoulder, she replied, "I know what you must be feeling right now, and I'm so sorry about what happened to you. I had no clue that was what we'd find. I had no clue you were so violated as a child. And in a way, I feel guilty for making you remember."

With my heart softening for her the longer she spoke. "It's not your fault Penny. It's no one's fault but my own. Because now that I'm beginning to remember what happened to me as a child, I'm beginning to think there had to be something I could've done different to stop all of the fear and abuse. There had to be something I could've done. Anything at all. And for the few moments I've been standing out here in the cool air, other memories have transformed into complete pictures. Now I know it didn't happen only once. It happened over and over again. But I guess the part I don't understand, is about my father. How could he let it happen? I saw it so clearly. He walked in and walked out of my room as if nothing was going on. He seemed to care less about me and my feelings. Penny, how could he do that to me? How could he?"

Sighing, she answered, "Dear, I don't know, but I do know one thing. You'll be just fine. Once you have time to let the rest of your past be put into its' place, then you'll be able to deal with it in a way that will be beneficial to your recovery. And I believe we've seen enough to know what was causing your distress. Now we know why you were having all those strange dreams, and who the person was in the shadows in each one of them. There's no question in my mind-it was your brother Lewis. And as horrible as it sounds, it's good for you to remember it. Because if you don't relive, remember and deal with it completely, then you'll never be the person you want to be."

While a tear rolled down my cheek, she wiped it away and asked, "Now, do you want to go inside and join your fiancé?"

"No. Would you please tell him I'll just meet him in the car. I'm sorry, but I just don't feel like talking right now, and if I know Eric, he'll want me to talk to him about everything. I don't know, I just can't right now. I just can't talk to anyone about it right this minute. It hasn't even had time to sink into my system yet. And I'm sure when it does, I'll feel like discussing it and analyzing it."

Nodding her head in accordance, she squeezed my hand and turned to go back inside. As she shut the front screen door, I wandered slowly and carefully down the steps, to the walkway. Trying to clear my mind of everything, it was impossible. In fact, I didn't know if I'd ever be able to get passed the thought of being molested by my own brother. And even though I knew he wasn't my real brother, it didn't matter, it was still a sick and inconceivable thought. Because the more I thought about it, the sicker I began to feel.

Leaning against the car feeling a cool breeze briskly brush by, I looked up to see Eric coming out of the house. He was holding his head down as if he were ashamed to look me in the eye. My first thought was that he looked down at me now, but without looking him directly in the eye, I couldn't tell that for sure. Of course, it wouldn't surprise me, because, at that moment, I looked down on myself for being so terrified and for giving in to a sorry son-of-a-bitch who I used to call my brother. I should've been strong enough to tell someone. But most of all, I should've known something wasn't right when my father gave sanction for him to tamper with my innocents.

Approaching me slowly, Eric looked up. His face was red, and his eyes were engulfed in large, expressive and caring tears.

"I had no idea Babe. I'm so sorry. I didn't know what to do or say when I finally realized what you were talking about in there. Now I know why it was hard for you to be with me sexually all those times. Now I understand everything. I wish I didn't, but I do."

Wiping his tears away, I began to cry as well. His emotional state of mind was contagious. I felt like bursting into tears before he came out, but when I saw the look on his face, I had no other choice than to show him exactly how much fear dwelled inside of me. And even though my inner secret was out in the open, I felt captive still. I felt like I was being held captive by the corpse lying in that old and ragged cemetery, in the middle of nowhere. And I knew that corpse would have a hold on my life until I got a grip on it myself.

"Eric, you need to be strong for me until I can be strong for myself. All of this is a shock to me as well as it is to you, but we've got to find a way to get past it somehow."

Then putting his hands on my face gently, he replied, "You're right, but I can't help but think what he did to you. I can't help but think of all of the horrible things you went through. And the worst part, is that no one was there to help you. There was no one there to protect you."

Lowering my head, "I know. My own father..."

Placing his finger over my lips, he stopped me, "No. Don't say it. Because the longer I think about it, the more I want to go and beat the hell out of that sorry, no good, uncaring, bastard father of yours. I would kill him if I ever got my hands on him. I'd just kill him Beth."

Then wrapping my arms around him, I tried to destroy part of his anger with my love, but it didn't seem to work. He broke away from me and walked over to the edge of the house. And following along behind him, I heard him mumbling.

"Why God? Why did this have to happen to her? Why her?" he muttered in a low, but furious voice.

Touching his shoulder, he flinched. It wasn't as though he didn't want me having contact with him, it was more like his nerves had gone crazy inside of him. He couldn't seem to stop shaking. It was very strange. It seemed to me I should've been the one acting in that way, but it was him.

Turning facing me, he grasped onto my shoulders, "Beth. I told you one time, every pain you feel, I feel it just as much, if not more. And until now, I wasn't sure exactly how true that was. But I feel so much pain for you. I feel enough pain for the both of us. It kills me knowing what happened to you. I can't stand it."

"Why don't we just go home and talk. Maybe we can focus on something else for the night. Maybe that's what we need to do, calm down a little." I said, even though I was shaking just as much as he was.

Taking my hand, he agreed, "Alright. Lets go."

Walking to the car, Eric didn't look at me, but instead, he held onto my hand as if he was afraid someone was going to steal me away. In a way, I felt like Eric was ashamed of me. I don't know why, I guess because I felt enough shame for the both of us. And even though I knew in my heart it wasn't my fault, I still felt responsible for letting it happen. I felt responsible for not telling someone about what Lewis had so horribly forced on me. But instead, I did nothing. I said nothing to no one. And to me, that was my fault, no one else's.

We got in the car and drove away. But when I looked back, I saw Penny standing on her front porch with her arms crossed. Once or twice she wiped her face as if she'd been crying, and I felt guilty. I felt like I had selfishly drug her into my complicated and terrible life. She had enough to worry about without having one more lost soul following her around looking for answers. So I decided I'd leave her alone for a while and try to work the rest of my recovery out, on my own. And although I needed her, I didn't want to drag her down with me. I wanted to wait until I had myself picked up out of my pity, before I re-entered her life once more.

We made it back to my room, and I started thinking. Deep down I wanted to be by myself for a while. Not just for an hour or two, but for a few days. Because if I didn't have some time to myself, I wasn't sure if I'd ever be able to sort out what I was feeling. Eric was only an obstacle in my thoughts. Though I loved thinking about him, as long as he was around, I wouldn't have the time to devote to putting together all of the pieces of my life.

Walking up to the front door of my dorm, with hesitation, I lowered my head and said, "I think I need a little time to think Eric. You know how much I love you, but this is one thing you can't help me with. Just think about it. I just found out what happened to me as a child which I made myself forget. My own brother, or someone I thought to be my brother for many years, took one thing from me I can never get back. He stole something from me that God gave to me- my innocence. And I'm afraid, little by little the rest will show itself to me. But when it does, I want to be able to handle it by myself. Because you're not always going to be with me, every second of every day. I've got to get a grip on reality and deal with my past. I hope you understand."

Kissing my forehead, he replied sweetly, "I understand. I can't argue with what you just said, but I do want you to remember where I am. I'll be there waiting for you whenever you get your head straight. And I want to be there whenever you're ready for me to come back around. It doesn't matter if it takes you two hours, two days, or two years. I'll be waiting."

His tender words touched me deeper than anything he'd ever said. And I believed every single word came from deep in his heart. I had no doubt about his sincerity. Then kissing him, I opened the door, went in, and shut it back. With him on one side and with me on the other, we both placed our hands on the glass as if our hands were touching one another. And when he smiled, I took a mental picture of that beautiful sight. I knew I would carry that picture around with me until I felt sane again. And although I had no idea how long it would take, I still had a glorious picture in my mind of the one man who never gave up on me. In fact, he was the only man who ever loved me unconditionally. And I loved him just the same.

Then walking to my room, I turned to see him getting driving away. It was hard watching him leave, but I knew it was something I had to do. I felt like I was doing the right thing. As I told Eric once, "I can't be happy with you until I'm happy with myself." And at that point, I wasn't happy with myself at all. In fact, shame filled each inch of me. I felt dirty and deprived of a happy childhood. And until I dealt with the whole picture, I knew I'd never be able to start another puzzle of my life without taking a look at the old one first.

Reaching my room, it seemed like memories of all sorts came zooming through my mind. Happy, sad, disturbing and appalling memories didn't seem to want to cease, but instead, got stronger and stronger. So, to sleep well for the night, I promised myself this would be the last time I'd take one of those pills to sleep. I opened the bottles, poured me a glass of water, and swallowed that tiny pill which seemed to work wonders for my slumber. And it was one time I really needed it. I wanted to remember everything eventually, but I wanted to rest in peace for the night. I wanted to be well rested so I could continue in my search for the remainder of the truth.

Only moments after I had swallowed that dream destroyer, my eyes began to get heavy, and the moment I laid on the bed, I was out like a light. In fact, a time or two, my own snoring half way woke me. But I would just fall back to sleep with no problem at all. Then as thoughts of Eric, my horrible dreams, and the rest of what I recollected earlier in the day, started to deteriorate little by little, nothing was left but a blank mind, heart and soul. I had drifted off into a land where nothing was wrong, and I didn't want to leave that land until that tiny bit of medication wore off the following morning. I wanted to stay in that place, but too soon, it wore off and I found a new day directly in front of me.

As soon as I sat up in my bed, the phone rang. I figured it was Eric checking on me, but as I picked up the phone, Penny's voice was on the other end of the line.

"Beth dear, how are you? I was really worried about you after you left last night. And Eric was even more worried. It looked like he was hurting the same as you. And to me, that's real love."

"He does love me. I know that. But Penny, like I told Eric, I need some time to think about all of this. I'm not sure how I'm gonna put together my past and build my future, but I can't do it with Eric or anyone else in my way. I can't be side tracked right now. This is something I have to do. And I was thinking about you last night." I said firmly but sensitively at the same time.

"What about me Beth?"

"I hate that I've put you in the middle of my problems. I know that's why you started helping me in the beginning, but after a while, I started looking at you as more of a friend than a doctor."

"So what's the problem? I think of you as a friend too, dear."

"I don't want to give you anything else to worry about. I'm the only one who needs to worry about my recovery from all of this. It's my life, no one else's."

Hesitantly, she replied, "Listen, I'm your friend, but as your doctor, I think it essential that you keep seeing me in therapy sessions until you resolve all of your harsh feelings inside. I can help you with that."

Trying to make her understand, I continued, "I know I need you, but you don't need someone else giving you something to worry about. You've got plenty of your own. And it's not fair for me to throw such dilemmas on you. I just don't think it's fair at all."

"Well, I'm here if you need me. I'm not going to force you to come and see me, but when you feel you need someone, you know where to find me, at home and at work. I want to be there for you dear. You've become like a...well, you've become very special to me." she said.

"Thank you Penny. You're special to me too. That's why I'm doing this. And if I need you, I promise I'll call. You can count on that." I replied.

"Call me anytime, day or night." she said hanging up the phone.

Feeling consoled, I went over, flipped on the television, and laid back on the bed. And as the night before, many incidents from my past jetted at me, one after another. I couldn't seem to stop them, and I wasn't so sure I wanted to. Because each time I'd remember something, I'd find a missing piece to my horrid puzzle of the past.

The day came and went, then the next day the same. Eric hadn't called and I spent my time filling empty holes in my memory. And with each hole filled, I felt more alive, more at ease. Each glance into years passed, I'd see something, then place it where it fit in my mind. Then as I had filled each and every puzzle piece, I sat in bewilderment. It was hard to believe that one last session with Penny caused such a flow of remembrance, but it did. And I was very grateful for that. Most of all, I was grateful to her for taking the time and effort to help someone like me.

Two days had passed since I'd talked to either Penny or Eric, and I felt like I'd had plenty of time by myself. So I picked up the phone and called Penny at home. She didn't answer, so I dialed her office number. After several rings, her secretary answered.

"Is Mrs. Downs in?" I asked timidly.

Hold please." she said professionally.

Then after listening to the radio playing in my ear for a moment or two, she answered.

"This is Mrs. Downs."

"Penny?"

"Beth. It's good to hear from you. It's been a few days, how's things goin'?"

"Good I guess. I think I finally worked everything out in my mind. Listen, do you mind if I come in and talk to you for a while. Do you have any openings today? She laughed and replied, "For you, I always have time. Just come in whenever you want. I make time."

"Thanks Penny. I'll see you after while." I said, hanging up the phone.

I went over to my desk and picked up a pen. It had been a while since I'd written anything, but I felt it was time I began to do things which came naturally to me. I had gotten out of my normal routine for so long, I almost forgot about writing. Besides, with each word written, I would give myself a little inner therapy along with the therapy Penny was providing. And between the two, I knew I'd be able to find a way out of such a perplexing state of mind.

And as my pen made contact with the wrinkled paper in front of me, I wrote:

I've found myself somehow,
After so many years of pain.
I feel more contented now,
When at first, I felt only shame.
Fault was no within my hands,
But in the hands of Lewis still.
Sometimes it's hard to tell just where I am,
Or exactly the way I feel.
But now I know the truth.
Now I know what's real.
I know Eric will always be with me,

And feel everything I feel.
I doubt not his feelings,
But instead I cherish and need him near.
I am alone for the moment,
But I know soon he will be here.
For I want to regain my life,
And continue to build our love.
For I'd never throw away
Something God sent from up above.
I would never deny my happiness,
If I knew things would stay that way.
I faced my fears head on
And said all I need to say.
Though I'll never know exactly why
I was chosen for this crime.
There's one thing that can heal my wounds,
And that one thing is time.

After writing every ounce of feeling inside of me at that moment, I went and got my purse and jacket. I couldn't wait to see Penny and thank her for everything. And while I was there, I knew it would be a good idea to tell her a little bit about a few of the other things my memory showed me. Because after she had released that one horrible recollection, then the rest followed like dominos falling in a row. And I was sure she wanted to see the entire picture of what I was seeing in my mind. She had the right to know the outcome of my discovery because she was the cause of it. She was the one who helped it to surface.

Then walking out my door, Eric's smile which I had pictured in my subconscious for days, showed itself to me once again in my mind. In fact, going to see him was one thing I needed to do after seeing my favorite doctor. I wanted to make sure I was okay before talking to Eric. And talking to Penny, I knew she'd be honest with me as far as my sanity went. There was no way she'd lie to me about my recovery. If anything she'd be too blunt and honest about it, whether it be good or bad.

Getting into my car, I felt completely free of every fear, pain, and confusion which had a tremendous hold on me for so long. Driving towards Penny's office, I knew I'd feel better and completely relaxed after talking with her. In fact, I had no doubt in my mind about that. So I drove along with nothing short of happy thoughts dancing around in my head. Happy thoughts was what I needed all along. The only problem was, up until then, I had nothing happy, other than Eric, to think of.

CHAPTER 22

Excited to tell Penny about how I'd handled the horrible fact of my past, I finally pulled into the small parking lot on the corner, by her office. But this time, when I pulled in, everything was as quiet and calm as it could be. There were no strangers lurking, and there was little traffic passing by. Just like everything else, the air was calm and placid. And for the first time in my life, I finally knew why I'd acted so crazy for so many years. I knew why I never wanted a man to touch me. But most of all, I had an excuse for the majority of my crazed actions. And with every step towards Penny's office, I felt each bit of uncertainty sifting out of my fragile body, little by little. It was like walking into a cloud, a safe, peaceful cloud, one I'd been in search of for far too long.

The first person I saw when I opened the door and walked in, was Penny's receptionists. I never knew her name, but she was always very friendly to everyone she'd come across. In fact, I couldn't remember one time when she wasn't in a good mood, or smiling from ear to ear. And for me, that meant a lot, especially the first time I walked into that place. I felt at home right off the bat because of that one smiling face. And every time thereafter, she always made each visit a pleasant experience.

Penny walked out into the waiting area where I was standing. And with no hesitation what-so-ever, she marched up to me and embraced me firmly.

"Welcome back dear. Come on in and sit down." she said, as she led me into her office, talking non-stop the entire way.

Then, as I sat back in that big, cushiony, velvet covered chair in front of her desk, I sighed a huge sigh. I closed my eyes for a moment without one single terrible fear slithering its' way into my thoughts.

"You look different Beth. I don't know what it is, but you look different somehow."

Tilting my head sideways, I replied, "I feel different. I feel free."

"Free. What do you mean?" she asked in a soft, soothing voice.

"Penny, ever since the other day, I don't know, but I've been able to see a light ahead of me. And for me, that's a first. I've been able to remember things I only wished I could remember. And with that, I put every single piece in its' place. Only a few weeks ago, there were so many missing pieces of my life, but now, those lost memories started coming at me faster and faster. It was strange, but I felt better once I knew the truth. And the funny thing, was that I was scared to find out the truth. I don't know what I was afraid of. If I'd only known the truth was going to free me, I would've done this a long, long, time ago."

With Penny sitting there quiet and attentive, I continued, "You know, I saw things in my mind about myself and my brother that was so incomprehensible, but at the same time, I was glad I saw those things. If I'd only come to the reality of them sooner, I never would've started having those horrible nightmares in the first place. I would've never been afraid of the unknown, because nothing would've been unknown. I guess the person I should be thanking is you Penny. I should thank you for all the help you've given me. If it weren't for you I'd still be climbing walls at night wondering what in the hell was happening to me. But instead, I'm dealing with each and every moment in my past and not running from them."

"Beth. You shouldn't be thanking me. I was just there for you as a friend. I know it all started out as more of a professional relationship, but you've sort of grown on me. And these past few days, I've worried day and night about how you were dealing with everything. I'm proud of you. I just can't tell you how proud I am of you for taking such pain and frustration with more than a calm attitude. Most anybody else would've already run away to hide from the world, but not you. You just kept searching and searching until you found the way out."

Leaning forward, I looked her dead in the eye and said, "I love you Penny. I love you for standing by me when everyone else thought I was crazy. I love you for being one of the best friends I've ever had.. But most of all, for giving me hope. You gave me all of the hope I needed to continue on each and every day. And even though there were days I just wanted to die, I didn't give up because I knew that someone believed in me. You believed in me."

Silence surrounded us for a moment or two, and the love we felt for one another was nothing short of obvious. I cared more about her than I ever cared about my parents the whole time I was growing up. She had given me reason to care about her. My parents never gave me one single reason to love them, only reason to hate them.

I guess curiosity had gotten the best of her, so she asked, "Do you want to tell me about some of the things you've remembered? Anything at all. Maybe you remembered something significant that you might want to share with me."

Thinking hard for a moment, I agreed, "Yeah, there is one thing you might wonder about. Have you thought about why my sister never did anything to help me?"

"Yes, I have. Did you remember something to explain her not wanting to get involved?"

"Unfortunately I did. You see Penny, I'm not the only one Lewis violated. I'm not the only one he hurt."

"What do you mean?"

"Well, when all those memories came at me one after another, one stood out in my mind. One incident replayed itself to me over and over again. I know I locked it away for sometime, but now, I don't believe I'll ever forget it.

I guess I was about eleven years old, or somewhere around there, and Melissa was about thirteen. Like many other times, I heard Lewis coming in late one night. I pulled the covers way over my head because I was scared he was coming for me, but he just walked passed my door. The next thing I knew, I heard Melissa telling him to leave her alone. And then there was nothing but silence. I wasn't sure if he had threatened her like he'd done to me, but he did something to make her quiet. I just laid there for a long time shaking. I knew how terrified I was of him, but it wasn't until then I realized I wasn't the only one being terrorized by that monster of a bastard.

Then when I heard his eerie footsteps down the hallway, I covered my head once more until he had passed by. And faint sounds of sobbing came echoing through the thin wall separating our rooms. I couldn't help but cry too. It was strange, but even though it didn't happen to me that particular time, I still felt like there was something I could do. Then I realized something. The reason Melissa didn't help me was because she feared him just as much as I did. I think his snide remarks and his boasting, only added to the hatred both me and my sister felt towards him.

Then after the crying stopped, I went to the door of her room and slowly opened the door. And when I saw her, it hurt me more than anything in the world. She was curled up in a ball, leaning up against the head-board of her bed. And her tension released when she saw it was me standing there instead of Lewis. I sat down on the side of her bed and we talked for hours. She told me how frightened she was for the both of us. She also stressed how much she wanted to stop him from hurting me, her baby sister. I don't know, all we could do was hold each other. That was all we could do." I concluded.

Tapping the pen she was holding, on her desk, it sounded like the ticking of a clock, then she took off her glasses, gently laid them down, and got up. Coming around to sit beside me, she had this bewildered look on her face. I wasn't quite sure what was going on in her mind, but I was sure anxious to find out.

"What are you thinking Penny? You've got the strangest look on your face."

Taking a deep breathe, she replied, "I'm just curious. Why didn't Melissa ever say thing about these incidents when you went home for Christmas."

"I think she might have, I just didn't know what she was talking about at the time. She told me at mom and dad's that she was sorry she didn't stop him. And until now, I didn't know what she was talking about. Now I know. Now I can ask her about all of it. Maybe she hasn't let herself deal with it. And maybe she needs to."

"You're probably right Beth. If she hasn't dealt with it, she could be digging the hole even deeper, just like you did. Maybe you do need to talk to her. She might not admit to it happening at first, but once you tell her you know and remember everything, then she might be able to set it free just like you have."

"Yeah, you're right. I mean it's plain to see he can't hurt us anymore. And if she'll give me the chance, maybe I can help her like you've helped me."

We talked for a while longer, and I hated to leave her, but I knew one thing I had to do right away. I had to find Eric. I knew he was probably wondering what was happening with me, and making him wait would do nothing but hurt our relationship. And finally, I felt like I could be happy. I was sure that was one thing he wanted to hear above anything else.

Giving Penny a hug before I left, it was the first time I felt so refreshed. Just her spirit gave me a wonderful feeling of rejuvenation. And I promised her I'd come see her very soon.

Just before I got into my car, a brisk, but cool air, swept through my hair. In fact, it felt like it had gone clear through me. It was as though God was telling me everything was going to be fine. And I took that caressing sign just as it was given, with love. It may not have been from God, but the serenity I felt was as if it were from the Almighty himself.

I drove carefully through that small town in the middle of Arkansas admiring each simple piece of beauty. Everything was so perfect. And even though the trees were lacking leaves, they still had an essence about them. A few birds still landed on their branches, and a few squirrels still made them their home. That was what made it perfect and special.

Entering the campus, I drove towards Eric's dorm, but was surprised when I saw him standing alone beside the pond. No one was around but him. He was standing there throwing small pebbles into the water trying to make them skip. If one didn't work, he'd try another. So I quickly turned in and parked on the side of the road. He must've heard my car because he turned around immediately. The frown which dwelled on his face when he was alone vanished when he saw me. And for a moment I felt like a child who'd found his lost puppy. We ran towards one another until we met in the middle. He lifted me high into the air until I seemed I to fly. And although I knew I couldn't, I'd learned something...anything's possible when you're in love.

"I've been so worried about you," he said.

Sighing, I replied, "There was no reason to worry. I'm fine. It just took me a few days to come to grips with what happened to me. And I think I've done that. I know I still have a lot of thinking to do, but I don't want to do it without you. I missed you, but you would've only distracted me. And I don't mean that in a bad way. I'm just saying, you would've kept me from having to deal with my past. And my past is what I needede to understand. I needed to know why it happened and what I can do to reverse its' affects on me."

"Well, no matter, I'm glad you were ready to see me. I was just about to go nuts without you. Sleeping alone does not make for a good night."

Kissing him on his cheek, I replied, "You won't have to sleep alone from now on. I want to get married right away. I want to be your wife, your friend and your lover. I want it all."

Swinging me around and around, he yelled out loud, "Beth Laney is going to be my wife!"

He was so happy he almost cried, but instead, he captivated me with his excitement. I never dreamed I would have the power to make someone that happy. But then again, I never dreamed I'd be lucky enough to find someone like him to love me. It was all too extraordinary to describe with words. I was happy, and Eric was the one responsible for it. From the first day I met him, he gave nothing short of all he had within him.

Arm in arm we walked back to my room. And all the way, he laughed and cut up. It was his way of showing his enthusiasm. It sounds kinda silly, but laughter is most often, the best medicine for any kind of sadness or pain. And a constant smile can make you believe you're as happy as you look. Eric was like that. If you were to look at him, you'd never think anything ever bothered him, but I knew better and so did he. But anybody from outside our love circle, was lost...completely lost.

We reached my room, but this time there were a few people coming back to school. I only saw one or two girls bringing suitcases in, and I was sure the others would come back soon. And with that, I knew Eric and I didn't have many more nights in my room, undisturbed. We had to hold our tongues no matter what we were doing. I didn't want to get caught with a man in my room, but in the back of my mind I didn't care. My only thought was that I wanted to be with him, and he wanted to be with me. Turning the key in the lock, I opened the door. And to my surprise, Amy was sitting on her bed. Her suitcases were lying by the door, and the look on her face was one of exhaustion.

Walking over to her, I sat down and hugged her, "You must've just gotten here. How was your Christmas vacation?"

She gave a little smirk and answered, "It was okay I guess. I don't know. I've never been one on large groups. And my family is quite large. The whole time I felt smothered or something. I know it sounds crazy, but I feel much more relaxed here. How was yours?"

Looking at Eric and back at her, I replied, "It was fine. The most important thing was that I spent it with the man I love."

"And who would that be?" Eric said kiddingly.

Glancing over to him out of the corner of my eye, I grinned as if to say, "You know it's you."

Yawning, Amy sat up and I noticed how red her eyes were. She looked like she'd been driving for days. Although she always had a happy look on her face. For once, the wrinkles surrounding her pretty blue eyes, showed exhaustion.

"Maybe you need to rest. It could do you some good. I know I could use a little more rest before school starts back."

"Yeah," she agreed, "I feel like I've been run over by a Mack truck. I guess the Christmas holiday drained me instead of letting me rest. Ole St. Nick should've brought me some sleeping pills instead of clothes." she said, returning back to her comedian self.

When she laid back down, Eric pulled me over to my bed and sat me down. Suddenly his face turned from smiling to serious in nothing flat. It scared me, but I sat there and listened just the same. And although I didn't know what he wanted to say to me, I always told him I'd be there any time he needed to talk to me, and I meant that with all my heart.

"What is it Eric? You look too serious. Is something wrong?" I asked.

Pausing, he answered, "Nothing's wrong at all. In fact, I think everything is turning out just right."

Raising my eyebrows, I continued, "Now don't leave me hangin' here. Tell me what's on your mind. You love to make me wonder, don't you?"

"Well..." he said as the phone began to blare.

I wanted to hear what he had to say, but I had to answer the phone too, so I told him, "Hold that thought. I'll be right back."

I took a couple of steps until I reached the phone, but when I answered all I heard was sobbing on the other end.

"Hello...hello." I said, trying to figure out who would be calling me in such a manner.

"Beth."

"Melissa?" I answered, recognizing her voice.

Afraid something was wrong with her, I snapped at her, "What's wrong? Tell me. What's going on?"

"Beth, It's mom and dad." she said continuing to cry.

"What about them. I told you once before..."

"They're dead! They're dead Beth. They got killed in a car wreck a few hours ago. My whole family is gone now. They're all gone."

Sliding down the wall to the floor, I crossed my legs and held the phone to me tightly, "Oh my God. My God. Melissa, I don't know what to say. I just don't know what to..."

"Say you're glad! I know that's what you want to say. You're glad they're dead, aren't you?"

Beginning to cry myself, I quickly retorted, "NO, I'm not. I wouldn't wish that on anyone Mel. You know that."

Continuing to weep heavily, she continued, "You hated them. I know you did."

"I didn't hate them, I only hated what they put me through, that's all. Don't you understand."

"It doesn't matter," she said, "The funeral's the day after tomorrow at two o'clock in the afternoon. Come if you ever felt anything for them at all. Remember Beth, they did feed and clothe you when you were growing up. If they didn't do anything else, they did that much. And I think you at least owe them the courtesy of telling them good-bye. At least you owe them that."

"I'll be there. And Melissa?"

"Yeah."

"I love you Sis. I always have," I said, trying to console her.

I could tell she was wiping away a few tears as she replied, "I know Beth. I know."

Releasing the phone, I carefully placed it back on the receiver. And all I could do was stare into space. I saw nothing, only darkness and emptiness, but I didn't know why. And Eric had come and sat down with me trying to get me to tell him what was happening. But for a moment or two I couldn't say a word. I felt paralyzed with the fear that my entire past had vanished completely. I felt like everything I'd lived as a child was just a fantasy and not reality at all. The man who I called daddy, the woman who I called mommy, and the boy I called my brother, were all dead and gone from the earth. And though I wasn't sure why it frightened me, I was shaking inside. My nerves were frazzled and were dancing around like crazy inside of me.

"Beth. What's wrong?"

Lowering my head solemnly, I answered, "My mom and dad, David and Alice."

"What about them? I thought you weren't going to talk about them."

For no reason, a tear or two were trying to trickle down my face, "They're dead Eric. That was Melissa. She told me they died a few hours ago. She wants me to come to the funeral. She thinks I should tell them good-bye one last time."

Rubbing my hand, he gave me some advice, "You do what you want to do Darlin''. Don't let someone else tell you what you need to do. If you want to go, we'll go, but if you think it would only hurt your recovery, then stay away."

Wiping my eyes, "I need to go. I need to be there for my sister. Melissa needs me now. And I promised her I'd always be there for her. I can't let her down now, can I?"

"Guess not," he replied rocking me back and forth on the floor.

It was hard to believe they were gone. It had only been days since I'd seen them. And I was so angry I didn't care whether they lived or died, but with the news, I wasn't sure what I wanted. Deep down I couldn't stand what I had been through because of their selfishness, but on the other hand, they did take care of me to a certain extent. I was so confused. The answer to the question, "What do I do?" was still something I needed to answer, and soon. And as Eric sat there glaring at me with those puppy dog eyes, I realized that I had cut him off in the middle of him telling me something.

"What was it you started to tell me?"

Hesitating for a few seconds, he answered, "It can wait. Besides, I don't think this is the best time to tell you such news."

"What news? Come on Eric. Don't just leave me hanging. You've already got me curious. And besides, if it's good news in the least, I'll be glad to hear it."

Standing up and walking away from me, he repeated what he'd just said, "It's just not the best time. I'll tell you when the timing is more appropriate."

Rushing over to him, I demanded, "Alright Eric Norris. I've been through hell and back, and I don't want you to add to that. Either tell me now or don't tell me at all!"

Without saying a word, he took my hand, "Come on. There's somewhere we need to go first."

"Where?"

"Don't ask any questions. Just trust me. I promise it'll be worth the wait." he said leading me out of the dorm and to his truck which was parked a block or so away.

Staring at him, intrigue began to fill my thoughts. I started thinking of a million and one things he could be wanting to tell me, but still I had no idea as to exactly what he was being so secretive about. He didn't say a word. It was as though he wanted to savor every bit of curiosity I had inside of me. And though the walk was short, it seemed like much farther.

When we finally got to his truck, he opened his door and let me in on his side as he always did. All he could do was grin at me, still not speaking. I wondered if he was scared to speak. He never was one to keep anything from me, and I believed he thought if he started talking, he would tell me what he had to say, prematurely. So he did nothing but enjoy the silence.

Once or twice I asked him where we were going, but he just kept on looking straight ahead as we traveled slowly down University Drive. After a moment or two I realized he wasn't going to tell me anything, so I watched the road ahead as well. But after we reached town, the direction in which he went, was quite familiar. And the further he drove the more familiar it became.

To my surprise, he pulled up to Penny's office and parked. Glancing over at me, he opened the door and helped me out carefully.

"What are we doing here?" I asked, but still he didn't say a word. All he could do was take my hand and walk towards the front door. The only car there was Penny's. I assumed her receptionist had left for the day. Penny always worked late most every night, but that still didn't explain why we were going to see her. She didn't even expect us, I didn't think, but Eric just kept right on walking as if he knew what he was doing.

Stopping him abruptly, I demanded, "Eric, what are you doing? Have you lost your mind? What are we doing here? I'm not going to ask you again."

Looking at me with loving eyes, he replied, "You won't have to. Your questions will be answered when we get inside. Just come on and stop being so stubborn."

Submitting to his requests, I followed him inside. And as we stepped in, I saw Penny sitting at her desk reading. Without hesitation, he walked up to her door, knocked, and she waved for us to come on in. Still curious why we were there, I waited to see what would happen next.

CHAPTER 23

My heart was racing with anticipation as I sat down. Eric didn't take a seat, but instead, he paced around the room as if he were trying to think of what he needed to say.

"What are you two doing here?" Penny asked.

Eric turned to her and replied, "Penny...Beth...there's something both of you need to know."

Turning to him, I waited to hear what he had to say next. And he acted more nervous than I had ever seen him.

"Eric. What's going on? Why are you acting so mysterious? It can't be that bad."

Walking over and kneeling down in front of me, he placed his gentle, but rough hands on my face, "It's not bad baby. I swear it's not bad. I just don't know how to say it without just blurting it out. There's no other way.."

Then he turned to Penny, smiled, and took a deep breath. Sitting down beside me, he continued, "For the past few days I've done a lot of checking and digging, probably in places I didn't belong. But all that digging paid off late yesterday afternoon. I found out something that neither of you will believe."

He stopped for a second, and I reached over and nudged him, "Finish. Tell us. Don't make us wait all day long."

"Okay." he said, placing a stack of documents on Penny's desk, "I got a hold of some papers that were hard to obtain, but I got them anyway. Well, I read them and was completely shocked at what I saw."

Turning to me, he took my hand, "Beth, remember I told you how much I wanted to help you find your real parents."

"Yeah."

"Well, I found them, or one of them anyway."

Turning to Penny, Eric continued, "Penny, you're baby didn't die when it was born. It was stolen from you. They just told you that your baby girl died. She was sold on the black market to a couple named David and Alice Laney. It was hard to find, but I found every last detail of what happened. I was unsure at first, but everything seems to fit in the missing pieces of the puzzle."

Penny's eyes got as big as saucers, and then they began to fill with tears, "You mean..."

"Yeah," Eric replied, "Beth. She's your daughter. She's the baby girl you gave birth to."

Speechless, I stood up, walked over and stared into the mirror hanging on the wall directly behind me. It was hard to believe. My mother, my real mother, had been the one helping me all this time. She was the one who helped me through all my pain from the past. But most of all, the woman who gave me birth, was in the room with me. And my reaction was the same as hers. Tears began to fill my eyes quickly, and before I knew it, I felt someone touch my shoulder. I looked into the mirror to see Penny...my mother. And seeing both of us side by side, I tried to find similarities in our facial features and expressions, but I was so overwhelmed about the whole thing, all I could do was stare at her.

She turned me around to her, "Beth, my sweet Beth. You're the baby I heard crying in my dreams every single night of my life. Your voice was the one I heard calling out to me when I thought I was only having a nightmare. For the longest time I wanted to believe the doctors were wrong, but then I made myself believe you were dead. I had to. There was no other way to deal with losing my only child."

"Penny, I told you one time that I wished my mom was more like you, and now I know. My wish has come true. That other woman was only a poor imitation of the real thing.

I don't know what to say. I don't know what to call you. All I know is that I'm glad I've gotten the chance to get to know you. Now I know what a wonderful mom you would've been to me as a child, if you'd been given the chance. Now I know who you are. Now I know who I am," I said, weeping the entire time.

She wrapped her caring arms around me, and I could see Eric leaning against her desk with a tear or two in his eyes as well. He felt the same happiness I felt. I could tell by the look in his eyes. And he was just as touched as I was at that particular moment.

After she embraced me so warmly, she walked over to Eric, "Eric, you've given me the greatest gift anyone's ever given me. You've given me my child back. And even though it's eighteen years too late, you did it. I'll never forget what you've done. I'll never forget it Eric...Never!" she said squeezing his hand and kissing him on his forehead.

That moment was so emotional. Still I didn't know what to say, but suddenly I thought of something I needed to tell her.

"Mom," I said, watching her turn to me with a glow about her I'll never forget.

"Melissa, my sister called me a little while ago. She told me that David and Alice, my mom and dad who raised me, died a few hours ago in a automobile accident. Will you go with Eric and me to the funeral. I promised Melissa I'd be there, and I don't want to let her down. In a way, I think she's been through as much as I have. She may not say so, but she has."

With no hesitation, she replied, "If you want me there, I'll go."

"I do. I want you...my mother to be there with me when I put my past completely to rest. And I believe that's what I'll be doing when they're buried deep into the ground.

Eric came up and put his arms around me firmly, "I'm sorry I couldn't tell you what I had to say until we got here, but it would've ruined the whole surprise. Besides, I thought it only fair for both of you to hear it at the same time."

Laughing, I replied, "Well, you are always right, aren't you?"

"Most the time." he said smugly but comically.

For the first time in my life, I felt like I had a real family. Even though I had only known who my real mother was for a few moments, it felt like a lifetime. Over and over, I replayed in my mind, how my life would've been with her as a mom growing up. And they were all pleasant thoughts. I could just see her coming out of the kitchen with freshly baked cookies, or dressing me in frilly dresses and bows. It all could've been so perfect.

Breaking the silence, Penny asked, "When do you want to leave for Dallas Beth? Because if you were ready to go now, I'd pack up and go with you."

"That's probably a good idea. I mean, Melissa's down there by herself. And I feel like she needs me."

"We can take my car," she said, "I'll go home and pack a few things and pick you kids up in about an hour. How does that sound?"

Nodding my head in agreement, she and I walked out arm in arm. Eric followed behind us, and I could almost hear his heart beating rapidly from all the excitement he'd caused.

Eric and I got into his truck, while Penny got in her car. And it was hard for me to take my eyes off her. I was still trying to find some spectacular resemblance between the two of us, but all I could see was that both she and I had a heart of gold. That was the most important similarity. And to me, having a warm and caring heart was the only similarity I needed to have with her.

We both left and hurried home to gather some things to carry with us on our unwanted trip to the land of the dead. That was the way I looked at it anyway.

Lewis was dead. Mom and dad were gone, and my fear of the past was dead and buried along with them. And that was exactly the way I wanted it to be. Although I had never wished anything bad on anyone intentionally, for once, I was glad about such a horrible thing. I was glad they were no longer there to torture me. The only thing I felt bad about, was the fact that Melissa's real mom and dad were gone. But as strong a person that she had always been, I knew it wouldn't take her long to adjust and deal with it to the best of her abilities. And I wanted to be a loving sister and stand beside her every step of the way.

Eric dropped me off at my room while he went to pack. I rushed in and threw my suitcase on the bed. Amy woke up as I was packing hurriedly.

"Slow down. Where ya goin' in such a hurry?" she said groggily.

Turning to her, I replied, "I have a lot to tell you when I come back. But I do want you to remember something. You're my best friend Amy. You have been since the day I moved in here. And I want to thank you for that."

She smiled and asked no more questions. But she did open up her suitcase and throw me that sweater I'd been looking for.

"Here. You might need this where ever you're goin'" she said.

"Thanks."

Time must have flown, because just about the time I shut my suitcase, the phone rang. I answered it quickly and heard the sweetest voice on the other end.

"Beth dear, you ready?"

"I'm ready. I'll call Eric and get him over here." I said.

I hung up the phone and picked it right back up to call Eric. The phone rang and rang over and over again, so I assumed he was on his way. And as soon as I hung it up, the door opened slowly.

"Is it safe to come in?" he said carefully.

"Come on in, I'm about ready. Just let me grab my purse and notepad."

"What do you need your notepad for?" he questioned.

Rolling my eyes away from him, I replied, "I need to write no matter where I am. If I get the urge, I want something to write on. Is that alright with you?"

"Alright, alright. Don't get snappy. I just asked a simple question."

Going up to him, I laid my head on his shoulder, "I'm sorry. I didn't mean to snap at you, but all of this has gotten to me a little."

"Don't worry about it. Let's just go outside and wait on Penny. I'm sure she's on her way."

Walking out the door, I turned to Amy and told her good-bye. And I knew once I got the chance to tell her about everything which had happened, she wouldn't believe it. It was hard for me to believe. But as good a friend as she was, I knew she would do her best to stand beside me until I felt I was fully recovered from every single thing I'd remembered, as well as the new information Eric so wonderfully told me. I had no doubt in my mind about her loyalty...none at all.

Just as we made it outside, Penny pulled up in front of the dorms. Meeting us half way, she took one of my bags and went and opened the trunk of her car. And after we loaded everything, I got in the front seat while Eric crawled into the back. He was fully prepared for a long drive. He laid his pillow up against the window and rested his head on it almost immediately after he got in. But I was still in shock from the fact that I'd found my real mom.

We started on our way to the small town outside of Dallas, and I kept staring over at Penny. I couldn't help it. I guess I kept trying to find some kind of resemblance. And after a while, I realized I must've looked more like my father than her. But we did have one thing in common. We both had a huge heart of gold. From the moment I first met her, I knew she and I were a lot alike. And I guess that was more important than being identical to her in looks. As I was always told, looks fade, but a good heart will last forever. And that is so very true.

After driving for almost an hour, the silence was overwhelming. Eric had fallen asleep, and Penny just kept looking straight ahead. I don't know if she was afraid to talk to me or if she just didn't have anything to say. The strange thing, was the feeling I had. Although I'd only known her for a few months, I had never felt uncomfortable around her in the least. But for some reason I was holding back. I wasn't sure what to say to her or even how to act. I think the main reason was I was scared I might say something stupid and end up looking like a dunce or something. And I didn't want my mom to think bad of me at all. So I rode out every bit of silence that twirled around me just waiting for a moment when I could break the ice a little.

The sun had fallen, and little by little the stars were showing clearer and clearer. I looked up and stared above for a moment admiring them.

"They're beautiful aren't they Beth?"

"Yeah, they are."

"You don't know what to think about all of this do you? Well, if it'll make you feel any better, neither do I. I'm just as lost as you are. All I know is that you're my daughter and I want to make up for all the time I didn't have with you. I want to let you know what kind of mother I could've been. And if you'll accept me as your mother, I promise you I'll be the happiest woman on this earth."

Glancing at her quickly, I hesitantly asked, "Tell me about my father. What was he like?"

"Oh Jerry...what a wonderful man. Beth I can't begin to tell you how happy he was when he found out we were going to have a child. He went out and bought every single stuffed animal he came across. After a while, it looked like we were carneys traveling with a circus. But he didn't stop buying things for our baby. He used to tell me he didn't care if it was a boy or a girl as long as it was healthy. But then I went and had a sonogram done. The doctor told us we were having a baby girl. And let me tell you, I've never seen a man any more excited than he was on that day. We left the doctor's office and went straight to this little place called "The Stork." Jerry loaded the counter with every frilly dress and outfit he saw. For a minute I thought he'd done lost his mind, but then I saw how happy he was. And I just couldn't take that happiness away. So I let him buy all he wanted."

Smiling, I kept on listening as she continued, "He was the kind of man who came home after work every single night with something special for me. Sometimes it was flowers. Other times it might have only been a small card. But whatever it was, I held them all precious to my heart.

Beth I can't say enough good things about your father. But I can say one thing. After the doctors told him our baby had died, he was never the same again. For a long time he fell way back inside of himself. And for the first time, he wouldn't talk to me. Sometimes it seemed like he was the one who had been carrying you. He acted that way anyway."

"He sounds like he was a terrific man." I replied.

"And you know what else?" she said sadly.

"What?"

"He would've been the best dad Beth. I just wish he would've had the chance. I wish I would've had the chance to be a mother to you. If I had, you wouldn't be having to go through all of what you're going through right now. But I know we still have plenty of time to make up all those lost hours, days and years. We have plenty of time."

Nodding and squeezing her hand, I replied, "We've got all the time in the world...Mom. Can I call you mom?"

Her eyes filled with tears until she could barely talk, "Oh my darling Beth, I wouldn't want you to call me anything else."

Sighing, once more I looked ahead of me. The road seemed so long, but I knew the drive would do both of us some good. If anything, I knew we'd have the chance to catch up on the past eighteen years. And little by little, I answered every question she had to ask me. Of course, through my therapy with her, she knew what most of my life was like, but there were a few things she had no idea about. And those were the things she was focusing on. She asked me about my junior prom, senior prom, my favorite subjects, and everything in-between. It astonished me. She was actually interested in what I liked to do. She was actually interested in me. Other than Eric, Melissa and Amy, no one else ever showed me that kind of caring.

Ever so often I looked into the back seat to see Eric tossing and turning. It was beyond me how he could sleep in such a position, but he was sound asleep. And just watching him, gave me the most peaceful feeling. I was riding with my new found mother and the man who would, one day, be my husband. How much more peaceful could I feel?

It crossed my mind to stop at that diner and see Belle, but it was already late and I wanted to get as much sleep as I possibly could when we reached our destination. I wanted to try to sleep in the car, but sitting there next to my mother, made it hard. I kept watching her for no reason. To me, she was beautiful. But above all, she was probably one of the most caring persons I'd ever met. Even when she thought I was just a stranger needing help, she gave her all to me. And since she found out who I really was, I knew she would treat me even better, if that was possible.

Hours passed quickly, much more quickly than when I drove it by myself. And when we were a few miles from my hometown, I gave Penny directions as to where we needed to stay for the night. It was far too late to phone Melissa, so I decided it would be best to wait until the morning.

We got to the hotel, Penny went inside to check us in, and I tried my best to wake up that gorgeous sleepy head in the back seat. And after shaking him a few times, he cracked open his eyes slightly and smiled.

"We here?" he said in a muffled voice.

"We're here. Wake up," I whispered.

He sat straight up with drooping eyes, and we both waited for Penny to return.

"Did you two get to talk any while I was asleep?"

With a smile, I answered, "We sure did. She told me about my father. And you know what Eric?"

"What babe?"

"I bet he was a one in a million."

"Just like you," he said tenderly.

With that lovable remark, I felt warm all over. And when Penny returned, she handed us our key and drove to the two rooms which adjoined one another. We quickly unpacked the car and settled in for the night. Eric carried our things into our room, but before I went in with him, I had to tell Penny good-night. I stepped into her room quietly and she turned to me after setting down her things.

"Good-night," I said in a sleepy voice.

Coming close to me, she embraced me tenderly and replied, "Goodnight Beth. And don't you worry about anything. Everything will be just fine tomorrow. It'll be hard, but Eric and I will right there beside you."

"I appreciate that more than both of you will ever know."

"Well, we love you. And I believe we'd both do anything for you. You are my daughter. And you'll soon be his wife. There's a lot of love there...a lot."

Kissing her on the cheek, I turned and joined Eric in our own room. But when I walked in, he was already in bed fast asleep. He was laid across the bed fully clothed. So I wrestled to get his clothes off before I got ready for bed myself. And the entire time, he didn't even half-way wake up. It was comical. I flipped and flopped him, and he never even knew it.

After getting him warmly tucked in, I slipped on my most comfortable gown and snuggled up next to him. And for once, I had no worries trampling through my mind. For once I didn't need something to keep me from dreaming horrible dreams. And it felt good to be free from all of that. My happiness had finally drenched every bit of fear which had me captured for way too long. And one of my securities was lying next to me. That was all I needed to know. The man who made me strong, was there beside me.

After lying there for only a short while, I passed out into a land of silence without any disturbing creatures following me in the dark. With each breath, in and out, I focused on nothing. The only thing going through my mind at all, was the thought of how much rest I needed. After all I'd been through in just one days time, I figured rest might possibly make some sense out of all of it. Only God knows I couldn't make any sense out of it on my own.

Then the light of day began to seep through the darkness little by little until a glimpse of the morning slowly showed itself through the small crack in the curtains in the corner. Rubbing my eyes intensely, I tossed and turned trying to deny the new day, but I knew I had to face it instead. I knew that Melissa had organized the funeral quickly. I'd never heard of only waiting one day after someone dies to have their funeral, but I guess Melissa wanted to get it over with as soon as possible. I didn't figure there would be that many people there. They didn't have very many friends. The friends they did have, they ended up running away in some form or fashion.

Eric and I got dressed, and when we were ready to go, I went over and knocked on Penny's door. When she came out, she looked beautiful. She was wearing an exquisite navy lace dress with off white trim. She was a sight to see.

"You look beautiful," I said hugging her.

She held my hands out and replied, "You look even more beautiful."

"Come on ladies, are we ready to go? I'll put the luggage in the car" Eric said.

Following along behind him, he turned around, "What time did you say the funeral was Beth?"

"I'm not really sure. I assume around one or two. We'll ask Melissa when we get to the house."

"What house are you talking about? Do you mean the house where you grew up?"

"Well, yeah. That's where Melissa is. And I'm sure by now, she's going nuts. So we best hurry before she does something crazy."

We checked out of the hotel and I gave Penny directions to where we were going. It wasn't far from where we were, but I could tell she felt a little uneasy about going there. I guess I could understand what she was feeling. The way she probably looked at the situation, was that she was driving me to the house where all of my childhood abuse was inflicted. And in a sense, that was correct. But the ones who inflicted all that pain were no longer there. They were all gone. And I had to make her realize, as well as myself, that no one could ever hurt me again.

A block away, I could see Melissa's car parked directly in front of the house. There were no other vehicles there. No one even wanted to pay their respects. In fact, I wasn't sure why I wanted to.

Parking in the driveway, Christmas day came back to me all over again. I could still hear the yelling and screaming, and I could still see my mother crying when she finally found out I knew about the adoption. She acted like it really hurt her, but on the other hand, my father was as mean and self-centered as he had ever been.

Trying to get those thoughts out of my mind, I stepped out as Eric opened my door for me. Melissa was standing on the front porch with her arms crossed and her hair pulled up in a bun. Penny waited a moment or two before getting out and I couldn't blame her for being nervous. But I wanted her to know Melissa, and I wanted Melissa to love her just as much as I did. I just kept thinking maybe she could be a substitute mother for my only sister. And although it seemed like a strange request, I kept my hopes alive.

We all walked up the few steps leading to the porch. I reached her first, and wrapped my arms around her. I must've held her for ten minutes or so. The strange thing, was she didn't cry at all. She was as calm as an ocean on a still summer night.

Kissing her on her forehead as we released one another, I introduced her to Penny, "Melissa, I want you to meet someone. Remember what I told you about my adoption?"

"Sure," she replied.

"Well, Eric found her. Melissa. This is my real mother...Penny Downs." I said as my hands were shaking from the nervousness of how she would accept her.

Glancing at me, her eyes watered, "Your mother? Beth, I'm so happy for you. I've prayed every night that you would find the person who gave you birth."

Then turning to Penny, "Mrs. Downs, it's so nice to meet you. I hope you know what a special daughter you have, and what a special sister I have."

"I know dear. I knew she was special even before I knew she was my daughter."

Giving me a look of quandary, she started to ask me something, but I interrupted.

"It's a long story Melissa. It's a long story."

We all went inside and drank a cup of coffee before the funeral. We had several hours to kill, so I told Melissa the whole story of my therapy and how I met Mrs. Downs. But when I told her about the part of my hypnotism, she got up and started cleaning off the table. It struck me as odd. The moment I told her about what Lewis had done to me, she began to shiver and shake all over.

I caught her in the kitchen and confronted her, "Melissa, stop! Stand still. I want to ask you something, and I want an honest answer. And believe me, telling the truth will only make you feel better."

About that time, Shane, Melissa's husband came in the back door with a handful of wood.

"I'll build a fire Hun, he said passing by us quickly."

She looked back at me and tried to walk away, but I grabbed her arm.

"Tell me. Did Lewis do the same to you. And if you lie to me, I'll know it. I remember everything. I remember it all. I don't know how I forgot it in the first place, but now I know the whole truth of my unforgettable childhood that I wished I'd never had in this house. I would've rather died at birth like the doctors told Penny. Now tell me. Please...please tell me the truth."

She walked a few feet away from me and turned facing the wall. "You're right. You're not the only one he hurt. He was doing it to me for a while before he decided to go to you as well. And when I realized he'd focused on you, I couldn't do a thing.

Mom and dad thought he was so perfect. They would've never believed me over him. And if I'd told them, they probably would've taken me to some foster home or something. I was scared Beth. I was more terrified of him than I was of ghosts and goblins. Because to me he was a creature of the night. I don't know about you, but I was scared to death to close my eyes at night for fear he'd come in and hover over me. I just didn't know what to do." she said.

Wiping away a tear which rolled down her cheek, I tried to comfort her, "It wasn't you fault, and it wasn't my fault. But if we don't deal with it and realize the only one at fault was Lewis, then we'll both wither away inside. I've just now come to the conclusion that I can be happy. And for a while my happiness was being held back by lost memories. Penny helped me bring those memories to surface. Melissa, I couldn't ask for a more precious mom. And I hope you try and get to know her as well. She may be able to help you if you ever have the need to talk."

Smiling an appreciative smile, she replied, "I'm glad you made me remember. For so long I've tried to forget. And when you mentioned your dreams to me last week, they all came real again. I guess I got mad because I really didn't want to think of what formidable things that were done to me. I just didn't want to think about it."

Slowly walking in to the living room together, I whispered, "I'm here now Sis. And I'll always be here for you."

I talked to Shane for a moment or two when Melissa informed us it was time to go. There was no family car to pick us up. And there was no one bringing food or flowers by the house. There were only the five of us attending that last good-bye scene for David and Alice Laney. And ironically, they were being buried next to their dearest son, Lewis. As sick as it may sound, I think that was the way they wanted it to be. In a way, I think they were glad to be able to greet their wonderful, do nothing wrong, son, in hell. That was the only place they could've gone. Because I didn't think God gave a passage for people as cruel and uncaring as they were.

We slowly drove to the cemetery as silence danced all around us. It was so quiet. And when we reached the grave side the only people standing beside those two coffins, was a preacher, and an old friend of my mothers. I guess you could say the better one between the two, was my mother. Although she wasn't a good mother, there were times she did show a little compassion. And the woman who stood there to bid her farewell, was one friend of Alice's that stood beside her through all the good and bad times. I was surprised to see anyone there, but then again, I was glad she touched someone's heart...because she never touched mine.

Hand in hand, Eric, me and Penny walked behind Melissa and Shane. And when they stopped, so did we. It felt strange to be there in that same place again because that was where all of my problems began. And with my strength along with Penny and Eric's, that place would be where it ended as well. No strange breeze was blowing through me as in my dreams, and my soul felt free. Looking on each side of me, I saw two people who cared about me more than anyone had ever cared before. And then looking ahead of me, I saw two caskets which were holding the two people who should've cared that much, but didn't. I felt no sorrow. I cried no tears, but instead, I thanked the lord for giving me a life by taking theirs away. As awful as it may sound, I felt it was a gift from God. Maybe he knew as well as I did how futile they were. In my opinion, they shouldn't have had the chance to ruin my life.

It was cool and windy on the day my mother, Alice, and my father, David, were laid to rest. The leaves were blowing like feathers in the wind as the caskets were being lowered. And a poem went trampling through my clear, unconfused mind as we walked away from such a tormenting atmosphere:

BURIED

Buried, not forgotten,
For your deeds will still live on.
They were cruel and careless
And still live though you are gone.
Buried, so beside you,
Your dear son, the precious one.
You patted his back so often
Through all that he had done.

Tammy D. Thompson

And now I find the identity,
Of the one who gave me life,
Who, when she thought I'd died that day,
Lived in agony and strife.
I stand here looking at the ground,
You're buried, not forgotten still,
But for all the wretched deeds you've done,
God took hell's empty glass to fill.
He placed you in the darkness,
Where eternity is your foe.
You're all buried, not forgotten,
For my life has to carry on.

Those lines of poetry flowed through my mind, and the feelings which went along with them, were overwhelming. They weren't feelings of grief, but more like feelings of doubt. In the back of my mind I doubted my own strength. I was afraid it would take me forever to be able to completely handle my past. And although I had people who loved me, the only person who could help me, was me. I was the one who counted. Eric and Penny could stand beside me forever, but until I believed in myself as much as they believed in me, then I would be lost just like Melissa. And I didn't want to be like that.

I had my mind made up that I would hold my head up high no matter what problems came my way, and if they were big problems, I would use my shield, my guardian, Eric, my love.

We traveled back to the old house and stood around outside for a few minutes saying our good-byes. It was hard for me to leave Melissa again, but we promised one another we'd keep in touch and visit. She seemed to really like Penny, and that meant more to me than anything. And as far as Eric goes,

Melissa was already calling him her 'brother-in-law.' They even hugged one another like they had know each other forever. And it was at that moment, I knew I hadn't lost my only sister. In fact, I think we had grown closer because of such an experience.

That day changed my whole life. After returning back to college, Eric and I moved in with Penny and enjoyed homemade dinners every single night. Eric did most of all. And after the year was up, we called the 'Mansion on Maine,' and asked Inez if she would allow us to get married in her beautiful home. She was even more excited than we were. And she told me over and over again how much she had missed us since we left.

Don't ask me why, but I called that little diner in the middle of nowhere and talked to Belle. I told her she was welcome to come to our wedding, and she gave an enthusiastic, "Ya Betcha Hun." I had started a fresh and wonderful life for myself. And I had the idea it was the beginning of new and beautiful friendships. Melissa learned to love Penny as a mother, and for once, I had the family I only dreamed of as a child.

Then the day for Eric and I marry, approached. Dressed in a beautiful, long, lacy, white gown, the music played as I carefully made my way down the winding staircase of that glorious Mansion on Main. And waiting at the foot of the stairs, was everyone I held close to my heart. Eric stood there looking more handsome than I'd ever seen him before. And Penny, Melissa, Shane and Amy were off to the side along with a few of Eric's family members who made a special trip to see us wed. Inez's husband, Lee, offered to play the role of my father and give me away, since I had no father to do so. And once the ceremony began, it didn't take long before I was introduced to everyone as Mrs. Eric Lee Norris.

It was cool and windy on the day Eric and I pledged our love to one another. The leaves were blowing like feathers in the wind as we made our way down the walk to meet our chariot of destiny. All of the fear and uncertainty that used to contain me, had been swept away. And all that remained was the feeling of love which had been taught to me by many new friends. There was a point when I thought I'd found the end, but I was wrong. My life was just beginning.

ABOUT THE AUTHOR

Tammy D. Thompson

Tammy D. Thompson was born in 1968 in Arkansas. When she was about ten years old, she realized her flare for writing, scribbling down silly little poems every chance she got. Then as the years passed, each line became more emotional from all the good times and hardships she had been through, from the death of her grandfather to graduation and starting a new life. She learned a lot from it all. And when she was twenty years old, she got married and had a son. But only a few short years later, she was left alone to raise her son as a single mother, but still determined to use her gift of writing one day.

That's when she sat down to write her first novel. Up until then then had only written short stories and poetry. And regretfully enough, that novel was much to be desired, not a wonderful piece of literature at all. But she learned from that and as she began to attend writing conferences and get together with her agent and other writers, everything fell into place. And her mistakes all seemed clear to her, making her learn from them all. Thompson went to bed one night and woke up after having a dream. She went straight to her computer and began to write "Buried, But Not Forgotten." That was the beginning of her dream trying to be reached. The dream of being a published author.

Printed in the United States
16029LVS00004B/195